THE CHILDREN'S HOUR

Volume One
FIRST STORY BOOK

Volume Two
FAVORITE FAIRY TALES

Volume Three
OLD TIME FAVORITES

Volume Four
CARAVAN OF FUN

Volume Five
BEST-LOVED POEMS

Volume Six
STORIES OF TODAY

Volume Seven
FAVORITE MYSTERY STORIES

Volume Eight
MYTHS AND LEGENDS

Volume Nine
FROM MANY LANDS

Volume Ten
SCHOOL AND SPORT

Volume Eleven
ALONG BLAZED TRAILS

Volume Twelve
STORIES OF LONG AGO

Volume Thirteen
ROADS TO ADVENTURE

Volume Fourteen
FAVORITE ANIMAL STORIES

Volume Fifteen
LEADERS AND HEROES

Volume Sixteen
SCIENCE FICTION–GUIDE

Myths and Legends

A BOOK TO GROW ON

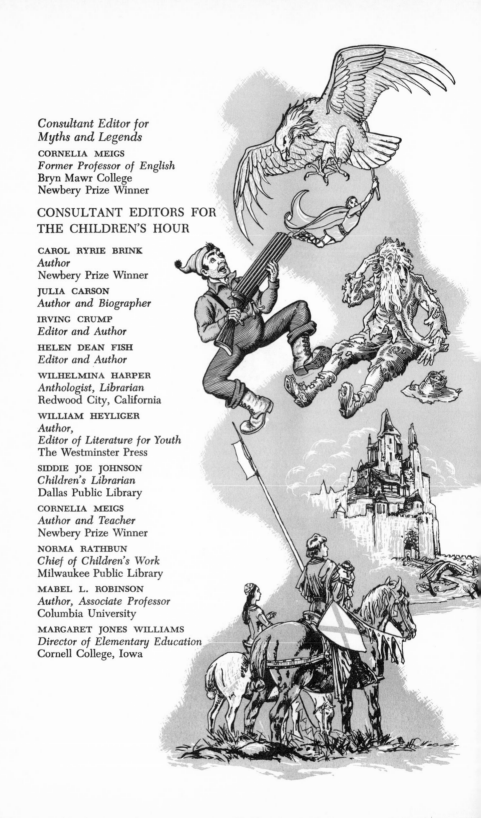

*Consultant Editor for
Myths and Legends*

CORNELIA MEIGS
Former Professor of English
Bryn Mawr College
Newbery Prize Winner

CONSULTANT EDITORS FOR THE CHILDREN'S HOUR

CAROL RYRIE BRINK
Author
Newbery Prize Winner

JULIA CARSON
Author and Biographer

IRVING CRUMP
Editor and Author

HELEN DEAN FISH
Editor and Author

WILHELMINA HARPER
Anthologist, Librarian
Redwood City, California

WILLIAM HEYLIGER
*Author,
Editor of Literature for Youth*
The Westminster Press

SIDDIE JOE JOHNSON
Children's Librarian
Dallas Public Library

CORNELIA MEIGS
Author and Teacher
Newbery Prize Winner

NORMA RATHBUN
Chief of Children's Work
Milwaukee Public Library

MABEL L. ROBINSON
Author, Associate Professor
Columbia University

MARGARET JONES WILLIAMS
Director of Elementary Education
Cornell College, Iowa

MARJORIE BARROWS, *Editor*

Myths and Legends

MATHILDA SCHIRMER
Associate Editor

DOROTHY SHORT
Art Editor

THE CHILDREN'S HOUR

PRINTED IN THE UNITED STATES OF AMERICA

Acknowledgments

The editor and publishers wish to thank the following publishers, agents, authors, and artists for permission to reprint the following stories, poems, and illustrations included in this book:

APPLETON-CENTURY-CROFTS, INC., for "Children of the Wolf" from *Mighty Men: From Achilles to Julius Caesar* by Eleanor Farjeon, copyright, 1925, D. Appleton & Company; "Uncle Remus and the Tar-Baby" by Joel Chandler Harris; and illustrations by A. B. Frost for "Uncle Remus and the Tar-Baby" by Joel Chandler Harris.

THOMAS Y. CROWELL COMPANY for "Cuchulain's Adventures in Shadow-land" from *The Boys' Cuchulain* by Eleanor Hull.

THE JOHN DAY COMPANY, INC., for "Bucca Boo's Little Merry Men" from *Piskey Folk* by Enys Tregarthen.

DOUBLEDAY & COMPANY, INC., for "Son of the South Wind" and "The White Horse of Volendam" from *Wonder Tales of Horses and Heroes* by Frances Carpenter, copyright, 1952, by Frances Carpenter Huntington; "A Tale of Three Tails" and "The Tale of the Lazy People" from *Tales from Silver Lands* by Charles J. Finger, copyright, 1924, by Doubleday & Company, Inc.

E. P. DUTTON & CO., INC., for "Capture of the Shen" from *Shen of the Sea* by Arthur Bowie Chrisman, published and copyright, 1925, by E. P. Dutton & Co., Inc., New York. Copyright renewed, 1953, Arthur Bowie Chrisman; and "The Cow Golden Horn" from *Hindu Fables for Little Children* by Dhan Gopal Mukerji, published and copyright, 1929, E. P. Dutton & Co., Inc., N. Y.

EXPOSITION PRESS, INC., for "I Hear Paul Bunyan" by Louise Leighton, first published by Henry Harrison.

HENRY HOLT AND COMPANY, INC., for "The One You Don't See Coming" and "Talk" from *The Cow-Tail Switch and Other West African Stories* by Harold Courlander and George Herzog, copyright, 1947, by Henry Holt and Company, Inc.; "The Apples of Iduna" from *Thunder of the Gods* by Dorothy Hosford, copyright, 1952, by Dorothy Hosford; "How Beowulf Rules the Geats" from *By His Own Might: The Battles of Beowulf*, by Dorothy Hosford, copyright, 1947, by Henry Holt and Company, Inc.; and one illustration by Claire and George Louden for "The Apples of Iduna" by Dorothy Hosford.

HOUGHTON MIFFLIN COMPANY for "Pecos Bill and His Bouncing Bride" and "Pecos Bill" from *Yankee Doodle's Cousins* by Anne Malcolmson, and illustrations by Robert McCloskey from the same book.

ALFRED A. KNOPF, INC., for "The Alphorn" from *The Three Sneezes* by Roger Duvoisin, copyright, 1945, by Alfred A. Knopf, Inc., and an illustration by Roger Duvoisin from the same book.

J. B. LIPPINCOTT COMPANY for "John Henry, Mighty Railroader" from *Clear the Track* by Louis Wolfe, copyright, 1952, by Louis Wolfe.

LONGMANS, GREEN AND COMPANY, INC., for "Three Golden Oranges" from *Three Golden Oranges and Other Spanish Folk Tales* by Ralph Steele Boggs and Mary Gould Davis, copyright, 1936, by Longmans, Green and Company, Inc.

THE MACMILLAN COMPANY for "The First Harp" from *The Big Tree of Bunlahy* by Padraic Colum; "The Broken Note" from *The Trumpeter of Krakow* by Eric Kelly; and illustrations by Maud and Miska Petersham for "Rip Van Winkle" from *The Legend of Sleepy Hollow and Rip Van Winkle* by Washington Irving.

THE VIKING PRESS, INC., New York, for "A Woman's Wit" from *The Cottage at Bantry Bay* by Hilda van Stockum, copyright, 1938, by Hilda van Stockum.

NORMA L. WALLER for "Why the Chipmunk's Back Is Striped" by Frank B. Linderman.

ALBERT WHITMAN & COMPANY for "Pecos Bill and His Bouncing Bride" and "Pecos Bill" from *Pecos Bill, The Greatest Cowboy of All Time* by James Cloyd Bowman, published by Albert Whitman & Company, which was the source of *Yankee Doodle's Cousins*.

KATE WOOLFOLK for "Big Music" by Margaret Prescott Montague.

PADRAIC COLUM for "Bellerophon" and "Phaeton."
CORNELIA MEIGS for "The Tale of Sir Gareth of Orkeney That Was Called Beaumains."
JAMES STEVENS for "Great Hunter of the Woods."

JOHN GEE for illustrations for "The Cow Golden Horn" by Dhan Gopal Mukerji.
MRS. DONN P. CRANE for illustrations by Donn P. Crane for "Phaeton" by Padraic Colum.

Great pains have been taken to obtain permission from the owners of reprint material. Any errors that may possibly have been made are unintentional and will gladly be corrected in future printings if notice is sent to the Spencer Press, Inc.

Contents

Introduction

The stories in this volume of "Myths and Legends" are like none others in the world. This is partly because they are, most of them, immensely old, older than any ancient buildings still standing, older than the battered swords or jewels or bits of patterned pavements or any relics of a visible kind that have been cherished from long past times. Many of these stories were old when all such things were new. Some old things dry up and fall to pieces and blow away in the winds of time, while some, when they have strength and life of their own, go on lustily through generation after generation of men's knowledge, from century to century still vivid, still deeply loved. They have life because they have to do so directly with living things.

Generally when one thinks of stories it is of some tale put down by someone who sat with pen in hand or before a typewriter and composed and wrote it, to be set on a printed page and bound into a book where it would not be lost, but might easily be forgotten. But the tales we have here were not written, they were told and retold, and not for hundreds of years did anyone worry for fear they might be put aside and lost. One would think that they were hardly safe when they were in no book at all, but lived only in the memories of people who loved them and kept in mind every word of them, to pass them on to their children when the time came. Some we know must have disappeared, but it was the best of them and the most loved which did not die. They were told by fathers and mothers to children and grandchildren, told by old soldiers to young soldiers in the camps at night, sung or recited by minstrels in the great halls of those castles which we see now in ruins but with the stories still going bravely on their way.

Some, although they were already old, were written down as soon as men knew how to write at all, more were put down to be gathered in books when printing began, five hundred years ago. But some went on, still unwritten and unforgotten into our own time, when writers, some very great ones, set themselves to retell the tales in words more fitted to our own day and especially more fitted for the tastes and interests of children. It is so that we have safe possession of our proper inheritance from the dimly distant past.

Besides living on so stoutly, the stories also traveled. When the Romans, in their days of greatest power, made conquests in Greece, they carried away young Greek men and women to be slaves in the noble houses of Rome. It was known that the Greeks were most of them well taught and that they, in turn, were the best of teachers and attendants for the Roman children. Captured slaves could take nothing with them so, as the young Greeks looked back longingly at the gray olive trees and the brilliant blue of the sea along their own shores, they carried nothing of their own except what was in their minds and hearts. But within them they had still the legends of heroes and great deeds, of dangers and high courage which they had heard so often and would never forget. And, as the years passed and they learned to be resigned, even a little contented and a little happy in the new land, we can think of them in the marble-paved halls, among the high columns in the great houses, lofty and cool even in the Italian summer; we can think of the children, who could not go out in the midday heat, gathering about and saying to the Greek tutor or the Greek nurse, "Tell us that story you told before, tell us about Phaeton and his runaway horses, tell us about Jason and the Argo and the Golden Fleece." No one ever grows tired of hearing about courage and greatness.

The tales began to belong as much to the Romans as the Greeks, and when the Roman legions conquered more widely they carried their stories even to far-off Britain, telling them around the camp-fires in that northern cold to which they were so little used. When the Romans left Britain, many of their stories vanished, but they were found and revived again when books and schools and scholars brought Greek and Latin poetry to England. The Angles and Saxons came with their own legends, of the hero Siegfried, of dwarfs and dragons and of Tom Thumb. They were followed by the Danes who told of giants, and of Odin, father of the northern gods, and of Thor and Balder, his children. And all the time there was story-telling among the Scotch, the Irish, the Welsh, and the Cornishmen, who knew about elves and pixies, about changelings and people who were carried away to fairyland to abide for years while they still thought they had been gone but a day. One can see that English children, and later those in America, had a rich treasure for their inheritance of stories, gathered for them out of the past. In America, Indian legends were old before any of our forefathers ever came to shore there, and later the tales of Brer Rabbit and Brer Fox came over from Africa and were told by slaves to listening children. So it can be seen that English and American children, more than any others, have long had, by their own right, a stock of stories to read, to have read to them, or to hear told, that is greater than what belongs to the children of any other country.

But now, authors and translators have taken such interest in these old tales that they have brought them home to us from other lands, just as other lands have borrowed from us. We see in the selections in this book that besides the Greek and Roman stories, like "The Children of the Wolf" and the tale of the Golden Fleece, besides the Scandinavian tales of Thor and Loki, besides the Cornish stories, the Irish, the Indian, and American ones, we have also legends from our neighboring countries of South America told by Charles Finger, we have Eric Kelly's "The Broken Note," which he brought home from a mission to Poland, we have tales from Arabia and China, all available for our own reading. And we can see, further, how this making of stories that are told and not written, goes on without end, for in our own country, whose history is short compared with the age of most of these legends, stories have arisen in just the same way that the old ones grew up and were told and told again.

In America, when it was the New World, there were great tasks to be carried out that took courage and endurance; the clearing of the forests, the mastering of the seas, the spanning of the west with railroads. Even though none of this was the work of one man, legends appeared out of the very greatness of what had been accomplished, out of the wish of older men to spur young ones to their highest efforts. So we have the accounts of Paul Bunyan which old lumbermen tell to new ones, of Captain Stormalong which young men, newly enlisted on board ship, heard from seasoned sailors, we have the tall tales of John Henry and Pecos Bill and Tony Beaver. From the earliest times men have been bound to make stories about the things that caught their admiration, about the God-given gifts of strength and boldness, resourcefulness, devotion to a cause, patience and determination and hope. Such tales are the beginnings of all literature, and they do not perish but live by their own force and beauty as they have lived since before the world of books began.

CORNELIA MEIGS
Consultant Editor, Myths and Legends

mister mckee

Part I: FOR YOUNGER READERS

A CORNISH TALE

Enys Tregarthen

BUCCA BOO'S
LITTLE MERRY MEN

ILLUSTRATED BY *John Dukes McKee*

NEARLY everybody in Mevagissey had heard of Bucca Boo, the Neptune of the Cornish sea, and how he had commanded his nine little mermen to row in their longboat to a large rock pool near one of Mevagissey's high cliffs. There, cormorants and gulls nested, and a rare weed called the Weed of Health grew. The Mevagissey people had also heard that whoever was lucky enough to see the wonderful little boat, curved like a moon on her back, and bring her inside Mevagissey Quay would bring good luck to himself and the whole fishing town.

No one believed the old whiddle any more except Merlin Legassick, an ancient fisherman, and his grandson and namesake. Old Merlin declared that his great-granfer had seen such a boat come into the basin, but as he was crippled in his legs he could not climb up the slippery sides of the rock and so lost the chance of getting the little craft and bringing her into the quay.

This old whiddle had made a great impression on the younger Merlin, and it was the one desire of his heart to see the little boat his great-great-grandfather had seen, so he watched for her coming at each flow of the tide.

In those days the people of Mevagissey were all fisherfolk and exceedingly poor, owing to the scarcity of fish. Most of them knew, more often than not, the pangs of hunger. Old Merlin Legassick and his children and grandchildren were some

1

of the worst sufferers, as they were a large family and, being so many to share the little food there was, they had often to go supperless to bed.

As the fishing grew worse and worse, Merlin the elder and Merlin the younger longed more and more for the coming of the little boat into Bucca Boo's Basin, for it would turn the luck of the fishing from bad to good if only one of them could see her there and get hold of her. But, in spite of all their watching and longing, she had not yet come into the pool.

The younger Merlin was beginning to despair of her ever coming at all. The elder Merlin was often a bit down in the mouth too, only he would not allow it and cheered his little grandson by telling him that she was bound to put into the basin sometime, adding impressively, " 'Tis a prize worth waiting for even if she don't come till you be as ould and gray-headed as your granfer."

Neither Merlin went fishing. The old man was too feeble and the boy too young, but the former mended the fishing nets, and the little lad got the bait to supply the hooks. Late one afternoon in the beginning of June when the larks were thrilling the blue air with their melodies and Mevagissey cliffs were a sight to see, with the pink of the thrifts and the red and gold of the lady's fingers, old Merlin sent his namesake to Polstreath beach to dig sprats in the great stretch of sand there.

As the lad was leaving the cottage on the cliffside, the grand-sire begged him to keep an extra lookout for the dinky longboat.

" 'Tis such handsome weather," he said, "an' the sea from Rame's Head to Chapel Point is like a millpond a'most. Which-ever way the little merry men be pleased to come, they will be able to get into the bay as easy as any of our own boats."

Old Merlin's manner was so eager and his voice so earnest that the boy, instead of going to Polstreath as he was bidden, went to Bucca Boo's Basin. When he got there the tide had not yet reached the rock where the pool was, but it was flowing fast toward it. The sea was rougher than his grandfather had allowed him to expect, and waves were breaking against the northern cliffs, which were by far the boldest in the bay.

2

"The wee chaps and their dinky longboat won't come today, that's certain," said the boy to himself, a look of disappointment on his bright young face as he stood gazing seaward. "If they don't make haste granfer an' me won't be alive to watch, for we shall soon die of hunger, an' all the other folk in Mevagissey will, too."

The words were hardly out of his mouth when a laugh from somewhere close to him stole upon his ear. At first he thought it was the giggle of a kittiwake, which often laughs as it flies over the cliffs, but as it was followed by a chorus of tiny voices singing he knew it could not be. Much wondering what it was, young Merlin listened intently, and as he listened it dawned upon him that it *might* be Bucca Boo's little merry men come into the basin at last.

No sooner had this idea taken possession of his mind than he climbed up the side of the rock and peeped into the pool. There, to his unspeakable delight, was a tiny boat not much bigger than a child's toy and curved like a moon on her back.

mister
mckee

3

The little craft was full of tiny men with scarlet caps on their dark heads, for all the world like inverted sea anemones. Jumpers clung tight to their slim figures which, when they moved, were all sparkle and color like a mackerel's back.

" 'Tis the boat I've been on the lookout for all this time," young Merlin said joyfully to himself as he watched her riding on the swirling water under the shadow of the basin's side, "an' my chance is come at last to bring good luck to Mevagissey and the fishing!"

As he said this, wondering how he could get hold of the tiny craft, all the little men began laughing and chaffing each other. Then one of them broke out into a rollicking song with a chorus in which they all joined.

"With a dally rally O!
With a rally dally O!
In their longboat O!"

Merlin, as he listened, could scarcely refrain from joining in, too, the air was so catching and as fresh as the breeze blowing in from the sea.

When they had finished their song, they gripped their oars and began to row the boat across the pool to where Merlin was looking over it, motionless as the basin itself. Merlin held his breath as she came, waiting to grip her when she got under the basin's brim. The dinky crew were so intent on their rowing that they did not notice the brown handsome face of the lad who was watching them. When the boat was within a yard or so from where Merlin was sitting, the little man at the helm suddenly pointed to something glowing like flame under the rim of the basin.

"It is the Weed of Health," he cried.

"So it is," responded all the little men, suspending their slender oars to gaze at the burning weed.

"How are we to get it?" asked one anxiously.

"That's the question," replied the helmsman. "If I can measure distance with my eye, I'm afraid it is far out of our reach."

4

"In that case our coming here is all in vain," said one of the crew in a dismal voice. "Our Bucca Boo will never be himself again, and that horrid Bee Bo will sit on the great pearl throne instead."

"It is terrible to think of," said another. "If only we had legs made for climbing, as those great men-creatures have who live in yonder town," he sighed, turning his face in the direction of Mevagissey.

"Do not look at the black side of things until you are so obliged," the helmsman commented severely.

"Let's go and have a closer view," piped a little voice. "It may not be so un-get-at-able as we fear."

"Yes, let us," they all cried.

When Merlin saw the boat turn round and make for the spot where the weed was burning as bright as a field of poppies, he pulled himself back very gently and crept round to where the little craft was close in to the basin's wall. As soon as he dared peep over the pool, he saw that the little merry men were looking anything but merry. Gazing at each other in silent dismay, they sat for five minutes or more, when a voice broke the silence with a cry of hope.

"Why, how stupid we are! The sea will flow into the basin soon after sundown, and the basin will be so full of water that it will be easy to reach the beautiful weed."

"You forget that the weed blossoms and ripens only two hours before the sun posts westward," said the steersman sadly, "and it is within half an hour of that time now."

"I had forgotten that," the small man murmured.

"And we must therefore give up all hope of taking back the Weed of Health to our dear Bucca Boo," piped another little voice, wisht as the cry of a gull proclaiming a storm.

"We shall never dare show our faces in Bucca Boo Town without the weed," said an oarsman, shaking his scarlet-capped head. "I, for one, could not bear to see the despair in Bucca's eyes nor the look of triumph in Bee Bo's. Bee must have known when we sailed away to this place that the Weed of Health was growing where we feetless little men could never get it "

5

When Merlin, who was a feeling-hearted little chap, heard what Bucca Boo's nine merry men said, he felt sorry for them and almost lost sight of his own troubles in theirs. The moment, however, they stopped talking and sat looking at each other, the thought of the hungry ones in Mevagissey came over him. Telling himself that now was his opportunity to bring good luck to everybody in the little fishing town, he crooked his bare feet in the outer rim of the basin and let himself gently down its seaweed-covered side.

As he hung head downward his full length and was stretching out his hands to grasp the boat, one of her crew looked up and saw him. He uttered a cry of warning, and in a moment of time the boat and her crew were far from the boy's outflung hands. Merlin pulled himself up from his undignified position amid roars of laughter from the nine little merry men.

"You thought you had got us nicely, didn't you?" asked the helmsman, doffing his bright cap in derision. "Perhaps you will be a bit slower in your movements the *next time* Bucca Boo's merry men in their longboat come into the basin."

"I can get you now if I like," cried Merlin, who was a quick-tempered lad and did not at all like the way the little cock-a-hoop spoke to him. "I can dive like a shag and swim like a fish, and if I dive down there into the pool I can get you quite easily. It was only the fear of upsetting your little craft an' drowning 'ee all that stopped me. There now!"

The nine little merry men seemed vastly amused at the boy's boast and laughed till the salt tears rolled down their faces.

"It is quite too funny," cried one, wiping his eyes on the hem of his jumper.

"Yes, isn't it?" cried another. "Fancy his being afraid of *our* drowning!" and again they roared with laughter.

" 'Tis no laughing matter," shouted Merlin, who was red as a boiled crab with anger. "I'll spring into the pool now and get 'ee."

"Do!" taunted the helmsman, who was evidently the spokesman of the longboat crew and a person of some importance. "But I think you will have as much difficulty in laying hold of our boat as you would of its reflection."

6

"I'll come all the same," cried the boy, diving into the pool as he spoke.

When Merlin came to the top of the water, the little craft was nowhere to be seen. After swimming about in the basin looking for the lost boat under all the seaweed and into every hole where he thought it was possible for so tiny a craft to hide, he reluctantly came to the conclusion that Bucca Boo's little merry men and their longboat had vanished forever.

It was a crestfallen lad that climbed up the basin's side, low-spirited indeed to think that he had had the chance of bringing good luck to his town and had lost it by his hasty temper and boasting. Like the merry men, he felt he could not go home and face his family and friends after missing such a splendid opportunity.

As he sat on the basin's brim with his bare legs dangling over, feeling as miserable as a gull with its wings clipped, a gurgle broke on his ear—just the sort of gurgle that had made him think of the laugh of the kittiwake half an hour before. It came *up* from the pool and, looking down, Merlin saw to his amazed delight the tiny longboat and its crew in their scarlet caps and shining jumpers. They were in the very spot where they had so strangely disappeared.

"So you are not so clever as you thought you were!" chorused the little merry men in voices which sounded like a company of hedge sparrows chirping.

7

"No," said the boy honestly, "I en't. And what is worse still, I'm afraid now I shall never get hold of 'ee an' bring good luck to our fishing."

"Whatever do you mean?"

So Merlin told them all about the strange whiddle, finishing up by saying that he supposed it wasn't a bit true and that the poor folks of Mevagissey would still go to bed with empty stomachs.

"Part of the story is true enough, or we would not be here in the basin now," said the helmsman, looking up not unkindly at the boy's sad face. "The rest of the story was born of a despairing hope in a man-creature's brain pan. I am sorry for you nevertheless," he added after a pause, "but you see it is quite useless to hope that you or anybody could ever bring us and our boat inside Mevagissey Quay *against* our will."

He took his gaze from the disconsolate lad as he was speaking and again looked with longing eyes at the weed almost touching the boy's bare legs. Merlin followed the glance, and, noticing the hopelessness of its expression, a kind thought came into his mind.

Leaning over the pool he said, "As it don't seem in my power to bring prosperity to our poor little Mevagissey an' make the folks there happy, I'll make you an' your Bucca Boo happy instead, if I can."

"You! What can you do to make us and our dear Boo happy?" asked all the nine little men in great amazement.

"I heard you talking just now 'bout the Weed of Health," answered the boy, touching the glowing fronds which, since he had climbed up on the basin's brim a second time, had put forth silvery looking berries with streakings of crimson and gold. "I heard you say you was in a terrible way 'cause it grew where you couldn't reach it."

The little men were listening with all their ears, watching the boy intently.

"Well," Merlin went on, "it has just come into my noddle that I can pick it for you, that is, if you will please let me, little misters."

8

"Will you really do that kindness for us and our Boo?" they asked eagerly, hope and delight spreading over their faces.

"Iss, of course I will," answered the boy. "Tell me when you want it picked, and I'll do it for 'ee."

The nine little men talked to each other, speaking so low that Merlin couldn't catch a word they said; besides, he was too much Nature's gentleman and a Cornishman to bend over and listen. They were holding a kind of privy council and were apparently of one mind, for when they had finished their say the little oarsmen straightened themselves, and the steersman stood up in the stern of the boat and saluted the boy after the manner of royal boatmen.

"In the name of his majesty, Bucca Boo of the Cornish Sea, we gratefully accept your kind offer to gather him the Weed of Health which we have come so far to get. At the same time we make you an offer under certain conditions, and, if you will fulfill them, we will allow you to take us in our longboat inside Mevagissey Quay and so bring good luck to the fishing there."

"Do 'ee really an' truly mean what you say?" gasped Merlin, almost tumbling into the pool in his excitement.

"Yes, really and truly," responded the steersman with a broad grin. "But under certain conditions," he nodded again impressively.

"What be they, little misters?" asked the boy.

"The conditions are that the moment you have gathered the Weed of Health and its berries and dropped it into the pool you will leave here at once. Return to your town or its neighborhood and there remain until we have rowed up to your quay, which we will do just before the tide turns. Come down to the quay then and bring the boat inside."

Merlin was about to speak, but the steersman went on. "In the meantime," he said, "you must not tell anybody, not even your parents, of our being here in the basin or that you have the power to bring good cheer to everybody in your town."

"Is that all you want me to promise?" asked the boy. "I reckon I can do that." Then he added with a broad smile, "It will be as easy as walking."

9

"Not so easy as you think," said the helmsman gravely. "You will be tempted to tell everyone you meet that you have seen Bucca Boo's nine little merry men in their longboat and that they have promised you to come up to the quay at the turning of the tide. Remember, if you do tell anyone your chance of bringing good luck to your town will be gone forever."

Merlin nodded solemnly, "I'll remember."

"Another thing we shall warn you against," the little man went on. "Should you be tempted, as you probably will, to detain our boat when you have brought us into your quay, you will be in danger of changing the good luck to bad. If you keep us against our will, even for an hour, Bucca Boo will turn all your fishing nets into boulders and your lines into stones."

"I won't tell the folks for anything if you don't want me to," said Merlin. "But I should like to tell my old granfer, who do take much interest in 'ee all. It will be dreadful hard not to tell him."

"Nevertheless you may not tell even your granfer until you have taken us into the quay. You may then. But now," the steersman spoke more briskly, "if you are willing to gather the weed, please be quick. It is ripe and ought to be plucked at once both for your sake and for our own. The waves are beginning to dash against the foot of the rock."

"I forgot the tide," cried Merlin, flinging himself flat on the basin's brim and gathering the scarlet weed with its bright berries. He plucked all there was and dropped it into the pool; then, as the little merry men were stowing it away in their longboat, he climbed down the basin's side.

If he had been five minutes later, he would not have been able to get away from the great rock at all for it was almost surrounded by the sea. Once clear of the rock Merlin made for Mevagissey. Distantly he heard the little merry men singing at the top of their voices the song which had so delighted him. Running up the narrow streets of the little town, Merlin found himself singing too and with as much gusto as the merry men.

Everyone he met asked what was the matter with him, and

10

mister
mckee

Merlin had, as the steersman foretold, the greatest difficulty
in the world to keep from telling that he had seen with his
own eyes Bucca Boo's little merry men in their longboat and of
all the luck and cheer the town was going to have. When he
reached home his grandfather quickly saw that something out
of the ordinary had happened to the boy and plied him with
questions.

Merlin would have answered the old man's questions gladly,
but he dared not because of what the helmsman had said to
him. To prevent himself from letting out all there was to tell, he
contorted his face so that his grandsire thought he was either
making faces at him on purpose or that he really had seen the
longboat in the rock pool and let go his chance of bringing her
up to the quay. Old Merlin threatened the boy that if he did
not let him hear all there was to hear he would give him the
rope's end.

11

"You have bewitched the cheeld with your nonsense about Bucca Boo's little boat coming into our bay," struck in the lad's mother after looking at her son. "Shame to 'ee, Granfer Legassick."

When the angry old man insisted that it was his belief the boy had seen the longboat and wouldn't tell, young Merlin to escape further questioning took to his heels and made for the top of the hill above the town where he knew his grandfather could not follow him.

The sun was sinking behind Mevagissey by this time, and all the beauty of the evening sky was reflected in the quiet waters of the bay. The whole harbor was lovely with reflected light, and even the northern cliffs shone with gold. As the sun sank lower and lower, the fishing boats came up the bay, catching the light on their weather-stained sails.

The lad watched the boats moving toward the quay, and as they came he saw the women and children go down on the quay walls to welcome them back and to see if they had a good catch of fish. But Merlin could tell by the very movements of the people that the fishermen's luck had been bad again.

"I'm glad as a bird that I didn't let out to anybody, nor to granfer nuther, that I saw the dinky longboat in Bucca Boo's Basin," said the lad to himself as his brown eyes followed the people on their homeward way, "for now there won't be any more starving folks in Mevagissey Town after tonight when I shall have brought the little craft and all her merry men into our quay!" He clapped his hands for the joy of it, then clapped them over his mouth lest he should be heard.

"Aw, I wonder what granfer an' all of 'em will say to me," he went on softly to himself, "when they have heard what I have seen with my own two eyes an' done with my own two hands. And that I, Merlin Legassick, have brought good luck to the fishing and good cheer to the people in our town." He laughed aloud at the thought of it.

The sun had dropped behind the hill by this time, but the clouds that stretched across the sky from Mevagissey to Goran Churchtown still held the sunlight. When the sun had set and

12

the afterglow had all gone and the little town, lying low in the valley below where Merlin sat, grew indistinct in the semi-darkness, the lad got up and went down the hill.

Mevagissey people went early to bed, and the narrow, twisting streets were very quiet as the lad made his way through them. His own people had retired even before the sun went down. Poor dears, they had nothing cheering to make them want to sit up. The catch of fish was unusually bad, not more than one small fish to a boat, and they all felt very miserable. Saying bed was the best place for starving people, to bed the Legassicks had gone, leaving the door on the latch for Merlin.

When the lad reached home he found even his old grandfather abed and apparently fast asleep, much to his thankfulness, for there was no one to ask him troublesome questions.

It was yet a good while to the ebb of the tide, but Merlin was loath to go to sleep, fearing he should not wake in time. He shared his room with several of his brothers, and, as he lay listening to their heavy breathing, a terrible misgiving took possession of him that Bucca Boo's little merry men had tricked him. The idea made him so miserable that he got into his clothes and crept out into the little street.

He had no sooner left the house than a pair of old eyes looked out of the window, watching eagerly to see what way the boy would go.

Once out on the street Merlin raced down to the quay and arrived there breathless. It was later than he thought, for a clock in the distance was striking the hour, and Merlin knew that the tide had already turned. There was still a great deal of ground swell on outside the little haven, but inside, where all the fishing boats were riding in safety, it was like a lake. The boy peered anxiously over the quay, but he could see nothing save the water heaving against its stone walls.

"I don't believe they meant to come when they sent me off like that," the boy cried aloud. " 'Twas a dirty trick to play on a poor little chap like me. I would a-kept my word."

"And we have kept ours," cried a little voice sweet and clear as a blackbird's whistle.

13

It was followed by a burst of hearty laughter, and, looking down again, Merlin saw on the dark water the longboat and her crew shining like a rising star.

"Aw, I *am* so glad you've come," exclaimed the boy, leaning over the quay wall in a transport of delight. "I was afraid you had gone along home. Shall I come down now an' bring the little boat an' you into the quay?"

"Have you kept your promise?" asked the steersman.

"Iss, faithful," answered the boy.

"Then come down and bring Bucca Boo's merry men inside Mevagissey Quay and win for the fisherfolk prosperity forever."

Young Merlin was down the quay's stone stairway in a jiffy. When he was about to lay his hands on the tiny boat and her crew, he paused, partly from fear and partly because she looked so beautiful: one moment she was a curve of crimson flame seeming to catch the water on fire around her, and the next she was like a rainbow lying on its back.

"Don't be afraid to touch the longboat," cried the nine little merry men. "She'll hurt nobody who plucked the scarlet Weed of Health. Be quick, please, for there is a faraway sound of an old man walking along the street."

For the sake of his beloved town and its people, Merlin took hold of the glowing little boat and brought her safely inside Mevagissey Quay. There she lay, a burning wonder on the quiet water, by the side of his father's fishing boat.

"Now," said the helmsman, standing up in the stern of the dinky craft, "speed away to meet the old man and tell him that at last Bucca Boo's little merry men have been brought inside Mevagissey Quay, and that the hand which brought her and us has won good luck to Mevagissey fishing forever."

"Don't send me away please, dear little sirs," pleaded the boy. "Let me keep the longboat here in the quay till the morning that the folks may see with their own eyes what a beauty she is with her dinky little oars and all."

"Away," said the little man sternly, "unless you wish to undo the blessing you have brought for this place and bring it a curse instead. Remember what we told you."

14

It was hard for Merlin to leave the little craft, which seemed to grow more and more beautiful as he gazed at it. Then he remembered all that he and the poor people in his town had suffered, and he made himself withdraw his gaze. Having done that, his passionate desire to detain her left him, and he rushed away to tell his grandfather, whom he saw walking toward him as quickly as his aged feet would let him.

"I guessed what was in the wind," said old Merlin, thumping his grandson's back in his joy when he had told him the great

news. "An' you was a sensible little chap to keep it dark, especially as they little merry men didn't want us to know."

He took young Merlin's hand in his. "Come along to the quay head," he said eagerly. "Maybe having give 'ee permission to tell me, they will wait by the quay that I may have the chance of seeing her."

The hope was vain. When they got to the quay and looked in, there was nothing to be seen except the fishing fleet riding on the dark, still water in its safe anchorage.

"An' she was down here by father's boat only ten minutes or so ago, burning like the moon away there," cried young Merlin, gazing out toward the sea, "an' now she is nowhere to be seen. 'Tis queer, sure 'nough."

15

"There is something or other glowing like a live coal on the horizon," said the old man, also gazing seaward where the moon was rippling the water. "Is it a star low down on the sea or is it the dinky longboat an' the nine little merry men going back home?"

It was a question young Merlin could not answer, and neither he nor the old fisherman was ever sure what the nature of that soft glow on the water's edge was. As they turned away from the quay, the wind blowing in from the open sea brought with it the sound of voices singing way faraway. The boy, listening with all his ears, thought he heard the last lines of the little merry men's song—

> "With a dally rally O!
> With a rally dally O!
> In their longboat O!"

All Mevagissey was in a ferment of excitement the next morning when young Merlin's story was noised about. Some believed it and some did not. Others declared that he had dreamed it all.

"True or not true, time will tell," said the old Merlin laconically. "But if it be true that Bucca Boo's nine little merry men and their dinky longboat have been in the rock pool and that my dear grandson and namesake saw her with his own eyes and brought her inside our quay, then prosperity has come to us."

If they laughed at the old man, as they had so often, he would nod and say, "You will all be wishing soon 'twas your eyes saw the little craft and your hands that brought her hither."

Young Merlin's story was soon verified, for, from the night that the lad declared the longboat and her crew had ridden safely on the water of Mevagissey Harbor, prosperity came to the little fishing town, to its fisherfolk, and particularly to the House of Legassick which flourished amazingly. If fish stayed away from the nets and lines of other Cornish fishermen, they did not from the fishermen of Mevagissey, and there was never any more need for anybody to go to bed with an empty stomach.

*Harold Courlander
and George Herzog*

TALK

ILLUSTRATED BY *Helen Prickett*

ONCE, not far from the city of Accra on the Gulf of Guinea, a country man went out to his garden to dig up some yams to take to market. While he was digging, one of the yams said to him,—

"Well, at last you're here. You never weeded me, but now you come around with your digging stick. Go away and leave me alone!"

The farmer turned around and looked at his cow in amazement. The cow was chewing her cud and looking at him.

"Did you say something?" he asked.

The cow kept on chewing and said nothing, but the man's dog spoke up.

"It wasn't the cow who spoke to you," the dog said. "It was the yam. The yam says leave him alone."

The man became angry, because his dog had never talked before, and he didn't like his tone besides. So he took his knife and cut a branch from a palm tree to whip his dog. Just then the palm tree said,—

17

"Put that branch down!"

The man was getting very upset about the way things were going, and he started to throw the palm branch away, but the palm branch said,—

"Man, put me down softly!"

He put the branch down gently on a stone, and the stone said,—

"Hey, take that thing off me!"

This was enough, and the frightened farmer started to run for his village. On the way he met a fisherman going the other way with a fish trap on his head.

"What's the hurry?" the fisherman asked.

"My yam said, 'Leave me alone!' Then the dog said, 'Listen to what the yam says!' When I went to whip the dog with a palm branch the tree said, 'Put that branch down!' Then the palm branch said, 'Do it softly!' Then the stone said, 'Take that thing off me!' "

"Is that all?" the man with the fish trap asked. "Is that so frightening?"

"Well," the man's fish trap said, "did he take it off the stone?"

"Wah!" the fisherman shouted. He threw the fish trap on the ground and began to run with the farmer, and on the trail they met a weaver with a bundle of cloth on his head.

"Where are you going in such a rush?" he asked them.

"My yam said, 'Leave me alone!' " the farmer said. "The dog said, 'Listen to what the yam says!' The tree said, 'Put that branch down!' The branch said, 'Do it softly!' And the stone said, 'Take that thing off me!' "

"And then," the fisherman continued, "the fish trap said, 'Did he take it off?' "

"That's nothing to get excited about," the weaver said, "no reason at all."

"Oh yes it is," his bundle of cloth said. "If it happened to you you'd run too!"

"Wah!" the weaver shouted. He threw his bundle on the trail and started running with the other men.

They came to the ford in the river and found a man bathing.

"Are you chasing a gazelle?" he asked them.

The first man said breathlessly,—

"My yam talked at me, and it said, 'Leave me alone!' And my dog said, 'Listen to your yam!' And when I cut myself a branch the tree said, 'Put that branch down!' And the branch said, 'Do it softly!' And the stone said, 'Take that thing off me!' "

The fisherman panted,—

"And my trap said, 'Did he?' "

The weaver wheezed,—

"And my bundle of cloth said, 'You'd run too!' "

"Is that why you're running?" the man in the river asked.

"Well, wouldn't you run if you were in their position?" the river said.

The man jumped out of the water and began to run with the others. They ran down the main street of the village to the house of the chief. The chief's servants brought his stool out, and he came and sat on it to listen to their complaints. The men began to recite their troubles.

"I went out to my garden to dig yams," the farmer said, waving his arms. "Then everything began to talk! My yam said, 'Leave me alone!' My dog said, 'Pay attention to your yam!' The tree said, 'Put that branch down!' The branch said, 'Do it softly!' And the stone said, 'Take it off me!' "

"And my fish trap said, "Well, did he take it off?' " the fisherman said.

"And my cloth said, 'You'd run too!' " the weaver said.

"And the river said the same," the bather said hoarsely, his eyes bulging.

The chief listened to them patiently, but he couldn't refrain from scowling.

"Now this is really a wild story," he said at last. "You'd better all go back to your work before I punish you for disturbing the peace."

So the men went away, and the chief shook his head and mumbled to himself, "Nonsense like that upsets the community."

"Fantastic, isn't it?" his stool said. "Imagine, a talking yam!"

19

Joel Chandler Harris

UNCLE REMUS AND THE TAR-BABY

ILLUSTRATED BY *A. B. Frost*

ONE evening recently, the lady whom Uncle Remus calls "Miss Sally" missed her little seven-year-old boy. Making search for him through the house and through the yard, she heard the sound of voices in the old man's cabin and, looking through the window, saw the child sitting by Uncle Remus. His head rested against the old man's arm, and he was gazing with an expression of the most intense interest into the rough, weather-beaten face that beamed so kindly upon him. This is what "Miss Sally" heard:

"Bimeby, one day, arter Brer Fox bin doin' all dat he could fer ter ketch Brer Rabbit, en Brer Rabbit bin doin' all he could fer to keep 'im fum it, Brer Fox say to hisse'f dat he'd put up a game on Brer Rabbit, en he ain't mo'n got de wuds out'n his mouf twel Brer Rabbit come a lopin' up de big road, lookin' des ez plump, en ez fat, en ez sassy ez a Moggin hoss in a barley-patch.

" 'Hol' on dar, Brer Rabbit,' sez Brer Fox, sezee.

" 'I ain't got time, Brer Fox,' sez Brer Rabbit, sezee, sorter mendin' his licks.

" 'I wanter have some confab wid you, Brer Rabbit,' sez Brer Fox, sezee.

"All right, Brer Fox, but you better holler fum whar you stan'. I'm monstus full er fleas dis mawnin',' sez Brer Rabbit, sezee.

" 'I seed Brer B'ar yistiddy,' sez Brer Fox, sezee, 'en he sorter

20

rake me over de coals kaze you en me ain't make frens en live naberly, en I told 'im dat I'd see you.'

"Den Brer Rabbit scratch one year wid his off hinefoot sorter jub'usly, en den he ups en sez, sezee,—

"'All a settin', Brer Fox. Spose'n you drap roun' ter-morrer en take dinner wid me. We ain't got no great doin's at our house, but I speck de old 'oman en de chilluns kin sorter scramble roun' en git up sump'n fer ter stay yo' stummuck.'

"'I'm 'gree'ble, Brer Rabbit,' sez Brer Fox, sezee.

"'Den I'll 'pen' on you,' sez Brer Rabbit, sezee.

"Nex' day, Mr. Rabbit an' Miss Rabbit got up soon, 'fo' day, en raided on a gyarden like Miss Sally's out dar, en got some cabbiges en some roas'n years, en some sparrer-grass, en dey fix up a smashin' dinner. Bimeby one er de little Rabbits, playin' out in de backyard, come runnin' in hollerin', 'oh, ma! oh, ma! I seed Mr. Fox a comin'!' En den Brer Rabbit he tuck de chilluns by der years en make um set down, en den him and Miss

Rabbit sorter dally roun' waitin' for Brer Fox. En dey keep on waitin', but no Brer Fox ain't come. Atter 'while Brer Rabbit goes to de do', easy like, en peep out, en dar, stickin' fum behime de cornder, wuz de tip-een'er Brer Fox tail. Den Brer Rabbit shot de do' en sot down, en put his paws behime his years en begin fer ter sing:

> " 'De place wharbouts you spill de grease,
>   Right dar youer boun' ter slide,
>   An' whar you fine a bunch er ha'r,
>   You'll sholy fine de hide.'

"Nex' day, Brer Fox sont word by Mr. Mink, en skuze hisse'f kaze he wuz too sick fer ter come, en he ax Brer Rabbit fer to come en take dinner wid him, en Brer Rabbit say he wuz 'gree-'ble.

"Bimeby, w'en de shadders wuz at der shortes', Brer Rabbit he sorter brush up en sa'nter down ter Brer Fox's house, en w'en he got dar, he hear somebody groanin', en he look in de do', en dar he see Brer Fox settin' up in a rockin' cheer all wrop up wid flannil, en he look mighty weak. Brer Rabbit look all 'roun', he did, but he ain't see no dinner. De dishpan wuz settin' on de table, en close by wuz a kyarvin' knife.

" 'Look like you gwineter have chicken fer dinner, Brer Fox,' sez Brer Rabbit, sezee.

" 'Yes, Brer Rabbit, deyer nice, en fresh, en tender,' sez Brer Fox, sezee.

"Den Brer Rabbit sorter pull his mustarsh, en say: 'You ain't got no calamus root, is you, Brer Fox? I done got so now dat I can't eat no chicken 'ceppin' she's seasoned up wid calamus root.' En wid dat Brer Rabbit lipt out er de do' and dodge 'mong de bushes, en sot dar watchin' fer Brer Fox; en he ain't watch long, nudder, kaze Brer Fox flung off de flannil en crope out er de house en got whar he could cloze in on Brer Rabbit, en bimeby Brer Rabbit holler out: 'Oh, Brer Fox! I'll des put yo' calamus root out yer on dish yer stump. Better come git it while hit's fresh,' and wid dat Brer Rabbit gallop off home. En Brer

22

Fox ain't never kotch 'im yit, en w'at's mo', honey, he ain't gwineter."

"Didn't the fox *never* catch the rabbit, Uncle Remus?" asked the little boy the next evening.

"He come mighty nigh it, honey, sho's you born—Brer Fox did. One day atter Brer Rabbit fool 'm wid dat calamus root, Brer Fox went ter wuk en got 'im some tar, en mix it wid some turkentime, en fix up a contrapshun wat he call a Tar-Baby, en he tuck dish yer Tar-Baby en he sot 'er in de big road, en den he lay off in de bushes fer to see what de news wuz gwineter be. En he didn't hatter wait long, nudder, kaze bimeby here come Brer Rabbit pacin' down de road—lippity-clippity, clippity-lippity—dez ez sassy ez a jaybird. Brer Fox, he lay low. Brer Rabbit come prancin' 'long twel he spy de Tar-Baby, en den he fotch up on his behime legs like he wus 'stonished. De Tar-Baby, she sot dar, she did, en Brer Fox, he lay low.

" 'Mawnin'!' sez Brer Rabbit, sezee—'nice wedder dis mawnin',' sezee.

"Tar-Baby ain't sayin' nothin', en Brer Fox, he lay low.

" 'How duz yo' sym'tums seem ter segashuate?' sez Brer Rabbit, sezee.

"Brer Fox, he wink his eye slow, en lay low, en de Tar-Baby, she ain't sayin' nothin'.

" 'How you come on, den? Is you deaf?' sez Brer Rabbit, sezee. 'Kaze if you is, I kin holler louder,' sezee.

"Tar-Baby stay still, en Brer Fox, he lay low.

" 'Youer stuck up, dat's w'at you is,' sez Brer Rabbit, sezee, 'en I'm gwineter kyore you, dat's w'at I'm a gwineter do,' sezee.

"Brer Fox, he sorter chuckle in his stummick, he did, but Tar-Baby ain't sayin' nothin'.

" 'I'm gwineter larn you howter talk ter 'specttubble fokes ef hit's de las' ack,' sez Brer Rabbit, sezee. 'Ef you don't take off dat hat en tell me howdy, I'm gwineter bus' you wide open,' sezee.

"Tar-Baby stay still, en Brer Fox, he lay low.

"Brer Rabbit keep on axin' 'im, en de Tar-Baby, she keep on sayin' nothin', twel present'y Brer Rabbit draw back wid his fis', he did, en blip he tuck 'er side er de head. Right dar's whar he broke his merlasses jug. His fis' stuck, en he can't pull loose. De tar hilt 'im. But Tar-Baby, she stay still, en Brer Fox, he lay low.

" 'Ef you don't lemme loose, I'll knock you agin,' sez Brer Rabbit, sezee, en wid dat he fotch 'er a wipe wid de udder han', en dat stuck. Tar-Baby, she ain't sayin' nothin', en Brer Fox, he lay low.

" 'Tu'n me loose, fo' I kick de natal stuffin' outen you,' sez Brer Rabbit, sezee, but de Tar-Baby, she ain't sayin' nothin'. She des hilt on, en den Brer Rabbit lose de use er his feet in de same way. Brer Fox, he lay low. Den Brer Rabbit squall out dat ef de Tar-Baby don't tu'n 'im loose he butt 'er cranksided. En den he butted, en his head got stuck. Den Brer Fox, he sa'ntered fort', lookin' des ez innercent ez one er yo' mammy's mockin'-birds.

24

" 'Howdy, Brer Rabbit,' sez Brer Fox, sezee. 'You look sorter stuck up dis mawnin','' sezee, en den he rolled on de groun', en laughed en laughed twel he couldn't laugh no mo'. 'I speck you'll take dinner wid me dis time, Brer Rabbit. I done laid in some calamus root, en I ain't gwineter take no skuse,' sez Brer Fox, sezee."

Here Uncle Remus paused and drew a two-pound yam out of the ashes.

"Did the fox eat the rabbit?" asked the little boy to whom the story had been told.

"Dat's all de fur de tale goes," replied the old man. "He mout, en den again he moutent. Some say Jedge B'ar come long en loosed 'im—some say he didn't. I hear Miss Sally callin'. You better run 'long."

Louis Wolfe

JOHN HENRY
MIGHTY RAILROADER

ILLUSTRATED BY *John Merryweather*

H IS name was John Henry. And what a man he was! Down South and even in other parts of the country railroaders still talk about, still sing about the famous Negro. He has become a part of our American railroad tradition. John Henry is remembered as the steel-driving man who challenged and beat them all.

West Virginia, especially, will never forget the fateful day in 1872 when John Henry challenged a steam drill to a contest. The young giant vowed he would drive a steel drill deeper into rock than the machine "even if I have to die with a hammer in my hand."

There are some things we don't know for certain about John Henry. He has become such a legendary figure that hundreds of Negroes who never even saw him claimed him as a close friend. Many families claimed him as a relative. Several southern states claimed him as a native son. Several cities claimed he died there—and at different times!

However, we are reasonably sure of some facts. We know that John Henry was the son of slave parents and grew up to manhood after the Civil War. He wandered from place to place, picking cotton, toting bales along the river front, shoveling coal on a locomotive, or helping build railroads by driving steel.

26

The brawny colossus liked people, and people liked him. He played cards, strummed a guitar, made up songs, and was popular with the girls. Whenever he strutted down the street, folks would gasp, "There goes John Henry. What a railroad man!"

John Henry himself was most proud of one thing—his reputation as a steel-driving man. Six feet three inches tall, solid as a steel beam, the strapping Hercules had muscles that bulged like knots on an oak tree. And when it came to swinging a hammer and driving steel, he took on all challengers and beat them in contests. And it was this reputation that made his name a household word from Atlanta to New Orleans and up to West Virginia.

Now a steel-driving man was a worker who swung a hammer and drove a sharp-edged steel bar or drill in solid rock. The drill was held by another worker, called a shaker. His job was to shake and turn the drill to keep the dust and gravel out of the hole. After the hole was made in the rock, it was filled with explosives which were set off. In this manner railroad tunnels were bored through mountains.

John Henry used to swing a 10- or 20-pound sheepnose hammer with a handle four feet long. Standing about six feet from the drill, he would sing in his deep bass voice and swing his mighty hammer with terrific force. Bill, his shaker, used to look up to him and gasp, "What power! What power!"

But Bill wasn't the only one who marveled at John Henry's superhuman strength. A blacksmith who sharpened the drills once said, "That man mountain sometimes needs six men running back and forth to supply him with drills." A steel driver drawled, "John Henry swings a hammer harder than an Alabama mule can kick." The foreman used to say, "He can swing two 20-pound hammers, one in each hand, for hours without losing a stroke."

And by 1870 John Henry's prowess was so well established down South that other steel-driving men were afraid to challenge him to a contest. It was a settled matter. John Henry was the champion of them all.

But as time passed and things changed—a new and different challenger turned up. It all happened in 1872 when the Chesapeake and Ohio Railroad was boring a tunnel through the Allegheny Mountains near the town of Talcott, West Virginia. Called the Big Bend, the tunnel was a mile and a quarter long through solid rock. John Henry and hundreds of other railroad workers were hammering, driving, and blasting their way through.

One day a salesman came around with a new-fangled machine. It was made of steel and was driven by steam. The salesman bragged that the machine could drive steel faster than any man. The foreman looked it over and rubbed his chin. "Hm, that's so," he said. "Maybe it's just what I need."

Meanwhile, a blacksmith, a few shakers, and some water boys gathered around the eight-horsepower machine and scornfully looked it over. John Henry also came over to take a look. He walked around the machine, gazing at the gauges, dials, and the rubber hose that was connected to the hammer. Placing his hands on his hips, he sneered, "So that's the contraption that can beat any man at driving steel, eh?"

"Of course," the salesman snapped. "No human being can beat this steam drill."

John Henry ran his wet handkerchief over his sweaty head and chuckled, "Well, Mister, you're looking right at the man who can beat it."

The salesman laughed, "John Henry, I've heard all about you being champion. But this is not a man . . . it's a machine . . . it's driven by steam . . . why . . ."

"I can still beat it," John Henry drawled, defiantly glaring at the salesman.

"That's impossible. Why . . ." the salesman sputtered.

"Well, if you're so cocksure," John Henry interrupted again, "how about a little contest?"

"That's a good idea," the foreman spoke up. "We'll hold a contest. The machine against our John Henry. And if the machine wins, I'll buy one."

"That's wonderful, wonderful," the salesman beamed, rub-

bing his hands together. "We'll hold a contest the first thing tomorrow morning." Then he walked away, still rubbing his hands as if he had already won the contest.

That night Talcott town buzzed with nothing else but chatter of the contest. Would John Henry beat the steam machine? Would he still hold the title of champion steel-driving man? Most railroaders were sure the big bruiser would win, but they talked and argued, talked and argued about the contest right into the middle of the night.

Early the next morning a hot August sun rose over the Allegheny hills. Excited shopkeepers and farmers as well as eager blacksmiths, shakers, steel-driving men, and water boys gathered at the east portal of Big Bend railroad tunnel. They could hardly wait for the big event to start. They still talked and argued, and some of them laid bets.

At 7 o'clock sharp Bill, John Henry's shaker, gripped a steel drill and took his position against the rock wall. The machine was then wheeled into position near by and steam got up. Stripped to the waist, John Henry huddled together with the foreman and salesman. They decided on the terms of the contest. It would last one hour. The one that drilled deepest into the rock would win. At the last minute the foreman bet the salesman $100 that John Henry would win.

Finally, everything was set. The machine operator had plenty of steam up and was raring to go. John Henry strode over to Bill. His black muscles glistened like patent leather in the bright sun as he bent down to rub some rock dust on his gnarled hands. A hush came over the crowd when the foreman took out his watch, raised his hand, and asked, "Are you ready?"

Digging his feet solidly into the dirt, the machine operator said, "Ready."

John Henry held his hammer in a viselike grip, tensed his muscles, then said, "Ready."

The foreman shouted, "Go."

John Henry raised his mighty hammer and with swift powerful strokes he swung away. Wham! Wham! Sparks flew from the drill, and dust shot up in tiny puffs.

30

Throbbing and hissing, the machine also banged away with mighty blows and pounded the drill down into the rock.

The race was on! Muscle against steam. John Henry against the machine!

"Come on, big fella," the blacksmith snarled. "Show 'em how to drive steel."

"Swing that hammer," a water boy yelled.

John Henry needed no coaxing. With his brawny arms and sturdy legs straining to the limit, he swung faster and faster. Bill turned and shook the drill as fast as he could.

But the machine pounded away and took an early lead. With steam way up, she clattered ra-ta-ta-ta . . . ra-ta-ta-ta.

Just then John Henry broke into song.

"Before that machine will beat me
I'll die with the hammer in my hand.
Before that machine will beat me
I'll die with my hammer in my hand."

Now his arm muscles bulged and sweat streamed down his broad back. His hammer swished through the air and the earth trembled beneath his feet. The tense crowd gathered closer. "Come on, John Henry, swing that hammer," they yelled.

Fifteen minutes had passed. The machine was still ahead and gaining. Bill looked up and pleaded, "Give it all you got."

The machine operator was smiling. He was sure of victory. The salesman was smiling too. He was sure of victory, the sale of the machine, and $100. Even the machine seemed to catch the spirit of victory as it purred with powerful strokes.

Then something happened! The machine . . . it coughed and sputtered . . . the drill was jammed in the hole. The operator angrily jerked the drill out, cleaned out the hole of dust and gravel, then jammed the drill back in again.

Meanwhile, Bill shouted, "Now's our chance, John Henry. Faster, faster." With a swifter and swifter stroke the Negro colossus swung the hammer round, up and down . . . round, up and down . . . round, up and down.

31

At the halfway mark John Henry asked, "How am I doing?" Bill glanced across the dusty tunnel entrance. "Still behind."

A frown came over John Henry's face. "Give me another hammer," he barked, without breaking the rhythm of his stroke. A blacksmith handed him another 20-pound hammer, and John Henry was now swinging away with a hammer in each hand. Wham! Wham! Wham! Wham!

"That's the stuff," the crowd yelled. "Now you're catching up."

The smile was gone from the machine operator's face. He grimly turned on every bit of steam he had. The salesman nervously adjusted the gauges and straightened out the rubber hose. The smile was gone from his face too.

"Fifteen minutes to go," the foreman announced.

The mountain seemed to tremble as John Henry and the machine let go with everything they had. Calling on his last ounce of strength, the muscle man whirled his two hammers at a killing pace. A tiny puddle of sweat formed near his feet. Again he broke into song. But now he was short of breath, and the words came haltingly.

> "Before . . . that machine . . . will beat me
> I'll die . . . I'll die . . ."

Now Bill was smiling. "You're ahead, big boy," he said. "Keep it up. Just keep it up."

Just then the foreman shouted, "Time's up!"

"Hurray! Hurray!" the crowd shouted. "Our man won!" Then they gathered around the foreman as he measured both holes to make it official. The machine had driven the drill six feet into the rock. John Henry had driven eight feet! He was still champion over all men—and machines.

Meanwhile, John Henry sat slumped down on a rock, dead tired. The two hammers still in his hands, he gasped for breath and barely had the strength to show a smile of victory. As some of the men paid off their bets and patted him on the back, he gazed blankly at the ground. Except for his heaving chest, he seemed as lifeless as the rock he sat on.

That night Talcott town planned a big celebration. But there was no celebration, and the town was quiet and sad. It was the quiet and sadness of mourning—for John Henry was dead.

After the contest John Henry complained of a pain in his head. That night he ate a light supper and went to bed early. Toward midnight a blood vessel burst in his head and he died. Three days later his weary body was laid to rest.

Yes, John Henry, the world's champion steel-driving man was dead. But his spirit will never be laid to rest. Today, wherever folks pick cotton, or tote cotton bales, or fire coal or drive steel, they still talk about, they still sing about the legendary Negro. Some railroaders even say that when trains speed through Big Bend Tunnel the wind can be heard sighing one of John Henry's tunes. And those with a little extra imagination listen closely and hear the tracks sing:

> "Before that machine will beat me
> I'll die with a hammer in my hands."

THE CHILDREN
OF THE WOLF

RETOLD BY *Eleanor Farjeon*

ILLUSTRATED BY *Helen Prickett*

IN THE city of Alba, in the lovely land of Italy, Aeneas was King. He had been a Prince in Troy, and when Troy was burned he sailed away to Italy with his men and his ships full of treasure. And when he came to Italy he married the King's daughter, and their sons became the Kings of Alba after them.

Now it happened that when the thirteenth King of Alba died, he left behind him two sons, whose names were Amulius and Numitor, and they could not decide which of the two should be King. So Amulius said to Numitor,—

"Let us divide what we have. Here, on the one hand, is the city and the land; and here, on the other, is all the treasure that Aeneas brought to Italy from Troy, hundreds of years ago. Which will you have, Numitor—the treasure or the land?"

"I will choose the land," said Numitor, "and you shall keep the treasure. You will be a richer man than I, but I will be the King of the land."

Amulius agreed to this, and the division was made. But Amulius longed for the land as well as the treasure, and he was now a rich man, while Numitor was only a poor King. So with his money Amulius paid the soldiers to fight for him, and he turned Numitor out of the city and became the King of Alba. In this way he had the money and the land as well.

From *Mighty Men from Achilles to Julius Caesar* by Eleanor Farjeon. Copyright, 1925, D. Appleton & Company. Reprinted by permission of the publishers Appleton-Century-Crofts, Inc.

Numitor went away with his friends and lived outside the city, keeping his cows and sheep like a poor man, as he now was. But he could not take with him his daughter Sylvia, for her uncle Amulius kept her a prisoner in the city. Amulius also had a beautiful daughter, Antho, who loved her cousin dearly.

One day an old servant came to King Amulius and said,—

"O King, there is danger to you. For the Princess Sylvia has twin babies, both boys, and who knows what they will not do to you when they are men?"

Then King Amulius was frightened and said,—

"Sylvia and her sons must be put to death."

But the Princess Antho fell on her knees before him and begged for Sylvia's life. "Do not kill her, father," she said, "for I love her."

She begged so hard that Amulius gave way. "Well, Sylvia shall live," said he, "but the babies must die."

And he told his servant to take the babies away in a little basket and cast them into the river Tiber.

The servant did as he was told—but when he got to the Tiber it was running high, with so strong a current that he was afraid

to go near it. So he laid the basket as close as he could to the water, thinking, "The river will rise and drown the children, or they will die of cold and hunger." And he went away.

The water in the river rose higher and higher, and came over the banks to where the basket was lying; but instead of drowning the babies, it lifted the basket as gently as though it were a mother rocking a cradle, and floated it away down the river, and brought it to shore in a pleasant grove. There it left the basket and flowed on while the children slept.

As they lay there, a tap-tap-tap was heard on the bark of the fig tree, and a woodpecker settled in the leaves and looked down on the children. And then a soft pad-pad-pad was heard in the woods, and through the trees came a big gray mother wolf, and she too stood over the basket and looked down at the children. "What lovely little cubs they are!" thought the wolf; and the woodpecker sang: "What lovely little birds!"

Then the two children woke, and were hungry, and seeing the wolf above them, they reached up their little hands and mouths as though she had been their own mother and they her cubs. And the woodpecker flew away into the woods to find berries for them to eat, and she too fed them as though they had been her own nestlings. So for a time the two babies were cared for by the wolf and the woodpecker, and they became strong and rosy babies and did not care whether they were boys or birds or little cubs.

Then one day an old man, one of Amulius's herdsmen, came by, and he found the two children and the basket. They were far away from the city of Alba, but he had heard all the tale of the Princess Sylvia's two sons, and he knew who the babies were. His heart was full of pity, and he took them away to his own hut. There he gave them the names of Romulus and Remus and brought them up as though they were peasants like himself. But they did not look like peasants; they grew up tall and strong and beautiful and carried themselves like Kings. But they were also wild and rough, from living in the woods, and when they were young men they went about the countryside with the herdsmen of King Amulius, looking after the cattle.

. . . a big gray mother wolf came and stood over the basket.

Now not far away lived their own grandfather, Numitor, with his servants who looked after *his* cattle; and one day there was a quarrel between the servants of Numitor and the servants of Amulius, who had tried to steal each other's cows. In the quarrel Remus was taken prisoner and was brought before his grandfather Numitor, who had never set eyes on him till then. And he was so tall and strong and kingly in his bearing that Numitor thought: "This boy cannot be a peasant." And he asked him who he was.

"I do not know who I am," said Remus. "I and my brother Romulus have been brought up by the herdsman as though we were his sons; but we do not feel like his sons, and we know that there is some secret about our birth."

Then he told Numitor the tale of the basket and the wolf and the woodpecker, and said that the herdsman still had the basket to prove the truth of the tale. And Numitor was over-joyed, and said: "You and your brother Romulus are my own grandsons, and your mother is my daughter Sylvia, whom Amu-lius keeps in prison." And he embraced Remus.

And now a great noise was heard, for Romulus, hearing that Remus had been taken, had gathered a company of men to come and save him. But when he saw his brother in Numitor's arms, and heard that he and Remus were the grandsons of a King, he went with all his men to Alba, where Amulius was still King. And he attacked the palace, and killed Amulius, and set his mother free.

Then he went back to Numitor and said,—

"Grandfather, you must now come and be King of Alba, as you should always have been. But as for me and Remus, we will go a little farther off and build another city, which we will rule."

So this was done, and Romulus and Remus went to the hills eighteen miles away to build the city of Rome. When it came to the building of the city, however, the two brothers quarreled, just as Numitor and Amulius had quarreled long ago; for Remus said the city should be built on one hill, but Romulus said it should be built on another, and each wanted to have his way.

37

Then Romulus and his friends marked out a great square on the ground, on which the walls of Rome were to be built, and when the square was marked they began to dig in it and make a ditch.

And Remus came up and watched them, very angry, and mocked at their work and tried to prevent it.

"Are these the walls of Rome?" cried Remus. "Why, the enemy will leap over them like this!" And as he spoke he jumped over the ditch into the midst of the workmen.

Then one of the men sprang up and cried: "And the men of Rome will drive them back like this!" And he struck a great blow at Remus, who fell down dead.

And the workman, seeing what he had done, fled far away as fast as he could, but Romulus cried out with grief and was so unhappy that he tried to kill himself too. However, his friends stopped him.

And so Romulus had to build the city of Rome alone. And into the ditch, before the walls were built, the men threw a little of everything good that grew in the land: olives, and corn, and grapes, and flowers. Then each man brought a handful of earth from his own part of Italy and threw that in too. So the city walls of Rome were built upon the best of everything that was in Italy, and Rome became the greatest city in the land, and then the greatest city in the world. And Romulus was its first King.

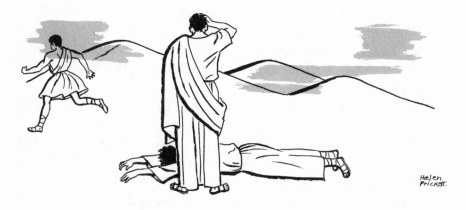

Helen
Prickett.

Dhan Gopal Mukerji
THE COW
GOLDEN HORN

ILLUSTRATED BY *John Gee*

HER real name was the Cow of Plenty. But after she was sold to Rajah the King, she came to be known as the royal cow Golden Horn.

She was bought for the royal stable from her master Krishaka, a farmer, because she was beautiful, wise, and fearless. It is said that Krishaka was paid with her weight in silver by Rajah. Not only that. In order to show how he loved her, the King had her horns covered with gold. After that had been done, he had set on the tips of her horns gems that shone like stars. That is how she came to be called Golden Horn.

Because everybody knew how wise and unusual she was, the whole kingdom allowed Golden Horn to go wherever she pleased and eat whatever fodder she chose. That, indeed, was a great honor.

Not a person in the royal household ever worried if Golden Horn did not come home at sundown. She could spend the night in the jungle full of tigers if she wanted to. Her fearless heart and wise head protected her everywhere.

Soon Golden Horn gave birth to a baby bull. He was named Ratna Singh or Jewel Horn. The reason they called him Jewel Horn, though he had no horns yet, was that after his birth for months his mother gave more milk than any ten cows put together.

Taken from *Hindu Fables for Little Children* by Dhan Gopal Mukerji, published and copyright, 1929, by E. P. Dutton & Co., Inc., New York.

Rajah, her owner, said, "Her son has brought us plenty of milk. Behold, she pours it like a stream of jewels into the bucket. Let us call her calf Jewel Horn."

Apart from giving floods of milk, Golden Horn had to do her duties of a mother. As soon as his horns had sprouted a little, she took Jewel Horn with her to many strange pastures in order to educate him.

She said, "You must go to school. My boy, I am your mother. I must teach you all I know. We cows are not like human beings who hire teachers; we have to educate our own children by ourselves.

"First of all, learn to think clearly. Always keep calm. And whenever you face an enemy, don't fear him. Remember that.

"I want you to learn the ways of men and beasts. You should know what befriends and what harms us. You should sharpen your wits. Strengthen your heart. And exercise your body."

"But mother," questioned Jewel Horn, "in order to succeed in fighting, all that I have to do is to use my horns."

"Not altogether," answered his mother. "You must use your brains, then your horns. If you use only horns, you may not succeed."

Thus conversing one day, they trotted off in the direction of the tiger-infested jungle. It was late afternoon. The wild animals were still sleepy. Those that were awake were stretching themselves in their dens. Black panthers sharpened their claws on the trees on which they had slept all day. Large leopards whined as they woke. Far off a *sher* (tiger) grunted as he leaped out of his lair. Darkness fell softly into the jungle.

When she noticed that the dusk was coming, Golden Horn said, "Come, Jewel, let us start homeward. It is getting late."

Slowly they sauntered back. But awhile after their backs had been turned to the deep forest resounding with the yell of wolves, the roar of tigers, and the trumpeting of elephants, Golden Horn felt that some beast was following them. She whispered, "Go slowly, my son. The calmer you are, the less anyone can frighten you. Don't be frightened. He who is frightened by any animal is killed by the same."

40

"And you, Mother, do you feel afraid?" questioned Jewel Horn.

"No, though I hear some fearful sounds," she answered.

"Look, Mother, what is that purple, black, now orange patch in the high grass before us—"

Golden Horn hissed at him, "Hush! Stop. Stand still." Hardly had she warned him when with a roar a tiger landed ten feet from where she had stood.

"Gr-rr," he roared again. A shock ran through both the cows. But clever Golden Horn stepped forward as if she was not at all disturbed. Stamping her hoofs on the ground she scolded the tiger, "Who are you? How dare you interrupt our evening walk?"

"Interrupt who, what?" growled the tiger in bewilderment. For he had never seen such horns on a cow nor heard such speech.

"Do you not know I am Golden Horn, the King's cow? I am the Cow of Plenty. I am walking with my son, Jewel Horn, a hero of the first water. Please be good enough to jump away from our path. We are on our way home to the King."

"Not a bit of it," growled the tiger. "Cow of Plenty, are you? Good. You will be plenty to eat!"

"How dare you insult my mother?" shouted Jewel Horn. "If you talk like that again, I will gore you, though my horns are only three inches long."

That speech from a mere calf puzzled the tiger more.

"Just a minute, Mr. Tiger," pleaded Golden Horn. "Forgive the rudeness of my son. He does not know who you are." Then, putting her mouth to her son's ear, she whispered, "The moment I bellow three times, attack him. Put your horns into his stomach. Leave me to do the rest." Then, quietly turning to the sinister beast whose stripes were like shining steel in the light of the risen moon, Golden Horn said, "O Sir, why destroy me, the Cow of Plenty? My horns are of gold. On their tips I wear diamonds. If you bite off those pieces of gold and diamond, you can sell them to a goldsmith. Then with the money you will be able to buy many cows. That will give you something to eat for many days."

"That is a good idea," chimed in the striped beast.

"Besides," continued Golden Horn, "the King will have my horns capped again with gold."

"Capital idea," shouted the tiger with joy. "Then again I will take the gold from your horns and buy some more cows to eat. Thus you will be mine own Cow of Plenty. What a name! Cow of Plenty!"

"If that pleases you," said Golden Horn.

"Now," said the tiger, "how can I get the gold off your horns?"

"That is easy. Come forward. I will lower my head. Then bite off the tips with your teeth while I hold my head steady. Do be kind enough not to wrench my horns too hard, won't you?" she begged.

"Of course anything to oblige such a good cow." Saying that Mr. Tiger advanced at her lowered head. . . . Though he was bewildered by the strangeness of all this, and his heart was full of strange fears, yet he moved on very slowly. Step by step, he came on. The earth seemed to tremble under his weight.

At last he stopped. It seemed to Golden Horn that an hour passed before he opened his mouth and closed his teeth slowly on the tip of one of her horns.

That instant she bellowed three times like three thunder claps, deafening his ears and almost freezing his muscles. At the same moment a sharp something pierced the roof of his mouth and his brain. From below something struck his side and knocked him over. Howling, he rolled on the ground once or twice.

He was so hurt and frightened that he did not dare to get on his feet. Instead he slunk away out of the sight of the two cows as if he were they, and they were two tigers. . . .

Seeing that they had not only saved themselves but also taught that tiger the lesson of his life, mother and son walked briskly towards the stable of the King.

"What an escape!" they exclaimed every few yards that they covered. And both Golden Horn and Jewel Horn knew that it was not by force that they had won.

The next day after they had been bathed and fed, Jewel Horn said, "Mother, you are right. Horns alone cannot protect a cow. He must use his brains."

Golden Horn answered, "Even our brains are not good enough unless our heart is calm. You must try to sharpen your wits. But above all be calm. If you are calm nothing can frighten you. And he who is not frightened can beat tigers or any other animal. Our fear kills us before we are killed by an enemy. He who is without fear has no enemy."

Padraic Colum

THE FIRST HARP

ILLUSTRATED BY *Decie Merwin*

UPON a time that was neither your time nor my time, a man and his wife were living at the back of the hills yonder. They had been happy together when they were young, but now that they were getting aged they were not so happy. Misfortunes had come on them, and each misfortune left them less and less forbearing with each other. So downcast did they become that they never went to a sport or a merry-making; they got no new things to wear; they would look with surprise on people dressed in their best and going to amusements; they did not know when holidays came round: Halloween would come, and they would have no apples to share with each other; Michaelmas would come, and they would kill no goose to feast themselves; May day would come, and they would wonder to see the children going from door to door with flowers in their hands.

And if the goats strayed away and there was no milk for the supper, "It's because my husband doesn't mind what happens about the place that I've to eat dry bread tonight," the woman would say. And if she lost three halfpence out of the shilling she had got for something she sold in the market, the man would keep on blaming her for the rest of the day. On times like these they would sit in the house remembering the miseries that had come on her or on him through the other. When they had been pleased with each other they had made no account of these miseries, but now when they were not pleased they remembered nothing else. One night as they sat in a house that had no fire they began going over the times when they had

44

comforts and when they could do pleasant things together. In everything one remembered there was blame for the other. They lay down, each thinking they would clear the score by forsaking the other. And in the morning each put a hand in the cold ashes of their hearth and went away from the house.

They came to the seashore, the man not knowing that the woman was behind him, and the woman not knowing that the man was before her. This is what befell the man that morning. He saw how the beach stretched away without a rock breaking through its yellow sand, and he saw how the clouds sailed above, big and white, without even a gull stretching its wings under them. The waves could not be seen, for the tide was very far out. There was no mark to go towards, but the man went on. Then he heard a sound and he went toward where it came from. It was a long, strong, soughing sound, and then it became a soft, sighing, sinking sound, and between the sinking and the swelling there were other sounds—a whirring sound and a whispering sound, a lifting sound and a lulling sound. He went on and on, and at last he came to what they came from. And lo and behold! there was a whale there, a great bulk upon the

45

sands. But it was a whale that was only bones now; the flesh had been stripped off it, and the wind was going through its ribs and touching upon the slight bones that were like river-reeds inside the skeleton. And the sounds changing ever never ceased—soughing, whirring, whispering, sighing. He stood listening to the music and forgetting everything that was upon his mind. And he saw his wife standing at the other end of the whale's bulk with wonder in her looks as she listened to the sinking and the swelling, the lifting and the lulling music that the wind made through the bones of the whale.

They went back talking about the wonder they had come upon. They had a meal in their house and still they talked about the wonder. Together they did the work that had to be done while they listened to the sounds that they thought they could hear. One evening the man made a frame of pine-wood, strung strings loosely across it, and left it hanging in the doorway of the house. The wind made music on the strings. Then he had a dream; he knew that pieces of wood across the frame would make the sounds come stronger: he put two boards in the frame, and the wind upon the strings had a deeper sound.

Neighbors came to listen; the man was praised for the wonder he had made; rich people made gifts to the couple. Then the man made a frame on which the strings were drawn tightly; he made the sounds by striking his fingers across the strings—louder and more piercing sounds. He went from place to place playing this instrument, his wife going with him. The King of the land heard about the instrument and the player; the man was brought to play before him. Sickness and sleeplessness left the King—so much did the music do for him. And the man and his wife were given riches so that they might stay always with him. They lived there content with themselves and content with each other. And the instrument that the man made was called a Harp, and the man himself was Cendfind, the first Harp-player in Ireland.

Roger Duvoisin

THE ALPHORN

ILLUSTRATED BY THE AUTHOR

LONG ago, high up on the Balisalp, Hans the herdsman tended his cows. His lonely chalet was always neat and tidy. A tight bunch of edelweiss hung over the door, and a single flower of the same plant was always stuck in Hans's little embroidered straw cap. This was to prove that he was a good climber, for the edelweiss only grows where clumsy feet dare not go.

Every evening, when the milking was done, Hans would climb to the ledge behind his chalet to wave to Frieda, his

47

fiancée, across on the Seealp. There he would remain, dreaming, and listening to the bells of his cows, until night crept slowly up from the deep valley below. Then he would return to his bed of straw, hoping to dream still of Frieda.

Every morning he would climb to the ledge again, and wave good morning to her, before starting the day's work.

But one night he was awakened by a strange sound, which seemed to be coming from the first floor of the chalet. It sounded as though several men were talking down there. They did not muffle their voices, but spoke loudly and freely as if they were in their own house. Hans went on tiptoe to the edge of the rough-hewn stairway. He was astonished at the sight that met his eyes.

A fire roared in the chimneyplace, while three men stood about it. They were dressed in long brown robes like monks, and their bald heads reflected the red light of the flames.

One was tall. The second was of medium size, while the third was very small.

The tall one was stirring the contents of a huge kettle which hung over the fire.

The second was pouring milk into the kettle.

The third was stacking wood upon the fire.

Then, as Hans watched, the tall man brought a small bottle from his pocket. After peering at its contents, he emptied it into the boiling milk.

The middle-sized man, having poured into the kettle all the milk he could find, went to the door. He picked up a strange, very long pipelike horn which was leaning there and began to play a lovely simple tune which echoed and re-echoed from the mountain. It must have been a magic horn, for all Hans's cows came lumbering to the door. They stood in a circle there, listening with deep attention.

Meanwhile the small man had poured the contents of the kettle into three different pails. Hans was surprised to see the boiling milk change color as he filled them. In one pail it was red. In the second green, but in the third it remained white.

Then, as if aware that Hans was watching, the tall man looked

48

up. With a sign of his hand he called the herdsman down.

Hans hesitated. Who were these mysterious men? Why had they come to his chalet to do these strange things? Perhaps his life was in danger.

But the tall man seemed impatient. He motioned again, and Hans, gathering his courage, went down into the room.

"Hans," said the small man, "do you see these three pails? I invite you to drink from one of them. If you choose the green one, you will become a very rich man. If you choose the red, you will become very, very strong. But if you drink from the white pail, you will be able to play the magic tune on the alphorn. Which will you take?"

Hans was not long in making his choice. He was charmed by the weird three-note melody that the middle-sized man was still playing upon the long horn. Bringing the pail of white liquid to his lips, he took a long draught from it.

"I congratulate you upon your choice," said the tall man. "For if you had chosen the red or the green, you would have died, and hundreds of years would have gone by before the Swiss mountaineers would be offered the alphorn again."

Then the three men vanished, like people in a dream.

Hans thought for a moment that it really had been a dream. Everything in the chalet seemed just as usual. But the long alphorn was still there. It was leaning against the door as the middle-sized man had left it.

Timidly the herdsman put it to his lips and blew. To his delight the same tune with the same charm came softly from the horn. Its three notes were repeated over and over, loud and soft, by the echoes of the mountain. Hans could play as well as the mysterious stranger.

Lovingly, Hans made a second horn exactly like the first, for Frieda, and they played to each other from one mountain to the next. They were married, and all their children and grandchildren learned how to play the horn.

And that is how the alphorn was given to the Swiss mountaineers to wake the echoes upon the Alps.

Frank B. Linderman

WHY THE CHIPMUNK'S
BACK IS STRIPED

ILLUSTRATED BY *John Dukes McKee*

WHAT a splendid lodge it was, and how grand War Eagle looked leaning against his backrest in the firelight! From the tripod that supported the backrest were suspended his weapons and his medicine bundle, each showing the wonderful skill of the maker. The quiver that held the arrows was combined with a case for the bow, and colored quills of the porcupine had been deftly used to make it a thing of beauty. All about the lodge hung the strangely painted linings, and the firelight added richness to both color and design. War Eagle's hair was white, for he had known many snows; but his eyes were keen and bright as a boy's, as he gazed in pride at his grandchildren across the lodge-fire. He was wise, and had been in many battles, for his was a warlike tribe. He knew all about the world and the people in it. He was deeply religious, and every Indian child loved him for his goodness and brave deeds.

About the fire were Little Buffalo Calf, a boy of eleven years; Eyes-in-the-Water, his sister, a girl of nine; Fine Bow, a cousin of these, aged ten, and Bluebird, his sister, who was but eight years old.

Not a sound did the children make while the old warrior filled his great pipe, and only the snapping of the lodge-fire broke the stillness. Solemnly War Eagle lit the tobacco that had been mixed with the dried inner bark of the red willow, and

50

for several minutes smoked in silence, while the children's eyes grew large with expectancy. Finally he spoke:

"Napa, *Old*-man, is very old indeed. He made this world, and all that is on it. He came out of the south and traveled toward the north, making the birds and animals as he passed. He made the perfumes for the winds to carry about, and he even made the war paint for the people to use. He was a busy worker, but a great liar and thief, as I shall show you after I have told you more about him. It was *Old*-man who taught the beaver all his cunning. It was *Old*-man who told the bear to go to sleep when the snow grew deep in winter, and it was he who made the curlew's bill so long and crooked, although it was not that way at first. *Old*-man used to live on this world with the animals and birds. There was no other man or woman then, and he was chief over all the animal-people and the bird-people. He could speak the language of the robin, knew the words of the bear, and understood the sign-talk of the beaver, too. He lived with the wolves, for they are the great hunters. Even today we make the same sign for a smart man as we make for the wolf; so you see he taught them much while he lived with them. *Old*-man made a great many mistakes in making things, as I shall show you after a while; yet he worked until he had everything good. But he often made great mischief and taught many wicked things. These I shall tell you about some day. Everybody was afraid of *Old*-man and his tricks and lies—even the animal-people, before he made men and women. He used to visit the lodges of our people and make trouble long ago, but he got so wicked that Manitou grew angry at him, and one day in the month of roses, he built a lodge for *Old*-man and told him that he must stay in it forever. Of course he had to do that, and nobody knows where the lodge was built, nor in what country, but that is why we never see him as our grandfathers did, long, long ago.

"What I shall tell you now happened when the world was young. It was a fine summer day, and *Old*-man was traveling in the forest. He was going north and straight as an arrow— looking at nothing, hearing nothing. No one knows what he was

51

after, to this day. The birds and forest-people spoke politely to him as he passed, but he answered none of them. The Pine-squirrel, who is always trying to find out other people's business, asked him where he was going, but *Old*-man wouldn't tell him. The woodpecker hammered on a dead tree to make him look that way, but he wouldn't. The Elk-people and the Deer-people saw him pass, and all said that he must be up to some mischief or he would stop and talk awhile. The pine trees murmured, and the bushes whispered their greeting, but he kept his eyes straight ahead and went on traveling.

"The sun was low when *Old*-man heard a groan" (here War Eagle groaned to show the children how it sounded), "and turning about he saw a warrior lying bruised and bleeding near a spring of cold water. *Old*-man knelt beside the man and asked: 'Is there war in this country?'

" 'Yes,' answered the man. 'This whole day long we have fought to kill a Person, but we have all been killed, I am afraid.'

" 'That is strange,' said *Old*-man; 'how can one Person kill so many men? Who is this Person, tell me his name!' but the man didn't answer—he was dead. When *Old*-man saw that life had left the wounded man, he drank from the spring and went on toward the north, but before long he heard a noise as of men fighting, and he stopped to look and listen. Finally he saw the bushes bend and sway near a creek that flowed through the forest. He crawled toward the spot and, peering through the brush, saw a great Person near a pile of dead men, with his back against a pine tree. The Person was full of arrows, and he was pulling them from his ugly body. Calmly the Person broke the shafts of the arrows, tossed them aside, and stopped the blood flow with a brush of his hairy hand. His head was large and fierce-looking, and his eyes were small and wicked. His great body was larger than that of a buffalo-bull and covered with scars of many battles.

"*Old*-man went to the creek, and with his buffalo-horn cup brought some water to the Person, asking as he approached:

" 'Who are you, Person? Tell me, so I can make you a fine present, for you are great in war.'

52

mister
mckee

" 'I am Bad Sickness,' replied the Person. 'Tribes I have met remember me and always will, for their bravest warriors are afraid when I make war upon them. I come in the night or I visit their camps in daylight. It is always the same; they are frightened, and I kill them easily.'

" 'Ho!' said *Old*-man, 'tell me how to make Bad Sickness, for I often go to war myself.' He lied; for he was never in a battle in his life. The Person shook his ugly head and then *Old*-man said,—

" 'If you will tell me how to make Bad Sickness I will make you small and handsome. When you are big, as you now are, it is very hard to make a living; but when you are small, little food will make you fat. Your living will be easy because I will make your food grow everywhere.'

" 'Good,' said the Person, 'I will do it; you must kill the fawns of the deer and the calves of the elk when they first begin to live. When you have killed enough of them you must make a robe of their skins. Whenever you wear that robe and sing—"Now you sicken, now you sicken," the sickness will come—that is all there is to it.'

" 'Good,' said *Old*-man, 'now lie down to sleep and I will do as I promised.'

"The Person went to sleep and *Old*-man breathed upon him until he grew so tiny that he laughed to see how small he had made him. Then he took out his paint sack and striped the Person's back with black and yellow. It looked bright and handsome and he waked the Person, who was now a tiny animal with a bushy tail to make him pretty.

" 'Now,' said *Old*-man, 'you are the Chipmunk and must always wear those striped clothes. All of your children and their children must wear them, too.'

"After the Chipmunk had looked at himself and thanked *Old*-man for his new clothes, he wanted to know how he could make his living, and *Old*-man told him what to eat and said he must cache the pine-nuts when the leaves turned yellow, so he would not have to work in the wintertime.

" 'You are a cousin to the Pine-squirrel,' said *Old*-man, 'and you will hunt and hide as he does. You will be spry and your living will be easy to make if you do as I have told you.'

"He taught the Chipmunk his language and his signs, showed him where to live, and then left him, going on toward the north again. He kept looking for the cow-elk and doe-deer, and it was not long before he had killed enough of their young to make the robe as the Person told him, for they were plentiful before the white man came to live on the world. He found a shady place near a creek, and there made the robe that would make Bad Sickness whenever he sang the queer song, but the robe was plain and brown in color. He didn't like the looks of it. Suddenly he thought how nice the back of the Chipmunk looked after he had striped it with his paints. He got out his old paint sack and with the same colors made the robe look very much like the clothes of the Chipmunk. He was proud of the work and liked the new robe better; but being lazy, he wanted

54

to save himself work, so he sent the South wind to tell all the doe-deer and the cow-elk to come to him. They came as soon as they received the message, for they were afraid of *Old*-man and always tried to please him. When they had all reached the place where *Old*-man was he said to them,—

" 'Do you see this robe?'

" 'Yes, we see it,' they replied.

" 'Well, I have made it from the skins of your children and then painted it to look like the Chipmunk's back, for I like the looks of that Person's clothes. I shall need many more of these robes during my life; and every time I make one, I don't want to have to spend my time painting it; so from now on and forever your children shall be born in spotted clothes. I want it to be that way to save me work. On all the fawns there must be spots of white like this (here he pointed to the spots on Bad Sickness's robe) and on all of the elk-calves the spots shall not be so white and shall be in rows and look rather yellow.' Again he showed them his robe, that they might see just what he wanted.

" 'Remember,' he said, 'after this I don't want to see any of your children running about wearing plain clothing, because that would mean more painting for me. Now go away, and remember what I have said, lest I make you sick.'

"The cow-elk and the doe-deer were glad to know that their children's clothes would be beautiful, and they went away to their little ones who were hidden in the tall grass, where the wolves and mountain lions would have a hard time finding them; for you know that in the tracks of the fawn there is no scent, and the wolf cannot trail him when he is alone. That is the way Manitou takes care of the weak, and all of the forest-people know about it, too.

"Now you know why the Chipmunk's back is striped, and why the fawn and elk-calf wear their pretty clothes.

"I hear the owls, and it is time for all young men who will some day be great warriors to go to bed, and for all young women to seek rest, lest beauty go away forever. Ho!"

55

*Harold Courlander
and George Herzog*

THE ONE
YOU DON'T SEE COMING

ILLUSTRATED BY *Helen Prickett*

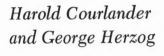

THE people who lived near the edge of the rain forest, in the country along the banks of the Cavally River, often talked about an animal of the forest called the One You Don't See Coming.

They said that all day long he lurked among the shadows of the great trees, waiting for night to fall. Then, when darkness came, he crept forward as silent as a leopard into the villages.

"Our best hunters have tried to capture this animal," they said. "We have set traps on the trails and at the water holes, but it is no use—he is the stealthiest of all the creatures of the forest. Each night he comes prowling among our houses. He is never heard and never seen."

"What does this animal do that we should be afraid of him?" the young people asked.

"The One You Don't See Coming is a thief," the older people said. "He steals everyone's brains and leaves them forgetful of everything until morning comes. One minute people are the way they are here now, talking back and forth. The next minute the One You Don't See Coming creeps upon them and steals their minds. They no longer talk or think, they simply lie motionless and stupid until the sun rises."

"What good are the dogs if they don't hear him and bark?" the children asked.

56

"They neither hear him nor smell him. When he comes he takes their brains too. The One You Don't See Coming has another name. Some people call him Sleep."

The young hunters talked about this curious animal among themselves, and one day a man named Biafu said,—

"What kind of hunters are we if we can't kill the One You Don't See Coming?"

"That's easy enough to say," a hunter named Gunde said. "But where will you find him? Our grandfathers were good hunters and they never caught him."

"I've heard that he leaves no footprints on the trail," a hunter named Deeba said. "What will you follow?"

"If he really lives in the forest, as the old people say, then we'll find him. We'll get rid of this nuisance once and for all!" Biafu said.

"I'm not afraid," Gunde said.

"I'll go too," Deeba said. "We'll catch this thing called Sleep, the One You Don't See Coming, and put an end to him. Then the old people will praise us and give us gifts."

So Gunde, Deeba, and Biafu took their hunting knives and spears and went deep into the shadows of the forest.

They listened, but they didn't hear Sleep. They searched the ground for footprints, but Sleep had left no footprints. All day they stalked Sleep. They came to a part of the forest where the villagers hardly ever went.

"He must lurk here among the tall ferns," Biafu said.

"I don't see him," Deeba said.

"I don't hear him," Gunde said.

"If there really is such an animal we shall certainly catch him at the water hole," Biafu said.

So they went down through the dense brush and the tall ferns until they came to where the river made its way through the jungle. The banks of the river were marked with the footprints of the gazelle, the antelope, the buffalo, and the leopard.

"We'll wait for him here, and when he comes to drink we shall kill him," Biafu said.

He found a tall tree by the edge of the water. It sloped outward over the river, so that any animal that came to drink would be under its branches.

"Climb the tree," Biafu said to Deeba. "When Sleep comes to drink you can throw yourself upon his back and we will finish him."

Deeba looked up and thought.

"Maybe *you* had better climb the tree," he said to Biafu.

"No, Gunde and I will stand guard below, and when we hear you shout we will come running."

Deeba shook his head. So Biafu turned to Gunde and said,—

"Then you climb the tree and wait. When Sleep comes to drink you can leap upon him. When we hear you shout, Deeba and I will come running."

Gunde thought a moment. He shook his head too.

"No, I would rather stay on the ground and come running myself."

Biafu became angry.

"What mighty hunters! Afraid of an animal you can't see!"

"Just the same, what if he likes to climb trees?" Deeba said.

"Yes, what if he likes to climb *this* tree?" Gunde said.

They argued and argued. Finally Biafu stamped his foot impatiently.

"All right, I'll climb the tree myself and wait. When you hear me shout, come as fast as you can!" he said. He went up into the branches of the tree overhanging the water and hid among the leaves. Gunde and Deeba crawled into the dense brush and waited.

Time passed. Antelope came down to the water and drank and went away. Night came, and owls called back and forth. Leopards came silently to drink and went away. Biafu clung to his tree and watched, his knife held tightly in his hand. Gunde and Deeba crouched in the brush and waited for Biafu to shout.

The misty night grew old, and the moon moved across the sky.

Biafu kept thinking about how pleased the old people would be when they had caught the One You Don't See Coming. But he was very tired. He began to nod. His eyes closed once, just

58

for a short moment. They closed again, just a little longer. Then he was aware that his mind was slipping away into the night. He jerked himself awake, and his heart beat fast, for he knew that the animal was there.

He waved his knife and shouted,—

"I see you! I see you!"

Deeba and Gunde ran as fast as they could to the edge of the water.

"Where is he?" they shouted. "Where is he?"

"Ah, he came and then he fled!" Biafu said. "Go back to your hiding place and wait."

Deeba and Gunde went back and crouched in the brush again. Biafu sat up very straight, waiting for the One You Don't See Coming to return. He peered through the darkness at the river. He heard nothing except the owls and the frogs in the distance. The moon moved across the sky.

A great heaviness came over Biafu's mind. No matter how hard he tried to keep them open, his eyes kept closing. For a moment he forgot everything. He seemed to be floating away. The tree swayed in the wind. Biafu clutched at the branches and opened his eyes. He waved his knife in the air and shouted,

"I see you! I see you!"

Again Deeba and Gunde came running, with their spears ready.

"Where is he! Where is he!" they shouted, trying to see in the darkness.

"He is near, he came up in the tree!" Biafu said. "He seized me, but I shook him off! Go back and hide again. Next time we will surely get him. But don't go so far, and run faster when you hear me shout!"

So Deeba and Gunde went back in the brush and waited.

Biafu talked to himself and rubbed his eyes to keep awake. He thought about the big celebration the village would have when he returned from the hunt. A cloud moved slowly across the sky and covered the moon. Things were very dark. There was no wind, and the leaves stopped rustling. The owls in the distance grew silent. The frogs stopped croaking.

And slowly, slowly, Biafu's eyes closed. His memory slipped away into the night. This time Sleep crept slowly upon him. Slowly, slowly, Sleep loosened Biafu's hold on the branches. Slowly Sleep pushed Biafu's head down on his chest. Biafu's knife slipped from his hand and fell into the water below. And slowly, slowly, Sleep pushed him, harder and harder, until he was leaning sideways. And suddenly Sleep seized Biafu and flung him down into the river below.

"Deeba! Gunde! He has me! He has me!" Biafu shouted.

They came running, ready for a great struggle, but they were too late, they only saw Biafu. Sleep was not there.

"Where is he! Where is he!" they shouted as Biafu came dripping out of the water.

"He climbed into the tree, and he threw me into the water!" Biafu said.

He sat down unhappily by the edge of the river and began to think. He was silent a long time, and then he said to Deeba and Gunde,—

"It's no use hunting Sleep. The old people are right. And anyway, he's not like the leopard, who steals our goats and doesn't bring them back. What Sleep steals he steals just for a few hours, and when morning comes you are whole again."

So the hunters took their weapons and hunted an antelope, and they carried it back to the village for a feast. The old people were glad, but they asked about Sleep.

"We almost saw him," Deeba said.

"I wrestled with him in a tree," Biafu said, "but I couldn't hold him."

"He threw Biafu into the river," Gunde said.

"It's the way I've always said," Biafu said with dignity. "You can't see the coming of Sleep. You almost see him but you never do."

Nathaniel Hawthorne

THE GOLDEN TOUCH

ILLUSTRATED BY *Helen Prickett*

ONCE upon a time, there lived a very rich man, and a king besides, whose name was Midas; and he had a little daughter, whom nobody but myself ever heard of, and whose name I either never knew or have entirely forgotten. So, because I love odd names for little girls, I choose to call her Marygold.

This King Midas was fonder of gold than of anything else in the world. He valued his royal crown chiefly because it was composed of that precious metal. If he loved anything better, or half so well, it was the one little maiden who played so merrily around her father's footstool. But the more Midas loved his daughter, the more did he desire and seek for wealth. He thought, foolish man! that the best thing he could possibly do for this dear child would be to bequeath her the immensest pile of yellow, glistening coin, that had ever been heaped together since the world was made. Thus, he gave all his thoughts and all his time to this one purpose. If ever he happened to gaze for an instant at the gold-tinted clouds of sunset, he wished that they were real gold and that they could be squeezed safely into his strongbox. When little Marygold ran to meet him with a bunch of buttercups and dandelions, he used to say, "Poh,

poh, child! If these flowers were as golden as they look, they would be worth the plucking!"

And yet, in his earlier days, before he was so entirely possessed of this insane desire for riches, King Midas had shown a great taste for flowers. He had planted a garden, in which grew the biggest and beautifulest and sweetest roses that any mortal ever saw or smelt. These roses were still growing in the garden, as large, as lovely, and as fragrant as when Midas used to pass whole hours in gazing at them and inhaling their perfume. But now, if he looked at them at all, it was only to calculate how much the garden would be worth if each of the innumerable rose-petals were a thin plate of gold. And though he once was fond of music (in spite of an idle story about his ears, which were said to resemble those of an ass), the only music for poor Midas, now, was the chink of one coin against another.

At length (as people always grow more and more foolish, unless they take care to grow wiser and wiser), Midas had got to be so exceedingly unreasonable, that he could scarcely bear to see or touch any object that was not gold. He made it his custom, therefore, to pass a large portion of every day in a dark and dreary apartment, under ground, at the basement of his palace. It was here that he kept his wealth. To this dismal hole— for it was little better than a dungeon—Midas betook himself, whenever he wanted to be particularly happy. Here, after carefully locking the door, he would take a bag of gold coin, or a gold cup as big as a washbowl, or a heavy golden bar, or a peck-measure of gold-dust, and bring them from the obscure corners of the room into the one bright and narrow sunbeam that fell from the dungeon-like window. He valued the sunbeam for no other reason but that his treasure would not shine without its help. And then would he reckon over the coins in the bag; toss up the bar and catch it as it came down; sift the gold-dust through his fingers; look at the funny image of his own face, as reflected in the burnished circumference of the cup; and whisper to himself, "O Midas, rich King Midas, what a happy man art thou!" But it was laughable to see how the

63

image of his face kept grinning at him out of the polished surface of the cup. It seemed to be aware of his foolish behavior and to have a naughty inclination to make fun of him.

Midas called himself a happy man, but felt that he was not yet quite so happy as he might be. The very tiptop of enjoyment would never be reached, unless the whole world were to become his treasure-room, and be filled with yellow metal which should be all his own.

Now, I need hardly remind such wise little people as you are, that in the old, old times, when King Midas was alive, a great many things came to pass, which we should consider wonderful if they were to happen in our own day and country. And, on the other hand, a great many things take place nowadays, which seem not only wonderful to us, but at which the people of old times would have stared their eyes out. On the whole, I regard our own times as the strangest of the two; but, however that may be, I must go on with my story.

Midas was enjoying himself in his treasure-room, one day, as usual, when he perceived a shadow fall over the heaps of gold; and, looking suddenly up, what should he behold but the figure of a stranger, standing in the bright and narrow sunbeam! It was a young man, with a cheerful and ruddy face. Whether it was that the imagination of King Midas threw a yellow tinge over everything, or whatever the cause might be, he could not help fancying that the smile with which the stranger regarded him had a kind of golden radiance in it. Certainly, although his figure intercepted the sunshine, there was now a brighter gleam upon all the piled-up treasures than before. Even the remotest corners had their share of it, and were lighted up, when the stranger smiled, as with tips of flame and sparkles of fire.

As Midas knew that he had carefully turned the key in the lock, and that no mortal strength could possibly break into his treasure-room, he, of course, concluded that his visitor must be something more than mortal. It is no matter about telling you who he was. In those days, when the earth was comparatively a new affair, it was supposed to be often the resort of beings endowed with supernatural power, and who used to interest themselves in the joys and sorrows of men, women, and children, half playfully and half seriously. Midas had met such beings before now, and was not sorry to meet one of them again. The stranger's aspect, indeed, was so good-humored and kindly, if not beneficent, that it would have been unreasonable to suspect him of intending any mischief. It was far more probable that he came to do Midas a favor. And what could that favor be, unless to multiply his heaps of treasure?

The stranger gazed about the room; and when his lustrous smile had glistened upon all the golden objects that were there, he turned again to Midas.

"You are a wealthy man, friend Midas!" he observed. "I doubt whether any other four walls, on earth, contain so much gold as you have contrived to pile up in this room."

"I have done pretty well,—pretty well," answered Midas, in a discontented tone. "But, after all, it is but a trifle, when you consider that it has taken me my whole life to get it together. If one could live a thousand years, he might have time to grow rich!"

"What!" exclaimed the stranger. "Then you are not satisfied?" Midas shook his head.

"And pray what would satisfy you?" asked the stranger. "Merely for the curiosity of the thing, I should be glad to know."

Midas paused and meditated. He felt a presentiment that this stranger, with such a golden luster in his good-humored smile, had come hither with both the power and the purpose of gratifying his utmost wishes. Now, therefore, was the fortunate moment, when he had but to speak, and obtain whatever possible, or seemingly impossible thing, it might come into his head to ask. So he thought, and thought, and thought, and heaped up one golden mountain upon another, in his imagination, without being able to imagine them big enough. At last, a bright idea occurred to King Midas. It seemed really as bright as the glistening metal which he loved so much.

Raising his head, he looked the lustrous stranger in the face.

"Well, Midas," observed his visitor, "I see that you have hit upon something that will satisfy you. Tell me your wish."

"It is only this," replied Midas. "I am weary of collecting my treasures with so much trouble, and beholding the heap so diminutive, after I have done my best. I wish everything that I touch to be changed to gold!"

The stranger's smile grew so very broad that it seemed to fill the room like an outburst of the sun, gleaming into a shadowy dell where the yellow autumnal leaves—for so looked the lumps and particles of gold—lie strewn in the glow of light.

"The Golden Touch!" exclaimed he. "You certainly deserve credit, friend Midas, for striking out so brilliant a conception. But are you quite sure that this will satisfy you?"

"How could it fail?" said Midas.

"And will you never regret the possession of it?"

"What could induce me?" asked Midas. "I ask nothing else, to render me perfectly happy."

"Be it as you wish, then," replied the stranger, waving his hand in token of farewell. "Tomorrow, at sunrise, you will find yourself gifted with the Golden Touch."

The figure of the stranger then became exceedingly bright, and Midas involuntarily closed his eyes. On opening them again, he beheld only one yellow sunbeam in the room, and, all around him, the glistening of the precious metal which he had spent his life in hoarding up.

Whether Midas slept as usual that night, the story does not say. Asleep or awake, however, his mind was probably in the state of a child's, to whom a beautiful new plaything has been promised in the morning. At any rate, day had hardly peeped over the hills, when King Midas was broad awake, and, stretching his arms out of bed, began to touch the objects that were within reach. He was anxious to prove whether the Golden Touch had really come, according to the stranger's promise. So he laid his finger on a chair by the bedside, and on various other things, but was grievously disappointed to perceive that they remained of exactly the same substance as before. Indeed, he felt very much afraid that he had only dreamed about the lustrous stranger, or else that the latter had been making game of him. And what a miserable affair would it be, if, after all his hopes, Midas must content himself with what little gold he could scrape together by ordinary means, instead of creating it by a touch!

All this while it was only the gray of the morning, with but a streak of brightness along the edge of the sky, where Midas could not see it. He lay in a very disconsolate mood, regretting the downfall of his hopes, and kept growing sadder and sadder, until the earliest sunbeam shone through the window and gilded the ceiling over his head. It seemed to Midas that this bright yellow sunbeam was reflected in rather a singular way on the white covering of the bed. Looking more closely, what was his astonishment and delight, when he found that this linen fabric has been transmuted to what seemed a woven texture of the purest and brightest gold! The Golden Touch had come to him with the first sunbeam!

Midas started up, in a kind of joyful frenzy, and ran about the room, grasping at everything that happened to be in his way. He seized one of the bedposts, and it became immediately a fluted golden pillar. He pulled aside a window-curtain, in order to admit a clear spectacle of the wonders which he was performing; and the tassel grew heavy in his hand,—a mass of gold. He took up a book from the table. At his first touch, it assumed the appearance of such a splendidly bound and gilt-edged volume as one often meets with, nowadays; but, on running his fingers through the leaves, behold! it was a bundle of thin golden plates, in which all the wisdom of the book had grown illegible. He hurriedly put on his clothes and was enraptured to see himself in a magnificent suit of gold cloth, which retained its flexibility and softness, although it burdened him a little with its weight. He drew out his handkerchief, which little Marygold had hemmed for him. That was likewise gold, with the dear child's neat and pretty stitches running all along the border, in gold thread!

Somehow or other, this last transformation did not quite please King Midas. He would rather that his little daughter's handiwork should have remained just the same as when she climbed his knee and put it into his hand.

But it was not worth while to vex himself about a trifle. Midas now took his spectacles from his pocket and put them on his nose, in order that he might see more distinctly what he was about. In those days, spectacles for common people had not been invented, but were already worn by kings; else, how could Midas have had any? To his great perplexity, however, excellent as the glasses were, he discovered that he could not possibly see through them. But this was the most natural thing in the world; for on taking them off, the transparent crystals turned out to be plates of yellow metal, and, of course, were worthless as spectacles, though valuable as gold. It struck Midas as rather inconvenient that, with all his wealth, he could never again be rich enough to own a pair of serviceable spectacles.

"It is no great matter, nevertheless," said he to himself, very philosophically. "We cannot expect any great good, without its being accompanied with some small inconvenience. The Golden Touch is worth the sacrifice of a pair of spectacles, at least, if not of one's very eyesight. My own eyes will serve for ordinary purposes, and little Marygold will soon be old enough to read to me."

Wise King Midas was so exalted by his good fortune that the palace seemed not sufficiently spacious to contain him. He therefore went downstairs, and smiled, on observing that the

Alas, what had he done?

balustrade of the staircase became a bar of burnished gold, as his hand passed over it in his descent. He lifted the doorlatch (it was brass only a moment ago, but golden when his fingers quitted it), and emerged into the garden. Here, as it happened, he found a great number of beautiful roses in full bloom, and others in all the stages of lovely bud and blossom. Very delicious was their fragrance in the morning breeze. Their delicate blush was one of the fairest sights in the world; so gentle, so modest, and so full of sweet tranquillity did these roses seem to be.

But Midas knew a way to make them far more precious, according to his way of thinking, than roses had ever been before. So he took great pains in going from bush to bush, and exercised his magic touch most indefatigably; until every individual flower and bud, and even the worms at the heart of some of them, were changed to gold. By the time this good work was completed, King Midas was summoned to breakfast; and as the morning air had given him an excellent appetite, he made haste back to the palace.

What was usually a king's breakfast in the days of Midas, I really do not know, and cannot stop now to investigate. To the best of my belief, however, on this particular morning, the breakfast consisted of hot cakes, some nice little brook trout, roasted potatoes, fresh boiled eggs, and coffee, for King Midas himself, and a bowl of bread and milk for his daughter Marygold. At all events, this is a breakfast fit to set before a king; and, whether he had it or not, King Midas could not have had a better.

Little Marygold had not yet made her appearance. Her father ordered her to be called, and, seating himself at table, awaited the child's coming, in order to begin his own breakfast. To do Midas justice, he really loved his daughter, and loved her so much the more this morning, on account of the good fortune which had befallen him. It was not a great while before he heard her coming along the passageway crying bitterly. This circumstance surprised him, because Marygold was one of the cheerfulest little people whom you would see in a summer's

day, and hardly shed a thimbleful of tears in a twelvemonth. When Midas heard her sobs, he determined to put little Marygold into better spirits, by an agreeable surprise; so, leaning across the table, he touched his daughter's bowl (which was a China one, with pretty figures all around it), and transmuted it to gleaming gold.

Meanwhile, Marygold slowly and disconsolately opened the door, and showed herself with her apron at her eyes, still sobbing as if her heart would break.

"How now, my little lady!" cried Midas. "Pray what is the matter with you, this bright morning?"

Marygold, without taking the apron from her eyes, held out her hand, in which was one of the roses which Midas had so recently transmuted.

"Beautiful!" exclaimed her father. "And what is there in this magnificent golden rose to make you cry?"

"Ah, dear father!" answered the child, as well as her sobs would let her; "it is not beautiful, but the ugliest flower that ever grew! As soon as I was dressed I ran into the garden to gather some roses for you; because I know you like them, and like them the better when gathered by your little daughter. But, oh dear, dear me! What do you think has happened? Such a misfortune! All the beautiful roses, that smelled so sweet and had so many lovely blushes, are blighted and spoilt! They are grown quite yellow, as you see this one, and have no longer any fragrance! What can have been the matter with them?"

"Poh, my dear little girl,—pray don't cry about it!" said Midas, who was ashamed to confess that he himself had wrought the change which so greatly afflicted her. "Sit down and eat your bread and milk! You will find it easy enough to exchange a golden rose like that (which will last hundreds of years) for an ordinary one which would wither in a day."

"I don't care for such roses as this!" cried Marygold, tossing it contemptuously away. "It has no smell, and the hard petals prick my nose!"

The child now sat down to table, but was so occupied with her grief for the blighted roses that she did not even notice the wonderful transmutation of her China bowl. Perhaps this was all the better; for Marygold was accustomed to take pleasure in looking at the queer figures, and strange trees and houses, that were painted on the circumference of the bowl; and these ornaments were now entirely lost in the yellow hue of the metal.

Midas, meanwhile, had poured out a cup of coffee, and, as a matter of course, the coffeepot, whatever metal it may have been when he took it up was gold when he set it down. He thought to himself that it was rather an extravagant style of splendor, in a king of his simple habits, to breakfast off a service of gold, and began to be puzzled with the difficulty of keeping his treasures safe. The cupboard and the kitchen would no longer be a secure place of deposit for articles so valuable as golden bowls and coffeepots.

Amid these thoughts, he lifted a spoonful of coffee to his lips and, sipping it, was astonished to perceive that the instant his lips touched the liquid, it became molten gold, and the next moment, hardened into a lump!

"Ha!" exclaimed Midas, rather aghast.

"What is the matter, father?" asked little Marygold, gazing at him, with the tears still standing in her eyes.

"Nothing, child, nothing!" said Midas. "Drink your milk."

He took one of the nice little trouts on his plate, and, by way of experiment, touched its tail with his finger. To his horror, it was immediately transmuted from an admirably fried brook trout into a goldfish, though not one of those goldfishes which people often keep in glass globes, as ornaments for the parlor. No; but it was really a metallic fish, and looked as if it had been very cunningly made by the nicest goldsmith in the world. Its little bones were now golden wires; its fins and tail were thin plates of gold; and there were the marks of the fork in it, and all the delicate, frothy appearance of a nicely fried fish, exactly imitated in metal. A very pretty piece of work, as you may suppose; only King Midas, just at that moment, would much rather have had a real trout in his dish than this elaborate and valuable imitation of one.

"I don't quite see," thought he to himself, "how I am to get any breakfast!"

He took one of the smoking-hot cakes, and had scarcely broken it, when, to his cruel mortification, though a moment before it had been of the whitest wheat, it assumed the yellow hue of Indian meal. To say the truth, if it had really been a hot Indian cake, Midas would have prized it a good deal more than he now did, when its solidity and increased weight made him too bitterly sensible that it was gold. Almost in despair, he helped himself to a boiled egg, which immediately underwent a change similar to those of the trout and the cake. The egg, indeed, might have been mistaken for one of those which the famous goose, in the story-book, was in the habit of laying; but King Midas was the only goose that had had anything to do with the matter.

72

"Well, this is a quandary!" thought he, leaning back in his chair and looking quite enviously at little Marygold, who was now eating her bread and milk with great satisfaction. "Such a costly breakfast before me, and nothing that can be eaten!"

Hoping that, by dint of great dispatch, he might avoid what he now felt to be a considerable inconvenience, King Midas next snatched a hot potato, and attempted to cram it into his mouth, and swallow it in a hurry. But the Golden Touch was too nimble for him. He found his mouth full, not of mealy potato, but of solid metal, which so burnt his tongue that he roared aloud and, jumping up from the table, began to dance and stamp about the room, both with pain and affright.

"Father, dear father!" cried little Marygold, who was a very affectionate child, "pray what is the matter? Have you burnt your mouth?"

"Ah, dear child," groaned Midas dolefully, "I don't know what is to become of your poor father!"

And, truly, my dear little folks, did you ever hear of such a pitiable case in all your lives? Here was literally the richest breakfast that could be set before a king, and its very richness made it absolutely good for nothing. The poorest laborer, sitting down to his crust of bread and cup of water, was far better off than King Midas, whose delicate food was really worth its weight in gold. And what was to be done? Already, at breakfast, Midas was excessively hungry. Would he be less so by dinnertime? And how ravenous would be his appetite for supper, which must undoubtedly consist of the same sort of indigestible dishes as those now before him! How many days, think you, would he survive a continuance of this rich fare?

These reflections so troubled wise King Midas, that he began to doubt whether, after all, riches are the one desirable thing in the world, or even the most desirable. But this was only a passing thought. So fascinated was Midas with the glitter of the yellow metal, that he would still have refused to give up the Golden Touch for so paltry a consideration as a breakfast. Just imagine what a price for one meal's victuals! It would have been the same as paying millions and millions of money (and as many millions more as would take forever to reckon up) for some fried trout, an egg, a potato, a hot cake, and a cup of coffee!

"It would be quite too dear," thought Midas.

Nevertheless, so great was his hunger, and the perplexity of his situation, that he again groaned aloud, and very grievously too. Our pretty Marygold could endure it no longer. She sat a moment, gazing at her father and trying with all the might of her little wits to find out what was the matter with him. Then, with a sweet and sorrowful impulse to comfort him, she started from her chair, and, running to Midas, threw her arms affectionately about his knees. He bent down and kissed her. He felt that his little daughter's love was worth a thousand times more than he had gained by the Golden Touch.

"My precious, precious Marygold!" cried he.

But Marygold made no answer.

Alas, what had he done? How fatal was the gift which the stranger bestowed! The moment the lips of Midas touched Marygold's forehead, a change had taken place. Her sweet, rosy face, so full of affection as it had been, assumed a glittering yellow color, with yellow teardrops congealing on her cheeks. Her beautiful brown ringlets took the same tint. Her soft and tender little form grew hard and inflexible within her father's encircling arms. Oh, terrible misfortune! The victim of his insatiable desire for wealth, little Marygold was a human child no longer, but a golden statue!

Yes, there she was, with the questioning look of love, grief, and pity, hardened into her face. It was the prettiest and most woeful sight that ever mortal saw. All the features and tokens of Marygold were there; even the beloved little dimple remained in her golden chin. But the more perfect was the resemblance, the greater was the father's agony at beholding this golden image, which was all that was left him of a daughter. It had been a favorite phrase of Midas, whenever he felt particularly fond of the child, to say that she was worth her weight in gold. And now the phrase had become literally true. And now, at last, when it was too late, he felt how infinitely a warm and tender heart, that loved him, exceeded in value all the wealth that could be piled up betwixt the earth and sky!

It would be too sad a story, if I were to tell you how Midas, in the fullness of all his gratified desires, began to wring his hands and bemoan himself; and how he could neither bear to look at Marygold, nor yet to look away from her. Except when his eyes were fixed on the image, he could not possibly believe that she was changed to gold. But stealing another glance, there was the precious little figure, with a yellow tear-drop on its yellow cheek, and a look so piteous and tender that it seemed as if that very expression must needs soften the gold, and make it flesh again. This, however, could not be. So Midas had only to wring his hands, and to wish that he were the poorest man in the wide world, if the loss of all his wealth might bring back the faintest rose-color to his dear child's face.

While he was in this tumult of despair, he suddenly beheld a stranger standing near the door. Midas bent down his head, without speaking; for he recognized the same figure which had appeared to him, the day before, in the treasure-room, and had bestowed on him this disastrous faculty of the Golden Touch. The stranger's countenance still wore a smile, which seemed to shed a yellow luster all about the room, and gleamed on little Marygold's image, and on the other objects that had been transmuted by the touch of Midas.

"Well, friend Midas," said the stranger, "pray how do you succeed with the Golden Touch?"

Midas shook his head.

"I am very miserable," said he.

"Very miserable, indeed!" exclaimed the stranger. "And how happens that? Have I not faithfully kept my promise with you? Have you not everything that your heart desired?"

"Gold is not everything," answered Midas. "And I have lost all that my heart really cared for."

"Ah! So you have made a discovery, since yesterday?" observed the stranger. "Let us see, then. Which of these two things do you think is really worth the most,—the gift of the Golden Touch, or one cup of clear cold water?"

"O blessed water!" exclaimed Midas. "It will never moisten my parched throat again!"

"The Golden Touch," continued the stranger, "or a crust of bread?"

"A piece of bread," answered Midas, "is worth all the gold on earth!"

"The Golden Touch," asked the stranger, "or your own little Marygold, warm, soft, and loving as she was an hour ago?"

"Oh, my child, my dear child!" cried poor Midas, wringing his hands. "I would not have given that one small dimple in her chin for the power of changing this whole big earth into a solid lump of gold!"

"You are wiser than you were, King Midas!" said the stranger, looking seriously at him. "Your own heart, I perceive, has not been entirely changed from flesh to gold. Were it so, your case would indeed be desperate. But you appear to be still capable of understanding that the commonest things, such as lie within everybody's grasp, are more valuable than the riches which so many mortals sigh and struggle after. Tell me, now, do you sincerely desire to rid yourself of this Golden Touch?"

"It is hateful to me!" replied Midas.

A fly settled on his nose, but immediately fell to the floor; for it, too, had become gold. Midas shuddered.

"Go, then," said the stranger, "and plunge into the river that

glides past the bottom of your garden. Take likewise a vase of
the same water and sprinkle it over any object that you may
desire to change back again from gold into its former substance.
If you do this in earnestness and sincerity, it may possibly re-
pair the mischief which your avarice has occasioned."

King Midas bowed low; and when he lifted his head, the lustrous stranger had vanished.

You will easily believe that Midas lost no time in snatching
up a great earthen pitcher (but, alas me! it was no longer
earthen after he touched it) and hastening to the riverside. As
he scampered along and forced his way through the shrubbery,
it was positively marvelous to see how the foliage turned yellow
behind him, as if the autumn had been there, and nowhere else.
On reaching the river's brink, he plunged headlong in, without
waiting so much as to pull off his shoes.

"Poof! poof! poof!" snorted King Midas, as his head emerged out of the water. "Well; this is really a refreshing bath, and I think it must have quite washed away the Golden Touch. And now for filling my pitcher!"

As he dipped the pitcher into the water, it gladdened his very heart to see it change from gold into the same good, honest earthen vessel which it had been before he touched it. He was conscious, also, of a change within himself. A cold, hard, and heavy weight seemed to have gone out of his bosom. No doubt his heart had been gradually losing its human substance and transmuting itself into insensible metal, but had now softened back again into flesh. Perceiving a violet that grew on the bank of the river, Midas touched it with his finger and was overjoyed to find that the delicate flower retained its purple hue, instead of undergoing a yellow blight. The curse of the Golden Touch had therefore really been removed from him.

King Midas hastened back to the palace; and I suppose the servants knew not what to make of it when they saw their royal master so carefully bringing home an earthern pitcher of water. But that water, which was to undo all the mischief that his folly had wrought, was more precious to Midas than an ocean of molten gold could have been. The first thing he did, as you need hardly be told, was to sprinkle it by handfuls over the golden figure of little Marygold.

78

No sooner did it fall on her than you would have laughed to see how the rosy color came back to the dear child's cheek! and how she began to sneeze and sputter!—and how astonished she was to find herself dripping wet, and her father still throwing more water over her!

"Pray do not, dear father!" cried she. "See how you have wet my nice frock, which I put on only this morning!"

For Marygold did not know that she had been a little golden statue; nor could she remember anything that had happened since the moment when she ran with outstretched arms to comfort poor King Midas.

Her father did not think it necessary to tell his beloved child how very foolish he had been, but contented himself with showing how much wiser he had now grown. For this purpose he led little Marygold into the garden, where he sprinkled all the remainder of the water over the rosebushes, and with such good effect that above five thousand roses recovered their beautiful bloom. There were two circumstances, however, which, as long as he lived, used to put King Midas in mind of the Golden Touch. One was, that the sands of the river sparkled like gold; the other, that little Marygold's hair had now a golden tinge, which he had never observed in it before she had been transmuted by the effect of his kiss. This change of hue was really an improvement and made Marygold's hair richer than in her babyhood.

When King Midas had grown quite an old man, and used to trot Marygold's children on his knee, he was fond of telling them this marvelous story, pretty much as I have now told it to you. And then would he stroke their glossy ringlets and tell them that their hair, likewise, had a rich shade of gold, which they had inherited from their mother.

"And to tell you the truth, my precious little folks," quoth King Midas, diligently trotting the children all the while, "ever since that morning, I have hated the very sight of all other gold, save this!"

79

William Elliot Griffis

THE ASHES THAT MADE TREES BLOOM

ILLUSTRATED BY *Robert Sinnott*

IN THE good old days of the daimios, there lived an old couple whose only pet was a little dog. Having no children, they loved it as though it were a baby. The old dame made it a cushion of blue crape, and at mealtime Muko—for that was its name— would sit on it as demure as any cat. The kind people fed the pet with tidbits of fish from their own chopsticks, and it was allowed to have all the boiled rice it wanted. Whenever the old woman took the animal out with her on holidays, she put a bright-red silk crape ribbon around its neck. Thus treated, the dumb creature loved its protectors like a being with a soul.

Now the old man, being a rice-farmer, went daily with hoe or spade into the fields, working hard from the first croak of the raven until O Tento Sama (as the sun is called) had gone down behind the hills. Every day the dog followed him to work and kept near by, never once harming the white heron that walked in the footsteps of the old man to pick up the worms. For the old fellow was kind to everything that had life, and often turned up a sod on purpose to give food to the sacred birds.

One day doggy came running to him, putting his paws against his straw leggings and motioning with his head to some spot behind. The old man at first thought his pet was only playing and did not mind it. But the dog kept on whining and running to-and-fro for some minutes. Then the old man followed the dog a few yards to a place where the animal began a lively

80

scratching. Thinking it only a buried bone or bit of fish, but wishing to humor his pet, the old man struck his iron-shod hoe in the earth, when, lo! a pile of gold gleamed before him.

He rubbed his old eyes, stooped down to look, and there was at least a half peck of *kobans,* or oval gold coins. He gathered them and hied home at once.

Thus in an hour the old couple were made rich. The good souls bought a piece of land, made a feast to their friends, and gave plentifully to their poor neighbors. As for doggy, they petted him till they nearly smothered him with kindness.

Now in the same village there lived a wicked old man and his wife, who had always kicked and scolded all dogs whenever any passed their house. Hearing of their neighbors' good luck, they coaxed the dog into their garden and set before him bits of fish and other dainties, hoping he would find treasure for them. But the dog, being afraid of the cruel pair, would neither eat nor move.

Then they dragged him out-of-doors, taking a spade and hoe with them. No sooner had doggy got near a pine tree growing in the garden than he began to paw and scratch the ground, as if a mighty treasure lay beneath.

"Quick, wife, hand me the spade and hoe!" cried the greedy old fool, as he danced with joy.

Then the covetous old fellow, with a spade, and the old crone, with a hoe, began to dig; but there was nothing but a dead kitten, the smell of which made them drop their tools and shut their noses. Furious at the dog, the old man kicked and beat him to death, and the old woman finished the work by nearly chopping off his head with the sharp hoe. They then flung him into the hole and stamped down the earth over his carcass.

The owner of the dog heard of the death of his pet and, mourning for him as if he had been his own child, went at night under the pine tree. He set up some bamboo tubes in the ground, such as are used before tombs, in which he put fresh camellia flowers. Then he laid a cup of water and a tray of food on the grave and burned several costly sticks of incense. He mourned a great while over his pet, calling him many dear names, as if he were alive.

That night the spirit of the dog appeared to him in a dream and said,—

"Cut down the pine tree over my grave, and make from it a mortar for your rice pastry and a mill for your bean sauce."

So the old man chopped down the tree and cut out of the middle of the trunk a section about two feet long. With great labor, partly by fire, partly by the chisel, he scraped out a hollow place as big as a half-bushel. He then made a great, long-handled hammer of wood, such as is used for pounding rice. When New Year's time drew near, he wished to make some rice pastry. So the white rice in the basket, and the fire and pot to boil the rice dumplings, and the pretty red lacquered boxes were got ready. The old man knotted his blue kerchief round his head, the old lady tucked up her sleeves, and all was ready for cake-making.

When the rice was all boiled, granny put it into the mortar, the old man lifted his hammer to pound the mass into dough, and the blows fell heavy and fast till the pastry was all ready for baking. Suddenly the whole mass turned into a heap of gold coins. When, too, the old woman took the hand-mill, and, filling it with bean sauce, began to grind, the gold dropped like rain.

Meanwhile the envious neighbor peeped in at the window when the boiled beans were being ground.

"Goody me!" cried the old hag, as she saw each dripping of sauce turning into yellow gold, until in a few minutes the tub under the mill was full of a shining mass of *kobans* (oval gold pieces). "I'll borrow that mill, I will."

So the old couple were rich again. The next day the stingy and wicked neighbor, having boiled a mess of beans, came and borrowed the mortar and magic mill. They filled one with boiled rice and the other with beans. Then the old man began to pound and the woman to grind. But at the first blow and turn, the pastry and sauce turned into a foul mass of worms. Still more angry at this, they chopped the mill into pieces, to use as firewood.

Not long after that, the good old man dreamed again, and
the spirit of the dog spoke to him, telling him how the wicked
people had burned the mill made from the pine tree.

"Take the ashes of the mill, sprinkle them on the withered
trees, and they will bloom again," said the dog-spirit.

The old man awoke and went at once to his wicked neighbor's house, where he found the miserable old pair sitting at
the edge of their square fireplace, in the middle of the floor,
smoking and spinning. From time to time they warmed their
hands and feet with the blaze from some bits of the mill, while
behind them lay a pile of the broken pieces.

The good old man humbly begged the ashes, and though the
covetous couple turned up their noses at him and scolded him
as if he were a thief, they let him fill his basket with the ashes.

On coming home, the old man took his wife into the garden.
It being winter, their favorite cherry tree was bare. He
sprinkled a pinch of ashes on it, and, lo! it sprouted blossoms
until it became a cloud of pink blooms which perfumed the air.
The news of this filled the village, and everyone ran out to see
the wonder.

The covetous couple also heard the story, and, gathering up the remaining ashes of the mill, kept them to make withered trees blossom.

The kind old man, hearing that his lord the daimio was to pass along the high road near the village, set out to see him, taking his basket of ashes. As the train approached, he climbed up into an old withered cherry tree that stood by the wayside. Now, in the days of the daimios, it was the custom, when their lord passed by, for all the loyal people to shut up their second-story windows. They even pasted them fast with a slip of paper, so as not to commit the impertinence of looking down on his lordship. All the people along the road would fall upon their hands and knees and remain prostrate until the procession passed by. Hence it seemed very impolite, at first, for the old man to climb the tree and be higher than his master's head.

The train drew near, with all its pomp of gay banners, covered spears, state umbrellas, and princely crests. One tall man marched ahead, crying out to the people by the way, "Get

84

down on your knees! Get down on your knees!" And every one kneeled down while the procession was passing.

Suddenly the leader of the van caught sight of the aged man up in the tree. He was about to call out to him in an angry tone, but, seeing he was such an old fellow, he pretended not to notice him and passed him by. So, when the daimio's palanquin drew near, the old man, taking a pinch of ashes from his basket, scattered it over the tree. In a moment it burst into blossom.

The delighted daimio ordered the train to be stopped and got out to see the wonder. Calling the old man to him, he thanked him and ordered presents of silk robes, sponge-cake, fans, a *nétsŭké* (ivory carving), and other rewards to be given him. He even invited him to visit him in his castle.

So the old man went gleefully home to share his joy with his dear old wife.

But when the greedy neighbor heard of it, he took some of the magic ashes and went out on the highway. There he waited until a daimio's train came along and, instead of kneeling down like the crowd, he climbed a withered cherry tree.

When the daimio himself was almost directly under him, he threw a handful of ashes over the tree, which did not change a particle. The wind blew the fine dust in the noses and eyes of the daimio and his Samurai. Such a sneezing and choking! It spoiled all the pomp and dignity of the procession. The man whose business it was to cry, "Get down on your knees," seized the old fool by the topknot, dragged him from the tree, and tumbled him and his ash-basket into the ditch by the road. Then, beating him soundly, he left him for dead.

Thus the wicked old man died in the mud, but the kind friend of the dog dwelt in peace and plenty, and both he and his wife lived to a green old age.

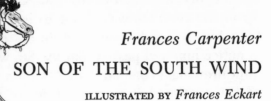

Frances Carpenter

SON OF THE SOUTH WIND

ILLUSTRATED BY *Frances Eckart*

THE Bedouin boy, Tamad, bent low over the flowing mane of his galloping brown horse. Now and then he looked back over his shoulder at two other boys. Their horses, like his, were racing over the gray Arabian Desert.

"Faster! Faster! Sa'da, Son of the South Wind," the Bedouin boy shouted. Almost as though he listened, the golden-brown horse lifted his pointed ears. Almost as though he understood, he laid his ears back again, close to his head. He galloped on faster.

The boy knew well that his horse, Sa'da, would win the race. Sa'da always was first to reach the black goat-hair tents of this Bedouin camp. In all Tamad's tribe, only the Sheik, his father, had horses that went faster than this one.

On, on Sa'da galloped. The horse's long tail floated behind him like the feathery frond of a date palm waving in a high wind. His flying hoofs threw small clouds of sand and pebbles toward the others racing to catch up with him.

The black tents of the Bedouin camp were reached at a full gallop. Tamad pulled hard on the camel-hair bridle ropes. He shouted a cry of victory. Sa'da reared high on his hind legs in a splendid salute.

"Riders! Oh, riders!" Other children shouted these words as they came running out of the black tents. It pleased them to pretend they were calling the news of strange horsemen riding into their camp.

All the children gathered around Tamad as he jumped down from the back of the prancing brown horse. This had been a special race on a special day. For it was only that morning that his father, the Sheik, had given Tamad this fine, brown horse for his own.

It was, however, by no means the first time that Tamad had raced on Sa'da's back across the gray Arabian Desert. Like all the other boys of this Bedouin tribe, he had ridden on horseback ever since he could sit alone in a saddle. Now that he was twelve years old, he could be trusted with almost any horse. Often the camp moved to a new water hole. The long line of camels and horses wound its way over the dry desert. Then Tamad would ride the gentle, spirited Sa'da for whole days at a time.

The boy stroked the silky mane of his golden-brown horse. He ran his hands fondly over the warm, velvety nose. Then he lifted the dainty hoofs, one after the other. He wanted to make sure that Sa'da's round, metal shoes had not picked up small stones that might make the horse lame.

Tamad led Sa'da to a quiet spot near the woman's half of his father's tent. Here he tied the horse's legs loosely together with his halter rope. Thus hobbled, Sa'da could not stray far away.

Sa'da whinnied gratefully when the boy brought him a bowl of sweet camel's milk, warm from the evening milking. Together, the children gathered wisps of desert grass for their hobbled horses. Then they squatted down on the ground near by to wait for their own suppers of camel's milk, cereal, and brown dates.

This evening, Tamad and his horse were the center of all their talk.

"Sa'da is truly a son of the South Wind," Tamad said proudly. "He can outrace an ostrich. He runs even more swiftly than the antelopes that bound over our desert. Look at his fine, shining coat! Has it not the color of the golden date? Everyone knows date-colored horses are the fastest of all."

The other boys nodded. They did not seem to mind Tamad's

boasting. They thought they, too, would be proud to own so fine a horse as this Sa'da.

"Now that you have a horse of your own, Tamad, good fortune will surely be yours," said one of the other boys. "My father says good fortune is woven into the mane of every Arabian horse."

"My father says that too," Tamad replied. "That is why he called my horse Sa'da. It is the same as 'Good Luck.'"

"And why do you call him 'Son of the South Wind'?" a very small boy demanded.

"Are you a baby that you do not know that all horses are sons of the South Wind?" Tamad cried. "Often and often, that tale is told in our coffee circle. I heard it again only last night when I poured coffee into the cups for my father's guests. But there, you are too young yet to serve at the coffee time; I will tell you the tale as I have heard it.

"The horse is the greatest gift men have from Allah-Who-Made-All-Things." Tamad spoke slowly, as should one who speaks of important happenings. "Praise be to Allah, the Lord of Heaven and Earth! Only Allah could have thought up so splendid a beast as a horse.

"It was in the very beginning. Allah was shaping the earth and its creatures. When he decided to make the horse, he called the South Winds before him.

"'Gather, ye South Winds,'" Allah commanded. "'Gather ye close together, and I shall make from thee a live creature that shall be above all other animals.'

"Then Allah bade his angel, Gabriel, put all the South Winds together. At the angel's touch, the winds became a thick mass. Allah took this mass into his own hands. With his own hands he shaped from it the very first horse.

"This one was, so the tale says, a date-colored mare, the Mother of All Horses. On her forehead she had a white star. On her legs she had white bands, just like my own Sa'da.

"'Thy name shall be *Horse*,' Allah said to his new creature, 'Thou hast no wings. Yet shalt thou fly. For thy people I give thee the Arabian tribes. They shall be to thee loving masters.

88

They shall ride on thy back. Ease in travel shalt thou give them. Safely and swiftly shalt thou carry them from water hole to water hole. Victory over their foes shalt thou help them to win. Good fortune for them shall be knit into thy forelock, O Arabian Horse.'

"So speak the tellers of tales in our goat-hair tents," Tamad explained to his listeners. "They say further that as soon as the

Mother of All Horses was made she raised her noble head. She gave a loud whinny, so happy was she to be in the free world.

" 'Blessed be thy whinny, O Arabian Horse,' Allah said to the Mother of Horses. 'Use thy shrill cry to frighten the foes of thy master. Thus shalt thou fill their hearts with fear so they shall turn and run away.' And that is why our horses always whinny when strangers draw near, or when they carry their riders into the battle.

"Oh, that was a handsome creature, that mare that was to be the mother of all our horses," Tamad told the other children. "Now when Allah made the donkey, it was a different affair. A donkey is, of course, somewhat like a horse. But a donkey cannot be called handsome, with its great flopping ears and its bare, ugly tail.

"Allah had already made the very first man, that one called Adam. He showed Adam the horse. And he showed him also the donkey. And he said, 'Adam, choose! Here are two of my creatures for thee to decide between. Which one wilt thou have for thy friend and helper?'

"Had I been Adam," Tamad declared, "I should have had no more trouble deciding than he did. 'I choose the handsome beast,' Adam said quickly. 'I choose the horse.'

" 'Well hast thou chosen, O Adam!' Allah was pleased. 'Thou hast chosen the creature which shall be to thee a glory so long as thou art on earth. And when thou art ready to go up to Heaven, I will send a Heavenly horse, with wings of fire to ride thee over the clouds.' "

In the men's side of the tent that night also, the talk was about the Sheik's gift of a horse to his son. For listening, Tamad found it hard to pour coffee into the wee brass cups.

"Tamad's horse, Sa'da, comes straight from one of the Five Mares of the Prophet," the Sheik told his guests, who sat on the soft tent rugs. At ease, leaning against their camel saddles, they listened intently.

By "the Prophet" Tamad knew his father meant Mahomet, the great messenger of Allah. These Bedouins of the Arabian Desert said their prayers to Mahomet. The Sheik often had told

90

his son about the Mahomet's five famous mares. From them
the very best Arabian horses had come.

"In the days of the Prophet," so the Sheik's story ran, "many
men offered their horses to him. Ten thousand was the number
of noble steeds which he had to choose from.

"One day Mahomet decided to pick out the finest among all
these ten thousand horses. He first chose one hundred of the
very best mares. Mares are as swift and as fierce in battle as
stallions. And besides this, they are the mothers of colts, and
our colts are our riches. It is right that we Arabians should prize
mares even above their brothers, the stallions.

"For four days and four nights, Mahomet kept the hundred
best mares penned up in one place. He gave them no water to
drink. He gave them no camel's milk, nor juicy, green grass to
eat. In the desert heat, the poor mares became almost crazy
from their terrible thirst.

"Then, on the fifth day, the Prophet had his men lead the
mares within sight of a distant stream. Those horses whinnied
and whinnied at the sight and smell of the water. Set free from
their hobbles, with flying hoofs they set off at full gallop toward

the stream. They had almost reached the water when suddenly Mahomet's trumpeter sounded the shrill call to halt.

"The hundred mares heard the familiar call of the trumpet. So well trained were they that all stopped short for a moment. But their thirst was so great that, almost at once, the stampede toward the water was on again. All galloped ahead, all save five splendid mares. Nobly, these five turned round to obey the trumpeter's call. They trotted back to the Prophet. Weak from thirst in the terrible heat of the noonday, they halted, panting, before him.

"Mahomet laid his hands on their forelocks and gave them his blessing. And ever since then men always speak of these peerless mares as the 'Five of the Prophet.' Their descendants, like Sa'da, are the most splendid horses in all the wide world."

Tamad and his people knew there were good horses in other lands too. But in their own minds they were sure that nowhere on earth were there horses to compare with their Arabian steeds. Did not Allah make the very first horse for the Arabians? Do not men come from all lands to seek the offspring of the Five Mares of the Prophet? "Surely," these Arabs said, "no other people love their horses as we do."

Many, many tales about horses are still told in the black goat-hair tents on the Arabian Desert. But many, many tales, too, are told in other lands. Ever since anyone can remember, wondrous stories about horses have been favorites the world over. Some are true tales of real horses such as Sa'da.

Padraic Colum

BELLEROPHON

ILLUSTRATED BY *Robert Sinnott*

OFTEN he watched the eagle in the air; as his gaze followed it on its way he would shout out his own name, "Bellerophon, Bellerophon." As his name came back to him from the high rocks it seemed to him to be a prophecy of the time when he, too, would mount up and go the way of the eagle. He owned a bright sword and he knew that his spirit was braver and stronger than the spirits of those who were around him. And yet he had to serve a grudging King, and fresh labors and harassments came to him every day.

Once as he came back from his labor the eyes of King Proetus' Queen rested upon the bright youth. "How beautiful he is, this Bellerophon," the Queen said. She spoke to him and would have him speak to her. But Bellerophon turned from Proetus' Queen—Proetus whom he had to serve. Then the Queen went to King Proetus and, falsely accusing Bellerophon, had him sent away. But she had him sent away from slavery into dangers. He was commanded to go to the King of Lykia, and he went bearing tablets that told that King to thrust him into danger and still more danger.

"Thou must slay the Chimera for me," said the King of Lykia, "thou must slay the Chimera that appears in the sky and affrights all of us." Even then the Chimera appeared in the sky. It had the head of a lion, the body of a goat, and the tail of a dragon. It filled the bright sky with horror and darkness. Then Bellerophon vowed that he would slay the monster; he would slay it, not because the King commanded him to slay it, but

93

because the monster filled the beautiful depth that he loved with blackness. "I will slay the Chimera for thee, O King," Bellerophon said, and he laid his hand on his bright sword as he spoke, "I will slay the Chimera, and I will bring its lion's head into thy hall."

But how would he come to the Chimera that went through the bright spaces of the sky? It came upon the tops of high mountains, and there Bellerophon would come upon it and slay it. But even as he sharpened his bright sword to go to the mountains and seek the Chimera there, a whisper came to Bellerophon and told him that he should mount up to slay the Chimera. And the whisper told him of a horse that grazed on far pastures, the horse Pegasus that had wings. And if he could come upon Pegasus and bridle him and mount him, he could slay with his bright sword the Chimera in the sky.

Then Bellerophon went forth bearing his sword and carrying the bridle that would hold Pegasus, the winged horse. He went forth, and in its own wild pastures he came upon Pegasus. The youth saw the winged horse feeding upon lotuses and springing across the water-courses. White was Pegasus, with white wings and dainty hoofs, and a heavy mane that tossed as it bounded along. It was easy to see that no bridle had ever gone upon the horse Pegasus, that had wings.

All day Bellerophon, the strong youth, followed after Pegasus. The horse bounded away, hardly noticing its pursuer. On the second day Bellerophon came suddenly upon Pegasus. It was drinking at a certain spring. He seized the winged horse by the mane, and he strove to hold it. But Pegasus trampled and kicked and at last broke away from Bellerophon. Afterwards he saw the winged horse only in the air, or drinking with his head raised from the spring every moment.

Often when he was worn out with watching and the chase, it would seem to Bellerophon that he never would be able to capture the horse Pegasus; he never would be able to slay the Chimera, and he would have to go back and bear whatever doom the King of Lykia would lay upon him. And then he would see the sky being filled with the blackness and horror of

the Chimera, and he would resolve once more that he would be
the one who would slay the monster.

One night a dream came to him. The goddess Pallas Athene
appeared in his dream, and she said to him that any mortal who
had such resolve as he had and who strove as he strove to carry
out his resolve would have help from the immortals. She
whispered to him of a philter that would tame the horse Pegasus. Then he awoke, and he found in the hollow of his shield
a cup that had a liquid in it—a liquid that was red like burning
iron.

Bellerophon waited, hidden, at the spring that Pegasus came
to. He seized the horse by the mane, and he poured into its
mouth and between its teeth the liquid that he had found. Then
Pegasus became tame under his hand. He put the bridle upon
it. With the bright sword in his hand he mounted up to slay
the Chimera that even then filled the sky with blackness and
horror.

And now he was in the air at last. As he went above the earth
he shouted out his name, "Bellerophon, Bellerophon!" He knew
now how magnificent that name was—the name for the rider of

the skies, the conqueror of the Chimera. He rose above where the eagle flew. He looked down and saw the fields and houses and towns of men. He would always soar above them, Bellerophon thought.

He saw the Chimera near him, the monster that had the head of a lion, the body of a goat, and the tail of a dragon. Pegasus screamed and would have kept back from the monster. But Bellerophon rode to meet the darkening thing. It breathed out fire that scorched him. But Bellerophon fought with it, using his bright sword. At last he struck into its body and brought the Chimera from the sky down to the ground.

He rode Pegasus beside where it lay. He sprung off and cut the lion head off the monster that lay there. Then Pegasus fled away. Bellerophon, as he saw the winged horse go, knew that he could never recapture it, and knew that he could never again soar above the fields and the houses and the towns of men.

Into the hall of the King of Lykia he went, bringing the lion-head of the Chimera. And then, because he saw an eagle soaring in the blue of the air, he wept. Before him, as he knew, there were long and weary wanderings over the face of the earth. He wept, knowing what was gone from him and what was before him. And then he knew that the pure spaces over him would never again be filled with the blackness and horror of the Chimera, and he rejoiced.

Dorothy Hosford

HOW BEOWULF
RULES THE GEATS

ILLUSTRATED BY *Walter R. Sabel*

NOW Beowulf became king of the Geats and ruled the people wisely and well. He ruled the land for fifty years, and the people prospered. When he was an old king, wise and beloved by his people, evil came to the realm. It came about in this way:

A dragon began to rage through the land and bring destruction far and wide. This dragon guarded a treasure-hoard that was hidden in a grave, a steep stone-barrow on a hill. A path unknown to men led to it. But by chance a man discovered that hidden hoard.

A guilty thrall fleeing from the wrath of his master came upon the barrow and sought shelter therein. Terror seized him when he saw the loathsome dragon asleep in the midst of his treasure, but before he turned to flee he snatched a golden goblet from the pile. There were many such riches, a great store of treasure which an earl, long dead, had hidden in this place. He, the last of his kin, piled high within this barrow all the treasure of his race, which there was none left to guard but him. Sorrowful of heart, he kept watch over it, grieving for those who had gone before and left him solitary, until death came to him also.

Then an evil dragon, of those that seek out the barrows and fly by night, folded in fire, found that treasure-hoard standing open. For three hundred winters the dragon held this treasure-

97

house in the earth. Then came the day when the thrall discovered the secret place and bore off the cup while the dragon slept. He thought by that gift to make peace with his master.

When the dragon awoke he saw the footprint of the man who had dared enter the cave. Angrily he snuffed along the rock that encircled the barrow, savagely seeking the intruder. But no man was there. When he entered the barrow again he found that some mortal had searched his treasure and stolen a golden cup. Then was the dragon filled with rage and scarce could wait for nightfall to take his vengeance.

When it grew dark the dragon fared forth wrapped in flames, spitting fire. It went abroad in the land and burned the homes of the people and brought terror to the hearts of men. That loathly thing left nought that was in its path alive. Night after night it wrought destruction upon the Geats, attacking the folk of the land with fire and burning. With the first light of dawn the dragon hastened again to his hidden lair, seeking refuge within the stone walls of the barrow.

Soon this terror that had come upon the land was made known to Beowulf. His own homestead, fairest of houses, throne-seat of the Geats, was burned to the earth. Great was the sorrow of the king.

The fire-dragon had laid in ashes the stronghold of the people; but Beowulf, the warlike king, the lord of the Geats, planned vengeance. He bade his clansmen make him a war-shield all of iron. He knew well that wood was of no avail against fire. When the shield was finished he made ready to meet the dragon.

Beowulf scorned to follow the far-flying dragon with a host of warriors, an army. He did not fear single combat, nor did he think overmuch of the dragon's strength and skill in battle. Beowulf had passed through many perils of war and desperate ventures since, a proud conqueror, he had cleansed the hall of Hrothgar and in hand-to-hand struggle killed Grendel and his kin.

Not the least of these encounters was the fight in which Hygelac fell, when the ruler of the Geats lost his life in the land

98

of the Frisians, struck down by the sword thrusts of the enemy. So fierce was Beowulf in that fight that few of the foe lived to return to their homes. Beowulf made his escape by his own great strength and power as a swimmer, though his arms were laden with thirty coats of mail as he swam the sea. Lonely and sorrowful, Beowulf swam over the ocean seeking his homeland.

There Hygd, Hygelac's queen, offered him the wealth and the throne of the kingdom. She doubted that her son would have strength to protect the land from hostile peoples now that Hygelac was gone. Yet she could not prevail upon Beowulf to make himself lord of the realm; instead he chose to support Heardred and to counsel and protect him until he came of age to rule the Geats in his own right.

But the time came when Heardred also fell in battle, leaving Beowulf lord of the Geats and master of the high-seat. He was a good king. And he made war and revenged the slaying of Heardred.

Thus had Beowulf passed safely through many perils and encounters and done daring deeds. Now he prepared to do battle with the dragon.

With eleven comrades, the lord of the Geats went to seek his foe. He had learned the cause of all this strife; how the cup had been stolen. They took the guilty culprit to show the way. Cringing and afraid, he was made to lead them to that burial-hall beneath the ground, near the sea and the tossing waters, within which were heaped jewels and woven gold-work. The fearful dragon kept guard over his lair. To enter there would be no easy task for any man.

Beowulf spoke to his men and made his battle-vow, "I have lived through many wars in my youth. Now once again, as defender of my folk, will I go forth to battle, if this dark destroyer will come from his cavern to fight me."

Then he greeted each of his men, saying, "I would carry no sword against the dragon, but count on my own strength as I did once with Grendel, but here I must fight against fire and poisonous breath. So I take with me shield and breastplate. I will not flee one step from the keeper of that barrow. Fate, which rules all men, shall decide the battle. I am ready.

"Wait here, my comrades, until the end. It is not your fight. It is fitting that I, the lord and defender of my people, alone should measure my strength against this monster. I shall win that gold and victory, or death will take your lord."

Then the sturdy champion took up his shield. Helmet on head and sword in hand he sought out the opening in that hill of rocks. No coward dared walk that path!

Beowulf soon spied an arch of stone, and beneath it a stream ran forth from the barrow. Those waves were steaming. He could never hope to reach his foe that way or pass through that narrow passage hot with the dragon's fire.

Then the prince of the Geats cried out in his wrath, and the shout went ringing clear and sure through the rocky cavern. The dragon heard the sound of a human voice, and his hate was kindled. His poisonous breath, streaked with fire, shot forth from the cave. The rocks resounded with his bellow.

Beowulf raised his shield and waited with drawn sword. Sharp was that weapon, a proud victor of many battles. The dragon coiled. The hero stood firm, ready for the onslaught. Uncoiling in long springs, the blazing serpent glided forth, moving speedily over the earth. As the dragon rushed upon him, Beowulf lifted his weapon and struck hard. But the burnished blade turned on the bone and cut less deeply than Beowulf had need of. The blow made the dragon wild with pain and rage. He thrashed savagely and spit forth deadly fire; the fierce flames shot far and wide. The lord of the Geats could boast no victor's glory yet; his sword had failed him in his utmost need.

Again the fighters closed in upon each other. Once more the dragon heaved his mighty breath, and Beowulf was in dire peril as the flames hemmed him in.

Then did the companions of Beowulf betray him. They came not to his aid when they saw his danger, but took to the woods to save their lives.

But the soul of one of them was troubled. His name was Wiglaf, a beloved thane and kinsman to Beowulf. He saw his king hard oppressed and struggling beneath his helmet against

Beowulf drove his sword into the dragon's head, but the sword broke.

the heat, and he remembered all that his prince had done for him. He drew his sword and spoke to his comrades,—

"I remember, when we drank our mead in the banquet-hall, the promises we made our lord. We would give him return, if ever he should need it, for all that he had bestowed upon us, for war-gear and battle-helmet and treasure. He chose us to be with him now because he counted us strong and quick with the spear, though he had hoped to finish this daring deed un-helped and alone.

"Now is the day come when our liege lord has need of stout warriors. Let us go to him and give him help while the heat and the flame are about him. God knows I would rather the fire should burn my body too, than that I should hide safely here. It is not meet that we should bear our shields home, unless we try our strength against the dragon and defend the life of our prince. It were shame to our land if the king alone of the Geatish warriors endured this struggle and sank in the strife.

101

My sword and helmet, breastplate and shield, shall serve us both."

So saying, Wiglaf turned and strode through the battle-smoke to the side of his chieftain. Quickly he spoke to his lord,—

"Dear Beowulf, fight well as you did in the days of your youth. Renowned are you for your deeds; now you must guard your life with all your might. I will help you."

As he spoke, the dragon came on once again, a fearful foe, mad with hate, breathing fire. The shield of the young spearsman burned to the boss in the waves of flame, and his breastplate gave him no shelter. Quickly he went under his kinsman's shield, since his own was consumed in the fire. Again Beowulf remembered his deeds of glory and with a mighty blow drove his sword into the dragon's head, a blow made strong with hate. But the sword broke. The sword of Beowulf failed him in the strife; it was not given to him that the edge of steel might help him much in battle. His hand was too strong, and the weight of his blow was often too great for the weapon he carried, no matter how sturdy the blade.

Then for the third time the fiery dragon rushed on the hero. Its bitter fangs sank in his neck, and the waves of blood gushed over Beowulf's breast.

It was now, when his prince was hard beset, that Wiglaf made known his skill and enduring courage. Heedless of danger, though his hand was burned, he came to his kinsman's aid. On the lower side of its body, beneath the scales, he smote the dragon with his sword and drove in the bright and burnished steel. It was a telling blow, and the flames of the dragon weakened. Then Beowulf gathered his strength once more and drew his war-knife, a sharp and biting dagger that hung from his breastplate. And the king of the Geats cut the dragon in two through the middle. So they felled their foe and flung forth its life. Thus they killed the dragon, the two kinsmen together.

James Stevens

THE GREAT HUNTER OF THE WOODS

ILLUSTRATED BY *John Dukes McKee*

"I WAS thinkin' of the most famous hunt of history," said old Larrity the bull cook. "That was when Paul Bunyan, the first great hunter of the woods, shouldered his scatter-cannon to bring down the wing-tailed turkey that had ravaged the Round River country of its game. A terrible turkey that was indade, for even such hunters as Paul Bunyan and Dublin, the wire-haired terror, who was tall as any tree. Such huntin' there was in that time long ago, a time too far away for even mention in the history books."

The old logger stopped there for a shrewd glance at the two by his side. They were Jeff Gavin, whose grandfather was the owner of the logging camp, and Mike, the boy's wire-haired terrier pup. Both were staring mournfully at the flaming leaves of dogwood thickets up the creek. There three men in red caps and brown coats with big spotted dogs sniffing and scampering at their heels, had vanished a few moments before.

"Whist, now, and you should be glad your grandpa left you with me. Pheasants they will be shootin'," said Larrity scornfully. "And the huntin' of chickens is too triflin' for the bother of old woodsmen like us, so it is. How much better, Jeff, to sun ourselves here on the creek bank and talk of the days of real huntin'."

Curiosity lightened the boy's eyes. On other Saturday afternoons he had listened to stories of Paul Bunyan from old Larrity, who had learned them many years ago in the faraway

103

Michigan woods. Here in the Oregon timber the stories would come to life. The Gavin grandson forgot his grief at being left in camp by the hunters. Mike, the terrier pup, also seemed resigned, as he stretched himself out in the rusty grass of the creek bank, crossed his paws, rested his chin on them, and shut his eyes.

Old Larrity was telling of the great hunter of the woods. As his voice drawled on, the boy saw a mighty figure rising dimly among the shadows of the trees. . . . Paul Bunyan, whose wiry black beard brushed the treetops . . . and at his heels trotted Dublin, wire-haired terror of the hunting trails. . . .

On the first day of a certain Christmas week (said old Larrity) the great hunter of the woods and his dog, Dublin, marched into the Round River country. This was the game country in the time when Ameriky was all one big timberland, and Paul Bunyan was the ruler of it and all the rest. In the black wild woods circled by Round River the famous logger always did his Christmas huntin'. That was only to provide rare holiday dinners for his seven hun'erd bully men. This huntin' season the reg'lar game was ruined. And all because the terrible turkey, the most ferocious fowl of the tall timber, had at last migrated to Round River from the mountains of the North.

Paul Bunyan had no hint of the trouble and grief ahead as he tramped through the autumn woods for Round River. He saw nothin' but a promise of cheer in the keen, bright mornin'. Above him shone the clean blue sky and about him blazed the fire colors of leaves. The frost made his breath steam till white clouds trailed him. Sunlight glinted from the forty-seven barrels of his scatter-cannon. At his heels the tremendous terror was a gay dog, ever waggin' his tree of a tail.

For Paul Bunyan talked to Dublin, even as you talk to your Mike when the two of you walk together. It was all gladness in the mighty voice, for Paul Bunyan spoke of the men in the camp behind. Of Johnny Inkslinger Paul spoke, that timekeeper who was such a big figger that his pens were made of peeled trees. He had kind words also for the Big Swede, his foreman, and a

104

mister mckee

man with legs so much like sawlogs that the reg'lar sized loggers were forever goin' after them with crosscuts and axes. Paul Bunyan spoke fondly to Dublin of Babe the Blue Ox, a beast that was even bigger than the dog, measurin' forty-two ax handles and a barrel of pickles betwixt the horns.

Of all these big figgers Paul Bunyan spoke kindly and well, but his best words were for his seven hun'erd men, who were no bigger than me or your grandfather. Never had his men done such fine loggin' as in this season. And for a reward they should have the grandest Christmas dinner ever heard of at all.

"What game shall it be for such a dinner?" said Paul Bunyan to Dublin, when they were to the bank of Round River. "The best meat will be none too good for my loggers' Christmas dinner, no sir! Should we bag some fat bucks for rabbit stews, Dublin? Or deer, to make a great steak dinner? Or cinnamon bears for the spicy roasts the loggers like so well? What do you say, you wire-haired terror, you?"

Dublin acted for all the world like he understood every one of Paul Bunyan's words. He sat down and slowly scratched his ear with his left foot, seemin' to be in the deepest thought.

"I know what you want to be huntin', first, last, and all the time, Dublin, I do." Paul Bunyan smiled down through his beard. "Yes, sir, mince-hunter that you are. You would have us go back with nothin' but mincemeat for the Christmas pies, you would. But we must hunt other game than minces."

Sayin' that, he leaned restfully on his scatter-cannon and gazed into the black wild woods across the river. Now he began to notice that they were silent, almost. Every other autumn the woods had been roarin' with sounds of wild life. The game of the country had never migrated beyond the river that circled their home.

We would think such a stream as Round River most peculiar nowadays, but sure, in the time of Paul Bunyan rivers were young and wild, and each one would run to suit itself. It suited this river to run always in a circle, bein' too proud, no doubt, to run into another river, or even into the great salt ocean.

Whatever the reason, I'm telling you now, that river was round. In its circle lived timber beasts like the hodag and sauger, which are remembered only by old loggers. And there were creatures like our deer, rabbits, bobcats, and bears, only mind you they all had tails in those times when the timberlands were young.

Fine and flourishin' tails were on all of them. The roarin' rabbit of the Round River woods was no such timorious, cowerin' and cringin' beastie as the rabbit of our time. Before he lost his tail the Round River rabbit would tackle a panther, he would, noosin' his powerful, long tail about the beast's neck, jerkin' him down, then kickin' the life out of the panther with both hind feet. In them days the blood-curdlin' roar of a rabbit was the most awful of all the wild woods sounds. The rabbits had run all the panthers out of the woods when the terrible turkey come to Round River.

The deer of them woods also had a fine tail for himself, one like a plume and the brightest spot of beauty in the forest. The bobcat's tail was more of a fightin' kind, like you'd expect. It was a fang tail, with sharp teeth in the tip, and with them the bobcat would strike like a snake at birds and small beasts for his prey. The black and cinnamon bears had stiff brushy tails, which they used mostly for the sweepin' of their caves. There were never cleaner creatures than the cave bears of Paul Bunyan's time; always hustlin' and bustlin' in every nook and cranny, keepin' everything spick and span.

Paul Bunyan did not dream that such a course had befallen the timber beasts as the loss of their tails. He had never even heard of the wing-tailed terrible turkey, so of course he did not know how this ferocious fowl made its meals. The dismal quiet of the black wild woods was all a mystery to Paul Bunyan, a quiet broken only by a whispering moan like the rustle of wind in trees at night. But this was no wind, indade; it was the timber beasts of Round River, hidin' away, and sighin' in sorrow and sadness for the lost tails of them.

Paul Bunyan wondered and worried, as he forded the river. Not even the mutter of a mince was heard, for that little beast, whose meat was so good for pies, was entirely gone. On no other huntin' trip had Paul Bunyan and Dublin come into the woods without hearin' minces mutterin' from their lairs. For the minces of Round River always muttered, so they did, just as the rabbits roared and the bears bellowed and growled. That mutter was the sweetest of music to the wire-haired terror's ears.

At last Dublin thought he heard it, when they had reached the inside bank of Round River. Paul Bunyan leaned on his scatter-cannon again, and wondered and worried still more about the dismal quiet of the black wild woods, with only that whisperin' moan to break it at all. But something else was soundin' in the terror's ears. He perked them up and made himself believe that this was a mince mutterin' out of the woods. So he came to a point, with the blunt muzzle of himself stuck out, and his tail wavin' and waggin' in the wind. For Dublin could never point a mince without h'istin' and waggin' his fine tail, such a gay dog he was when huntin' his favorite game.

Then it happened. What Dublin thought was the mutter of a mince suddenly growed into growlin' thunder. Paul Bunyan stiffened up, but before he could bring the scatter-cannon to his shoulder a coppery streak touched with red at the head of it and with a whirlin' blur behind, flashed from sight along the circle of the river. In the same instant there rose a fearful howl of grief from the wire-haired terror.

Pore dog, indeed pore Dublin, sure he had a right to howl, for all but a stub of his tail was gone, clipped clean away before he could wink an eye. Now he was a sad dog, with tears tricklin' from his eyes as he looked up at Paul Bunyan. He whimpered and moaned with a sound which melted into that whisperin' from the forest, and now that was a mystery no longer to Paul Bunyan. He knew the reason for the sorrowful sound. Certainly all the timber beasts had been denuded of their tails, and like Dublin all were bemoanin' their loss. And the robber of all was none other than this red-headed thunderbolt in coppery feathers, this ferocious fowl who drove like lightin' through the air by the power of his whirlin' wing tail.

Paul Bunyan figgered that out as he doctored Dublin's hurt with arnicky, stanched it, and bound it. Then with kind words he comforted the grievin' terror. As he did so, he again heard that sound like the mutter of a mince from its lair; and it soon growed into rolls of thunder.

The great hunter of the woods stared up at the sound, his head turnin' back till the tip of his wiry black beard waved at the sky. And here was the roar and the rush again; but now it was Paul Bunyan's time to howl; for all of his beard was gone, so it was, nipped and clipped slick away from his chin.

But Paul Bunyan did not howl with grief, nor did he roar with rage or sigh with sorrow or anything like that at all. Paul Bunyan was not that kind of a man. Enough had happened, indade, to drive anybody distracted—the ruin of the game, the loss of the grand Christmas dinner he had planned for his men, the thievery of Dublin's fine tail, and the snippin' and pluckin' away of his famous beard. Disaster and disgrace it all was, enough to make even a hero like Paul Bunyan despair.

But sure the great hunter would not give up, not even when he realized that he could do no thinkin' until his beard growed out again. Paul Bunyan could think only when he brushed his beard with a young pine tree. Now he had no beard to brush at all.

"If I cannot think, then I must act," said Paul Bunyan, makin' the best of things. "And I'll do that soon and sudden."

What to do was plain enough. Paul Bunyan could see it all without thinkin'. Both times the wing-tailed terrible turkey had flown in a perfect circle, follyin' the course of Round River. To get the feathered thunderbolt on the wing, he must shoot in a circle. So Paul Bunyan first bent the forty-seven barrels of his scatter-cannon so that they would do just that—shoot their loads of cannon balls in an in-curve that would exactly folly the course of Round River.

Next, it was plain that he must set up a lure, to bring the ferocious fowl swoopin' down again. Paul Bunyan fixed a lure by pluckin' a colossyal cattail from the riverbank and bindin' it to the pore stump left to Dublin. The dog whimpered, and he shed more tears at such a fake of a tail; he felt disgraced, indade, to have a cattail foisted on such a tremenjus dog as himself, and would have stuck it betwixt his hind legs and crept off in shame. But Paul Bunyan spoke to him stern-like, and Dublin, obejient wire-haired terror that he was, set up and took notice, flourishin' the shameful fake of a tail to please his master.

Well, the fake fooled the terrible turkey, who had no more brains than the small gobblers of our own time. Soon there was the mutter again, and then the thunder. A coppery streak bolted down from the blue sky, and the false tail was snipped up like lightin'. So fast was it grabbed and gobbled that Paul Bunyan's scatter-cannon would have been no use at all, had not the terrible turkey gone red with wrath over the deceit played on him. He stopped in mid-air to spit the cattail out of his beak, and also to strut and pout—and that was the chance for the great hunter to bring him down.

For two seconds Paul Bunyan took careful aim. The terrible turkey hovered low, and so was on a level with Paul Bunyan's shoulders. While he hovered, he puffed and swelled, the terrible turkey did, till only his wattles showed like flames from his ruffle of coppery feathers. His wrathy gobbles sounded like the

mister mckee

stormiest thunder now. The wing tail of him, spread like a windmill, whirled slow, just holdin' him above the trees.

Paul Bunyan's aim was set. He squeezed the trigger, and the forty-seven barrels roared as one cannon. The balls whistled and screamed, powder smoke fogged up like a stormcloud, the earth shook, the timber shivered, and waves rolled over the river from the mighty blast of Paul Bunyan's scatter-cannon. The terrible turkey took alarm in the instant of an instant, so he did.

The cloud of balls was hardly out of the muzzles before he was off at full speed, his side wings spread, his wing tail a whirlin' blur again, his body a red-headed coppery streak.

"A second too late," groaned Paul Bunyan. "He is out-flyin' my cannon balls, a curse on me now for bein' too careful and slow!"

The terrible turkey was gone. The streak and blur of him disappeared around the curve of the river. The cloud of cannon balls curved after him, but slower, and they were soon left behind.

Paul Bunyan was like to give up at that. He was minded to turn his back on the huntin' woods at once and return to his loggers with an empty bag. Never had he been so grieved, to know that this year he could give his loggers no fine Christmas dinner. Dublin stood by him and licked his hand, tryin' also, pore dog, to wag the stub of a tail which was left to him.

"So we must go back, Dublin," said Paul Bunyan sadly, "without even a mince for the loggers. Dear, oh, dear, and such a curse!"

He swung his gun over his shoulder to go. Just then the terrible turkey thundered down the river again. It was roarin' thunder indade this trip, for the fowl had his wing tail whirlin' at the speed limit. Down the river he curved and was gone. And now, from away back up the river, sounded the whistle and screech of the cannon balls, too slow indade for that feathered thunderbolt. Paul Bunyan blushed with shame to see them so far behind.

Now they were beginnin' to fall. White spouts of water and foam gushed up from the river as spent cannon balls dropped, the spray flashin' in the sunlight, makin' rainbows bright to see. But Paul Bunyan took no joy in the sight. He was ashamed to think that his cannon balls were so slow that the terrible turkey might catch 'em from behind in the great circle of the river.

Paul Bunyan raised his eyes, to look behind the cannon balls which still whistled and whined down the river. And now Paul Bunyan got a hope, a flimsy and scrawny hope, but he needed no more. Paul Bunyan was that kind of a man.

"Up and ready, Dublin!" he roared. "Sic 'em, boy! *Up* the river!"

That was enough for Dublin. What was up the wire-haired terror didn't know, but he lepped up river. And with that Paul Bunyan threw up his scatter-cannon with the forty-seven barrels of it curved like a hoop; and he let fly. After the terrible turkey? Not at all. Sure, he'd tried that once. The bird was too fast for that. Paul Bunyan turned his back and fired in the opposite direction. For when he said to Dublin, "*Up* the river, boy," he'd bent the forty-seven barrels to the other side. Down the river curved the big bird and was gone. So *up* the river curved the shot, whistling and screeching. And Dublin after them.

There was a great sound as the terrible turkey flew head on into them new cannon balls. Feathers flew in clouds, and the river boiled and foamed as the cannon balls splashed down. The terrible turkey fell, but in a great rainbow curve, for his speed carried him on, turnin' him over and over, while the dog lepped in frantic chase of him.

Paul Bunyan, runnin' after both, saw the terrible turkey sail down like a coppery cloud, while Dublin lunged up like a black-spotted white cloud to meet him. The great hunter reached the death-grapple just in time. With one snap Dublin had taken off the terrible turkey's head in return for his tail and was goin' after the rest of him. Paul Bunyan had to grope his way to the dog through a snowstorm of feathers, but he got there in time.

Dublin soon had the terrible turkey well plucked. And when Paul Bunyan saw the royal drumsticks of the fowl, the rich meat of his breast, the grandeur of his giblets, and all the rest, his gladness was so great that he was like to sheddin' tears of joy.

"Would you but look at the drumsticks of him, Dublin!" cried Paul Bunyan. "What logger would ask for a rabbit stew, deer steak, or cinnamon bear roast, when he can have such fine eatin' as this for his Christmas dinner? Tender and plump, juicy and drippin', crisped to a fine golden brown, stuffed till he bulges, this behemoth of a bird will be enough for twice seven hun'erd men. Here is the meat for the finest Christmas dinner ever heard of; yes, sir!"

Yet the Dublin dog looked troubled. And Paul Bunyan knew why.

"Never mind," said the great logger cheerily. "I'll invent a recipe for mincemeat which will beat that from the mutterin' minces of the Round River woods. You leave it to me, Dublin."

112

mister
mckee

And so Paul Bunyan did. He invented such fine mince meat that cooks have used it ever since, and minces are never hunted any more for their meat at all. And the dinner from the terrible turkey was so ravishin' to Paul Bunyan's seven hun'erd men that they took his breast bone and made a mountain out of it, to stand as a moniment to the first Christmas turkey dinner.

And so we have had turkey dinners for Christmas ever since. To be sure, they are not terrible turkeys nowadays, for Paul Bunyan glued up the tails of all the young ones of the turkey tribe, and soon they had forgot how to fly with any but their side wings. But even our tame turkeys of today will pout and strut and spread their stiff tails, just like the terrible turkey of old. And their tails look like windmills, but never can they twist and turn, to make turkeys fly like lightnin' and thunder. Nor can our tame turkeys bite off dogs' tails, but they will peck at them every chance, in memory of what the daddy of 'em all used to do.

There is a bit of sadness to remember, too. For the rabbit was made a coward by the loss of the tail with which he choked panthers in the old times, and the rabbit roars no more. Nor did deer, bobcats, and bears ever grow fine tails again. Neither do you see tails worth the mention on wire-haired terrors, these tiny descendants of Dublin, the tremendous terror who follied the first great hunter of the woods.

But sure it was worth it all to discover the glory of turkey for Christmas dinner. For that you must ever remember Paul Bunyan.

Old Larrity was silent. Jeff stroked his dog's head and stared out into the timber. Now, here in the autumn woods, he could imagine that he was Paul Bunyan and that Mike the pup was Dublin, a wire-haired terrier as tall as a tree.

●

Anne Malcolmson

PECOS BILL
AND HIS BOUNCING BRIDE

ILLUSTRATED BY *Robert McCloskey*

G RANDY COYOTE was out for his afternoon run along the bank of the Pecos River. Grandy was the honored grandfather and chief wise man of all the coyotes of Texas. As he loped along, snuffing in the sagebrush, the sharp warning smell of human struck his nose. Ordinarily that was the signal for a smart coyote to head in the opposite direction. But Grandy didn't turn away. He had heard a baby cry from the direction of the smell. He went to see what was up.

In a clump of sagebrush lay a little boy about two years old. There were no grown-up humans near by. The child must have fallen out of a prairie schooner as it jounced up the bank. The pioneers had families so large that one child could easily be lost without being missed for several days.

Grandy took a fancy to little Crop Ear, as he called the baby. He picked him up and trotted him home to the pack. He fed him and played with him until his foundling was as happy as any coyote cub.

As the years went on Grandy adopted Crop Ear as his own and favorite son. He taught him all the tricks of the desert and the prairie. Crop Ear learned to sit on his haunches and bay at the moon. He ran on four legs as did the other cubs. He hunted with the pack. He learned the animal language and the bird language. He could speak with any living creature, except man, in his own tongue.

In order to protect his foster child, Grandy called a council of all the animals of the plains. From each one he asked a

115

pledge that Crop Ear would not be injured. For he knew that the boy was at a disadvantage. All but the rattlesnake and the wowser agreed.

These two were the most bitter of all man's natural enemies. They were famous for their bad dispositions. The wowser was a cross between a mountain lion and a grizzly bear and had all the meanness and ill temper of both.

Fortunately Crop Ear soon learned to stay away from them. He listened for their warnings—the rattle of the snake and the snarl of the wowser—and so grew up to be a strong young coyote-man without mishap.

The only thing that Grandy refused to teach the boy was the fact that he was a human. No member of the tribe was allowed to tell Crop Ear the story of his adoption. So far as he knew, he was a coyote cub and had been born into the pack.

He might have gone through life without learning the truth if it hadn't been for a cowboy named Chuck. Chuck was riding the range when he saw a strange wild creature. It certainly looked like a man. But when it saw Chuck and his pony it slunk off into the bushes on all fours, just like a coyote. The cowpuncher tried to get a closer view. After a day of tempting it with bits of jerked beef from his lunch, he was able to pat its ugly matted hair.

He tried to talk to it in every language he could think of. He spoke in cowpuncher American, high-brow English, and *vaquero* Spanish. The creature sat on its haunches listening with interest. It seemed unable to understand. But Chuck could see that it was trying to recall something to mind. At last its face lit up with a smile. Out gushed a torrent of words such as "Ga-ga. Ma-ma, Wa-wa." Baby talk!

Yes, Crop Ear was talking baby talk. It was the only human speech he had known before his life with the coyotes. Naturally, when he started to speak like a human again, he started in where he had left off.

"Well, tan my hide!" exclaimed Chuck. He "goo-gooed" back in great style. For several hours the two men stood there, gurgling and calling each other "itsy-bitsy," like babies in a nursery.

116

Then Chuck began to experiment. He branched out into kindergarten and first-grade language. Crop Ear had learned the secret of imitating from a mockingbird. He caught on quickly. By sundown he had mastered the art of speaking cultured English as well as any lecturer.

Then the real conversation began. Crop Ear told Chuck about his life with the coyotes. Chuck told him about the outside world. They talked for several days.

At noon on the fourth day, Chuck noticed that Crop Ear had a blue mark on his left arm. He looked at it carefully. It was a five-pointed star, just like the one on his own arm.

"Yippee, ti-yi!" he yelled. "If you aren't my brother Bill, the one that fell out of the wagon on the Pecos bank! We always wondered what had become of you."

Crop Ear asked Chuck to explain this outburst. Chuck then told him all about his family. Their mother had had trouble telling her children from the neighbors'. So she had them all tattooed with blue stars on their left arms. Whenever she saw a blue star, she knew the child was hers.

Although Bill, as he called himself now, hated to leave his dear friends the coyotes, he knew it was his duty to return to the human race. Chuck bought him an outfit of clothes and took him to his own ranch, the I.X.L.

The cow hands were amazed at their strange new mate. They were even more amazed at the things he could do. He never had to rope a cow. He talked to her politely in her own language. When the boys raced their ponies up and down the range, Bill took off his shoes and loped along on all fours. Even so he outran the fastest mustangs.

Soon he was elected the boss of the ranch. He took to the life as a duck takes to water. Before long he was making improvements.

Before Bill came to the I.X.L., a cowboy's life was very easy. The herds looked after themselves. Nobody cared whether or not they wandered off. All the hands had to do was to sit in the bunkhouse. They played cards and rolled cigarettes all day long. If they wanted exercise they raced their ponies. On Satur-

117

day nights they roared into the nearest village and shot it up.

Once in a long while a steer had to be roped and butchered for food. The method of roping was very poor. A cowboy laid out a loop of rope on the ground and hid behind a tree. When a steer stepped into the loop, the man pulled his end of the rope. Sometimes he had to stand all day before a steer would step in.

Bill changed all this. He invented the lasso. He practiced whirling it around his head and slinging the loop over the steer's necks. He became so clever at it he could lasso an owl out of the top of a tree while his broncho was galloping at full speed. Then he taught this trick to the I.X.L. boys.

He thought it was wasteful to allow the cattle to wander off into the hills without any mark of ownership. The star on his arm gave him an idea. He had Bean Hole, the cook, bend an iron into the shape of I.X.L. Then he heated it over the kitchen stove until it glowed like a ruby. He held it against the flank of a steer until the hair burned off. When the scar healed no one could mistake his animal. He had invented branding.

His next invention was the roundup. Every spring and every fall he had the boys ride out to the range and bring in all the cattle marked with his brand. It was simpler this way to keep track of the herd.

As you can see, the cowboys had no time left for their former lazy life. Bill kept them busy. Some of them resented all the work. They grew cross and tired and complained that they had no fun any more. So Bill had to scratch his head and think up another invention. This one was the rodeo. After every roundup he held a big party. Every hand in the outfit had a chance to show off. This made them all completely happy.

A few gangs of cowpunchers refused to take Bill's new method of cowpunching. They said the life was too hard. They much preferred their old lazy habits of playing cards and being tough and shooting up the towns on Saturday nights.

The worst of these gangs was the Devil's Cavalry. It had a hideout in a canyon called Hell's Gate Gulch. Old Satan was the name of the leader. He claimed that Bill was a sissy and that

118

no coyote could tell him what to do. In defiance he rode into the town of Dallas and shot all the glass out of the windows. Furthermore he took to stealing cattle. He roped several of Bill's prize bulls and sold them to an Indian.

This made Bill mad. He vowed to make Old Satan listen to reason. He knew it would be a rough trip to Hell's Gate Gulch. He didn't want his boys to be hurt, so he went alone.

It was to be more of a trip than he bargained for. He had gone not more than a day's journey when he met his old enemy Granddaddy Rattler. The big old snake was coiled in the middle of his road. It sprang at his horse. The pony lunged aside and fell, breaking his leg. Immediately Bill was on his feet and grasped the snake.

The rattler was a strong fellow. But he was not strong enough for Pecos Bill. After an hour's terrible battle, the cowman had his enemy by the throat.

"Are you going to obey me?" roared Bill.

The snake gagged. "Y-yes, sir," he said meekly.

"That's better," said the cowpuncher, cooling off a little. "Now wrap yourself around my arm and come along."

With the snake coiled around his arm, Bill loped off down the road, on all fours this time. He'd had to shoot his horse.

At the end of the second day's journey Bill heard a snarl above his head. He looked up just in time to see the King of the Wowsers leaping down on top of him from an overhanging cliff. He jumped aside, but now he had another fight on his hands. Quickly the snake unwound itself and slid to the side of the road. The fight with the wowser was even worse than the fight with the snake. But at the end, Pecos Bill had his enemy's promise to come along meekly. Bill saddled him and bridled him. Then when the snake had coiled itself around his arm again, he set out riding the wowser.

At last the strange party came to Hell's Gate Gulch. Old Satan and the Devil's Cavalry were having a merry time. They were sitting around their campfire roaring and bragging. They were telling all the terrible things they would do to Pecos Bill when they met him.

120

Bill moved up quietly behind them. With a terrible yell he stepped out. In that yell were all the animal and bird screams and roars and bellows he had learned as a cub among the coyotes. The wowser gave his own terrifying howl. The rattler shook his rattles.

The Devil's Cavalry were so frightened they couldn't move. They turned as white as a salt lick. Their knees shook so that their six-guns and cutlasses clinked like Christmas-tree ornaments in a strong wind.

Bill strode into the midst of the party. "Who's the boss of this outfit?" he growled.

Poor Old Satan fainted on the ground. When he came to he looked up timidly and murmured, "I was, but you be now."

That was all there was to it. Bill lassoed the gang together and carried them back to I.X.L., where he taught them to be good, modern cowpunchers. The rattler and the wowser came along too, as pets.

One summer, Bill had trouble with the weather. First came a drought. The range grass dried up, and the cattle had nothing to eat. All the springs and rivers dried up. Bill dug a canal, hoping that this would solve his problem. It was a lovely canal, but no water flowed into it. Then Bill took his lasso and roped a ten-mile piece of the Rio Grande River. This was enough to last the ranch a day. Every morning before breakfast Bill had to rope himself another length.

As though this were not bad enough, the sky grew green. From the mountains came the wild roar of a tornado. The boys divided the cattle to keep them from stampeding. They did their best to keep them out of the hurricane's path. It wasn't any use. The tornado headed for them whichever way they went.

To save his ranch, Bill risked his own life. He swung his lasso around his head and let fly. The noose caught the tornado and Bill was yanked up, up, up into the middle of the ugly green cloud.

The thought that a human had roped it was unbearable to the cyclone. It whipped around and around, bucked up and down, tried side-kicking and sky-walking, all the tricks of a

121

bucking steer. Bill held on for dear life. Over plains and mountains they raced. The cyclone tried to brush him off against the Rockies. It slapped him against the walls of the Grand Canyon. It bumped his head against the sky. Still Pecos Bill kept his seat.

At last, seeing that there was no other means of shaking off its rider, the tornado headed for the Pacific Ocean and tried to rain out from under him. Bill decided he had had enough. He picked out a pleasant spot in California and jumped. The force with which he landed dug a big hole. Today this is known as Death Valley.

One of the strange things the cyclone did was almost too much for Bill. Before he threw his lasso he put two things into his pocket, a twenty-dollar gold piece and a bowie knife. With these he knew he could get along wherever the tornado landed him. As soon as he hit the earth, he felt in his pocket. The twenty-dollar gold piece had been changed into a couple of half-dollars and a plugged nickel. The bowie knife had shrunk. It was changed into a lady's pearl-handled penknife.

There were two loves in the life of Pecos Bill. The first was his horse Widow-Maker, a beautiful creamy white mustang. The second was a girl, a pretty, gay creature named Slue-Foot Sue.

Widow-Maker was the wildest pony in the West. He was the son of the White Mustang. Like his father he had a proud spirit which refused to be broken. For many years cowboys and *vaqueros* had tried to capture him. At last Pecos Bill succeeded. He had a terrible time of it. For a whole week he lay beside a water hole before he could lasso the white pony. For another week he had to ride across the prairies, in and out of canyons and briar patches, before he could bring the pony to a walk. It was a wild ride indeed. But after Bill's ride on the cyclone it was nothing.

At last the white stallion gave up the struggle. Pecos patted his neck gently and spoke to him in horse language. "I hope you will not be offended," he began as politely as possible, "but beauty such as yours is rare, even in this glorious state of Texas.

I have no wish to break your proud spirit. I feel that together you and I would make a perfect team. Will you not be my partner at the I.X.L. Ranch?"

The horse neighed sadly. "It must be," he sighed. "I must give up my freedom. But since I must, I am glad that you are the man who has conquered me. Only Pecos Bill is worthy to fix a saddle upon the son of the great White Stallion, the Ghost King of the Prairie."

"I am deeply honored," said Pecos Bill, touched in his heart by the compliment.

"It is rather myself who am honored," replied the mustang, taking a brighter view of the situation.

The two of them went on for several hours saying nice things to each other. Before they were through, the pony was begging Pecos to be his master. Pecos was weeping and saying he was not fit to ride so magnificent a beast. In the end, however, Pecos Bill made two solemn promises. He would never place a bit in the pony's mouth. No other human would ever sit in his saddle.

When Bill rode back to I.X.L. with his new mount, the second promise was broken. Old Satan, the former bad man, had not completely recovered from his badness. He was jealous of Bill. When he saw the beautiful white stallion he turned green and almost burst wtih jealousy. One night he stole out to the corral. Quietly he slipped up beside the horse and jumped into the saddle.

Pegasus, as the horse was called, knew right away that his rider was not Pecos Bill. He lifted his four feet off the ground and bent his back into a perfect semicircle. Old Satan flew off like an arrow from a bow. He flew up into the air, above the moon, and came down with a thud on top of Pike's Peak. There he sat howling with pain and fright until the boys at I.X.L. spotted him.

Bill was angry. He knew, however, that Old Satan had had enough punishment. In his kind heart he could not allow the villain to suffer any more than he had to. So he twirled his lasso around his head, let it fly, and roped Old Satan back to the Texas ranch. The former desperado never tried to be bad again.

The cowhands were so impressed by the pony's bucking they decided to change his name. From that time on they dropped the name of Pegasus and called him Widow-Maker. It suited him better.

The story of Bill's other love, Slue-Foot Sue, is a long one. It began with the tale of the Perpetual Motion Ranch. Bill had bought a mountain from Paul Bunyan. It looked to him like a perfect mountain for a ranch. It was shaped like a cone, with smooth sides covered with grassy meadows. At the top it was always winter. At the bottom it was always summer. In between it was always spring and fall. The sun always shone on one side; the other was always in shade. The cattle could have any climate they wished.

Bill had to breed a special kind of steer for his ranch. These had two short legs on one side and two long legs on the other. By traveling in one direction around the mountain, they were able to stand up straight on the steep sides.

The novelty wore off, however, and at last Bill sold the Perpetual Motion Ranch to an English duke. The day that the I.X.L. boys moved out, the lord moved in. He brought with him trainload after trainload of fancy English things. He had featherbeds and fine china and oil paintings and real silver and linen tablecloths and silk rugs. The cowboys laughed themselves almost sick when they saw these dude things being brought to a cattle ranch.

Pecos Bill didn't laugh. He didn't even notice the fancy things. All he could see was the English duke's beautiful daughter. She was as pretty as the sun and moon combined. Her hair was silky and red. Her eyes were blue. She wore a sweeping taffeta dress and a little poke bonnet with feathers on it. She was the loveliest creature Pecos Bill had ever seen.

She was as lively and gay as she was pretty. Bill soon discovered that Slue-Foot Sue was a girl of talent. Before anyone could say "Jack Robinson," she changed into a cowboy suit and danced a jig to the tune of *Get Along, Little Dogies*.

Bill soon lost all his interest in cowpunching. He spent his

124

afternoons at the Perpetual Motion Ranch, teaching Sue to ride a broncho. Sue could ride as well as anyone, but she pretended to let him teach her. After several months of Bill's lessons, she put on a show. She jumped onto the back of a huge catfish in the Rio Grande River and rode all the way to the Gulf of Mexico, bareback. Bill was proud of her. He thought she had learned her tricks all from him.

Sue's mother was terribly upset by her daughter's behavior. She didn't care much for Bill. She was very proper. It was her fondest hope that Sue would stop being a tomboy and marry an earl or a member of Parliament.

As soon as she realized that her daughter was falling in love with a cowboy, she was nearly heartbroken. There was nothing she could do about it, however. Slue-Foot Sue was a headstrong girl who always had her own way.

At last the duchess relented. She invited Bill to tea and began to lecture him on English manners. She taught him how to balance a teacup, how to bow from the waist, and how to eat scones and marmalade instead of beans and bacon. He learned quickly, and soon the duchess was pleased with him. She called him "Colonel."

When the boys from the I.X.L. Ranch saw what was going on they were disgusted. Here was their boss, their brave, big, cyclone-riding Pecos Bill, mooning around in love like a sick puppy. They laughed at his dude manners. They made fun of his dainty appetite. When he dressed up in his finery to call on his girl, they stood in the bunkhouse door. They simpered and raised their eyebrows and said to one another, "La-dee-da, dearie, ain't we fine today!"

But for all their kidding they were broken-hearted. None of them had anything against Sue. They admired the way she rode a horse and played a guitar and danced a jig. But the thought of losing Bill to a woman was too much. Even worse was the thought that Bill might get married and bring a woman home to live with them. That was awful.

In spite of their teasing and the duchess's lessons, Bill asked Slue-Foot Sue to marry him. She accepted before he could back out. Her father, the lord, had always liked Bill and was terribly pleased at the match.

On his wedding day Pecos Bill shone like the sun in his new clothes. His boys were dressed in their finest chaps and boots for the occasion. Half of them were going to be groomsmen. The other half were going to be bridesmen. At first Bill asked them to be bridesmaids, but they refused. They said that was going too far.

They rode to the Perpetual Motion Ranch in a fine procession, Bill at the head on Widow-Maker. The white horse pranced and danced with excitement.

At the ranchhouse waited the rest of the wedding party. The lord had sent back to England for a bishop to perform the ceremony. There stood His Eminence in his lace robes. On his one hand stood the duke in a cutaway coat. On his other hand stood the duchess in a stiff purple gown right from Paris.

Down the stairs came the bride. She was a vision of beauty. She wore a white satin dress cut in the latest fashion. It had a long lace train, but its chief glory was a bustle. A bustle was a wire contraption that fitted under the back of the dress. It made the skirt stand out and was considered very handsome in those days.

As Slue-Foot Sue danced down the steps even the cowhands forgot their sorrow. They jumped down from their horses and swept their sombreros from their heads. Pecos Bill lost his head. He leapt down from Widow-Maker and ran to meet her. "You are lovely," he murmured. "I promise to grant you every wish you make."

That was a mistake. A devilish gleam twinkled in Sue's eye. For months she had been begging Bill to let her ride Widow-Maker. Bill, of course, had always refused.

Now Sue saw her chance. Before she allowed the wedding to proceed, she demanded that Bill give her one ride on his white mustang.

"No, no!" cried Pecos Bill. Before he could stop her Sue dashed down the drive and placed her dainty foot into the stirrup. The duchess screamed. The bishop turned pale.

Widow-Maker gave an angry snort. This was the second time the promise to him had been broken. He lifted his four feet off the ground and arched his back. Up, up, up shot Slue-Foot Sue. She disappeared into the clouds.

"Catch her, catch her!" roared Bill at the boys. They spread themselves out into a wide circle. Then from the sky came a

127

scream like a siren. Down, down, down fell Sue. She hit the earth with terrible force. She landed on her bustle. The wire acted as a spring. It bounced. Up again she flew.

Up and down, up and down between the earth and sky Sue bounced like a rubber ball. Every time she fell, her bustle hit first. Back she bounced. This went on for a week. When at last she came back to earth to stay, she was completely changed. She no longer loved Pecos Bill.

The wedding was called off, and the boys returned to the I.X.L. with their unhappy boss. For months he refused to eat. He lost interest in cowpunching. He was the unhappiest man Texas had ever seen.

At last he called his hands together and made a long speech. He told them that the days of real cowpunching were over. The prairie was being fenced off by farmers. These "nesters," as he called them, were ruining the land for the ranchers. He was going to sell his herd.

The I.X.L. had its last roundup. Bill gathered all the prime steers together and put them on the train for Kansas City. Then he divided the cows and calves among his boys. He himself mounted Widow-Maker and rode away.

The boys hated to see him go, but they knew how he felt. "Nesters" or no "nesters," the real reason for his going was his broken heart.

None of them ever saw him again. Some of them thought he had gone back to the coyotes. Others had an idea that Slue-Foot Sue had changed her mind and that she and Bill were setting up housekeeping in some private canyon. But they never knew.

Some years later an old cowhand claimed that Bill had died. The great cowpuncher had met a dude rancher at a rodeo. The dude was dressed up in an outfit he had bought from a movie cowboy. The dude's chaps were made of doeskin. His boots were painted with landscapes and had heels three inches high. The brim of his hat was broad enough to cover a small circus. Bill took a good look at him and died laughing.

128

Charles J. Finger

THE TALE
OF THE LAZY PEOPLE

ILLUSTRATED BY *John Merryweather*

IN COLOMBIA, it seems, there were always monkeys, or if not always, at least as far as the memory of man goes. An old historian named Oviedo noted that and wrote: "When the Christians make an expedition to the interior and have to pass by woods, they ought to cover themselves well with their bucklers . . . for the monkeys throw down nuts and branches at them. . . . I knew one, a servant. This man threw a stone at a monkey, who caught it and returned it with such force that it knocked out four or five of Francisco's teeth, and I know this to be true for I often saw the said Francisco, always without his teeth."

Now one day a man told me the tale of the monkeys, and he talked and talked as he smoked, until the stars came out and shone clear and steady and the air was heavy with perfume, and owls and bats floated strangely, as they will do, and when he had finished he still talked, taking up forgotten ends of his tale and winding in and about, making a long affair of a short matter. But then he had nothing else to do but to talk and was mighty pleased, it seemed, to have someone to listen to him. Then, when we should have been sleeping, he went on talking, picking out a piece of the tale here and another piece there, and explaining until I was well nigh like to get the story tangled myself. But here is the meat of it:

Long, long ago there were no monkeys, and the trees were so full of fruit, and the vines of grapes, that the people became lazy, and at last did little but eat and sleep, being too idle to

129

carry away the rinds and skins of the fruit that they lived on, and certainly too lazy to clean their thatched houses.

It was very pleasant at first, but soon not so pleasant, for winged things that bit and stung came in thousands to feed on the things thrown aside, and they, too, grew lazy, finding so much to eat ready at hand, and when people tried to brush them away there was a loud and angry buzz and much irritated stinging, so that soon everyone was wonder-struck, not knowing exactly what to do. For a time it seemed easier to move the little village to a new spot and to build new houses, for the dwellings were light affairs and in a day or less a good house could be built. But then they lived by a lake from which the water for drinking was taken, and as it was but a little body of water, it was not long before the people had built right round the still pool and so were back again at the starting place. As for the stinging flies, they were soon worse than the mosquitoes, while a great wasp with pink head and legs and bands of black and gold on its body, though very pretty to see, was worst of all. So it was no easy matter to know what to do, and there was much talk and much argument, and all that the people agreed on was that something had to be done, and that, very soon.

One day there came to the village a queer and rather faded kind of man, ragged and tattered and torn as though he had scrambled for miles through the thorn-bush forest. He had rough yellow hair and queer wrinkles at the corners of his eyes which made him look as if he were smiling. It was late in the afternoon when he came, and the people were taking their rest after the noon meal, so no one took much notice of him although he went here and there, looking at things, and so walked round the lake. But the curiosity of everyone was excited when he was seen to make a basket, which he did quickly, and then commence to gather up the fruit skins and rinds in one place. Now and then some one or other raised himself in his hammock, with a mind to talk to him, but it seemed almost too much trouble, and when some great blue-winged butterfly fluttered past or some golden-throated hummingbird flashed in the sunlight, their eyes wandered away from the old man, and they forgot him again. So the sunlight died and the forest was a velvet blackness and everyone slept, though the old man still worked on, and the next morning when the people awoke he was still working diligently, though he had but a small place cleared after all.

The very thought that anyone would work all night made the headman shiver with a kind of excitement, yet he was very curious to know why the stranger went to so much trouble, seeing that he neither lived there nor was of the lake men. At the same time it made his spirit droop to think that if the place was to be cleared up, he and everyone else had a mountain of work in sight. So Tera, the head man, called to Cuco, who was his servant, telling him to bring the stranger to him, and Cuco, who was very respectful, said that he would attend to it. Then Cuco did his part by calling Yana and delivering the message to him. And Yana in turn told his servant, Mata, who told his servant, Pera, who told his servant, Racas, who told a boy, so that at last the message reached the old man. Then back went the old man, handed by the boy to Racas, by Racas to Pera, by Pera to Mata, by Mata to Yana, and by Yana to Cuco, so that at last he stood before Tera, the headman, and the others, being curious to know what was afoot, gathered about.

"What is your name, from where do you come, and what do you want?" asked Tera, putting his three questions at once, to save trouble. Then the headman looked at those about him with a little frown, as much as to say, "Note how wisely I act," and each man who had heard, seeing that the headman looked his way, nodded at his neighbor, as though calling attention to the wisdom of the headman, so all went very well. But the little old man stood there very simply, making no fuss at all and quite unimpressed with the greatness of the great man.

"I want to work," he answered. "I want to be told what you want done and to see that it is done."

To be sure, the language that he spoke was one new to those who listened, but somehow they seemed to understand. But the thing that he said they found truly astonishing and could hardly believe their ears. But the headman, though as aston-

131

ished as anyone there, quickly regained his composure and asked this question:

"What is your trade?"

"I have no trade," said the old man. "But I get things done."

"What kind of things?"

"All kinds of things."

"Do you mean big things, like house-building and all that?" asked the headman.

"Yes. And little things too, which are really big things when you come to consider," said the old man, but that seemed an odd if not a silly thing to say, the headman thought.

"Little things left undone soon become big things," explained the old man, and waved his hand in the direction of a heap of fruit skins and husks near by.

"Yes. Yes. But you must not preach to us, you know," said Tera a little testily. "Tell me the names of the trades you have."

So the little old man began to tell, naming big things and very little things, things important and things not important at all, and having finished, asked very politely whether anyone there had anything to be done. As for pay, he said that he wanted none at all and would take none, and he said that because some of those gathered about him began offering him things.

For instance, Pera said: "If you work for me, I will let you have one fish out of every ten that you catch, for I am a fisherman." And Racas pushed him aside, saying: "But I will do better, for I am supposed to be fruit gatherer and will give you two things for every ten you gather." And so it went, each bidding higher than his neighbor, until it came to the turn of the man whose duty it was to gather the rinds and fruit skins. He said, "I will let you have, not one out of ten, nor two out of ten, nor five out of ten that you gather, but ten out of ten, if you will work for me." At that the old man said quite positively that he would take no pay at all.

No more was said then, and the little old man turned away without as much as bowing to the headman, seeing which, the headman waved his hand and said: "You may go, and so that you will lose no time, you need not bow to me." And all the rest gathered there said very hastily: "Nor need you bow to me, either."

The old man took small notice of anyone, but went away singing, for he had a gay, light-hearted disposition, and having reached the place he had cleared, he took flat pieces of wood and began cutting out figures like little men, and each figure had a kind of handle that looked like a long tail. Nor did he cease whittling until he had made at least twenty wooden figures for each man in the village. Being finished he stood up to stretch his legs and straighten his back, and when the people asked him what the little figures were for, he shrugged his shoulders but spoke never a word. Then he lifted the figures that he had made, one by one, and set them upright in the sand until there was a long row of them, and took his place in front of them, like a general before his army. It was beautiful to look at, for one figure was as like another as one pin is like another, and for a moment even the old man stood admiring the line. After a moment he waved his hand in a peculiar way,

133

spoke some magic word, and waved his hand again, at which each of the figures came to life and nodded its head, seeing which all the people laughed and clapped their hands. The ragged man bade them make no noise, but watch.

"Since you do not like to work," he said, "I have made twenty figures for each of you, and they will work for you without pay, doing what you require them to do; only observe this, you must not give any figure more than one particular job. And now let each man or woman clap his hands three times, then call out the name of the thing to be done."

When he had said this, the figures started running, twenty gathering in a circle about each man there, bowing from the hips and straightening themselves again, so that their tails of wood went up and down like pump-handles.

"Now see," said the ragged man, "you have things to work for you, and as I call out, the figures will stand forth, each ready to do his task." And he began calling, thus:

"Armadillo hunters, stand forth!" and a hundred and more active figures ran together like soldiers.

So he named others in order, as:

Bread makers.

Cassava gatherers.

Despolvadores, who would gather up dust.

Esquiladors, who would shear the goats.

Farsante men, whose work was to amuse tired men.

Guardas, to keep order about the place.

Horneros, or bakers.

Industriosos, who were to do odd jobs everywhere.

Jumentos, whose work it was to carry burdens.

Labradores, to do heavy work and clear away garbage.

Moledores, to grind the corn.

Narradores, who told stories, related gossip and so on.

Olleros, or pot makers.

Pocilga figures, to attend to the pigs.

Queseros, to make cheese from goat's milk.

Rumbosos, or proud-looking things to walk in parades.

Servidores, or food carriers.

Trotadores, to run errands.

Vaqueros, to attend to the cows.

So everyone was well pleased and each one had his twenty figures to do all that needed to be done, and all that day there was a great scraping and cleaning and carrying and currying and hurrying and scurrying. Silently the little figures worked, never stopping, never tiring, never getting in one another's way, and all that the living people had to do was to rest, and watch the men of wood, and keep their brains free for higher things. For it must be remembered that before the old man came there with his wonderful gift, the people had complained that there was so much to be done that they had no time to write poems or to make songs or to create music, and that with the daily tasks abolished their brains would be more active.

Not two days had passed before the children of the place complained that they did not have a chance and that they had so much to do, what with hunting for things lost, looking after their small brothers and sisters, keeping things in order, trying to remember things they were told, cleaning things, and a dozen other tasks, that they really had no time to play, much less to study. So they went in a body to the old man and asked him to give each child twenty figures to do odd things. There was a great deal of fire and expression in his eyes when he made answer that if the children really needed help he would lose no time in providing it. But the young people were quite positive that they were overworked, and the long and short of it was that the old man whittled out many, many more figures, and in twenty-four hours each and every boy and girl had his own

Abaniquero, or fan maker, so that none had to pluck a palm leaf.

Baliquero figure, to carry letters and messages.

Cabrero, to look after the goats.

Desalumbrado, to hunt for things in the dark.

Enseñador, or private teacher, who was never to scold.

Florista, to save them the trouble of gathering flowers.

Guasón figure, to amuse them.

Hojaldarista, whose work it was to make cakes.

136

Juego figure, to arrange games.
Keeper of things.
Lector, to read and tell stories.
Mimo, to act as clown.
Niñera, to look after younger children.
Obediencia figure, to make others obey.
Postor, to buy things for them.
Quitar figures, to take things away when children tired.
Recordación figures, or rememberers.
Solfeadors, to sing to them.
Tortada men, to make pies.
Volantes, as servants.

So things seemed to be going very well, and before a month had passed in all that place there was not a thing out of order, soiled, broken, bent, lost, misplaced, undone, unclean, or disorderly. Neither man nor woman nor child had to worry; dinners were always prepared, fruits gathered, beds made, houses in perfect order, and all was spick and span. All that the grown-up people had to do was to look on, and no one was proud of the order in his house because every other house in the place was as orderly. As for the children, they had nothing at all to do but to eat, drink, rest, and sleep. Then, presently, more figures were called for as this one or that wanted a larger house, a finer garden, or grander clothes.

137

But as the wooden figures became more numerous and as no figure could do more than one task, the ragged man had to make figures for the figures and servants for the servants, for as things went on, there had to be more fruit gatherers, more water carriers, more scavengers, more cooks, because the figures had to eat and drink. Thus it came to pass that before long, instead of their being twenty figures for each man, there were sixty or seventy, with new ones coming from the old man's knife every day. Soon the lively manikins were everywhere, inside houses as well as outside, thick as flies in summer and certainly a great deal more persistent, for there could be no closing of doors against the manikins. Indeed, had anything like that been attempted there would have been a great cry for special door-openers. So, many houses were quite cluttered with wooden men, those who were on duty rushing about until it made the head swim to look at them, and those who were resting or sleeping, for soon they learned to rest and to sleep, lying about the floors, piled up in corners, or hanging to rafters by their tails. All that increase in help had made for the production of a thousand or more guardas, whose task it was to keep order, and they were everywhere, alert and watchful and officious, and the real people had to step about very gingerly sometimes, to avoid treading on them and annoying them.

At last there came a day when the people began to grow a little tired of doing nothing, and they told one another that a little help was a very good thing, but help in excess, too much of a good thing altogether. So there was a meeting and much talk and the manikin narradors, whose duty it was to carry gossip and the news, were very busy, rushing from here to there with their scraps of information.

"It is very clear that something must be done," said Tera, the headman.

"But everything *is* being done," answered the little old man. "If *everything* is done, something *must* be done."

"I did not mean that," said Tera, who seemed a little testy. "I meant to say that these wooden men must be kept in their places."

"But they *are* in their places," replied the old man. "Their place is everywhere because they do everything, so they are in their places."

"You see, the days are so very long, so very dull," said the man who wished to have time that he might become a poet. "At the shut of day we are not weary."

"We do not want to be petted," said another.

"The trouble is," sighed a fat man, "you can't be happy when everything is done for you."

"And we don't want to be nobodies," shouted another.

Another said very mournfully: "It seems to me that when these wooden things do things with our things, then the things that they do and make and care for are not our things."

"Too many 'things' in that speech," said the fat man.

"Well, there are too many things," answered the other. "Look at me. I used to be gardener and now I'm nothing. When my garden is dug and planted and tended and watered and the very flowers plucked by these wooden things, and when other wooden things pick up the leaves and pull the weeds and do everything, then my garden does not seem to be mine." He added after awhile: "I hope you know what I mean, because it is not very clear to me, yet it is so. I remember—"

At that the little old man put up his hand and said: "But that is against the contract. You must not try to remember, really you must not, because there are manikins to do all the remembering, if you please."

"Well, but I think____" began the man, when he was again interrupted.

"Please do not think," said the little old man. "We have things to do the thinking, if you please." He thought for a moment, his bent forefinger on his lips, then he said: "I'll see what can be done. It is clear that you are not satisfied, although you have everything that you asked for and certainly all the time that you want."

"Let us do something," murmured Tera.

"I'm afraid there is nothing that you can do," said the little old man, "because, as you see, everything is done, and when

139

everything is done it is quite clear that something cannot be
left to be done. The only thing that is clear is that there is
nothing to be done."

At that the meeting broke up and each went to his own
hammock to think things over, and soon the general cry was:
"We must have elbow room." And hearing that, the little old
man went to work and whittled more figures of wood, a whole
army of them, ten for each living man, woman, and child, and in
voices that creaked like wooden machinery they marched hither
and thither, crying: "Elbow room. Elbow room!"

Soon there was confusion. It was manikin against manikin for
a time, the Elbow-room-ers thrusting and pushing the other
working manikins, some going about their work with frantic
haste, others interfering with them, clutching at them and at
the things they carried, a tangled knot of them sometimes
staggering, to go down with a crash. Soon in every house was
a jangling tumult, manikins and men running about in houses

and dashing out into the open spaces outside; the noise of slamming doors and breaking pots; the clamor of animals. Above all could be heard everywhere cries of "We want elbow room! We want elbow room!" Soon men were running away from the houses with those strange swift manikins hanging to them sometimes beating them, while other manikins threw things out of the doors and through windows, food and household things. And excited children fled too, while their manikins ran at their sides, some chattering, some acting the clown as was their duty, some telling stories as they ran, while other strange little figures of wood ran bearing heavy burdens. It was all a dreadful mix-up with no one knowing what to do, no one knowing where to go, and everywhere the manikins who were guardas, or order keepers, ran about, tripping people and manikins alike in the effort to stop the rush. But when the day was near its end there were no people in the houses and the hammocks swung idly, for all the men and women and children, even the white-haired grandfathers and grandmothers, had fled to the further side of the lake, where they could have elbow room, leaving the houses and all that was in them to the manikins.

The next day, the people plucked their fruit for themselves, and it seemed as though fruit was never sweeter. The water that they carried from the lake tasted better and cooler than water had for many a long day, and when night came they were happily tired and slept well, without any manikin to swing their hammocks and sing to them. And in the morning they woke early to discover the pink and gold of the sunrise most wonderful to see, and there was music in the sound of the wind among the grasses. So as the day passed they were both amazed and astonished at the wonderful and beautiful things that they had almost forgotten, the sight of butterflies fluttering from flower to flower, the shadows chasing across the hills, the richness of the green earth and the blueness of the sky, the gold of sunlight on the leaves, the rippling water and the bending trees; indeed the memory of the manikin days was like a fearful nightmare. Very light-hearted then they grew, and the world was

141

full of the music of their laughter and song, and briskly they worked, enjoying it all, building new houses and making things to put in them.

Meanwhile in the village things had gone queerly. For one thing the Elbow-room-ers kept up their crowding and pushing, so that the manikins trying to work at their old tasks (and there were many who went on just as before) were sadly hindered. There were other figures of wood with nothing to do, since the people they served were gone, and these fell to quarrelling among themselves and grew mischievous. For instance, the pot makers and the pot cleaners fell out, and the pot cleaners started to break the pots so that the pot makers would have more work to do. That meant that the clay gatherers and the clay diggers had to work harder, then because they worked harder, though to be sure all their work meant nothing and was little more than idle bustle, they grew hungrier and wanted more to eat. Because of all that, the fruit gatherers had more to do and the water carriers had to work harder and the cassava bread makers had to bake as they had never baked before. That brought the fire builders into it, and of course the wood gatherers also, for they too had to work harder and to eat more, so still more work came on the food bringers. And all the time the Elbow-room-ers rushed about, always in groups of ten, driving and commanding, rushing on workers and sweeping them aside. So everywhere were little figures hurrying one after the other, going to and fro, busy about nothing, quarrelling about nothing, fighting about nothing.

The trouble came when the Elbow-room-ers interfered with the dogs and the cats, the goats and the hens, pushing and hustling them. For the animals, disliking all the disorder and clatter, fell upon the manikins, workers and idlers alike. Seeing that, the household utensils took a hand, and the very pots and kettles ran or rolled or fell, spilling hot water over the wooden things with pump-handle tails. The very embers from the fires leaped into the fray. All the while from the metates in which the corn had been ground came a low growling, and the growling formed itself into words:

142

"Day by day you tortured us——
Grind, grind, grind.

"Holi! Holi!
Huqui! Huqui!
Grind, grind, grind.

"Bring to us the torturers——
Grind, grind, grind.

"Let them feel our power now——
Grind. *Grind.* GRIND!"

So the metates turned and turned, going round and round without hands, and presently an Elbow-room-er that was struggling with a corn-grinder stumbled, and both fell between the grinding stones and in a moment were crushed to powder. In a flash house utensils and animals learned the new trick, and in every house manikins were pushed into the grinding stones. Then sparks began to fly and roofs to catch on fire and manikins bolted here and there in confusion, sometimes jamming in doorways, there were so many and all in such disorder. Then came dazzling, flickering lightning and a great rain, so that for very safety the manikins fled to the forest and climbed the trees. And there they have lived ever since, for they grew hair and became monkeys. But the remembrance of all that passed stayed with them, and in their hearts to this very day is no love for man, and for that very reason when a Christian passes through a forest he must look well to himself, lest the manikins in revenge try to hurt him by casting nuts and branches at his head.

Padraic Colum

PHAETON

ILLUSTRATED BY *Donn P. Crane*

HIS fiery steeds and his gleaming chariot, Helios, because he had sworn an oath that might not be broken, gave to the young man Phaeton. The shining doors were rolled open and the steeds stood there, pawing the ground and sniffing the wind that blew towards them; yoked to the steeds was the gleaming chariot.

These were the horses and that was the chariot that, journeying through the heavens, brought light and warmth to men. None but Helios himself had ever driven them before. Now Helios stood there and the light was gone from his face. "O Phaeton, O my son," he cried, "thou art being given what thou hast claimed. But before thou dost take the reins, stay and consider. Thou art half mortal, and only immortals may drive these fiery steeds and this gleaming chariot through the course of the heavens."

But the young man Phaeton sprang into the chariot and took in his hands the reins that were across the necks of the

144

fiery steeds. "Long did I live on earth," he said, "without name and without honor; now I would have the world know that I am indeed the son of bright Helios. Thou didst swear to let me have a token that I, Phaeton, am indeed thy son, and this is the token that I claim—to be let drive thy steeds and thy chariot through the course of the heavens for a single day."

"Renounce thy desire before it is too late, and in my shining halls stay, known to mortals and immortals as my son, the son of Helios who brings light and warmth to the world."

But already the young man had shaken the reins; the fiery steeds sprang forward, and the shining doors of their stable rolled back. Something more his father said to him but Phaeton did not hear his words: the bright wheels spun round and the chariot of Helios took its course through the sky.

The brightness of their tossing manes made Phaeton exultant; the swiftness of the steeds, as they swept along the brightening path through the heavens, filled him with delight, and his heart was lifted with pride as he held the reins that guided the course of the horses. "I, I," he cried in his pride, "I, the nameless son of Klymene, my mother, have the horses of Helios under my hands; I drive my father's gleaming chariot through the heavens; I, Phaeton, will be remembered, and all men must speak of me, because for a single day, I am bringing them light and warmth."

He thought of the time he had bade farewell of Klymene, his mother; he thought of how he had come into the bright halls of Helios; he thought of how he had heard his father speak of him, praising his beauty, and of how pride had grown in him then and a resolve to have his father grant him a token that would make the world know that he, Phaeton, was indeed the son of Helios. His father had sworn that he would grant him any token that he might ask.

"And what other token might I ask than this token—to have their reins in my hands and these fiery steeds sweeping forward upon the brightening path? O brightness of fire! What was it that my father said about none but an immortal being able to drive the steeds of Helios? I drive them. I am half mortal, but

145

now that I have driven the fiery steeds and the gleaming chariot I feel that I am become immortal! Immortal, immortal, immortal!" he cried as he went through the brightening heavens, "Immortal Phaeton!"

But the immortal horses knew that hands that were not immortal held their reins. They knew that the weakness of one who dies was in the hold that was upon them. They swerved aside from their path in the heavens. They plunged and plunged, going further off their course. And upon earth men looked up and said, "A portent in the heavens! The steeds of Helios are rushing here and there!"

To Phaeton the horses were but tossing their manes; the bright wheels were but spinning as they should spin. He stood upright in his chariot, holding the reins, and he spoke.

"Are these the hands of one who is half-immortal? These hands that hold and guide the horses of Helios! But must men speak always of the horses of Helios? Would that there was a way of making men below wonder at their course today! Wonder and then know that not Helios but another, one younger and more daring than he, has hands upon the reins today!"

Plunging and plunging, the horses went farther and farther off their course. They went too far from their course in the blue heavens. Earth withered as they came too near. Fire sprang up, fire, and again, fire! The trees on the plains crackled, and dropped branches, and burned. On the mountains the forests took fire. Now there were mountains burning with fires that went up to the sky.

He knew now that the steeds had gone from their course. He tried to guide them back. The fiery steeds turned savage eyes and bared teeth upon him. They tossed their heads; the wheels spun faster and faster, and the chariot rocked as they rushed and plunged along.

Fires went up in the cities of men; in the rivers and lakes the waters dried up; men lay dying upon the earth. The young man Phaeton, knowing his hands too weak to guide them, shouted to the fiery steeds.

146

Zeus, the ever-watchful, saw Phaeton's course through the heavens, saw the plunging steeds and the fires going up on the earth, and he knew that all life might be destroyed by the horses and chariot coming nearer and nearer to the earth. He gathered the clouds together, making a veil between the chariot and the world of men. And then he flung his lightning on young Phaeton. The lightning of Zeus tore him from the chariot and the horses, now that they no longer felt his hands upon the reins, staggered back to their course. Feebly now they went on. Feebly they finished their journey, but they won back to the shining stables that had been built for them by Hephaestos beside the gleaming halls of Helios, and there the dark-robed Hours tended them.

Down, down, into the seething sea young Phaeton fell. But he was not lost in the sea. The daughters of Hesperus found him and lifted his body out of the depths of the sea. They made a tomb for him on the seashore, and they wrote above his tomb, "Young Phaeton fell from his father's chariot, but even so he lost nothing of his glory, for his heart was set upon the doing of great things."

147

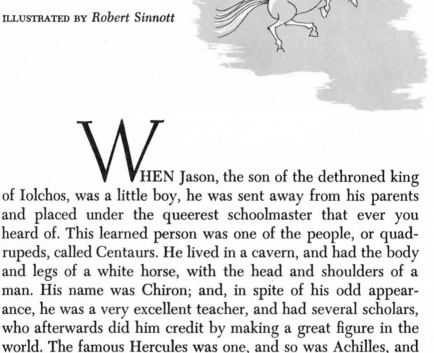

Nathaniel Hawthorne

THE GOLDEN FLEECE

ILLUSTRATED BY *Robert Sinnott*

WHEN Jason, the son of the dethroned king of Iolchos, was a little boy, he was sent away from his parents and placed under the queerest schoolmaster that ever you heard of. This learned person was one of the people, or quadrupeds, called Centaurs. He lived in a cavern, and had the body and legs of a white horse, with the head and shoulders of a man. His name was Chiron; and, in spite of his odd appearance, he was a very excellent teacher, and had several scholars, who afterwards did him credit by making a great figure in the world. The famous Hercules was one, and so was Achilles, and Philoctetes, likewise, and Aesculapius, who acquired immense repute as a doctor. The good Chiron taught his pupils how to play upon the harp, and how to cure diseases, and how to use the sword and shield, together with various other branches of education, in which the lads of those days used to be instructed, instead of writing and arithmetic.

I have sometimes suspected that Master Chiron was not really very different from other people, but that, being a kindhearted and merry old fellow, he was in the habit of making believe that he was a horse, and scrambling about the school-room on all fours, and letting the little boys ride upon his back. And so, when his scholars had grown up, and grown old, and were trotting their grandchildren on their knees, they told them about the sports of their schooldays; and these young folks took the idea that their grandfathers had been taught their letters by a Centaur, half man and half horse. Little children, not quite understanding what is said to them, often get such absurd notions into their heads, you know.

Be that as it may, it has always been told for a fact (and always will be told, as long as the world lasts) that Chiron, with the head of a schoolmaster, had the body and legs of a horse. Just imagine the grave old gentleman clattering and stamping into the schoolroom on his four hoofs, perhaps tread-ing on some little fellow's toes, flourishing his switch tail instead of a rod, and, now and then, trotting out-of-doors to eat a mouthful of grass! I wonder what the blacksmith charged him for a set of iron shoes.

So Jason dwelt in a cave, with this four-footed Chiron, from the time that he was an infant, only a few months old, until he had grown to the full height of a man. He became a very good harper, I suppose, and skillful in the use of weapons, and tolerably acquainted with herbs and other doctor's stuff, and, above all, an admirable horseman; for, in teaching young people to ride, the good Chiron must have been without a rival among schoolmasters.

At length, being now a tall and athletic youth, Jason resolved to seek his fortune in the world, without asking Chiron's advice, or telling him anything about the matter. This was very unwise, to be sure . . . But, you are to understand, he had heard how that he himself was a prince royal, and how his father, King Aeson, had been deprived of the kingdom of Iolchos by a certain Pelias, who would also have killed Jason, had he not been hidden in the Centaur's cave. And, being come to the strength of a man, Jason determined to set all this business to rights, and to punish the wicked Pelias for wronging his dear father, and to cast him down the throne, and seat himself there instead.

149

With this intention, he took a spear in each hand and threw a leopard's skin over his shoulders, to keep off the rain, and set forth on his travels, with his long yellow ringlets waving in the wind. The part of his dress on which he most prided himself was a pair of sandals that had been his father's. They were handsomely embroidered and were tied upon his feet with strings of gold. But his whole attire was such as people did not very often see; and as he passed along, the women and children ran to the doors and windows, wondering whither this beautiful youth was journeying, with his leopard's skin and his golden-tied sandals, and what heroic deeds he meant to perform, with a spear in his right hand and another in his left.

I know not how far Jason had traveled, when he came to a turbulent river, which rushed right across his pathway with specks of white foam among its black eddies, hurrying tumultuously onward, and roaring angrily as it went. Though not a very broad river in the dry seasons of the year, it was now swollen by heavy rains and by the melting of the snow on the sides of Mount Olympus; and it thundered so loudly, and looked so wild and dangerous, that Jason, bold as he was, thought it prudent to pause upon the brink. The bed of the stream seemed to be strewn with sharp and rugged rocks, some of which thrust themselves above the water. By and by, an uprooted tree, with shattered branches, came drifting along the current and got entangled among the rocks. Now and then a drowned sheep, and once the carcass of a cow, floated past.

In short, the swollen river had already done a great deal of mischief. It was evidently too deep for Jason to wade and too boisterous for him to swim; he could see no bridge; and as for a boat, had there been any, the rocks would have broken it to pieces in an instant.

"See the poor lad," said a cracked voice close to his side. "He must have had but a poor education, since he does not know how to cross a little stream like this. Or is he afraid of wetting his fine golden-stringed sandals? It is a pity his four-footed schoolmaster is not here to carry him safely across on his back!"

Jason looked round greatly surprised, for he did not know

150

that anybody was near. But beside him stood an old woman, with a ragged mantle over her head, leaning on a staff, the top of which was carved into the shape of a cuckoo. She looked very aged, and wrinkled, and infirm; and yet her eyes, which were as brown as those of an ox, were so extremely large and beautiful that, when they were fixed on Jason's eyes, he could see nothing else but them. The old woman had a pomegranate in her hand, although the fruit was then quite out of season.

"Whither are you going, Jason?" she now asked.

She seemed to know his name, you will observe; and, indeed, those great brown eyes looked as if they had a knowledge of everything, whether past or to come. While Jason was gazing at her, a peacock strutted forward and took his stand at the old woman's side.

"I am going to Iolchos," answered the young man, "to bid the wicked king Pelias come down from my father's throne and let me reign in his stead."

"Ah, well, then," said the old woman, still with the same cracked voice, "if that is all your business, you need not be in a very great hurry. Just take me on your back, there's a good youth, and carry me across the river. I and my peacock have something to do on the other side, as well as yourself."

"Good mother," replied Jason, "your business can hardly be so important as the pulling down a king from his throne. Besides, as you may see for yourself, the river is very boisterous; and if I should chance to stumble, it would sweep both of us away more easily than it has carried off yonder uprooted tree. I would gladly help you if I could; but I doubt whether I am strong enough to carry you across."

"Then," said she, very scornfully, "neither are you strong enough to pull King Pelias off his throne. And, Jason, unless you will help an old woman at her need, you ought not to be a king. What are kings made for, save to succor the feeble and distressed? But do as you please. Either take me on your back, or with my poor old limbs I shall try my best to struggle across the stream."

Saying this, the old woman poked with her staff in the river,

as if to find the safest place in its rocky bed where she might make the first step. But Jason, by this time, had grown ashamed of his reluctance to help her. He felt that he could never forgive himself, if this poor feeble creature should come to any harm in attempting to wrestle against the headlong current. The good Chiron, whether half horse or no, had taught him that the noblest use of his strength was to assist the weak; and also that he must treat every young woman as if she were his sister and every old one like a mother. Remembering these maxims, the vigorous and beautiful young man knelt down and requested the good dame to mount upon his back.

"The passage seems to me not very safe," he remarked. "But as your business is so urgent, I will try to carry you across. If the river sweeps you away, it shall take me too."

"That, no doubt, will be a great comfort to both of us," quoth the old woman. "But never fear. We shall get safely across."

So she threw her arms around Jason's neck; and lifting her from the ground, he stepped boldly into the raging and foamy current and began to stagger away from the shore. As for the peacock, it alighted on the old dame's shoulder. Jason's two spears, one in each hand, kept him from stumbling and enabled him to feel his way among the hidden rocks; although, every instant, he expected that his companion and himself would go down the stream, together with the driftwood of shattered trees, and the carcasses of the sheep and cow. Down came the cold, snowy torrent from the steep side of Olympus, raging and thundering as if it had a real spite against Jason, or, at all events, were determined to snatch off his living burden from his shoulders. When he was halfway across, the uprooted tree (which I have already told you about) broke loose from among the rocks and bore down upon him, with all its splintered branches sticking out like the hundred arms of the giant Briareus. It rushed past, however, without touching him. But the next moment, his foot was caught in a crevice between two rocks, and stuck there so fast that, in the effort to get free, he lost one of his golden-stringed sandals.

At this accident Jason could not help uttering a cry of vexation.

"What is the matter, Jason?" asked the old woman.

"Matter enough," said the young man. "I have lost a sandal here among the rocks. And what sort of a figure shall I cut at the court of King Pelias, with a golden-stringed sandal on one foot and the other foot bare!"

"Do not take it to heart," answered his companion, cheerily. "You never met with better fortune than in losing that sandal. It satisfies me that you are the very person whom the Speaking Oak has been talking about."

There was no time, just then, to inquire what the Speaking Oak had said. But the briskness of her tone encouraged the young man; and besides, he had never in his life felt so vigorous and mighty as since taking this old woman on his back. Instead of being exhausted, he gathered strength as he went on; and, struggling up against the torrent, he at last gained the opposite shore, clambered up the bank, and set down the old dame and her peacock safely on the grass. As soon as this was done, however, he could not help looking rather despondently at his bare foot, with only a remnant of the golden string of the sandal clinging round his ankle.

"You will get a handsomer pair of sandals by and by," said the old woman, with a kindly look out of her beautiful brown eyes. "Only let King Pelias get a glimpse of that bare foot, and you shall see him turn as pale as ashes, I promise you. There is your path. Go along, my good Jason, and my blessing go with you. And when you sit on your throne, remember the old woman whom you helped over the river."

With these words, she hobbled away, giving him a smile over her shoulder as she departed. Whether the light of her beautiful brown eyes threw a glory round about her, or whatever the cause might be, Jason fancied that there was something very noble and majestic in her figure, after all, and that, though her gait seemed to be a rheumatic hobble, yet she moved with as much grace and dignity as any queen on earth. Her peacock, which had now fluttered down from her shoulder, strutted behind her in prodigious pomp, and spread out its magnificent tail on purpose for Jason to admire it.

When the old dame and her peacock were out of sight, Jason set forward on his journey. After traveling a pretty long distance, he came to a town situated at the foot of a mountain, and not a great way from the shore of the sea. On the outside of the town there was an immense crowd of people, not only men and women, but children, too, all in their best clothes, and evidently enjoying a holiday. The crowd was thickest towards the seashore; and in that direction, over the people's heads, Jason saw a wreath of smoke curling upward to the blue sky. He inquired of one of the multitude what town it was, near by, and why so many persons were here assembled together.

"This is the kingdom of Iolchos," answered the man, "and we are the subjects of King Pelias. Our monarch has summoned us together, that we may see him sacrifice a black bull to Neptune, who, they say, is his Majesty's father. Yonder is the king,

154

where you see the smoke going up from the altar."

While the man spoke he eyed Jason with great curiosity; for his garb was quite unlike that of the Iolchians, and it looked very odd to see a youth with a leopard's skin over his shoulders, and each hand grasping a spear. Jason perceived, too, that the man stared particularly at his feet, one of which, you remember, was bare, while the other was decorated with his father's golden-stringed sandal.

"Look at him! only look at him!" said the man to his next neighbor. "Do you see? He wears but one sandal!"

Upon this, first one person, and then another, began to stare at Jason, and everybody seemed to be greatly struck with something in his aspect; though they turned their eyes much oftener towards his feet than to any other part of his figure. Besides, he could hear them whispering to one another.

"One sandal! One sandal!" they kept saying. "The man with one sandal! Here he is at last! Whence has he come? What does he mean to do? What will the king say to the one-sandaled man?"

Poor Jason was greatly abashed and made up his mind that the people of Iolchos were exceedingly ill bred, to take such public notice of an accidental deficiency in his dress. Meanwhile, whether it were that they hustled him forward, or that Jason, of his own accord, thrust a passage through the crowd, it so happened that he soon found himself close to the smoking altar, where King Pelias was sacrificing the black bull. The murmur and hum of the multitude, in their surprise at the spectacle of Jason with his one bare foot, grew so loud that it disturbed the ceremonies; and the king, holding the great knife with which he was just going to cut the bull's throat, turned angrily about, and fixed his eyes on Jason. The people had now withdrawn from around him, so that the youth stood in an open space near the smoking altar, front to front with the angry King Pelias.

"Who are you?" cried the king, with a terrible frown. "And how dare you make this disturbance, while I am sacrificing a black bull to my father Neptune?"

155

"It is no fault of mine," answered Jason. "Your Majesty must blame the rudeness of your subjects, who have raised all this tumult because one of my feet happens to be bare."

When Jason said this, the king gave a quick, startled glance down at his feet.

"Ha!" muttered he, "here is the one-sandaled fellow, sure enough! What can I do with him?"

And he clutched more closely the great knife in his hand, as if he were half a mind to slay Jason instead of the black bull. The people round about caught up the king's words indistinctly as they were uttered; and first there was a murmur among them, and then a loud shout.

"The one-sandaled man has come! The prophecy must be fulfilled!"

For you are to know that, many years before, King Pelias had been told by the Speaking Oak of Dodona, that a man with one sandal should cast him down from his throne. On this account, he had given strict orders that nobody should ever come into his presence, unless both sandals were securely tied upon his feet; and he kept an officer in his palace, whose sole business it was to examine people's sandals and to supply them with a new pair, at the expense of the royal treasury, as soon as the old ones began to wear out. In the whole course of the king's reign, he had never been thrown into such a fright and agitation as by the spectacle of poor Jason's bare foot. But, as he was naturally a bold and hard-hearted man, he soon took courage and began to consider in what way he might rid himself of this terrible one-sandaled stranger.

"My good young man," said King Pelias, taking the softest tone imaginable, in order to throw Jason off his guard, "you are excessively welcome to my kingdom. Judging by your dress, you must have traveled a long distance; for it is not the fashion to wear leopard-skins in this part of the world. Pray what may I call your name? and where did you receive your education?"

"My name is Jason," answered the young stranger. "Ever since my infancy, I have dwelt in the cave of Chiron the Centaur. He was my instructor and taught me music, and horse-

157

manship, and how to cure wounds, and likewise how to inflict wounds with my weapons!"

"I have heard of Chiron the schoolmaster," replied King Pelias, "and how that there is an immense deal of learning and wisdom in his head, although it happens to be set on a horse's body. It gives me great delight to see one of his scholars at my court. But, to test how much you have profited under so excellent a teacher, will you allow me to ask you a single question?"

"I do not pretend to be very wise," said Jason. "But ask me what you please, and I will answer to the best of my ability."

Now King Pelias meant cunningly to entrap the young man and to make him say something that should be the cause of mischief and destruction to himself. So with a crafty and evil smile upon his face, he spoke as follows.

"What would you do, brave Jason," asked he, "if there were a man in the world by whom, as you had reason to believe, you were doomed to be ruined and slain,—what would you do, I say, if that man stood before you, and in your power?"

When Jason saw the malice and wickedness which King Pelias could not prevent from gleaming out of his eyes, he probably guessed that the king had discovered what he came for and that he intended to turn his own words against himself. Still he scorned to tell a falsehood. Like an upright and honorable prince, as he was, he determined to speak out the real truth. Since the king had chosen to ask him the question, and since Jason had promised him an answer, there was no right way, save to tell him precisely what would be the most prudent thing to do, if he had his worst enemy in his power.

Therefore, after a moment's consideration, he spoke up, with a firm and manly voice.

"I would send such a man," said he, "in quest of the Golden Fleece!"

This enterprise, you will understand, was, of all others, the most difficult and dangerous in the world. In the first place, it would be necessary to make a long voyage through unknown seas. There was hardly a hope, or a possibility, that any young man who should undertake this voyage would either succeed in obtaining the Golden Fleece, or would survive to return home and tell of the perils he had run. The eyes of King Pelias sparkled with joy, therefore, when he heard Jason's reply.

"Well said, wise man with the one sandal!" cried he. "Go, then, and, at the peril of your life, bring me back the Golden Fleece."

"I go," answered Jason, composedly. "If I fail, you need not fear that I will ever come back to trouble you again. But if I return to Iolchos with the prize, then, King Pelias, you must hasten down from your lofty throne, and give me your crown and scepter."

"That I will," said the king, with a sneer. "Meantime, I will keep them very safely for you."

The first thing that Jason thought of doing, after he left the king's presence, was to go to Dodona and inquire of the Talking Oak what course it was best to pursue. This wonderful tree stood in the center of an ancient wood. Its stately trunk rose up a hundred feet into the air and threw a broad and dense shadow over more than an acre of ground. Standing beneath it, Jason looked up among the knotted branches and green leaves and into the mysterious heart of the old tree, and spoke aloud, as if he were addressing some person who was hidden in the depths of the foliage.

"What shall I do," said he, "in order to win the Golden Fleece?"

At first there was a deep silence, not only within the shadow of the Talking Oak, but all through the solitary wood. In a moment or two, however, the leaves of the oak began to stir and rustle, as if a gentle breeze were wandering amongst them, although the other trees of the wood were perfectly still. The sound grew louder and became like the roar of a high wind. By and by, Jason imagined that he could distinguish words, but very confusedly, because each separate leaf of the tree seemed to be a tongue, and the whole myriad of tongues were babbling at once. But the noise waxed broader and deeper, until it resembled a tornado sweeping through the oak and making one

159

great utterance out of the thousand and thousand of little murmurs which each leafy tongue had caused by its rustling. And now, though it still had the tone of mighty wind roaring among the branches, it was also like a deep bass voice, speaking, as distinctly as a tree could be expected to speak, the following words:

"Go to Argus, the shipbuilder, and bid him build a galley with fifty oars."

Then the voice melted again into the indistinct murmur of the rustling leaves and died gradually away. When it was quite gone, Jason felt inclined to doubt whether he had actually heard the words, or whether his fancy had not shaped them out of the ordinary sound made by a breeze, while passing through the thick foliage of the tree.

But on inquiry among the people of Iolchos, he found that there was really a man in the city, by the name of Argus, who was a very skillful builder of vessels. This showed some intelligence in the oak; else how should it have known that any such person existed? At Jason's request, Argus readily consented to build him a galley so big that it should require fifty strong men to row it; although no vessel of such a size and burden had heretofore been seen in the world. So the head carpenter, and all his journeymen and apprentices, began their work; and for a good while afterwards, there they were, busily employed, hewing out the timbers and making a great clatter with their hammers; until the new ship, which was called the Argo, seemed to be quite ready for sea. And, as the Talking Oak had already given him such good advice, Jason thought that it would not be amiss to ask for a little more. He visited it again, therefore, and standing beside its huge, rough trunk, inquired what he should do next.

This time, there was no such universal quivering of the leaves, throughout the whole tree, as there had been before. But after a while, Jason observed that the foliage of a great branch which stretched above his head had begun to rustle, as if the wind were stirring that one bough, while all the other boughs of the oak were at rest.

160

"Cut me off!" said the branch, as soon as it could speak distinctly, "cut me off! cut me off! and carve me into a figurehead for your galley."

Accordingly, Jason took the branch at its word and lopped it off the tree. A carver in the neighborhood engaged to make the figurehead. He was a tolerably good workman, and had already carved several figureheads, in what he intended for feminine shapes, and looking pretty much like those which we see nowadays stuck up under a vessel's bowsprit, with great staring eyes, that never wink at the dash of the spray. But (what was very strange) the carver found that his hand was guided by some unseen power, and by a skill beyond his own, and that his tools shaped out an image which he had never dreamed of.

When the work was finished, it turned out to be the figure of a beautiful woman with a helmet on her head, from beneath which the long ringlets fell down upon her shoulders. On the left arm was a shield, and in its center appeared a lifelike representation of the head of Medusa with the snaky locks. The right arm was extended, as if pointing onward. The face of this wonderful statue, though not angry or forbidding, was so grave and majestic, that perhaps you might call it severe; and as for the mouth, it seemed just ready to unclose its lips and utter words of the deepest wisdom.

Jason was delighted with the oaken image and gave the carver no rest until it was completed and set up where a figure-head has always stood, from that time to this, in the vessel's prow.

"And now," cried he, as he stood gazing at the calm, majestic face of the statue, "I must go to the Talking Oak and inquire what next to do."

"There is no need of that, Jason," said a voice which, though it was far lower, reminded him of the mighty tones of the great oak. "When you desire good advice, you can seek it of me."

Jason had been looking straight into the face of the image when these words were spoken. But he could hardly believe either his ears or his eyes. The truth was, however, that the oaken lips had moved, and, to all appearance, the voice had proceeded from the statue's mouth. Recovering a little from his surprise, Jason bethought himself that the image had been carved out of the wood of the Talking Oak, and that, therefore, it was really no great wonder, but on the contrary, the most natural thing in the world, that it should possess the faculty of speech. It would have been very odd, indeed, if it had not. But certainly it was a great piece of good fortune that he should be able to carry so wise a block of wood along with him in his perilous voyage.

"Tell me, wondrous image," exclaimed Jason,—"since you inherit the wisdom of the Speaking Oak of Dodona, whose daughter you are,—tell me, where shall I find fifty bold youths, who will take each of them an oar of my galley? They must

162

have sturdy arms to row and brave hearts to encounter perils, or we shall never win the Golden Fleece."

"Go," replied the oaken image,—"go, summon all the heroes of Greece."

And, in fact, considering what a great deed was to be done, could any advice be wiser than this which Jason received from the figurehead of his vessel? He lost no time in sending messengers to all the cities and making known to the whole people of Greece that Prince Jason, the son of King Aeson, was going in quest of the Fleece of Gold, and that he desired the help of forty-nine of the bravest and strongest young men alive, to row his vessel and share his dangers. And Jason himself would be the fiftieth.

At this news, the adventurous youths, all over the country, began to bestir themselves. Some of them had already fought with giants and slain dragons; and the younger ones, who had not yet met with such good fortune, thought it a shame to have lived so long without getting astride of a flying serpent, or sticking their spears into a Chimera, or, at least, thrusting their right arms down a monstrous lion's throat. There was a fair prospect that they would meet with plenty of such adventures before finding the Golden Fleece. As soon as they could furbish up their helmets and shields, therefore, and gird on their trusty swords, they came thronging to Iolchos, and clambered on board the new galley. Shaking hands with Jason, they assured him that they did not care a pin for their lives, but would help row the vessel to the remotest edge of the world, and as much farther as he might think it best to go.

Many of these brave fellows had been educated by Chiron, the four-footed pedagogue, and were therefore old schoolmates of Jason, and knew him to be a lad of spirit. The mighty Hercules, whose shoulders afterwards held up the sky, was one of them. And there were Castor and Pollux, the twin brothers, who were never accused of being chicken-hearted, although they had been hatched out of an egg; and Theseus, who was so renowned for killing the Minotaur; and Lynceus, with his wonderfully sharp eyes, which could see through a millstone, or

163

look right down into the depths of the earth and discover the treasures that were there; and Orpheus, the very best of harpers, who sang and played upon his lyre so sweetly, that the brute beasts stood upon their hind legs and capered merrily to the music. Yes, and at some of his more moving tunes, the rocks bestirred their moss-grown bulk out of the ground, and a grove of forest trees uprooted themselves, and, nodding their tops to one another, performed a country dance.

One of the rowers was a beautiful young woman, named Atalanta, who had been nursed among the mountains by a bear. So light of foot was this fair damsel that she could step from one foamy crest of a wave to the foamy crest of another, without wetting more than the sole of her sandal. She had grown up in a very wild way, and talked much about the rights of women, and loved hunting and war far better than her needle. But, in my opinion, the most remarkable of this famous company were two sons of the North Wind (airy youngsters, and of rather a blustering disposition), who had wings on their shoulders, and, in case of a calm, could puff out their cheeks and blow almost as fresh a breeze as their father. I ought not to forget the prophets and conjurers, of whom there were several in the crew, and who could foretell what would happen to-morrow, or the next day, or a hundred years hence, but were generally quite unconscious of what was passing at the moment.

Jason appointed Tiphys to be helmsman, because he was a star-gazer, and knew the points of the compass. Lynceus, on account of his sharp sight, was stationed as a lookout in the prow, where he saw a whole day's sail ahead, but was rather apt to overlook things that lay directly under his nose. If the sea only happened to be deep enough, however, Lynceus could tell you exactly what kind of rocks or sands were at the bottom of it; and he often cried out to his companions that they were sailing over heaps of sunken treasure, which yet he was none the richer for beholding. To confess the truth, few people believed him when he said it.

Well! But when the Argonauts, as these fifty brave adven-

"Look yonder," she whispered. "Do you see it?"

turers were called, had prepared everything for the voyage, an unforeseen difficulty threatened to end it before it was begun. The vessel, you must understand, was so long, and broad, and ponderous, that the united force of all the fifty was insufficient to shove her into the water. Hercules, I suppose, had not grown to his full strength, else he might have set her afloat as easily as a little boy launches his boat upon a puddle. But here were these fifty heroes pushing, and straining, and growing red in the face, without making the Argo start an inch. At last, quite wearied out, they sat themselves down on the shore, exceedingly disconsolate, and thinking that the vessel must be left to rot and fall in pieces, and that they must either swim across the sea or lose the Golden Fleece.

All at once, Jason bethought himself of the galley's miraculous figurehead.

"O daughter of the Talking Oak," cried he, "how shall we set to work to get our vessel into the water?"

"Seat yourselves," answered the image (for it had known what ought to be done from the very first, and was only waiting for the question to be put), "seat yourselves, and handle your oars, and let Orpheus play upon his harp."

Immediately the fifty heroes got on board, and seizing their oars, held them perpendicularly in the air, while Orpheus (who liked such a task far better than rowing) swept his fingers across the harp. At the first ringing note of the music, they felt the vessel stir, Orpheus thrummed away briskly, and the galley slid at once into the sea, dipping her prow so deeply that the figurehead drank the wave with its marvelous lips and rose again as buoyant as a swan. The rowers plied their fifty oars; the white foam boiled up before the prow; the water gurgled and bubbled in their wake; while Orpheus continued to play so lively a strain of music that the vessel seemed to dance over the billows by way of keeping time to it. Thus triumphantly did the Argo sail out of the harbor, amidst the huzzas and good wishes of everybody except the wicked old Pelias, who stood on a promontory, scowling at her and wishing that he could blow out of his lungs the tempest of wrath that was in his heart, and so sink the galley with all on board. When they had sailed about fifty miles over the sea, Lynceus happened to cast his sharp eyes behind, and said that there was this bad-hearted king, still perched upon the promontory and scowling so gloomily that it looked like a black thundercloud in that quarter of the horizon.

In order to make the time pass away more pleasantly during the voyage, the heroes talked about the Golden Fleece. It originally belonged, it appears, to a Boeotian ram, who had taken on his back two children, when in danger of their lives, and fled with them over land and sea, as far as Colchis. One of the children, whose name was Helle, fell into the sea and was drowned. But the other (a little boy, named Phrixus) was brought safe ashore by the faithful ram, who, however, was so exhausted that he immediately lay down and died. In memory of this good deed, and as a token of his true heart, the fleece of the poor dead ram was miraculously changed to gold and became one of the most beautiful objects ever seen on earth. It was hung upon a tree in a sacred grove, where it had now been kept I know not how many years, and was the envy of mighty kings, who had nothing so magnificent in any of their palaces.

If I were to tell you all the adventures of the Argonauts, it would take me till nightfall, and perhaps a great deal longer. There was no lack of wonderful events, as you may judge from what you may have already heard. At a certain island they were hospitably received by King Cyzicus, its sovereign, who made a feast for them, and treated them like brothers. But the Argonauts saw that this good king looked downcast and very much troubled, and they therefore inquired of him what was the matter. King Cyzicus hereupon informed them that he and his subjects were greatly abused and incommoded by the inhabitants of a neighboring mountain, who made war upon them, and killed many people, and ravaged the country. And while they were talking about it, Cyzicus pointed to the mountain and asked Jason and his companions what they saw there.

"I see some very tall objects," answered Jason; "but they are at such a distance that I cannot distinctly make out what they are. To tell Your Majesty the truth, they look so very strangely that I am inclined to think them clouds, which have chanced to take something like human shapes."

"I see them very plainly," remarked Lynceus, whose eyes, you know, were as far-sighted as a telescope. "They are a band of enormous giants, all of whom have six arms apiece, and a club, a sword, or some other weapon in each of their hands."

"You have excellent eyes," said King Cyzicus. "Yes; they are six-armed giants, as you say, and these are the enemies whom I and my subjects have to contend with."

The next day, when the Argonauts were about setting sail, down came these terrible giants, stepping a hundred yards at a stride, brandishing their six arms apiece, and looking very formidable, so far aloft in the air. Each of these monsters was able to carry on a whole war by himself, for with one of his arms he could fling immense stones, and wield a club with another, and a sword with a third, while the fourth was poking a long spear at the enemy, and the fifth and sixth were shooting him with a bow and arrow. But, luckily, though the giants were so huge, and had so many arms, they had each but one heart, and that no bigger nor braver than the heart of an ordinary man. Besides, if they had been like the hundred-armed Briareus, the brave Argonauts would have given them their hands full of fight. Jason and his friends went boldly to meet them, slew a great many, and made the rest take to their heels, so that, if the giants had had six legs apiece instead of six arms, it would have served them better to run away with.

Another strange adventure happened when the voyagers came to Thrace, where they found a poor blind king, named Phineus, deserted by his subjects, and living in a very sorrowful way, all by himself. On Jason's inquiring whether they could do him any service, the king answered that he was terribly tormented by three great winged creatures, called Harpies, which had the faces of women, and the wings, bodies, and claws of vultures. These ugly wretches were in the habit of snatching away his dinner, and allowed him no peace of his life. Upon hearing this, the Argonauts spread a plentiful feast on the seashore, well knowing, from what the blind king said of their

greediness, that the Harpies would snuff up the scent of the victuals, and quickly come to steal them away. And so it turned out; for hardly was the table set, before the three hideous vulture women came flapping their wings, seized the food in their talons, and flew off as fast as they could. But the two sons of the North Wind drew their swords, spread their pinions, and set off through the air in pursuit of the thieves, whom they at last overtook among some islands, after a chase of hundreds of miles. The two winged youths blustered terribly at the Harpies (for they had the rough temper of their father), and so frightened them with their drawn swords that they solemnly promised never to trouble King Phineus again.

Then the Argonauts sailed onward and met with many other marvelous incidents, any one of which would make a story by itself. At one time, they landed on an island, and were reposing on the grass, when they suddenly found themselves assailed by what seemed a shower of steel-headed arrows. Some of them stuck in the ground, while others hit against their shields and several penetrated their flesh. The fifty heroes started up, and looked about them for the hidden enemy, but could find none, nor see any spot, on the whole island, where even a single archer could lie concealed. Still, however, the steel-headed arrows came whizzing among them; and, at last, happening to look upward, they beheld a large flock of birds, hovering and wheeling aloft and shooting their feathers down upon the Argonauts. These feathers were the steel-headed arrows that had so tormented them. There was no possibility of making any resistance; and the fifty heroic Argonauts might all have been killed or wounded by a flock of troublesome birds, without ever setting eyes on the Golden Fleece, if Jason had not thought of asking the advice of the oaken image.

So he ran to the galley as fast as his legs would carry him.

"O daughter of the Speaking Oak," cried he, all out of breath, "we need your wisdom more than ever before! We are in great peril from a flock of birds, who are shooting us with their steel-pointed feathers. What can we do to drive them away?"

"Make a clatter on your shields," said the image.

On receiving this excellent counsel, Jason hurried back to his companions (who were far more dismayed than when they fought with the six-armed giants), and bade them strike with their swords upon their brazen shields. Forthwith the fifty heroes set heartily to work, banging with might and main, and raised such a terrible clatter that the birds made what haste they could to get away; and though they had shot half the feathers out of their wings, they were soon seen skimming among the clouds, a long distance off, and looking like a flock of wild geese. Orpheus celebrated this victory by playing a triumphant anthem on his harp, and sang so melodiously that Jason begged him to desist, lest, as the steel-feathered birds had been driven away by an ugly sound, they might be enticed back again by a sweet one.

While the Argonauts remained on this island, they saw a small vessel approaching the shore, in which were two young men of princely demeanor, and exceedingly handsome, as young princes generally were in those days. Now, who do you imagine these two voyagers turned out to be? Why, if you will believe me, they were the sons of that very Phrixus, who, in his childhood, had been carried to Colchis on the back of the golden-fleeced ram. Since that time, Phrixus had married the king's daughter; and the two young princes had been born and brought up at Colchis, and had spent their playdays in the outskirts of the grove, in the center of which the Golden Fleece was hanging upon a tree. They were now on their way to Greece, in hopes of getting back a kingdom that had been wrongfully taken from their father.

When the princes understood whither the Argonauts were going, they offered to turn back and guide them to Colchis. At the same time, however, they spoke as if it were very doubtful whether Jason would succeed in getting the Golden Fleece. According to their account, the tree on which it hung was guarded by a terrible dragon, who never failed to devour, at one mouthful, every person who might venture within his reach.

"There are other difficulties in the way," continued the young princes. "But is not this enough? Ah, brave Jason, turn back

170

before it is too late. It would grieve us to the heart, if you and your nine-and-forty brave companions should be eaten up, at fifty mouthfuls, by this execrable dragon."

"My young friends," quietly replied Jason, "I do not wonder that you think the dragon very terrible. You have grown up from infancy in the fear of this monster, and therefore still regard him with the awe that children feel for the bugbears and hobgoblins which their nurses have talked to them about. But, in my view of the matter, the dragon is merely a pretty large serpent, who is not half so likely to snap me up at one mouthful as I am to cut off his ugly head and strip the skin from his body. At all events, turn back who may, I will never see Greece again unless I carry with me the Golden Fleece."

"We will none of us turn back!" cried his nine-and-forty brave comrades. "Let us get on board the galley this instant; and if the dragon is to make a breakfast of us, much good may it do him."

And Orpheus (whose custom it was to set everything to music) began to harp and sing most gloriously, and made every mother's son of them feel as if nothing in this world were so delectable as to fight dragons, and nothing so truly honorable as to be eaten up at one mouthful, in case of the worst.

After this (being now under the guidance of the two princes, who were well acquainted with the way), they quickly sailed to Colchis. When the king of the country, whose name was Aeetes, heard of their arrival, he instantly summoned Jason to court. The king was a stern and cruel-looking potentate; and though he put on as polite and hospitable an expression as he could, Jason did not like his face a whit better than that of the wicked King Pelias, who dethroned his father.

"You are welcome, brave Jason," said King Aeetes. "Pray, are you on a pleasure voyage?—or do you meditate the discovery of unknown islands?—or what other cause has procured me the happiness of seeing you at my court?"

"Great sir," replied Jason, with an obeisance,—for Chiron had taught him how to behave with propriety, whether to kings or beggars,—"I have come hither with a purpose which I now beg

171

your Majesty's permission to execute. King Pelias, who sits on my father's throne (to which he has no more right than to the one on which your excellent Majesty is now seated), has engaged to come down from it, and to give me his crown and scepter, provided I bring him the Golden Fleece. This, as your Majesty is aware, is now hanging on a tree here at Colchis; and I humbly solicit your gracious leave to take it away."

In spite of himself, the king's face twisted itself into an angry frown; for, above all things else in the world, he prized the Golden Fleece, and was even suspected of having done a very wicked act, in order to get it into his own possession. It put him into the worst possible humor, therefore, to hear that the gallant Prince Jason, and forty-nine of the bravest young warriors of Greece, had come to Colchis with the sole purpose of taking away his chief treasure.

"Do you know," asked King Aeetes, eying Jason very sternly, "what are the conditions which you must fulfill before getting possession of the Golden Fleece?"

"I have heard," rejoined the youth, "that a dragon lies beneath the tree on which the prize hangs, and that whoever approaches him runs the risk of being devoured at a mouthful."

"True," said the king, with a smile that did not look particularly good-natured. "Very true, young man. But there are other things as hard, or perhaps a little harder, to be done, before you can even have the privilege of being devoured by the dragon. For example, you must first tame my two brazen-footed and brazen-lunged bulls, which Vulcan, the wonderful blacksmith, made for me. There is a furnace in each of their stomachs; and they breathe such hot fire out of their mouths and nostrils, that nobody has hitherto gone nigh them without being instantly burned to a small, black cinder. What do you think of this, my brave Jason?"

"I must encounter the peril," answered Jason, composedly, "since it stands in the way of my purpose."

"After taming the fiery bulls," continued King Aeetes, who was determined to scare Jason if possible, "you must yoke them to a plough, and must plough the sacred earth in the grove of

172

Mars, and sow some of the same dragon's teeth from which Cadmus raised a crop of armed men. They are an unruly set of reprobates, those sons of the dragon's teeth; and unless you treat them suitably, they will fall upon you sword in hand. You and your nine-and-forty Argonauts, my bold Jason, are hardly numerous or strong enough to fight with such a host as will spring up."

"My master Chiron," replied Jason, "taught me, long ago, the story of Cadmus. Perhaps I can manage the quarrelsome sons of the dragon's teeth as well as Cadmus did."

"I wish the dragon had him," muttered King Aeetes to himself, "and the four-footed pedant, his schoolmaster, into the bargain. Why, what a foolhardy, self-conceited coxcomb he is! We'll see what my fire-breathing bulls will do for him. Well, Prince Jason," he continued, aloud, and as complaisantly as he could, "make yourself comfortable for today, and tomorrow morning, since you insist upon it, you shall try your skill at the plough."

While the king talked with Jason, a beautiful young woman was standing behind the throne. She fixed her eyes earnestly upon the youthful stranger and listened attentively to every word that was spoken; and when Jason withdrew from the king's presence, this young woman followed him out of the room.

"I am the king's daughter," she said to him, "and my name is Medea. I know a great deal of which other young princesses are ignorant and can do many things which they would be afraid so much as to dream of. If you will trust to me, I can instruct you how to tame the fiery bulls, and sow the dragon's teeth, and get the Golden Fleece."

"Indeed, beautiful princess," answered Jason, "if you will do me this service, I promise to be grateful to you my whole life long."

Gazing at Medea, he beheld a wonderful intelligence in her face. She was one of those persons whose eyes are full of mystery; so that, while looking into them, you seem to see a very great way, as into a deep well, yet can never be certain whether

173

you see into the farthest depths, or whether there be not something else hidden at the bottom. If Jason had been capable of fearing anything, he would have been afraid of making this young princess his enemy; for, beautiful as she now looked, she might, the very next instant, become as terrible as the dragon that kept watch over the Golden Fleece.

"Princess," he exclaimed, "you seem indeed very wise and very powerful. But how can you help me to do the things of which you speak? Are you an enchantress?"

"Yes, Prince Jason," answered Medea, with a smile, "you have hit upon the truth. I am an enchantress. Circe, my father's sister, taught me to be one, and I could tell you, if I pleased, who was the old woman with the peacock, the pomegranate, and the cuckoo staff, whom you carried over the river; and, likewise, who it is that speaks through the lips of the oaken image that stands in the prow of your galley. I am acquainted with some of your secrets, you perceive. It is well for you that I am favorably inclined; for, otherwise, you would hardly escape being snapped up by the dragon."

"I should not so much care for the dragon," replied Jason, "if I only knew how to manage the fiery-lunged bulls."

"If you are as brave as I think you, and as you have need to be," said Medea, "your own bold heart will teach you that there is but one way of dealing with a mad bull. What it is I leave you to find out in the moment of peril. As for the fiery breath of these animals, I have a charmed ointment here, which will prevent you from being burned up and cure you if you chance to be a little scorched."

So she put a golden box into his hand and directed him how to apply the perfumed unguent which it contained and where to meet her at midnight.

"Only be brave," added she, "and before daybreak the brazen bulls shall be tamed."

The young man assured her that his heart would not fail him. He then rejoined his comrades, and told them what had passed between the princess and himself, and warned them to be in readiness in case there might be need of their help.

At the appointed hour he met the beautiful Medea on the marble steps of the king's palace. She gave him a basket, in which were the dragon's teeth, just as they had been pulled out of the monster's jaws by Cadmus, long ago. Medea then led Jason down the palace steps, and through the silent streets of the city, and into the royal pasture-ground, where the two brazen-footed bulls were kept. It was a starry night, with a bright gleam along the eastern edge of the sky, where the moon was soon going to show herself. After entering the pasture, the princess paused and looked around.

"There they are," said she, "reposing themselves and chewing their fiery cuds in that farthest corner of the field. It will be excellent sport, I assure you, when they catch a glimpse of your figure. My father and all his court delight in nothing so much as to see a stranger trying to yoke them, in order to come at the Golden Fleece. It makes a holiday in Colchis whenever such a thing happens. For my part, I enjoy it immensely. You cannot imagine in what a mere twinkling of an eye their hot breath shrivels a young man into a black cinder."

"Are you sure, beautiful Medea," asked Jason, "quite sure, that the unguent in the gold box will prove a remedy against those terrible burns?"

"If you doubt, if you are in the least afraid," said the princess, looking him in the face by the dim starlight, "you had better never have been born than go a step nigher to the bulls."

But Jason had set his heart steadfastly on getting the Golden Fleece; and I positively doubt whether he would have gone back without it, even had he been certain of finding himself turned into a red-hot cinder, or a handful of white ashes, the instant he made a step farther. He therefore let go Medea's hand, and walked boldly forward in the direction whither she had pointed. At some distance before him he perceived four streams of fiery vapor, regularly appearing, and again vanishing, after dimly lighting up the surrounding obscurity. These, you will understand, were caused by the breath of the brazen bulls, which was quietly stealing out of their four nostrils, as they lay chewing their cuds.

At the first two or three steps which Jason made, the four fiery streams appeared to gush out somewhat more plentifully; for the two brazen bulls had heard his foot-tramp, and were lifting up their hot noses to snuff the air. He went a little farther, and by the way in which the red vapor now spouted forth, he judged that the creatures had got upon their feet. Now he could see glowing sparks and vivid jets of flame. At the next step, each of the bulls made the pasture echo with a terrible roar, while the burning breath, which they thus belched forth, lit up the whole field with a momentary flash. One other stride did bold Jason make; and, suddenly as a streak of lightning, on came these fiery animals, roaring like thunder and sending out sheets of white flame, which so kindled up the scene that the young man could discern every object more distinctly than by day-light. Most distinctly of all he saw the two horrible creatures galloping right down upon him, their brazen hoofs rattling and ringing over the ground, and their tails sticking up stiffly into the air, as has always been the fashion with angry bulls. Their breath scorched the herbage before them. So intensely hot it was, indeed, that it caught a dry tree, under which Jason was now standing, and set it all in a light blaze. But as for Jason himself (thanks to Medea's enchanted ointment), the white flame curled around his body, without injuring him a jot more than if he had been made of asbestos.

Greatly encouraged at finding himself not yet turned into a cinder, the young man awaited the attack of the bulls. Just as the brazen brutes fancied themselves sure of tossing him into the air, he caught one of them by the horn, and the other by his screwed-up tail, and held them in a grip like that of an iron vise, one with his right hand, the other with his left. Well, he must have been wonderfully strong in his arms, to be sure. But the secret of the matter was, that the brazen bulls were enchanted creatures, and that Jason had broken the spell of their fiery fierceness by his bold way of handling them. And, ever since that time, it has been the favorite method of brave men, when danger assails them, to do what they call "taking the bull by the horns"; and to grip him by the tail is pretty much the

same thing,—that is, to throw aside fear and overcome the peril by despising it.

It was now easy to yoke the bulls and to harness them to the plough, which had lain rusting on the ground for a great many years gone by; so long was it before anybody could be found capable of ploughing that piece of land. Jason, I suppose, had been taught how to draw a furrow by the good old Chiron, who, perhaps, used to allow himself to be harnessed to the plough. At any rate, our hero succeeded perfectly well in breaking up the greensward; and, by the time that the moon was a quarter of her journey up the sky, the ploughed field lay before him, a large tract of black earth, ready to be sown with the dragon's teeth. So Jason scattered them broadcast, and harrowed them into the soil with a brush-harrow, and took his stand on the edge of the field, anxious to see what would happen next.

"Must we wait long for harvest-time?" he inquired of Medea, who was now standing by his side.

"Whether sooner or later, it will be sure to come," answered the princess. "A crop of armed men never fails to spring up, when the dragon's teeth have been sown."

The moon was now high aloft in the heavens, and threw its bright beams over the ploughed field, where as yet there was nothing to be seen. Any farmer, on viewing it, would have said that Jason must wait weeks before the green blades would peep from among the clods, and whole months before the yellow grain would be ripened for the sickle. But by and by, all over the field, there was something that glistened in the moonbeams, like sparkling drops of dew. These bright objects sprouted higher and proved to be the steel heads of spears. Then there was a dazzling gleam from a vast number of polished brass helmets, beneath which, as they grew farther out of the soil, appeared the dark and bearded visages of warriors, struggling to free themselves from the imprisoning earth. The first look that they gave at the upper world was a glare of wrath and defiance. Next were seen their bright breastplates; in every right hand there was a sword or a spear, and on each left arm a shield; and when this strange crop of warriors had but half grown out

178

of the earth, they struggled,—such was their impatience of restraint,—and, as it were, tore themselves up by the roots. Wherever a dragon's tooth had fallen, there stood a man armed for battle. They made a clangor with their swords against their shields and eyed one another fiercely; for they had come into this beautiful world, and into the peaceful moonlight, full of rage and stormy passions, and ready to take the life of every human brother, in recompense of the boon of their own existence.

There have been many other armies in the world that seemed to possess the same fierce nature with the one which had now sprouted from the dragon's teeth; but these, in the moonlit field, were the more excusable, because they never had women for their mothers. And how it would have rejoiced any great captain, who was bent on conquering the world, like Alexander or Napoleon, to raise a crop of soldiers as easily as Jason did!

For a while, the warriors stood flourishing their weapons, clashing their swords against their shields, and boiling over with the red-hot thirst for battle. Then they began to shout, "Show us the enemy! Lead us to the charge! Death or victory! Come on, brave comrades! Conquer or die!" and a hundred other outcries, such as men always bellow forth on a battlefield, and which these dragon people seemed to have at their tongues' ends. At last, the front rank caught sight of Jason, who, beholding the flash of so many weapons in the moonlight, had thought it best to draw his sword. In a moment all the sons of the dragon's teeth appeared to take Jason for an enemy; and crying with one voice, "Guard the Golden Fleece!" they ran at him with uplifted swords and protruded spears. Jason knew that it would be impossible to withstand this bloodthirsty battalion with his single arm, but determined, since there was nothing better to be done, to die as valiantly as if he himself had sprung from a dragon's tooth.

Medea, however, bade him snatch up a stone from the ground.

"Throw it among them quickly!" cried she. "It is the only way to save yourself."

179

The armed men were now so nigh that Jason could discern
the fire flashing out of their enraged eyes, when he let fly the
stone and saw it strike the helmet of a tall warrior, who was
rushing upon him with his blade aloft. The stone glanced from
this man's helmet to the shield of his nearest comrade, and
thence flew right into the angry face of another, hitting him
smartly between the eyes. Each of the three who had been
struck by the stone took it for granted that his next neighbor
had given him a blow; and instead of running any farther towards Jason, they began a fight among themselves. The confusion spread through the host, so that it seemed scarcely a moment before they were all hacking, hewing, and stabbing at
one another, lopping off arms, heads, and legs, and doing such

180

memorable deeds that Jason was filled with immense admiration; although, at the same time, he could not help laughing to behold these mighty men punishing each other for an offense which he himself had committed. In an incredibly short space of time (almost as short, indeed, as it had taken them to grow up), all but one of the heroes of the dragon's teeth were stretched lifeless on the field. The last survivor, the bravest and strongest of the whole, had just force enough to wave his crimson sword over his head, and give a shout of exultation, crying, "Victory! Victory! Immortal fame!" when he himself fell down, and lay quietly among his slain brethren.

And there was the end of the army that had sprouted from the dragon's teeth. That fierce and feverish fight was the only enjoyment which they had tasted on this beautiful earth.

"Let them sleep in the bed of honor," said the Princess Medea, with a sly smile at Jason. "The world will always have simpletons enough, just like them, fighting and dying for they know not what, and fancying that posterity will take the trouble to put laurel wreaths on their rusty and battered helmets. Could you help smiling, Prince Jason, to see the self-conceit of that last fellow, just as he tumbled down?"

"It made me very sad," answered Jason, gravely. "And, to tell you the truth, princess, the Golden Fleece does not appear so well worth the winning, after what I have here beheld."

"You will think differently in the morning," said Medea. "True, the Golden Fleece may not be so valuable as you have thought it; but then there is nothing better in the world; and one must needs have an object, you know. Come! Your night's work has been well performed; and tomorrow you can inform King Aeetes that the first part of your allotted task is fulfilled."

Agreeably to Medea's advice, Jason went betimes in the morning to the palace of King Aeetes. Entering the presence-chamber, he stood at the foot of the throne and made a low obeisance.

"Your eyes look heavy, Prince Jason," observed the king; "you appear to have spent a sleepless night. I hope you have been considering the matter a little more wisely, and have con-

181

cluded not to get yourself scorched to a cinder, in attempting to tame my brazen-lunged bulls."

"That is already accomplished, may it please your Majesty," replied Jason. "The bulls have been tamed and yoked; the field has been ploughed; the dragon's teeth have been sown broadcast and harrowed into the soil; the crop of armed warriors has sprung up, and they have slain one another, to the last man. And now I solicit your Majesty's permission to encounter the dragon, that I may take down the Golden Fleece from the tree and depart, with my nine-and-forty comrades."

King Aeetes scowled and looked very angry and excessively disturbed; for he knew that, in accordance with his kingly promise, he ought now to permit Jason to win the fleece, if his courage and skill should enable him to do so. But, since the young man had met with such good luck in the matter of the brazen bulls and the dragon's teeth, the king feared that he would be equally successful in slaying the dragon. And therefore, though he would gladly have seen Jason snapped up at a mouthful, he was resolved (and it was a very wrong thing of this wicked potentate) not to run any further risk of losing his beloved fleece.

"You never would have succeeded in this business, young man," said he, "if my undutiful daughter Medea had not helped you with her enchantments. Had you acted fairly, you would have been, at this instant, a black cinder or a handful of white ashes. I forbid you, on pain of death, to make any more attempts to get the Golden Fleece. To speak my mind plainly, you shall never set eyes on so much as one of its glistening locks."

Jason left the king's presence in great sorrow and anger. He could think of nothing better to be done than to summon together his forty-nine brave Argonauts, march at once to the grove of Mars, slay the dragon, take possession of the Golden Fleece, get on board the Argo, and spread all sail for Iolchos. The success of the scheme depended, it is true, on the doubtful point whether all the fifty heroes might not be snapped up, at so many mouthfuls, by the dragon. But, as Jason was hastening down the palace steps, the Princess Medea called after him

182

and beckoned him to return. Her black eyes shone upon him with such a keen intelligence that he felt as if there were a serpent peeping out of them; and although she had done him so much service only the night before, he was by no means very certain that she would not do him an equally great mischief before sunset. These enchantresses, you must know, are never to be depended upon.

"What says King Aeetes, my royal and upright father?" inquired Medea, slightly smiling. "Will he give you the Golden Fleece, without any further risk or trouble?"

"On the contrary," answered Jason, "he is very angry with me for taming the brazen bulls and sowing the dragon's teeth. And he forbids me to make any more attempts and positively refuses to give up the Golden Fleece, whether I slay the dragon or no."

"Yes, Jason," said the princess, "and I can tell you more. Unless you set sail from Colchis before tomorrow's sunrise, the king means to burn your fifty-oared galley and put yourself and your forty-nine brave comrades to the sword. But be of good courage. The Golden Fleece you shall have, if it lies within the power of my enchantments to get it for you. Wait for me here an hour before midnight."

At the appointed hour, you might again have seen Prince Jason and the Princess Medea, side by side, stealing through the streets of Colchis, on their way to the sacred grove, in the center of which the Golden Fleece was suspended to a tree. While they were crossing the pasture-ground, the brazen bulls came towards Jason, lowing, nodding their heads, and thrusting forth their snouts, which, as other cattle do, they loved to have rubbed and caressed by a friendly hand. Their fierce nature was thoroughly tamed; and, with their fierceness, the two furnaces in their stomachs had likewise been extinguished, insomuch that they probably enjoyed far more comfort in grazing and chewing their cuds than ever before. Indeed, it had heretofore been a great inconvenience to these poor animals, that, whenever they wished to eat a mouthful of grass, the fire out of their nostrils had shriveled it up, before they could manage to

crop it. How they contrived to keep themselves alive is more than I can imagine. But now, instead of emitting jets of flame and streams of sulphurous vapor, they breathed the very sweetest of cow breath.

After kindly patting the bulls, Jason followed Medea's guidance into the grove of Mars, where the great oak trees, that had been growing for centuries, threw so thick a shade that the moonbeams struggled vainly to find their way through it. Only here and there a glimmer fell upon the leaf-strewn earth, or now and then a breeze stirred the boughs aside and gave Jason a glimpse of the sky, lest, in that deep obscurity, he might forget that there was one, overhead. At length, when they had gone farther and farther into the heart of the duskiness, Medea squeezed Jason's hand.

"Look yonder," she whispered. "Do you see it?"

Gleaming among the venerable oaks, there was a radiance, not like the moonbeams, but rather resembling the golden glory of the setting sun. It proceeded from an object, which appeared to be suspended at about a man's height from the ground, a little farther within the wood.

"What is it?" asked Jason.

"Have you come so far to seek it," exclaimed Medea, "and do you not recognize the meed of all your toils and perils, when it glitters before your eyes? It is the Golden Fleece."

Jason went onward a few steps farther and then stopped to gaze. Oh, how beautiful it looked, shining with a marvelous light of its own, that inestimable prize, which so many heroes had longed to behold, but had perished in the quest of it, either by the perils of their voyage, or by the fiery breath of the brazen-lunged bulls.

"How gloriously it shines!" cried Jason, in a rapture. "It has surely been dipped in the richest gold of sunset. Let me hasten onward and take it to my bosom."

"Stay," said Medea, holding him back. "Have you forgotten what guards it?"

To say the truth, in the joy of beholding the object of his desires, the terrible dragon had quite slipped out of Jason's

185

memory. Soon, however, something came to pass that reminded him what perils were still to be encountered. An antelope, that probably mistook the yellow radiance for sunrise, came bounding fleetly through the grove. He was rushing straight towards the Golden Fleece, when suddenly there was a frightful hiss, and the immense head and half the scaly body of the dragon was thrust forth (for he was twisted round the trunk of the tree on which the fleece hung), and seizing the poor antelope, swallowed him with one snap of his jaws.

After this feat, the dragon seemed sensible that some other living creature was within reach on which he felt inclined to finish his meal. In various directions he kept poking his ugly snout among the trees, stretching out his neck a terrible long way, now here, now there, and now close to the spot where Jason and the princess were hiding behind an oak. Upon my word, as the head came waving and undulating through the air, and reaching almost within arm's length of Prince Jason, it was a very hideous and uncomfortable sight. The gape of his enormous jaws was nearly as wide as the gateway of the king's palace.

"Well, Jason," whispered Medea (for she was ill-natured, as all enchantresses are, and wanted to make the bold youth tremble), "what do you think now of your prospect of winning the Golden Fleece?"

Jason answered only by drawing his sword and making a step forward.

"Stay, foolish youth," said Medea, grasping his arm. "Do not you see you are lost, without me as your good angel? In this gold box I have a magic potion, which will do the dragon's business far more effectually than your sword."

The dragon had probably heard the voices; for, swift as lightning, his black head and forked tongue came hissing among the trees again, darting full forty feet at a stretch. As it approached, Medea tossed the contents of the gold box right down the monster's wide-open throat. Immediately, with an outrageous hiss and a tremendous wriggle,—flinging his tail up to the tiptop of the tallest tree and shattering all its branches as it crashed heavily down again,—the dragon fell at full length upon the ground and lay quite motionless.

"It is only a sleeping potion," said the enchantress to Prince Jason. "One always finds a use for these mischievous creatures, sooner or later; so I did not wish to kill him outright. Quick! Snatch the prize and let us be gone. You have won the Golden Fleece."

Jason caught the Fleece from the tree and hurried through the grove, the deep shadows of which were illuminated as he passed by the golden glory of the precious object that he bore along. A little way before him, he beheld the old woman whom he had helped over the stream, with her peacock beside her. She clapped her hands for joy, and beckoning him to make haste, disappeared among the duskiness of the trees. Espying the two winged sons of the North Wind (who were disporting themselves in the moonlight, a few hundred feet aloft), Jason bade them tell the rest of the Argonauts to embark as speedily as possible. But Lynceus, with his sharp eyes, had already caught a glimpse of him, bringing the Golden Fleece, although several stone walls, a hill, and the black shadows of the grove of Mars intervened between. By his advice, the heroes had seated themselves on the benches of the galley, with their oars held perpendicularly, ready to let fall into the water.

As Jason drew near, he heard the Talking Image calling to him with more than ordinary eagerness, in its grave, sweet voice:—

"Make haste, Prince Jason! For your life, make haste!"

With one bound he leaped aboard. At sight of the glorious radiance of the Golden Fleece, the nine-and-forty heroes gave a mighty shout, and Orpheus, striking his harp, sang a song of triumph, to the cadence of which the galley flew over the water, homeward bound, as if careering along with wings!

THREE GOLDEN ORANGES

RETOLD BY *Mary Gould Davis*
and Ralph Steele Boggs

ILLUSTRATED BY *Robert Sinnott*

ONCE upon a time there lived in the old city of Granada a widow who had one son. His name was Diego. He was tall and strong and handsome, and it was high time for him to marry.

Now Diego was of an independent spirit and he did not care for any of the girls whom his mother had selected to be a possible bride. He determined to win a bride of his own choosing. And nothing would suit him but the most beautiful girl in the world.

So he went one day to an old wise woman who lived on the road leading out toward the Sierra Nevada.

"Tell me, old woman," he said, "how can I find the most beautiful girl in all the world?"

The old woman cackled.

"So that is it, is it?" she said. "Well, well! You will find what you seek if you do exactly as I tell you. Follow the road that leads into the mountains. Follow it until you come to the Garden of the Three Golden Oranges. If you can pluck the three oranges without climbing the tree, your quest will be well started. Bring them here to me and I will tell you what to do next."

The next morning Diego said good-bye to his mother and set out along the way that led toward the mountains. All day he walked, following the curves of the hard white road deeper and deeper into the hills. Toward nightfall he came to a golden castle that was surrounded on all sides by a high wall. There

188

was a tall iron gate, and beside it, a bell. Diego rang the bell and instantly the gate swung open. No sooner had he passed through than it shut behind him. There on the pathway that led to the Castle stood a tall young girl. She was fair, with hair as golden as ripe corn, and her blue eyes looked frightened. Diego made her his most graceful bow.

"Can you tell me," he said, "where I shall find the Garden of the Three Golden Oranges?"

The girl shook her head.

"I do not know," she answered. "My father is the Sun and he may know. He will be home very soon now, but you must go away before he comes. He will be very angry if he finds you here."

But Diego laughed and refused to go. He followed the girl into the Castle of the Sun and talked to her so charmingly that she forgot her fear and became as gay and happy as a child. Suddenly a deep golden light flooded the room, and the Sun himself stood in the doorway.

"Who is this stranger, my daughter?" he demanded. "Let him explain himself, or it will be the worse for you both."

The frightened look came back into the girl's eyes.

"Father," she said, "he means no harm. He seeks the Garden of the Three Golden Oranges. Can you tell him where it is?"

The Sun shook his great head.

"I do not know," he said. "Let him go still higher and ask my sister, the Moon. And let him go quickly before I lose my temper."

Bidding farewell to the daughter of the Sun, Diego hurried to the great gate which opened silently to let him through. On and upward he went, following the curves of the road ever higher and higher. At last he saw on the slope above him a Castle that was made of silver. Like the Castle of the Sun it had a great wrought iron gate, and when Diego rang the bell the gate swung open. On the path that led to the door of the Castle there stood a tall young girl. Her hair was so fair that it looked like silver and her eyes were gray.

"Can you tell me," said Diego, not forgetting to bow, "where

I shall find the Garden of the Three Golden Oranges?"

The girl shook her head.

"I do not know," she answered, "but I will ask my mother, the Moon."

She went quickly into the Castle from which a silvery light shone. Presently she returned.

"You are to go at once," she told Diego. "Go along the road until you come to a Castle that is built of gray rock. There dwells my uncle, the East Wind. He blows everywhere, all over the world, and surely he will know where your Garden is to be found."

Diego thanked her and started out again. He was tired and hungry, his throat was dry with the white dust before he saw above him the great gray Castle of the East Wind. Again he rang a bell and again a great gate swung open. The girl who stood on the pathway this time was so pretty that Diego's heart beat faster. Her brown eyes were bright with mischief and she wore a red carnation in her dark hair.

"You are a very foolish youth to come here," she told him. "If my father, the East Wind, sees you he will probably blow you over the top of the Sierra Nevada."

"Perhaps it is there that I want to go," Diego answered boldly. "I am seeking the Garden of the Three Golden Oranges. Do you know where it lies?"

The girl raised her black eyebrows.

190

"Why should I bother to know that?" she said. "My father knows, of course. He knows everything. If you will entertain me all the afternoon, if you will eat with me and drink with me and tell me about the world below the mountains, I will hide you in the chest beside the fireplace when my father comes home. Then I will ask him where this Garden is, and you can listen to his answer. And if you are brave and clever you can get away without his seeing you."

The hours of the day passed very quickly for them both. The daughter of the East Wind was so charming that Diego forgot his quest and thought only of her. Was she, perhaps, the most beautiful girl in all the world?

Toward night there was a great clatter and bustle in the courtyard, and a chill wind blew in through doors and windows.

"That is my father," said the girl quickly. "Go and hide in the chest beside the fireplace."

Diego crouched down inside the great chest, and the girl threw over it a gaily embroidered blanket. "Now listen well," she whispered.

Presently Diego heard the East Wind come into the room. In spite of his rough manners he seemed to be a kindly person. He pinched his daughter's cheek and pulled a lock of her dark hair.

"And what have you been doing today while I have been blowing my way across the world?" he asked.

His daughter seemed not at all afraid of him. "Father," she said, "I have a question to ask you. Where lies the Garden of the Three Golden Oranges?"

The East Wind laughed until the great wooden rafters shook. "Now what care have you for the Three Golden Oranges?" he shouted. "That is a quest for a man, not for a woman. The Garden lies just on the other side of the crest of the highest peak in the Sierra Nevada. If you stand on the top you can look down and see the Garden and the Orange Tree below you. But enough of this chatter! I am hungry. Bring me meat and drink!"

That night while East Wind slept Diego made his way out of the Castle, the gate opening silently to let him through. All

191

that day and the next day, and the next and the next, he worked his way up the highest peak of the Sierra Nevada, through fields starred with wild flowers, through drifts of snow. There was no sound in his ears but the lonely cry of a bird or the trickle of the clear, cold stream. He seemed quite alone in a strange, silent world.

At dawn on the fifth day he stood on the crest of the highest peak, and looking down, he saw the Garden.

Surely it was the loveliest Garden in all the world. It was like an emerald set in the snow. Tall cypress trees guarded it, roses and lilies and carnations bloomed, fountains threw up their sparkling jets of water. And in the center of the Garden there stood an Orange Tree. Even from his height Diego could see that only three oranges grew on its branches and that these three shone and glistened like the purest gold.

Eagerly he ran down the slope and rang the bell in the Garden wall, and silently the gate swung open. It was very still in the Garden, and there was no living soul in sight. Diego went up to the tree. Remembering what the wise woman had said, he did not try to climb it, but leaped in the air until he had leaped high enough to catch the branch that bore the fruit. Quickly he broke it off. They were his, the Three Golden Oranges!

Thrusting them into his pouch, he hurried through the Garden to the gate. Would it open for him? For an instant he waited, listening. Then the gate swung silently open, and he was free. Wrapping his cloak about him he slept. And the next day he started on his homeward journey.

If the way to the Garden had seemed long, the way back seemed even longer. One day when Diego could see below him the white roofs and square red towers of Granada he sat down to rest beside the road. His mouth was so parched with thirst that he took from his pouch one of the Three Golden Oranges. He looked at it longingly.

"It could do no harm," he said to himself, "if I ate just one of them."

He broke the skin of the orange—and out of it there stepped a tiny maiden!

Slender and delicate, just as tall as his little finger, she stood there on the palm of his hand. My, but she was lovely! Her eyes were as bright as the stars in a June sky, her hair was as black as a crow's wing, her curved mouth as red as a passion flower. Her long, ruffled dress was of yellow muslin and on her tiny arched feet she wore golden shoes.

Light as thistledown, she sprang from Diego's hand to the ground. And there she stood—as tall as he!

Diego could only stand and gape at her. Surely this was the most beautiful girl in all the world!

Lifting her yellow fan so that it hid her lips, she looked at him over its rim.

"Will you give me some bread?" she asked.

Diego was so dazed with her beauty that he could only answer stupidly, "I have none."

"Then," said the girl, "I will creep back into my Golden Orange and return to my tree."

With that she became small again and curled up inside the orange. And both girl and orange disappeared.

Now Diego had a head on his shoulders, and you must know by this time that he was not easily discouraged. He felt in his pouch to be sure that the other two oranges were there. Then he went on until he came to a goatherd's hut, where he begged a piece of bread. Sitting down on the hillside under an olive tree, he took the second Golden Orange from his pouch and broke the skin. And out there stepped a second maiden. My but she was lovelier than the first!

Her hair was as gold as the flowers of the broom, her eyes as blue as the wild lupin and her lips like the curved petals of a pink rose. Her long, ruffled dress was of blue, and her shoes were silver.

Lightly she leaped to the ground, and there she stood just as high as Diego's shoulder.

"Will you give me some bread?" she asked, resting the edge of her fan against her lips.

Diego took the bread from his pouch and handed it to her.

"And now," she said, "will you give me some water?"

193

Diego's heart sank.

"I have none," he answered.

"Then," said the girl, "I will creep back into my little Orange and return to my tree."

And with that she grew small again, curled up inside the orange skin, and girl and orange disappeared.

And now Diego wished that he had heeded the words of the old wise woman and had brought the oranges to her. But something made him feel that he would like to finish the adventure for himself. So he walked to where a brook flowed down the hillside. Taking the bread from his pouch, he laid it on the grass beside him and opened the third Golden Orange.

My, but the tiny maiden who stepped out of this one was the loveliest of all! Diego knew now that he had found the most beautiful girl in all the world!

Her hair, under the black lace mantilla, was red gold, she had the long gray eyes of Andalusia, and her eyebrows and lashes were as black as night. Her dress was snow white, the many ruffles edged with scarlet, and on her slender feet she wore scarlet shoes. When she jumped to the ground she stood just as high as Diego's heart.

"Will you give me some bread?" she asked, her eyes smiling at him over her scarlet fan.

Diego's fingers trembled with eagerness as he gave her the bread.

"And now," she said, "will you give me some water?"

He scooped the clear water from the brook and gave it to her.

"And now," she said, "we will eat together and drink together and live happily ever afterward."

Diego's heart leaped with joy. They ate and drank, and then, with the girl's cool hand clasped in his, her white skirts rustling crisply as she walked, they went on down the road toward Granada.

Just before they reached the town they passed an Inn. In the patio there was a fountain and over the basin of the fountain there grew an olive tree.

194

"See," said the girl, "you cannot bring your bride into Granada on foot. Go into the Inn and ask them to let you have a carriage and a pair of horses. Bargain well for it, and I will wait for you up in the olive tree."

And with that she climbed up into the tree and settled down there, looking for all the world like a great scarlet and white bird.

Diego went on into the Inn, and what with bargaining with the shrewd landlord for a carriage and pair, and celebrating the happy ending of his quest with a glass or two of *valdepeñas*, it was some time before he came out again.

No sooner had he disappeared than out of the shadow of the wall there came a woman dressed as a gypsy. And how was the gray-eyed girl to know that she was really a wicked witch? As the gypsy bent over to fill her pitcher at the fountain she saw the face of the girl reflected in the water, and jealousy of the beauty of that face filled her.

"If that face were mine," she thought, "there would be no end to my power."

Long she looked at the reflected face, and then, in a frenzy of rage, she lifted the pitcher and threw it into the basin, thus breaking both the pitcher and the reflection. Now, for her own purposes, the witch was acting as a servant at the Inn. When she came back without the pitcher, the Innkeeper gave her another one and told her, impatiently, to fill that. For the second time she saw the reflected face, and for the second time in her rage she destroyed both pitcher and image. This time when she returned to the kitchen with empty hands the Innkeeper scolded her soundly. Then he gave her a pitcher that was made of metal. In a frenzy the witch banged it against the fountain, but it would not break.

Up in the olive tree the gray-eyed girl of the third Golden Orange laughed at her.

This, to the witch, was the last straw. Climbing the tree as swiftly as a cat she stuck a magic pin into the girl's head. And there in the branches of the olive tree sat, not a gray-eyed maiden, but a little white dove.

When Diego came out of the Inn and discovered that the most beautiful girl in all the world had disappeared, he was distracted. Vainly he hunted for her through the Inn and the orchard and along the road. Then he threw himself in despair on the grass under the olive and mourned aloud, while his mourning was echoed by the plaintive cry of the white dove in the branches above him. Finally Diego drew the dove down and held it against his breast.

"Come with me, little dove," he said. "Together we will go to the wise woman and ask her how I can find my lost love."

For days and for weeks the old wise woman had sat at the entrance of her cave and watched for Diego. And now she saw him coming, his face sad and downcast, the glistening white dove held against his breast.

And instantly, in her wisdom, she knew what had happened. And her anger at the witch, who was in truth her enemy, made her old eyes glow like live coals. Stretching out her hands she took the dove from Diego without a word. Her thin, brown fingers felt about under its feathers and touched almost at once

196

the head of the magic pin. Swiftly she drew it out—and there before them stood the gray-eyed girl of the third Golden Orange!

Gratefully Diego thanked the wise old woman; proudly he led his bride to his mother's house. A fine pair they made standing before the altar. The wedding festivities lasted three days and three nights. I, myself, was there as a guest. And I came away with nothing in my pouch but the skin of a golden orange.

I HEAR PAUL BUNYAN

Louise Leighton

When the night is still and the wind,
    that ancient squatter
Claiming the timeless land of the
    sky-blue water,
Sleeps in his weathered wigwam of birch bark,
I hear Paul Bunyan tramping through the dark.
I hear the sibilance of aspens quaking,
I feel the tremor his mighty feet are making,
I can almost see him striding by,
Parting the Norway pines to clear the sky.
Between the boughs the star-combed waters
    glisten,
And vibrant, breathing forests pause to listen,
As throb, throb, throbbing through the night,
Paul Bunyan haunts the land of his delight.

A DUTCH TALE

Frances Carpenter

THE WHITE HORSE OF VOLENDAM

ILLUSTRATED BY *Frances Eckart*

IN THE early days, there were farms where the Netherlands fishing town of Volendam now stands. Men of those times wore wooden shoes, as they do today. But their wooden shoes were for walking on the damp, grassy pasture lands along the ocean rather than on the wet floors of their fishing boats and their boat landings.

One of the farmers in that part of the Netherlands had a daughter as fair as any spring tulip field. We may as well call her Katrinka, although I do not know that that was her name.

Well, this Katrinka was always running away from the meadows down to the seashore. Day after day, she would go there to watch the big waves rolling in.

198

"What do you do there by the ocean, my daughter?" the girl's mother asked when she came home at nightfall.

"I watch the white horses leaping over the high waves," Katrinka replied. In vain her mother told the girl that what she saw on the waves was only the water breaking into foam.

"I can see white horses," Katrinka insisted. "And one day a white horse will ride straight out on the beach. I shall climb on his back, and we shall go like the wind."

Nothing could keep Katrinka from going again and again down to the seashore. Each afternoon when her work of making butter and cheese was done for the day, she would run as fast as she could to the edge of the ocean.

"My White Horse rode up out of the sea waves today," Katrinka at last told her mother. "It galloped along the seashore before my very eyes. I shall take it some oats tomorrow."

The next day when the girl came home from the beach, she carried a great fish in her arms.

"The White Horse ate the oats," she cried. "Then it turned round and galloped back into the ocean. When it returned, it brought me this fish for us to eat." And she told how the flounder had rolled out of the sea at the hoofs of the horse.

"The girl is bewitched. She does not know what she says." Her friends shook their heads. But when, each day, Katrinka brought home another fine flounder, they began to wonder.

Katrinka's family had never before eaten fish, so this old legend says. But they cooked the flounders as the White Horse taught the girl. And they found their taste good. With her bringing home a fresh fish every night, they now had no need to worry about food for their supper.

But one day Katrinka did not come home from the seashore.

"She rode away on a great white horse," a farmer reported. "I saw the White Horse come out of the sea. I saw him leap onto the shore over the top of a great wave. The girl climbed on his back. The horse turned about. Then he galloped off again into the ocean."

Her father gathered his neighbors from the farms round about. All working, the men nailed pieces of wood together

199

into a boat. They put a cloth sail above it, and they set it to float on the ocean. The winds blew into the sail, and the boat moved hither and yon. The men in it looked and looked into the water for the lost girl. But they did not find her.

Then, with the women to help them, the men made a huge net. They dragged this through the ocean waters, hoping and hoping that it would draw Katrinka back from the watery land of the White Horse.

That net did not find the girl either, so the story says, but each time it was drawn up on the beach, there spilled out of it a fine catch of silvery fish. These fish, too, were good for food, so these farming folk soon discovered.

At last, they gave up all hope of bringing the girl, Katrinka, back from her new home with the White Horse. But the Volendam men did not give up going out in their little boats and dropping their strong nets into the ocean. More and more fish they caught. More and more houses were built near the seashore. More and more boats went out from the little landings of the fishing town of Volendam.

Visitors from many lands come to see the town of Volendam of today. Its fisherfolk still wear the costumes of bygone times. The men and the boys keep to the old-fashioned, baggy pantaloons and the tight jackets with their big, round silver buttons. Their winter hats are like stovepipes made out of fur, and their summer caps of black cloth have shiny black visors to keep off the sun. The women and girls like the full skirts and bright shawls and the gay little lace caps their grandmothers wore.

Saturdays, in the harbor of Volendam, the masts of the fishing boats are thick as trees in a forest. Along its wharves, the brown nets are hung high to dry in the sun and the wind. Women carry baskets on their heads, selling fish from door to door.

The faces of the boys and girls of this seashore village are rosy and tanned from the sea air. Their bright eyes grow even brighter when they show visitors pictures of the famous White Horse of Volendam. At its back is the sea. At its feet lies a flounder. These pictures remind them of the story of the White Horse that taught their forefathers how to fish.

200

Hilda van Stockum

A WOMAN'S WIT

ILLUSTRATED BY *Rosemary Buehrig*

IN THE days long ago, before Saint Patrick banished the snakes, there were giants in Ireland so big that they could swallow an ox whole. They were strong but they were just like any other body in their hearts. So when a Connemara giant, called Fergus McGrath, who was champion of all Ireland, heard of another, stronger giant in Donegal he grew pale with jealousy, just as you or I would. He was getting old, and there had been no need for him to fight for such a long time that he had gotten out of practice.

"Must I fight this new giant and prove I am stronger?" he asked of his little wife, his voice quavering as he said it. His wife said nothing as she sat by the fire with her knitting. She knew he was not what he had been, but she didn't mind that. She set no store by muscular strength. "What's strength to a woman's wit?" she'd say. She just sat and knitted and counted stitches till her husband stamped out of the house in a rage.

Well, the other giant—Donal was his name—was like a young bull, bursting to test his mettle. He had heard of Fergus McGrath's fame and he said it was all put up. He didn't believe it.

"I'm going to find out meself if he'll stand up in a fight," he said, and he meant it. When Fergus heard this he quaked so the house shook.

201

"Must I fight him?" he asked of his wife, but his wife kept on knitting and counting stitches. Suddenly there was a big bang on the door and when Fergus peeped through the window he saw a man twice the size of himself waiting to be let in.

"It's Donal!" he cried, running around in a circle like a dog that's mad. "It's not meself that'll knock the likes of him down! Ochone! Me reputation is ruined!" And he burst into tears. Then his wife saw that she must put by her knitting. "Go to bed," she said, "and don't say a word. Leave it all to me!" Before the visitor knocked the second time she had lifted the latch.

"How are ye, ma'am?" the giant said. "I'm Donal O'Mahoney from Donegal." He tugged at his forelock, for he didn't carry a hat, and he had been taught manners by his mother. "Is Fergus McGrath at home?"

"He is not," said the missus. "But you're welcome all the same, and he may be in any minute now. Sit ye down and make yourself comfortable." So Donal scraped his boots on the threshold and went in. "What might you be wanting of himself now?" asked Mrs. McGrath. "It's not often we have visitors in these parts."

"Have ye never heard him speak of me?" asked Donal in a disappointed voice. Mrs. McGrath pretended to think deeply. She wrinkled her forehead.

"No," she said, "unless you be the man that promised to call for the old suit he's grown out of."

"How can I be him?" cried Donal with flashing eyes, pushing out his chest. "Sure, ye can't have looked at me properly, ma'am, or ye wouldn't be saying such a thing." Mrs. McGrath took up her knitting again and settled herself beside the fire.

"It is true," she said, glancing at him. "The old suit would not fit you; you're too narrow in the shoulders." Donal snorted, but awe crept into his eyes.

"Well, if so, it's your husband'll find a smaller man can beat him." Donal puffed himself up with pride until he was a formidable sight. Fergus peered through the curtains of the press-bed and groaned.

202

"What's that?" asked Donal, who had sharp ears. "Did I hear a man's voice?"

"No," said Mrs. McGrath, dropping a stitch. "It's only me wee babe has the colic."

"Oh!" And Donal sank back in his chair. "Will your husband be here soon?" he asked.

"He will, so. He has only gone out to the woods to root out some trees," she said and, as she noticed the rumbling of thunder in the distance, she put up a finger. "Do ye hear them falling? He has the wood nearly plowed up now. He pulls the trees out like radishes. 'Why don't you use a hatchet?' says I to him often and often. 'What for,' says he, 'when this way is simpler and saves trouble in the end?' So I let him be; he must have his own way in everything." Mrs. McGrath shook her head. "It's terrible to be wedded to a man with a temper," she went on with a sigh.

Donal's cheeks paled, and he began to fidget on his chair. "What's the matter?" asked Mrs. McGrath. "Aren't ye comfortable? Come, take a cake. They're me husband's favorite." She handed him a stale dog biscuit. Donal took a bite and broke two teeth.

"Thank ye," said he, putting the biscuit down. "I'm not fond of sweets."

"I'm sorry to hear it," said Mrs. McGrath. "If I had known you were coming I'd have made you something heartier; but me husband likes soft food."

"Do ye think he'll be here soon?" asked Donal hastily, with a timid glance at the door.

"He'll be here as soon as he has loaded the trees on his back," said the missus. "Come and have a look at me babe to while away the time. He's a bit puny; all his brothers were handsome fellows, but he, being the last and a trifle sickly, he's not much to look at for a six months' child. Still, have a peep." And she led her visitor to the bed where her husband was lying and pulled the covers from his terrified face. When Donal saw the huge bearded fellow and heard he was only a six months' infant, he put a hand to his head.

"If so, what'll the father be like!" he thought, and terror came over him like a whirlwind. "Don't let me keep ye any longer, ma'am!" he said to Mrs. McGrath. "I don't think I'll wait for your husband after all!" and he ran to the door, stumbling over a pitchfork.

"Och! I'm sorry now," murmured Mrs. McGrath picking it up. "Me husband *will* leave his pocket combs lying about. . . ." Donal didn't listen. He ran out of the door and down the road and up hill and down hill all the way until he reached his mother's kitchen, where he fell gasping on a chair and asked for a glass of water. Fergus crawled cautiously out of his bed.

"Is he gone?" said he. His wife had taken up her knitting and paid no attention to him.

"What's strength to a woman's wit?" she thought.

Howard Pyle

ROBIN HOOD TURNS BEGGAR

ILLUSTRATED BY *John Dukes McKee*

AFTER jolly Robin had left Little John at
the forking of the roads, he walked merrily
onward in the mellow sunshine that shone
about him. Ever and anon he would skip and leap or sing a
snatch of song, for pure joyousness of the day; for, because of
the sweetness of the springtide, his heart was as lusty within
him as that of a colt newly turned out to grass. Sometimes he
would walk a long distance, gazing aloft at the great white
swelling clouds that moved slowly across the deep blue sky;
anon he would stop and drink in the fullness of life of all things,
for the hedgerows were budding tenderly, and the grass of the
meadows was waxing long and green; again he would stand
still and listen to the pretty song of the little birds in the thickets
or hearken to the clear crow of the cock daring the sky to rain,
whereat he would laugh, for it took but little to tickle Robin's
heart into merriment. So he trudged manfully along, ever willing to stop for this reason or for that, and ever ready to chat
with such merry lasses as he met now and then. So the morning
slipped along, but yet he met no beggar with whom he could
change clothes. Quoth he, "If I do not change my luck in haste,
I am like to have an empty day of it, for it is well nigh half
gone already, and, although I have had a merry walk through
the countryside, I know nought of a beggar's life."

Then, after a while, he began to grow hungry, whereupon
his mind turned from thoughts of springtime and flowers and
birds and dwelt upon boiled capons, Malmsey, white bread,
and the like, with great tenderness. Quoth he to himself, "I

205

would I had Willie Wynkin's wishing coat; I know right well what I should wish for, and this it should be." Here he marked upon the fingers of his left hand with the forefinger of his right hand those things which he wished for. "Firstly, I would have a sweet brown pie of tender larks; mark ye, not dry cooked, but with a good sop of gravy to moisten it withal. Next, I would have a pretty pullet, fairly boiled, with tender pigeons' eggs, cunningly sliced, garnishing the platter around. With these I would have a long, slim loaf of wheaten bread that hath been baked upon the hearth; it should be warm from the fire, with glossy brown crust, the color of the hair of mine own maid, Marian, and this same crust should be as crisp and brittle as the thin white ice that lies across the furrows in the early winter's morning. These will do for the more solid things; but with these I must have three pottles, fat and round. One full of Malmsey, one of Canary, and one brimming full of mine own dear lusty sack." Thus spoke Robin to himself, his mouth growing moist at the corners with the thoughts of the good things he had raised in his own mind.

So, talking to himself, he came to where the dusty road turned sharply around the hedge, all tender with the green of the coming leaf, and there he saw before him a stout fellow sitting upon a stile, swinging his legs in idleness. All about this lusty rogue dangled divers pouches and bags of different sizes and kinds, a dozen or more, with great, wide, gaping mouths, like a brood of hungry daws. His coat was gathered in at his waist, and was patched with as many colors as there are stripes upon a Maypole in the springtide. On his head he wore a great tall leathern cap, and across his knees rested a stout quarter-staff of blackthorn, full as long and heavy as Robin's. As jolly a beggar was he as ever trod the lanes and byways of Notting-hamshire, for his eyes were as gray as slate, and snapped and twinkled and danced with merriment, and his black hair curled close all over his head in little rings of kinkiness.

"Halloa, good fellow," quoth Robin, when he had come nigh to the other, "what art thou doing here this merry day, when the flowers are peeping and the buds are swelling?"

Then the other winked one eye, and straightway trolled forth in a merry voice:

> "I sit upon the stile,
>   And I sing a little while
>   As I wait for my own true dear, O,
>   For the sun is shining bright,
>   And the leaves are dancing light,
>   And the little fowl sings she is near, O.

"And so it is with me, bully boy, saving that my doxy cometh not."

"Now that is a right sweet song," quoth Robin, "and, were I in the right mind to listen to thee, I could bear well to hear more; but I have two things of seriousness to ask of thee; so listen, I prythee."

At this the jolly Beggar cocked his head on one side, like a rogue of a magpie. Quoth he, "I am an ill jug to pour heavy things into, good friend, and, if I mistake not, thou hast few serious words to spare at any time."

"Nay," quoth jolly Robin, "what I would say first is the most serious of all thoughts to me, to wit, 'where shall I get somewhat to eat and drink?'"

"Sayst thou so?" quoth the Beggar. "Marry, I make no such serious thoughts upon the matter. I eat when I can get it, and munch my crust when I can get no crumb; likewise, when there is no ale to be had I wash the dust from out my throat with a trickle of cold water. I was sitting here, as thou camest upon me, bethinking myself whether I should break my fast or no. I do love to let my hunger grow mightily keen ere I eat, for then a dry crust is as good to me as a venison pasty with suet and raisins is to stout King Harry. I have a sharp hunger upon me now, but methinks in a short while it will ripen to a right mellow appetite."

"Now, in good sooth," quoth merry Robin, laughing, "thou hast a quaint tongue betwixt thy teeth. But hast thou truly nought but a dry crust about thee? Methinks thy bags and pouches are fat and lusty for such thin fare."

"Why, mayhap there is some other cold fare therein," said the Beggar, slyly.

"And hast thou nought to drink but cold water?" said Robin.

"Never so much as a drop," quoth the Beggar. "Over beyond yon clump of trees is as sweet a little inn as ever thou hast lifted eyelid upon; but I go not thither, for they have a nasty way with me. Once, when the good Prior of Emmet was dining there, the landlady set a dear little tart of stewed crabs and barley-sugar upon the window sill to cool, and, seeing it there, and fearing it might be lost, I took it with me till that I could find the owner thereof. Ever since then they have acted very ill toward me; yet truth bids me say that they have the best ale there that ever rolled over my tongue."

At this Robin laughed aloud. "Marry," quoth he, "they did ill toward thee for thy kindness. But tell me truly, what hast thou in thy pouches?"

"Why," quoth the Beggar, peeping into the mouths of his bags, "I find here a goodly piece of pigeon pie, wrapped in a cabbage leaf to hold the gravy. Here I behold a dainty streaked piece of brawn, and here a fair lump of white bread. Here I find four oaten cakes and a cold knuckle of ham. Ha! in sooth 'tis strange; but here I behold six eggs that must have come by accident from some poultry yard hereabouts. They are raw, but roasted upon the coals, and spread with a piece of butter that I see"—

"Peace, good friend!" cried Robin, holding up his hand. "Thou makest my poor stomach quake with joy for what thou tellest me so sweetly. If thou wilt give me to eat, I will straightway hie me to that little inn thou didst tell of but now and will bring a skin of ale for thy drinking and mine."

"Friend, thou hast said enough," said the Beggar, getting down from the stile; "I will feast thee with the best that I have and bless Saint Cedric for thy company. But, sweet chuck, I prythee bring three quarts of ale at least, one for thy drinking and two for mine, for my thirst is such that methinks I can drink ale as the sands of the River Dee drink salt water."

So Robin straightway left the Beggar, who, upon his part,

mister
mckee

went to a budding lime bush back of the hedge and there spread his feast upon the grass and roasted his eggs upon a little fagot fire, with a deftness gained by long labor in that line. After a while back came Robin bearing a goodly skin of ale upon his shoulder, which he laid upon the grass. Then, looking upon the feast spread upon the ground—and a fair sight it was to look upon—he slowly rubbed his hand over his stomach, for to his hungry eyes it seemed the fairest sight that he had beheld in all his life.

"Friend," said the Beggar, "let me feel the weight of that skin."

"Yea, truly," quoth Robin, "help thyself, sweet chuck, and meantime let me see whether thy pigeon pie is fresh or no."

So the one seized upon the ale and the other upon the pigeon pie, and nothing was heard for a while but the munching of food and the gurgle of ale as it left the skin.

At last, after a long time had passed thus, Robin pushed the food away from him and heaved a great sigh of deep content, for he felt as though he had been made all over anew.

"And now, good friend," quoth he, leaning upon one elbow, "I would have at thee about that other matter of seriousness of which I spoke not long since."

"How!" said the Beggar, reproachfully; "thou wouldst surely not talk of things appertaining to serious affairs upon such ale as this!"

"Nay," quoth Robin, laughing. "I would not check thy thirst, sweet friend; drink whilst I talk to thee. Thus it is: I would have thee know that I have taken a liking to thy craft and would fain have a taste of a beggar's life mine own self."

Said the Beggar: "I marvel not that thou hast taken a liking to my manner of life, good fellow, but 'to like' and 'to do' are two matters of different sorts. I tell thee, friend, one must serve a long apprenticeship ere one can learn to be even so much as a clapper-dudgeon, much less a crank or an Abraham-man. I tell thee, lad, thou art too old to enter upon that which it may take thee years to catch the hang of."

"Mayhap that may be so," quoth Robin, "for I bring to mind that Gaffer Swanthold sayeth Jack Shoemaker maketh ill bread; Tom Baker maketh ill shoon. Nevertheless, I have a mind to taste a beggar's life and need but the clothing to be as good as any."

"I tell thee, fellow," said the Beggar, "If thou wert clad as sweetly as good Saint Wynten, the patron of our craft, thou wouldst never make a beggar. Marry, the first jolly traveler that thou wouldst meet would beat thee to a pudding for thrusting thy nose into a craft that belongeth not to thee."

"Nevertheless," quoth Robin, "I would have a try at it; and methinks I shall change clothes with thee, for thy garb seemeth to be pretty, not to say gay. So not only will I change clothes, but I will give thee two golden angels to boot. I have brought my stout staff with me, thinking that I might have to rap some one of the brethren of thy cloth over the head by way of argument in this matter, but I love thee so much for the feast thou hast given me that I would not lift even my little finger against thee, so thou needst not have a crumb of fear."

210

To this the Beggar listened with his knuckles resting against his hips, and when Robin had ended he cocked his head on one side and thrust his tongue into his cheek.

"Marry come up," quoth he at last. "Lift thy finger against me, forsooth! Art thou out of thy wits, man? My name is Riccon Hazel, and I come from Holywell, in Flintshire, over by the River Dee. I tell thee, knave, I have cracked the head of many a better man than thou art, and even now I would scald thy crown for thee but for the ale thou hast given me. Now thou shalt not have so much as one tag-rag of my coat, even could it save thee from hanging."

"Now, fellow," said Robin, "it would ill suit me to spoil thy pretty head for thee, but I tell thee plainly, that but for this feast I would do that to thee would stop thy traveling the country for many a day to come. Keep thy lips shut, lad, or thy luck will tumble out of thy mouth with thy speech!"

"Now out, and alas for thee, man, for thou hast bred thyself ill this day!" cried the Beggar, rising and taking up his staff. "Take up thy club and defend thyself, fellow, for I will not only beat thee but I will take from thee thy money and leave thee not so much as a clipped groat to buy thyself a lump of goose-grease to rub thy cracked crown withal. So defend thyself, I say."

Then up leaped merry Robin and snatched up his staff also. "Take my money, if thou canst," quoth he. "I promise freely to give thee every farthing if thou dost touch me." And he twirled his staff in his fingers till it whistled again.

Then the Beggar swung his staff also and struck a mighty blow at Robin, which the yeoman turned. Three blows the Beggar struck, yet never one touched so much as a hair of Robin's head. Then stout Robin saw his chance, and, ere you could count three, Riccon's staff was over the hedge, and Riccon himself lay upon the green grass with no more motion than you could find in an empty pudding-bag.

"How now!" quoth merry Robin, laughing. "Wilt thou have my hide or my money, sweet chuck?" But to this the other answered never a word. Then Robin, seeing his plight, and that

211

he was stunned with the blow, ran, still laughing, and brought the skin of ale and poured some of it on the Beggar's head and some down his throat, so that presently he opened his eyes and looked around as though wondering why he lay upon his back.

Then Robin, seeing that he had somewhat gathered the wits that had just been rapped out of his head, said: "Now, good fellow, wilt thou change clothes with me, or shall I have to tap thee again? Here are two golden angels if thou wilt give me freely all thy rags and bags and thy cap and things. If thou givest them not freely I much fear me I shall have to—" and he looked up and down his staff.

Then Riccon sat up and rubbed the bump on his crown. "Now, out upon it!" quoth he. "I did think to drub thee sweetly, fellow. I know not how it is, but I seem, as it were, to have bought more beer than I can drink. If I must give up my clothes, I must, but first promise me, by thy word as a true yeoman, that thou wilt take nought from me but my clothes."

"I promise on the word of a true yeoman," quoth Robin, thinking that the fellow had a few pennies that he would save.

Thereupon the Beggar drew a little knife that hung at his side, and, ripping up the lining of his coat, drew thence ten bright golden pounds, which he laid upon the ground beside him with a cunning wink at Robin. "Now thou mayst have my clothes and welcome," said he, "and thou mightest have had them in exchange for thine without the cost of a single farthing, far less two golden angels."

"Marry," quoth Robin, laughing, "thou art a sly fellow, and I tell thee truly, had I known thou hadst so much money by thee maybe thou mightest not have carried it away, for I warrant thou didst not come honestly by it."

Then each stripped off his clothes and put on those of the other, and as lusty a beggar was Robin Hood as e'er you could find of a summer's day. But stout Riccon of Holywell skipped and leaped and danced for joy of the fair suit of Lincoln green that he had so gotten. Quoth he, "I am a gay feathered bird now. Truly, my dear Moll Peascod would never know me in this dress. Thou mayst keep the cold pieces of the feast, friend, for

I mean to live well and lustily while my money lasts and my clothes are gay."

So he turned and left Robin and, crossing the stile, was gone, but Robin heard him singing from beyond the hedge as he strode away:—

> "For Polly is smiling and Molly is glad
> When the beggar comes in at the door,
> And Jack and Dick call him a fine lusty lad,
> And the hostess runs up a great score.
> Then hey, Willy Waddykin,
> Stay, Billy Waddykin,
> And let the brown ale flow free, flow free,
> The beggar's the man for me."

Robin listened till the song ended in the distance, then he also crossed the stile into the road, but turned his toes away from where the Beggar had gone. The road led up a gentle hill and up the hill Robin walked, a half score or more of bags dangling about his legs. Onward he strolled for a long time, but other adventure he found not. The road was bare of all else but himself, as he went kicking up little clouds of dust at each footstep; for it was noontide, the most peaceful time of all the day, next to twilight. All the earth was silent in the restfulness of eating-time; the plough-horses stood in the furrow munching, with great bags over their noses holding sweet food, the plough-man sat under the hedge and the plough-boy also, and they, too, were munching, each one holding a great piece of bread in one fist and a great piece of cheese in the other.

So Robin, with all the empty road to himself, strode along whistling merrily, his bags and pouches bobbing and dangling at his thighs. At last he came to where a little grass-grown path left the road and, passing through a stile and down a hill, led into a little dell and on across a rill in the valley and up the hill on the other side, till it reached a windmill that stood on the cap of the rise where the wind bent the trees in swaying motion. Robin looked at the spot and liked it, and, for no reason but that his fancy led him, he took the little path and walked down

213

mister
mc kee

the grassy sunny slope of the open meadow, and so came to the
little dingle and, ere he knew it, upon four lusty fellows that
sat with legs outstretched around a goodly feast spread upon
the ground.

Four merry beggars were they, and each had slung about
his neck a little board that rested upon his breast. One board
had written upon it, "I am blind," another, "I am deaf," another, "I am dumb," and the fourth, "Pity the lame one." But
although all these troubles written upon the boards seemed so
grievous, the four stout fellows sat around feasting as merrily
as though Cain's wife had never opened the pottle that held
misfortunes and let them forth like a cloud of flies to pester us.

The deaf man was the first to hear Robin, for he said, "Hark,
brothers, I hear someone coming." And, the blind man was the
first to see him, for he said, "He is an honest man, brothers, and
one of like craft to ourselves." Then the dumb man called to him
in a great voice and said, "Welcome, brother; come and sit
whilst there is still some of the feast left and a little Malmsey in
the pottle." At this the lame man, who had taken off his wooden
leg and unstrapped his own leg, and was sitting with it stretched

214

out upon the grass so as to rest it, made room for Robin among them. "We are glad to see thee, brother," said he, holding out the flask of Malmsey.

"Marry," quoth Robin, laughing, and weighing the flask in his hands ere he drank, "methinks it is no more than seemly of you all to be glad to see me, seeing that I bring sight to the blind, speech to the dumb, hearing to the deaf, and such a lusty leg to a lame man. I drink to your happiness, brothers, as I may not drink to your health, seeing ye are already hale, wind and limb."

At this all grinned, and the Blind beggar, who was the chief man among them and was the broadest shouldered and most lusty rascal of all, smote Robin upon the shoulder, swearing he was a right merry wag.

"Whence comest thou, lad?" asked the Dumb man.

"Why," quoth Robin. "I came this morning from sleeping overnight in Sherwood."

"Is it even so?" said the Deaf man. "I would not for all the money we four are carrying to Lincoln Town sleep one night in Sherwood. If Robin Hood caught one of our trade in his woodlands he would, methinks, clip his ears."

"Methinks he would, too," quoth Robin, laughing. "But what money is this that ye speak of?"

Then up spake the Lame man: "Our king, Peter of York," said he, "hath sent us to Lincoln with those moneys that—"

"Stay, brother Hodge," quoth the Blind man, breaking into the talk; "I would not doubt our brother here, but bear in mind we know him not. "What art thou, brother? Upright-man, Jurkman, Clapper-dudgeon, Dommerer, or Abram-man?"

At these words Robin looked from one man to the other with mouth agape. "Truly," quoth he, "I trust I am an upright man, at least, I strive to be; but I know not what thou meanest by such jargon, brother. It were much more seemly, methinks, if yon Dumb man, who hath a sweet voice, would give us a song."

At these words a silence fell on all, and after a while the Blind man spoke again. Quoth he, "Thou dost surely jest when thou sayest that thou dost not understand such words. Answer me this: Hast thou ever fibbed a chouse quarrons in the Rome pad for the loure in his bung?"

"Now out upon it," quoth Robin Hood, testily; "an ye make sport of me by pattering such gibberish, it will be ill for you all, I tell you. I have the best part of a mind to crack the heads of all four of you, and would do so, too, but for the sweet Malmsey ye have given me. Brother, pass the pottle lest it grow cold."

"But all the four beggars leaped to their feet when Robin had done speaking, and the Blind man snatched up a heavy knotted cudgel that lay beside him on the grass, as did the others likewise. Then Robin, seeing that things were like to go ill with him, albeit he knew not what all the coil was about, leaped to his feet also, and, catching up his trusty staff, clapped his back against the tree and stood upon his guard against them. "How, now!" cried he, twirling his staff betwixt his fingers, "would you four stout fellows set upon one man? Stand back, ye rascals, or I will score your pates till they have as many marks upon them as a pot-house door! Are ye mad? I have done you no harm."

"Thou liest!" quoth the one who pretended to be blind, and who, being the lustiest villain, was the leader of the others; "thou liest! for thou hast come amongst us as a vile spy. But thine ears have heard too much for thy body's good, and thou goest not forth from this place unless thou goest feet foremost, for this day thou shalt die! Come, brothers, all together! Down with him!" Then, whirling up his cudgel, he rushed upon Robin as an angry bull rushes upon a red rag. But Robin was ready for any happening. "Crick! Crack!" he struck two blows as quick as a wink and down went the Blind man, rolling over and over upon the grass.

At this the others bore back and stood at a little distance scowling upon Robin. "Come on, ye scum!" cried he, merrily. "Here be cakes and ale for all. Now, who will be next served?"

To this speech the beggars answered never a word, but they looked at Robin as great Blunderbore looked upon stout Jack, the slayer of giants, as though they would fain eat him, body and bones; nevertheless, they did not care to come nigher to

216

him and his terrible staff. Then, seeing them so hesitate, Robin of a sudden leaped upon them, striking even as he leaped. Down went the Dumb man, and away flew his cudgel from his hand as he fell. At this the others ducked to avoid another blow, then, taking to their heels, scampered, the one one way and the other the other, as though they had the west wind's boots upon their feet. Robin looked after them, laughing, and thought that never had he seen so fleet a runner as the Lame man; but neither of the beggars stopped nor turned around, for each felt in his mind the wind of Robin's cudgel about his ears.

Then Robin turned to the two stout knaves lying upon the ground. Quoth he, "These fellows spake somewhat about certain moneys they were taking to Lincoln; methinks I may find it upon this stout blind fellow, who hath as keen sight as e'er a trained woodsman in Nottingham or Yorkshire. It were a pity to let sound money stay in the pockets of such thieving knaves." So saying he stooped over the burly rascal and searched among his rags and tatters, till presently his fingers felt a leathern pouch slung around his body beneath his patched and tattered coat. This he stripped away, and, weighing it in his hands, bethought himself that it was mightily heavy. "It were a sweet thing," said he to himself, "if this were filled with gold instead of copper pence." Then, sitting down upon the grass, he opened the pocket and looked into it. There he found four round rolls wrapped up in dressed sheepskin; one of these rolls he opened; then his mouth gaped, and his eyes stared, I wot, as though they would never close again, for what did he see but fifty pounds of bright golden money! He opened the other pockets and found in each one the same, fifty bright new-stamped golden pounds. Quoth Robin, "I have oft heard that the Beggars' Guild was over rich, but never did I think that they sent such sums as this to their treasury. I shall take it with me; for it will be better used for charity and the good of my merry band than in the enriching of such knaves as these." So saying he rolled up the money in the sheepskin again, and putting it back in the purse, he thrust the pouch into his own bosom. Then taking up the flask of Malmsey he held it toward the two fellows

mister mckee

lying on the grass, and quoth he, "Sweet friends, I drink your health and thank you dearly for what ye have so kindly given me this day, and so I wish you good den." Then, taking up his staff, he left the spot and went merrily upon his way.

But when the two stout beggars that had been rapped upon the head roused themselves and sat up, and when the others had gotten over their fright and come back, they were as sad and woebegone as four frogs in dry weather, for two of them had cracked crowns, their Malmsey was all gone, and they had not so much as a farthing to cross their palms withal. As for the treasury of the Beggars' Guild at the Inn of the Beggar's Bush, near Lincoln Town, it was two hundred pounds poorer than it would have been had bold Robin not met the Blind man, the Deaf man, the Dumb man, and the Lame man nigh to the highroad that led to Blyth.

But after Robin left the little dell he strode along merrily, singing as he went; and so blithe was he and such a stout beggar, and, withal, so fresh and clean, that every merry lass he met had a sweet word for him and felt no fear, whilst the very dogs, that most times hate the sight of a beggar, snuffed at his legs in friendly wise and wagged their tails pleasantly; for dogs know an honest man by his smell, and an honest man Robin was —in his own way.

Thus he went along till at last he had come to the wayside cross nigh Ollerton, and, being somewhat tired, he sat him down to rest upon the grassy bank in front of it. "It groweth nigh time," quoth he to himself, "that I were getting back again to Sherwood; yet it would please me well to have one more merry adventure ere I go back again to my jolly band." So he looked up the road and down the road to see who might come, until at last he saw someone drawing near, riding upon a horse. When the traveler came nigh enough for him to see him well, Robin laughed, for a strange enough figure he cut. He was a thin, weazened man, and, to look upon him, you could not tell whether he was thirty years old or sixty, so dried up was he even to skin and bone. As for the nag, it was as thin as the rider, and both looked as though they had been baked in Mother Huddle's Oven, where folk are dried up so that they live forever. The poor nag's neck bent down instead of up, as most horses' do, and his mane was as ragged as though the mice had made nests in it; his backbone stood up sharp and jagged, like a new-turned furrow when the plough first passes, and his ribs showed beneath his skin like the hoops on a barrel of five-year-old ale. Thus the horse came hobbling along, and at every step the rider popped up and down in his saddle, so that his head bobbed and wagged upon his lean neck all in time to the motion of the nag. At this sight merry Robin laughed till the tears stood on his cheeks, for, as though to make the sight still more droll, the rider wore great clogs upon his feet instead of shoon, the soles whereof were made of wood half a palm's breadth in thickness, and studded all over with great nails.

But although Robin laughed, he knew the wayfarer to be a
219

certain rich Corn Engrosser of Worksop, who more than once had bought all the grain in the countryside and held it till it reached even famine prices, thus making much money from the needs of poor people, and for this he was hated far and near by everyone that knew aught of him.

Quoth Robin to himself, when he saw who it was that came, "Oho, my thieving magpie! It is thou, is it? Now I would that I could pluck thee bare, even to the naked skin! But thou art so sly that I misdoubt finding aught of thy ill-gotten gains upon thee so nigh to Sherwood. Nevertheless, I will see what can be done; for, as Gaffer Swanthold says, 'If Ned never tries, Ned never does.' "

So, after a while, the Corn Engrosser came riding up to where Robin sat; whereupon merry Robin stepped straightway forth, in all his rags and tatters, his bags and pouches dangling about him, and laid his hand upon the horse's bridle-rein, calling upon the other to stop.

"Who art thou, fellow, that doth dare to stop me thus upon the King's highway?" said the lean man, in a dry, sour voice.

"Pity a poor beggar," quoth Robin. "Give me but a farthing to buy me a piece of bread."

"Now, out upon thee!" snarled the other. "Such sturdy rogues as thou art are better safe in the prisons or dancing upon nothing, with a hempen collar about the neck, than strolling the highways so freely."

"Tut," quoth Robin, "how thou talkest! Thou and I are brothers, man. Do we not both take from the poor people that which they can ill spare? Do we not make our livings by doing nought of any good? Do we not both live without touching palm to honest work? Have we either of us ever rubbed thumbs over honestly-gained farthings? Go to! We are brothers, I say; only thou art rich and I am poor; wherefore, I prythee once more, give me a penny."

"Dost thou prate so to me, sirrah?" cried the Corn Engrosser, in a rage. "Now I will have thee soundly whipped if ever I catch thee in any town where the law can lay hold of thee! As for giving thee a penny, I swear to thee that I have not so much

mister
mckee

as a single groat in my purse. Were Robin Hood himself to take me, he might search me from crown to heel without finding the smallest piece of money upon me. I trust I am too sly to travel so nigh to Sherwood with money in my pouch and that thief at large in the woods."

Then merry Robin looked up and down, as if to see that there was no one nigh, and then, coming close to the Corn Engrosser, he stood on tiptoe and spake in his ear: "Thinkest thou in sooth that I am a beggar, as I seem to be? Look upon me. There is not a grain of dirt upon my hands or my face or my body; didst thou ever see a beggar so? I tell thee I am as honest a man as thou art. Look, friend." Here he took the purse of money from his breast and showed to the dazzled eyes of the Corn Engrosser the bright golden pieces. "Friend, these rags serve but to hide an honest rich man from the eyes of Robin Hood."

"Put up thy money, lad," cried the other, quickly. "Art thou a fool, to trust to beggar's rags to shield thee from Robin Hood? If he caught thee he would strip thee to the skin, for he hates a lusty beggar as he doth a fat priest or those of my kind."

"Is it indeed so?" quoth Robin. "Had I known this, mayhap I had not come hereabouts in this garb. But I must go forward now, as much depends upon my journeying. Where goest thou, friend?"

"I go to Grantham," said the Corn Engrosser; "but I shall lodge tonight at Newark; if I can get so far upon my way."

"Why, I myself am on the way to Newark," quoth merry Robin; "so that, as two honest men are better than one in roads beset by such a fellow as this Robin Hood, I will jog along with thee, if thou hast no dislike to my company."

"Why, as thou art an honest fellow and a rich fellow," said the Corn Engrosser, "I mind not thy company; but, in sooth, I have no great fondness for beggars."

"Then forward," quoth Robin, "for the day wanes and it will be dark ere we reach Newark." So off they went, the lean horse hobbling along as before, and Robin running beside, albeit he was so quaking with laughter within him that he could hardly

222

stand; yet he dared not laugh aloud, lest the Corn Engrosser should suspect something. So they traveled along till they reached a hill just on the outskirts of Sherwood. Here the lean man checked his lean horse into a walk, for the road was steep, and he wished to save his nag's strength, having far to go ere he reached Newark. Then he turned in his saddle and spake to Robin again, for the first time since they had left the cross. "Here is thy greatest danger, friend," said he, "for here we are nighest to that vile thief, Robin Hood, and the place where he dwells. Beyond this we come again to the open honest country, and so are more safe in our journeying."

"Alas!" quoth Robin, "I would that I had as little money by me as thou hast, for this day I fear that Robin Hood will get every groat of my wealth."

Then the other looked at Robin and winked cunningly. Quoth he, "I tell thee, friend, that I have nigh as much by me as thou hast, but it is hidden so that never a knave in Sherwood could find it."

"Thou dost surely jest," quoth Robin. "How could one hide so much as two hundred pounds upon his person?"

"Now, as thou art so honest a fellow, and, withal, so much younger than I am, I will tell thee that which I have told to no man in all the world before, and thus thou mayst learn never again to do such a foolish thing as to trust to beggar's garb to guard thee against Robin Hood. Seest thou these clogs upon my feet?"

"Yea," quoth Robin, laughing; "truly, they are large enough for any man to see, even were his sight as foggy as that of Peter Patter, who never could see when it was time to go to work."

"Peace, friend," said the Corn Engrosser, "for this is no matter for jesting. The soles of these clogs are not what they seem to be, for each one is a sweet little box; and by twisting the second nail from the toe, the upper of the shoe and part of the sole lifts up like a lid, and in the spaces within are fourscore and ten bright golden pounds in each shoe, all wrapped in hair, to keep them from clinking and so telling tales of themselves."

When the Corn Engrosser had told this, Robin broke into a roar of laughter, and, laying his hands upon the bridle-rein, stopped the sad-looking nag. "Stay, good friend," quoth he, between bursts of merriment; "thou art the slyest old fox that e'er I saw in all my life!—In the soles of his shoon, quotha! —If ever I trust a poor seeming man again, shave my beard and paint it blue! A corn factor, a horse jockey, an estate agent, and a jackdaw for cunningness, say I!" And he laughed again till he shook in his shoes with mirth.

All this time the Corn Engrosser had been staring at Robin, his mouth agape with wonder. "Art thou mad," quoth he, "to talk in this way, so loud and in such a place? Let us forward, and save thy mirth till we are safe and sound at Newark."

"Nay," quoth Robin, the tears of merriment wet on his cheeks, "on second thoughts I go no farther than here, for I have good friends hereabouts. Thou mayst go forward if thou dost list, thou sweet pretty fellow, but thou must go forward barefoot, for I am afraid that thy shoon must be left behind. Off with them, friend, for I tell thee I have taken a great fancy to them."

At these words the Corn Factor grew pale as a linen napkin. "Who art thou that talkest so?" said he.

Then merry Robin laughed again, and quoth he, "Men hereabouts call me Robin Hood; so, sweet friend, thou hadst best do my bidding and give me thy shoes, wherefore hasten, I prythee, or else thou wilt not get to fair Newark Town till after dark."

At the sound of the name of Robin Hood the Corn Factor quaked with fear, so that he had to seize his horse by the mane to save himself from falling off its back. Then straightway, and without more words, he stripped off his clogs and let them fall upon the road. Robin, still holding the bridle-rein, stooped and picked them up; then he said, "Sweet friend, I am used to ask those that I have dealings with to come and feast at Sherwood with me. I will not ask thee, because of our pleasant journey together; for I tell thee there be those in Sherwood that would not be so gentle with thee as I have been. The name of Corn Engrosser leaves a nasty taste upon the tongue of all honest men. Take a fool's advice of me and come no more so nigh to Sherwood, or mayhap some day thou mayst of a sudden find a clothyard shaft betwixt thy ribs. So, with this, I give thee good den." Hereupon he clapped his hand to the horse's flank and off went nag and rider. But the man's face was all bedewed with the sweat of fright, and never again, I wot, was he found so close to Sherwood Forest as he had been this day.

Robin stood and looked after him, and, when he was fairly gone, turned, laughing, and entered the forest carrying the shoes in his hand.

That night in sweet Sherwood the red fires glowed brightly in wavering light on tree and bush, and all around sat or lay the stout fellows of the band to hear Robin Hood and Little John tell their adventures. First Little John began and told about his meeting with the three lasses, amid great shouts of laughter, for he was quaint of speech and told his doings merrily. Then Robin told of his meeting the stout beggar, and what befell behind the hedge under the lime tree. Then Little John told of meeting the good fellows at the inn, and Robin told of his adventure with the four beggars, and showed the money he had taken from them. Last of all, Little John told how he had prayed to Saint Dunstan with the Gray Friars and showed the gold that the Saint had sent him. This Robin matched with his story of meeting the Corn Engrosser at the cross near Ollerton, and held up the shoes that he had taken from the lean man. All listened closely, and again and again the woods rang with shouts of laughter.

When all was told, Friar Tuck spoke up, "Good master," said he, "thou hast had a pretty time, but still I hold to my saying, that the life of the barefoot friar is the merrier of the two."

"Nay," quoth Will Stutely, "I hold with our master, that he hath had the pleasanter doings of the two, for he hath had two stout bouts at quarterstaff this day."

So some of the band held with Robin Hood and some with Little John. As for me, I think— But I leave it with you to say for yourselves which you hold with.

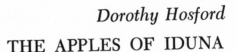

Dorothy Hosford

THE APPLES OF IDUNA

ILLUSTRATED BY *Claire and George Louden*

DIN often traveled forth from Asgard to take part in the affairs of men and to see what was going on in all the wide expanses of the world. One day he set out on such a journey, taking Loki and Hoenir with him. They wandered a long way over mountains and wasteland and at length they grew hungry. But food was hard to find in that lonely country.

They had walked many miles when they saw a herd of oxen grazing in a valley.

"There is food for us at last," said Hoenir.

They went down into the valley, and it was not long before they had one of the oxen roasting on a fire. While their meal cooked they stretched out on the ground to rest. When they thought the meat had cooked long enough they took it off the fire. But it was not yet ready. So they put it back over the embers and waited.

"I can wait no longer," cried Loki at last. "I am starving. Surely the meat is ready."

The gods scattered the fire once more and pulled forth the ox, but it seemed as though it had not even begun to cook. It was certainly not fit for eating.

This was a strange thing, and not even Odin knew the mean-

226

ing of it. As they wondered among themselves, they heard a voice speak from the great oak tree above them.

"It is because of me," said the voice, "that there is no virtue in your fire and your meat will not cook."

They looked up into the branches of the tree, and there sat a huge eagle.

"If you are willing to give me a share of the ox, then it will cook in the fire," said the eagle.

There was little the gods could do but agree to this. The eagle let himself float down from the tree and alighted by the fire. In no time at all the ox was roasted. At once the eagle took to himself the two hindquarters and the two forequarters as well.

This greediness angered Loki. He snatched up a great pole, brandished it with all his strength, and struck the eagle with it. The eagle plunged violently at the blow and whirled into the air. One end of the pole stuck fast to the eagle's back, and Loki's hands stuck fast to the other end. No matter how he tried he could not free them. Swooping and turning, the eagle dragged Loki after him in his flight, flying just low enough that Loki's feet and legs knocked against stones and rock heaps and trees. Loki thought his arms would be torn from his shoulders. He cried out for mercy.

"Put me down! Put me down!" begged Loki. "Free me and you shall have the whole ox for your own."

"I do not want the ox," cried the eagle. "I want only one thing —Iduna and her apples. Deliver them into my power, and I will set you free."

Iduna was the beautiful and beloved wife of the god Bragi. She guarded the most precious possession of the gods, the apples of youth. Unless they might eat of them the gods would grow old and feeble like mortal men. They kept the gods ever young. Iduna and her apples were priceless beyond words.

"Iduna and her apples! Such a thing cannot be done," shouted Loki.

"Then I will fly all day," screamed the eagle. "I will knock you against the rocks until you die." And he dragged Loki

227

through rough tree branches and against the sides of mountains and over the rocky earth. Loki could endure it no longer.

"I will do as you ask," he cried. "I will bring Iduna to you, and her apples as well."

"Give me your oath," said the eagle. Loki gave his oath. A time was set when Loki should put Iduna in the eagle's power.

The eagle straightway made Loki free and flew off into the sky. A much-bruised Loki returned to his companions, and all three set off on their homeward journey. But Odin and Hoenir did not know the promise which Loki had made.

Loki pondered how he could keep his word to the eagle, whom he now knew to be the giant Thjazi in disguise. When the appointed day came Loki approached Iduna.

"Iduna," he said, speaking gently, "yesterday I found a tree on which grow wondrous apples. It is in the wood to the north of Asgard. They are like your apples in color and shape. Surely they must have the same properties. Should we not gather them and bring them to Asgard?"

"There are no apples anywhere," said Iduna, "like to my apples."

"These are," said Loki. "They are very like. Come and look for yourself. If you bring your apples we can put them side by side and you will see."

So Iduna went with Loki to the wood, taking her apples with her. While they were in the wood the giant Thjazi swooped down in his eagle's plumage and carried Iduna and her apples off to his abode.

The gods soon missed Iduna. And they knew her apples were gone, for the signs of old age began to show among them. They grew bent and stiff and stooped.

Odin called a hasty council of the gods. They asked each other what they knew of Iduna.

"Where was she last seen?" asked Odin.

Heimdal had seen her walking out of Asgard with Loki. That was the last that was known of her.

Odin sent Thor to seize Loki and to bring him to the council. When Loki was brought the gods threatened him with tortures

They looked up into the tree and there sat a huge eagle.

and death unless he told what he knew of Iduna. Loki, frightened, admitted that Iduna had been carried off to Jötunheim.

"I will go in search of her," he cried, "if Freyja will lend me her falcon wings."

Freyja was more than willing. When Loki had put on the feather dress he flew to the north in the direction of Jötunheim.

He flew for a long time before he came to the home of Thjazi, the giant. Then he circled slowly overhead and saw Iduna walking below. She carried in her arms her golden casket of apples. Thjazi was nowhere to be seen, for he had rowed out to sea to fish. Loki quickly alighted on the ground beside Iduna.

"Hasten, Iduna," he cried, "I will rescue you." And he changed Iduna into the shape of a nut and flew off with her in his claws.

Loki had no sooner gone than Thjazi arrived home. At once he missed Iduna and her precious apples. Putting on his eagle's plumage, he flew into the air. Far off in the distance he saw the falcon flying. Instantly he took after him. The eagle's wings beat powerfully, making a deep rushing sound like a great wind. Thjazi drew nearer and nearer to Loki. Loki flew with all his might, but the eagle was bearing down upon the falcon just as the towers of Asgard came into view. With a last burst of strength Loki hastened toward the shining battlements.

The gods were on watch for Loki's return. They saw the falcon bearing the nut between his claws, with the eagle in close pursuit. Quickly they built a great pile of wood shavings just outside the wall of Asgard. As Loki came near he swooped down low over the shavings. Thjazi swooped down too, hoping to seize the falcon before he reached the safety of Asgard. Just as the eagle came close to the pile, the gods set fire to the shavings. Instantly the fire blazed up, but Thjazi could not stop himself. He plunged into the flames, and the feathers of his wings took fire. Then he could fly no more, and the gods slew him where he was.

There was great rejoicing within the walls of Asgard to have Iduna safe once more. And the gods grew young and bright again.

THOR'S
WONDERFUL JOURNEY

RETOLD BY *Hamilton Wright Mabie*

ILLUSTRATED BY *Walter R. Sabel*

THOR made many journeys and had many strange adventures; but there was one journey which was more wonderful than all the others, and which proves, moreover, that the strongest and truest are sometimes deceived by those who are weaker than themselves. The giants in old Norse times were not easy to conquer; but generally it was when they hid themselves behind lies and appeared to be what they were not that they succeeded for a time. Thor's strength was a noble thing because he used it to help men; but his truthfulness and honesty were nobler still.

One morning just as the sun was beginning to shine through the mists that overhung the world, the gates of Asgard opened, and Thor's chariot, drawn by the goats, rattled along the road. Thor and Loki were evidently off for a journey; but Thor was always going off somewhere, and nobody who saw him now thought that he was starting out to try his strength with the most powerful things in the whole earth. Nor did he know it. All day long the chariot rolled across the level stretches of meadow and through the valleys, leaving the echoes shouting to each other from the overhanging mountains as it passed by. At night it stopped at the house of a poor peasant, and Thor stepped down and stood in the doorway.

"Can you lodge two travelers over night?" he asked.

230

"Certainly," said the peasant, "but we can give you nothing to eat, for we have nothing for ourselves."

"Give yourselves no trouble about that," answered Thor cheerfully; "I can provide for all."

He went back to Loki, who got out of the chariot; and then to the great astonishment of the people in the house, Thor killed both his goats, and in a minute they were ready for cooking. The great pot was soon sending savory odors through the house, and the whole family with their strange guests sat down shortly to a bountiful supper.

"The more you eat the better I shall like it," said Thor, as they took their places at the table, "but do not on any account break the bones; when you have done with them throw them into the skins which I have spread out on the hearth."

The peasant and his wife and Thjalfe and Roskva, their two children, ate bountifully; but Thjalfe broke one of the bones to get the marrow. The next morning Thor was up with the sun, and when he dressed himself he took the hammer and held it over the goatskins: and immediately the bones flew into place, and the skins covered them, and there were the two goats as full of life as when they started out the day before. But one of the goats limped; and when Thor saw it he was so angry that he looked like a thundercloud, and his fingers closed so tightly round Mjolner that his knuckles were white. Thjalfe, who had been looking with the rest of the family in speechless wonder, was frightened half out of his wits when he saw Thor's rage, and would have run away if he could. The poor peasant and his wife were equally terrified and besought Thor that he would not destroy them. Seeing them in such misery Thor's anger died out, and he said he would forgive them, but Thjalfe and Roskva must henceforth be his servants. So taking the two children, and leaving the goats with their parents for safe keeping, Thor and Loki set out again.

Thor had decided to go to Jötunheim, and all the morning they traveled eastward until they reached the shore of the sea. They crossed the wide waters quickly and climbed up on the further shore of Jötunheim. Mists floated over the land, and

231

great rocks rose along the coast so stern and black from the wash of the sea and the fury of storms that they seemed like strong giants guarding their country against the giant-queller. Thor led the way, and they soon entered a deep forest through which they traveled until nightfall, Thjalfe, who was very fleet of foot, carrying the sack of provisions. As night came on they looked about for shelter, and came upon an immense building with a whole side opening into a great room off which they found five smaller rooms. This was just what he wanted, although they could not imagine why anyone had built such a house in that lonely place. After supper, weary with the long journey, they were soon in a deep sleep.

Three or four hours went by quietly enough, but about midnight they were suddenly awakened by an awful uproar, which shook the building to its foundations and made the whole earth tremble. Thor called the others and told them to go into the further rooms. Half dead with fright they did so, but Thor stretched himself, hammer in hand, at the wide entrance. As soon as there was light enough to see about him, Thor went into the woods, and had gone but a little way when he came upon an enormous giant, fast asleep, and snoring so loudly that the very trees shook around him. Thor quickly buckled on his belt of strength, and had no sooner done so than the giant awoke and sprang to his feet. The whole earth shook under him, and he towered as far over Thor, as a great oak does over the fern that grows at its foot. Thor was never frightened, but he had never heard of such a giant before and he looked at him with honest surprise.

"Who are you?" he asked, after looking up to the great face.

"I am Skrymer," answered the giant, "but I don't need to ask your name. You are Thor. But what have you done with my glove?"

And stretching out his great hand the giant picked up his glove, which was nothing less than the building Thor and the others had spent the night in.

"Would you like to have me travel with you?" continued the giant.

"Certainly," said Thor, although it was plainly to be seen that neither Thjalfe nor Roskva wanted such a companion. Skrymer thereupon untied his sack and took out his breakfast, and the others followed his example, taking care, however, to put a comfortable distance between themselves and their dangerous fellow-traveler. After breakfast Skrymer proposed that they should put all their provisions into one bag, to which Thor consented, and they started off, the giant tramping on ahead and carrying the sack on his broad back.

All day long he walked steadily on, taking such tremendous strides that the others could hardly keep up with him. When night came he stopped under a great oak.

"There," said he, throwing down the sack; "take that and get some supper; I am going to sleep."

The words were hardly out of his mouth before he began to snore as loudly as the night before. Thor took the sack, but the harder he tried to loosen the string the tighter it drew, and with all his strength he could not untie a single knot. Finding he could not get into the sack, and hearing the giant snore so peacefully at his side, Thor's anger blazed out, and grasping the hammer he struck the giant full on the head. Skrymer opened his eyes drowsily.

"Did a leaf fall on my head?" he called out sleepily, without getting up. "Have you had your supper yet, and are you going to bed?"

In a minute he was snoring again. Thor went and lay down under another oak; but at midnight the giant began to snore so heavily that the forest resounded with the noise. Thor was fairly beside himself with rage, and swinging his hammer struck Skrymer such a tremendous blow that the hammer sank to the handle in his head. The giant opened his eyes and sat up.

"What is the matter now?" he called out; "did an acorn fall on my head? How are you getting on, Thor?"

"Oh, I am just awake," said Thor, stepping back quickly. "It is only midnight, and we may sleep awhile longer."

Thor watched until the giant had fallen asleep again and just at daybreak dealt him the most terrible blow that he had ever

given with the hammer. It flashed through and buried itself out of sight in Skrymer's forehead. The giant sprang on his feet and began to stroke his beard.

"Are there any birds up there?" he asked, looking into the oak. "I thought a feather dropped on my head. Are you awake, Thor? It is full time to dress, and you are near the end of your journey. The city of Utgard is not far off. I heard you whispering together that I was a man of great stature, but you will find much larger men in Utgard. Take my advice, and when you get there don't boast very much, for they will not take boasting from such little fellows as you are. You would do well to turn back and go home while you have a chance; but if you will go on, take the road to the eastward—my way takes me to the north." And, swinging the sack of provisions over his shoulder, Skrymer plunged into the forest and was soon out of sight.

Thor and his companions pushed on as fast as they could until noon, when suddenly a great city rose before them, on a vast plain, the walls of which were so high that they had to lean back as far as they could to see the top. A great gate, heavily barred, stopped them at the entrance; but they crept between the bars. After going a little distance they came upon a palace and, the doors being open, went in and found themselves in a great hall with long seats on either side, and on these seats rows of gigantic men larger than Skrymer. When they saw Utgard-Loki, who was the king of that country, they saluted him; but he sat for a long time without taking any notice of them. At last smiling contemptuously he said: "It is tiresome for travelers to be asked about a long journey; but if I am not mistaken this little fellow is Thor. Perhaps, however, you are really larger than you seem to be. What feats of strength can you show us? No one is permitted to stay here unless he excels in some difficult thing."

Hearing these words, in a very insulting tone, Loki answered loudly, "There is one feat in which no one can equal me, and I am ready to perform it at once. I can devour food faster than any one here."

"Truly, that would be a feat if you could do it," said the

scornful king; and he called to a man named Loge to contend with Loki.

A great trough full of meat was placed in the center of the hall, and, commencing at either end, the contestants began to eat voraciously; and so fast that it is disagreeable even to think of it. They reached the middle of the trough at exactly the same moment; but Loki had eaten only the meat, while Loge had devoured meat, bones, trough, and all. There was nothing left on his side, and Loki had to confess himself beaten.

Then the king, looking at Thjalfe, asked, "What can you do, young man?"

"I will run a race with anyone you will select," answered Thjalfe promptly.

"If you can outrun anyone I can select, it will certainly be a splendid feat," said Utgard-Loki; "but you must be very swift-footed to do it."

There was a noble race-ground just outside the palace, and everyone hurried out to see the race. The king called a slender young fellow named Huge and told him to run with Thjalfe.

There was never such running since the world began. Thjalfe ran like the wind; but Huge reached the goal first and turned about to meet Thjalfe as he came breathless to the post.

"You must use your legs better than that if you intend to win," said the king, as Thjalfe walked back; "although you are the fastest runner that ever came here."

They ran a second time, but when Huge reached the goal and turned around, Thjalfe was a full bow-shot behind.

"Well run!" shouted Utgard-Loki; "well run! a third race shall decide it."

A third time they were at the starting-place and again they were speeding down the course, while everybody strained his eyes to look at them; and a third time Huge reached the goal and turned to find Thjalfe not halfway.

"We have had racing enough!" cried the giants, and they all went back into the palace again.

And now it was Thor's turn to show his wonderful strength, but he did not dream that he was going to measure strength

236

with the most tremendous forces in the whole earth.

"Your fame fills all the worlds, Thor," called out Utgard-Loki, when they had seated themselves on the benches along the great hall; "give us some proof of your wonderful power."

Thor never waited to be asked a second time.

"I will contend in drinking with anyone you may select," was his prompt acceptance of the challenge.

"Well answered," said the king. "Bring out the great horn."

A giant went out, and speedily came back bearing a very deep horn, which the king said his men were compelled to empty as a punishment.

"A good drinker will empty that horn at a single draft," said Utgard-Loki, as it was filled and handed to Thor, "but a few men need to drink twice, but only a milksop needs a third pull at it."

Thor thought the horn not overlarge, although very long, and as he was very thirsty he put it to his lips without further ado, and drank so long and deep that he thought it certainly must be empty, but when he set the horn down and looked into it he was astonished to find that the liquor rose almost as high as when he set his lips to it.

"That was fairly well drunk," said the king, "but not unusually so; if anybody had told me Thor could do no better than that I would not have believed him. But of course you will finish it at a second draft."

Thor said nothing, although he was very angry, but setting the horn to his lips a second time he drank longer and deeper than before. When he had stopped to take breath, and looked at it again, he had drunk less than the first time.

"How now, Thor," cried Utgard-Loki, "you have left more for the third draft than you can manage. If there are no other feats which you can perform better than this, you must not expect to be considered as great here as among the gods."

Thor became very angry when he heard these words, and seizing the horn he drank deep, fast, and furiously until he thought it certainly must be empty; but when he looked into it the liquor had fallen so little that he could hardly see the

237

difference; and he handed it to the cupbearer, and would drink no more.

"It is plain," spoke up the king in a very insulting tone, "that you are not so strong as we thought you were; you cannot succeed in this strife, certainly; will you try something else?"

"I will certainly try something else," said Thor, who could not understand why he had failed to drain the horn; "but I am sure that even among the gods such drafts would not be counted small. What game do you propose now?"

"Oh, a very easy one," replied the king, "which my youngsters here make nothing of; simply to lift a cat from the floor. I should not think of asking you to try it if I did not see that you are much less of a man than I have always supposed."

He had no sooner said this than a large gray cat ran out into the hall. Thor put his hand under it and tried to lift it, but the cat arched its back as high as Thor stretched his hands and, do his best, he could only get one foot off the floor.

"It is just as I expected," cried Utgard-Loki in a loud voice, "the cat is very large, and Thor is a very little fellow compared with the rest of us."

Thor's eyes flashed fire. "Little as I am," he shouted, "I challenge any of you to wrestle with me."

Utgard-Loki looked up and down the benches as if he would call out someone from the two rows of giants. Then he shook his head, saying, "There is no one here who would not think it child's play to wrestle with you; but let someone call in Ellie, my old nurse; she shall try her strength with you. She has brought many a stronger man than you to earth."

An old woman came creeping into the hall, bent, wrinkled, and toothless. Thor seized her, but the tighter his grasp became the firmer she stood. Her thin arms gripped him like a vise, her strength seemed to grow as she put it forth, and at last after a hard struggle, in which Thor strained every muscle to the breaking point, he sank on one knee.

"That is enough," said Utgard-Loki, and the old woman crept feebly out of the hall, leaving Thor stunned and bewildered in the midst of the silent giants. There were no more trials of strength, and Thor and his companions were generously feasted after their defeats.

The next morning, after they had partaken of a bountiful breakfast of meat and drink, they started on their journey homeward. Utgard-Loki went with them as far as the gate of the city, where he stopped.

"How do you think your journey has turned out?" he asked Thor; "and have you met any men stronger than yourself?"

"I have brought shame upon myself," answered Thor frankly and honestly, after his nature, "and it vexes me to think that you will hereafter speak of me as a weak fellow."

"Now that you are out of the city, I will tell you the truth about these things," said Utgard-Loki. "If I had known how mighty you are, I would never have allowed you to enter the gates, and you may be very sure you will never get in a second time. I have beaten you by deception, not by strength. I have been deluding you from the start. In the forest I tied the sack with a tough iron wire in such a way you could not discern the secret of the knot. Thrice you struck at me with your hammer, and the first blow, though the lightest, would have killed me had it fallen on me; but each time I slipped a mountain between myself and the hammer, and the blows made three deep clefts in its stony sides. I have deluded you, too, in all the trials of strength and skill. Loki was very hungry and ate voraciously, but he contended against fire itself, which goes like the wind and devours everything in its path; Thjalfe ran as man never ran before, but Huge, who raced with him, was no other than my thought, and what man is so swift as thought? The horn which you strove in vain to empty had its further end in the sea, and so mighty were your drafts that over the wide sea the waters have sunk to the ebb. Your strength was no less wonderful when you lifted the cat; when we saw one foot raised from the floor our hearts sank in terror, for it was the Midgard-serpent, encircling the whole earth, which you really contended against, and you held it aloft so near heaven that the world was hardly enclosed by its folds. Most marvelous of all was the wrestling with Ellie, who was none other than old age itself, who sooner or later must bring all things to the ground. We must part, I hope never to meet again; for I can only defend myself against you by spells of magic such as these."

Thor was so enraged when he heard these words that he swung his hammer high in the air to crush the lying Utgard-Loki, but he had vanished, and when Thor turned to look for the city he saw only a beautiful plain spreading its blossoming meadows to the far mountains; and he went thoughtfully back to Asgard.

Charles J. Finger

A TALE OF THREE TAILS

ILLUSTRATED BY *John Merryweather*

OWN in Honduras there is a town called Pueblo de Chamelecón, which is not much of a town after all. There is only one street in it, and the houses are like big beehives that have been squared up, and the roofs are of straw. There is no sidewalk, no roadway, and the houses are unfenced, so that you step from the room into the sandy street and, because of the heat, when you are inside you wish that you were out, and when you are outside you wish that you were in. So the children of the place spend much time down at the little river. At least they did when I was there.

I rode there on a donkey and, the day being hot, let the animal graze, or sleep, or think, or dream, or work out problems —or whatever it is that a donkey does with his spare time—and I watched the children in the water. There was one, a little baby just able to toddle around, who crawled down to the water's edge, rolled in, and swam about like a little dog, much as the babies of Tierra del Fuego will swim in the icy waters of the Far South. He came out on my side of the water, as lively as a grig, smiling every bit as friendly as any other little chap of his age, white, brown, or yellow.

I stayed there that night because the day did not get cool, and in the evening the people sat outside of their houses and played the guitar and sang. Now I had with me a little musical instrument like a tiny organ, which I bought in France, and it was so compact and handy that I could carry it everywhere as

241

easily as I could a blanket. In fact, I used to ride with it behind my saddle, wrapped in my bedding. Well, as the people seemed to like their music, I brought out mine, so we had a very jolly concert, in spite of my poor voice, which they politely pretended not to notice. Then later, from curiosity, the children came about me and, to amuse them as well as myself, having done so badly at the singing, I did a few tricks with wads of rolled paper and a couple of tin cups, and the little boy who had swum across the pond laughed as loudly as anyone there. That pleased his father mightily, so much indeed that he brought me a cup of goat's milk and some cassava bread and told me that I was a fine fellow. To please me further, he sang a very, very long song. It was all about the parrot and the wonderful things it did, a parrot that had lived long among people and learned their songs, and when the bird flew back to the forest, it still sang, and so well that all the other parrots in the forest learned to sing the song from beginning to end. But what was curious was that at the end of every other verse, there was this line:

"When the rat had a tail like a horse."

So when he had done I asked him about that, for all the rats I had seen had tails which were far from beautiful, according to my notion.

The man listened gravely, then said: "But certainly, once the rat had a tail like a horse."

"When was that?" I asked.

"When the rabbit had a tail like a cat," he said.

"But I am still puzzled," I told him. "Was it long ago?"

"It was when the deer's tail was plumed like the tail of a dog," he told me.

As we talked, a kind of polite silence was upon all the people gathered about us; then a very, very old woman who was smoking a cigar nodded her head and said: "But Tio Ravenna is right. It was in the days of Hunbatz, who lived on beetles and spiders, and I heard it from my mother's mother, and she from

242

the mother of her mother." Then the old woman went on smoking with her eyes closed, and all who were there nodded at one another thinking, I suppose, that the old grandmother would presently tell the story. But of course, they who knew her well were wiser than to ask her to tell the Tale of Three Tails, so everyone waited.

Presently, a little girl gave the old grandmother a piece of sugar and asked: "Was it two brothers, or three, who had to clear the great forest? I am not sure."

At that the little old lady's eyes were bright, and she threw away her cigar and said,—

"Two brothers. That I have told you before." After a little sigh, which was only pretending that she was weary of telling the tale, she said: "You know that I have told it to you before, and it is wrong that I should have to tell it so often. But you see this."

So saying, she took from her bosom, where she had it fastened to a silk thread, a little piece of jade and let us see it. It was broken from a larger piece, but we could make out on it a carving which I saw to be a deer with a tail like a sheep dog's. We passed it about, and everyone looked at it carefully, although certainly all of them must have seen it time and time again, and when it came to the old grandmother again she replaced it and told us the Tale of Three Tails, just as I have written it here.

Once, long ago, the rat had a beautiful tail like a horse, with long sweeping hairs, though it was before my time of life. It was in the days of old Hunbatz, and he was a wizard who lived in the dark of the great forest that used to be on the other side of the big river. In those days things were not as now and animals were different; some larger, some smaller. The deer, as you have seen on the stone I showed you, had a tail like a dog, and the rabbit's tail was long and furry like the tail of a cat.

Now in that land there was a hunter with whom neither lasso nor arrow ever failed, and he had two sons, beautiful to look at and brave of heart, stout and quick of foot. Not only did the

243

brothers work better than any men had ever worked, but they could play ball and sing, throwing the ball higher than birds could fly and singing in a way that brought the wild things to hear them. Nor was there living creature able to run as swiftly as the two brothers. The birds alone could outrace them.

The brothers being grown, their father thought that it was time for them to make a home for themselves, so chose a place on the farther side of the forest and told them to clear it, which, he said, could be done in seven days. It was no little forest, you must remember, but a vast place, where sunlight never pierced, and the roots of trees were like great ropes; a jungle that stretched for miles and miles and the tangle in it was so thick that a monkey could barely get through without squeezing. Deep in the forest there was a blackness like the blackness of night. The trunks of the trees were so large that three men holding hands could not circle them, and where there were no trees, there were vines and snakelike lianas and flowers so great that a man could lie down to sleep in the shade of them.

The first day the brothers took a great space, piling the trees at one corner, clearing the tangle and leaving all as smooth as the water of a lake. They sang as they worked, and they sang as they rested in the heat of the day, and the organ bird and the flute bird answered them from the gold-green shade. So pleasant was their music that the old iguana, though he was as big as a man, came from his resting-place in the trees to listen.

Seeing how things were going, old Hunbatz in the dark of the forest grew very angry, fearing that his hiding-place would soon dwindle and vanish. So he went to the great gray owl, his friend, and they talked the matter over between them. The owl told Hunbatz that he must set the father's heart against the brothers, telling him that the boys were lazy and instead of working spent their time in playing with the ball and in singing.

"Go," said the owl, "to their father, and when he asks how the lads fare with their work, say to him:

"They sing and they play
For half of the day."

244

It may fall out that he will grow angry and cut off their heads, and thus the forest will be safe for us."

That seemed to the wizard to be good advice, and before the close of the day's work, old Hunbatz, who could fly by flapping his hands in a certain way like a swimmer, cast himself into the air and flew with great swiftness to the place where the father lived. But he took care to dress himself like a woodman.

"Well met," said the father, seeing Hunbatz, but thinking him no wizard of course. "From where do you come?"

"From the other side of the forest," was the reply.

"Then perchance you saw my two sons who are clearing the forest," said the father.

"I did," said Hunbatz.

"And how are the boys doing?" asked the father.

At that old Hunbatz shook his head sadly and answered, as the owl had told him:

> "They sing and they play
> For half of the day."

That, you know, was quite untrue, for while they sang, there was no stopping of work, and as for the play, it is true that they threw the ball from one to the other, but so clever were they that one would throw the ball so high that it would take hours and hours before it came down again, and of course, while it was in the air, the brothers went on working.

"I would cut off their heads to teach them a lesson," said Hunbatz, "if they were sons of mine." Then he turned on his heel and went away, not flying until he was out of the father's sight, for he did not wish any man to know that he was a wizard.

To be sure, the good man was grieved and his face clouded, when he heard the tale of Hunbatz, but he said nothing, and, a short time after, the brothers came home. He was much surprised when, asking the lads how much work they had done that day, they told him that they had cleared off the space of forest he had bidden them to. After much thought he told them that the next day they would have to do twice as much as before. The brothers thought the new task hard, but they went to work with a good will and on the second day the trees fell like corn before a man with a machete, and before night they had finished that which they had been given to do.

Again old Hunbatz flew through the air to the father and tried to set him against the boys, and again that night, when the boys were home, their task was set for the next day twice as much as the day before.

It was the same the third day, and the fourth, until at last the boys came to a point where by the mightiest working they could not move a stick or a blade of grass more. And yet, because of old Hunbatz, the father set them a task still greater.

On the fifth day things looked very hopeless for the boys, and their hearts were sad as they looked at the forest and saw the task that their father had set them to do. They went to work feeling for the first time it would be impossible for the sun to go down on their finished task, and the heart of old Hunbatz was glad. But the birds in the forest were silent that morning, for they too knew that there were sad hearts in the brothers. Even the grasshoppers and the mosquitoes and the bees were still, and as for the boys, not a note of joy could they raise.

Then to them came the iguana, wise old lizard who knew everything that went on in the forest, and as soon as he had heard what the brothers had to say he smiled and called on them to listen, after making sure that there was no living creature to hear except the birds, for of them he had no fear, knowing that the birds tell no secrets.

"Be cheerful," said the iguana, "and I will tell you a charm. It is this: mark about the handles of your working tools rings of black, white, red, and green, and before you start to work, sing:

> "I must do what I can,
> Is the thought of a man."

and if your hearts are brave, you will see what happens."

247

Having said this and smiled on the brothers, the old iguana climbed into a tree and stretched himself along the branch of it where he could best see, and the birds gathered in a great circle, a matchless melody going up to the sky.

So the brothers took their axes, their spades, their hoes, and their machetes, and painted about the handles of them rings of black and of white and of red and of green, and their voices rang sweet and clear as they sang, as the iguana had told them:

> "I must do what I can,
> Is the thought of a man."

No sooner had the last words passed than the whole company of birds broke out into a chorus, singing, chattering, chirping, whistling, screaming, each according to its manner and, without hands touching them, axes went to work cutting down trees, machetes chopped at lianas and vines, spades cleared and dug; and trees, bushes, and weeds piled themselves in great heaps at the edge of the clearing, so that in less than an hour the whole task was done. Then it was that all things in the forest were glad and the good iguana smiled broadly. The very monkeys joined in and, catching the ball which the brothers threw, tossed it from tree to tree until it passed through the whole jungle and back again.

But old Hunbatz was angry beyond measure, so angry that he whirled about on his heels three hundred times, turning so rapidly that he looked like a stormcloud, and his long whiskers were tangled about him like a mantle. But the faster he whirled, the more his anger boiled, and, flapping his hands, he shot into the air, going so swiftly that his very clothes were scorched.

"How are the boys?" asked the father, when Hunbatz stood before him.

For answer, Hunbatz screamed: "Your boys are idle fellows!

"They sing and they play
For half of the day."

Had I such sons, I would cut their heads off to teach them a lesson."

Said the father: "Tomorrow I shall go to the forest, and if you have not spoken truth, then this arrow which has never yet missed a mark shall find one in your heart. But if it is as you say, then my sons shall feel my anger."

Old Hunbatz did not like that at all, for well he knew that the hunter's arrows were never wasted. So back he flew to the owl, and the two of them whispered together. That night there was a great gathering of the animals: of the hare, the deer, the rat, the jaguar, the puma, the oppossum, and many others. The rat, the deer, and the rabbit led them, and in a wonderfully short time, not only were all things restored and the work of the day undone, but the trees and the bushes and the vines and the lianas that had been moved on the other days were put back in their old places, growing and blooming, so that all was as though the brothers had never been at the forest at all.

249

Sad was the hour the next morning when the hunter came with his two sons and saw the forest as though hand had never touched it. The brothers could not believe their eyes. Grinning from the thick of a rubber tree was the face of Hunbatz, and on his shoulder was the owl. For a moment the father thought to cut off the heads of the lads to teach them a lesson, but on second thought he told them that he would give them another chance.

"What should have been done is not done," he said. "I will grant you a day and a night to clear all the forest as you told

me it was cleared. Tomorrow morning I will come again, and see whether all is well done." At that he left them and went his way.

No sooner had he gone than the two brothers went to see the iguana, who told them of the witchery of the owl and Hunbatz and bade them to act as before. So they made the ring about the handles of their working tools once more and sang:

"I must do what I can,
Is the thought of a man."

and, as on the day before, axes, machetes, and spades went to work and in a short time all was clear again. Then the iguana told the brothers of the evil that Hunbatz had done and bade them set traps and keep watch that night. So three traps were made and set, and when night fell, from all parts of the forest there came animals led by the rat, the deer, and the rabbit, and old Hunbatz and the owl watched from the dark caves of the leaves.

No sooner had the first three animals stepped into the clearing than they were caught fast in the traps, whereupon the rest of the animals turned and fled. Then the brothers rushed to the traps. The rabbit gave a great jump when he felt the jaws close upon his beautiful catlike tail, but it was chopped off close to the body. The deer, with his tail like a plume, fared no better. So both deer and rabbit fled to the woods ashamed, and, as you see for yourself, have had no tails ever since. As for the rat, he was far too wise to jump as the rabbit and deer had done. But seeing the brothers coming, he pulled and pulled and pulled so that all the beautiful hair was stripped, leaving him with but a bare and ugly thing of a tail as you see today.

The next morning when the hunter-father came, there was the forest cleared and all in good order as the boys had said. So he sought out old Hunbatz, who flapped his hands and flew for very fear. But so fast he went that his clothes were burnt off, and his skin was baked into a hard crust by the great heat, and he fell to the earth and so became what we call an armadillo. As for the two brothers, they lived very happily for many, many years, and things went well with them, and the land they lived in was a land of good harvest and fruit trees.

So now you know the Tale of Three Tails, and if you do not believe it, look at the rat and the deer and the rabbit and the armadillo, and see for yourself.

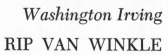

Washington Irving

RIP VAN WINKLE

ILLUSTRATED BY *Maud and Miska Petersham*

WHOEVER has made a voyage up the Hudson must remember the Catskill Mountains. They are a dismembered branch of the great Appalachian family and are seen away to the west of the river, swelling up to a noble height and lording it over the surrounding country.

Every change of season, every change of weather, indeed every hour of the day, produces some change in the magical hues and shapes of these mountains; and they are regarded by all the good wives, far and near, as perfect barometers. When the weather is fair and settled, they are clothed in blue and purple, and print their bold outlines on the clear evening sky; but sometimes, when the rest of the landscape is cloudless, they will gather a hood of gray vapors about their summits, which, in the last rays of the setting sun, will glow and light up like a crown of glory.

At the foot of these fairy mountains the voyager may have descried the light smoke curling up from a village, whose shingle roofs gleam among the trees, just where the blue tints of the upland melt away into the fresh green of the nearer landscape. It is a little village, of great antiquity, having been founded by some of the Dutch colonists in the early times of the province, just about the beginning of the government of the good Peter Stuyvesant (may he rest in peace!), and there were some of the houses of the original settlers standing within a few years, built of small yellow bricks brought from Holland, having latticed windows and gable fronts, surmounted with weathercocks.

In that same village, and in one of these very houses (which, to tell the precise truth, was sadly time-worn and weatherbeaten), there lived many years since, while the country was yet a province of Great Britain, a simple, good-natured fellow, of the name of Rip Van Winkle. He was a descendant of the Van Winkles who figured so gallantly in the chivalrous days of Peter Stuyvesant and accompanied him to the siege of Fort Christina. He inherited, however, but little of the martial character of his ancestors. I have observed that he was a simple, good-natured man; he was, moreover, a kind neighbor, and an obedient, henpecked husband. Indeed, to the latter circumstance might be owing that meekness of spirit which gained him such universal popularity; for those men are most apt to be obsequious and conciliating abroad who are under the discipline of shrews at home. Their tempers, doubtless, are rendered pliant and malleable in the fiery furnace of domestic tribulation; and a curtain lecture is worth all the sermons in the world for teaching the virtues of patience and long-suffering. A termagant wife may, therefore, in some respects be considered a tolerable blessing, and if so, Rip Van Winkle was thrice blessed.

Certain it is, that he was a great favorite among all the good wives of the village, who, as usual with the amiable sex, took his part in all family squabbles; and never failed, whenever they talked those matters over in their evening gossipings, to lay all the blame on Dame Van Winkle. The children of the village, too, would shout with joy whenever he approached. He assisted at their sports, made their playthings, taught them to fly kites and shoot marbles, and told them long stories of ghosts, witches, and Indians. Whenever he went dodging about the village, he was surrounded by a troop of them, hanging on his skirts, clambering on his back, and playing a thousand tricks on him with impunity; and not a dog would bark at him throughout the neighborhood.

The great error in Rip's composition was an insuperable aversion to all kinds of profitable labor. It could not be from the want of assiduity or perseverance; for he would sit on a wet rock, with a rod as long and heavy as a Tartar's lance, and fish all day without a murmur, even though he should not be encouraged by a single nibble. He would carry a fowling-piece on his shoulder for hours together, trudging through woods and swamps, and up hill and down dale, to shoot a few squirrels or wild pigeons. He would never refuse to assist a neighbor, even in the roughest toil, and was a foremost man at all country frolics for husking Indian corn, or building stone fences; the women of the village, too, used to employ him to run their errands and to do such little odd jobs as their less obliging husbands would not do for them. In a word, Rip was ready to attend to anybody's business but his own; but as to doing family duty and keeping his farm in order, he found it impossible.

In fact, he declared it was of no use to work on his farm; it was the most pestilent little piece of ground in the whole country; everything about it went wrong, and would go wrong, in spite of him. His fences were continually falling to pieces; his cow would either go astray or get among the cabbages; weeds were sure to grow quicker in his fields than anywhere else; the rain always made a point of setting in just as he had some outdoor work to do; so that though his patrimonial estate had dwindled away under his management, acre by acre, until there was little more left than a mere patch of Indian corn and potatoes, yet it was the worst-conditioned farm in the neighborhood.

His children, too, were as ragged and wild as if they belonged to nobody. His son Rip, an urchin begotten in his own likeness, promised to inherit the habits, with the old clothes of his father. He was generally seen trooping like a colt at his mother's heels, equipped in a pair of his father's cast-off galligaskins, which he had much ado to hold up with one hand, as a fine lady does her train in bad weather.

Rip Van Winkle, however, was one of those happy mortals, of foolish, well-oiled dispositions, who take the world easy, eat

254

white bread or brown, whichever can be got with least thought or trouble, and would rather starve on a penny than work for a pound. If left to himself, he would have whistled life away in perfect contentment; but his wife kept continually dinning in his ears about his idleness, his carelessness, and the ruin he was bringing on his family. Morning, noon, and night her tongue was incessantly going, and everything he said or did was sure to produce a torrent of household eloquence. Rip had but one way of replying to all lectures of the kind, and that, by frequent use, had grown into a habit. He shrugged his shoulders, shook his head, cast up his eyes, but said nothing. This, however, always provoked a fresh volley from his wife; so that he was fain to draw off his forces, and take to the outside of the house—the only side which, in truth, belongs to a henpecked husband.

Rip's sole domestic adherent was his dog Wolf, who was as much henpecked as his master; for Dame Van Winkle regarded them as companions in idleness, and even looked upon Wolf with an evil eye, as the cause of his master's going so often astray. True it is, in all points of spirit befitting an honorable dog, he was as courageous an animal as ever scoured the woods —but what courage can withstand the ever-during and all-besetting terrors of a woman's tongue? The moment Wolf entered the house his crest fell, his tail drooped to the ground, or curled between his legs, he sneaked about with a gallows air, casting many a sidelong glance at Dame Van Winkle, and at the least flourish of a broomstick or ladle he would fly to the door with yelping precipitation.

Times grew worse and worse with Rip Van Winkle as years of matrimony rolled on; a tart temper never mellows with age, and a sharp tongue is the only edged tool that grows keener with constant use. For a long while he used to console himself, when driven from home, by frequenting a kind of perpetual club of the sages, philosophers, and other idle personages of the village, which held its sessions on a bench before a small inn, designated by a rubicund portrait of His Majesty George the Third. Here they used to sit in the shade through a long lazy

255

summer's day, talking listlessly over village gossip, or telling endless sleepy stories about nothing. But it would have been worth any statesman's money to have heard the profound discussions that sometimes took place, when by chance an old newspaper fell into their hands from some passing traveler. How solemnly they would listen to the contents, as drawled out by Derrick Van Bummel, the schoolmaster, a dapper learned little man, who was not to be daunted by the most gigantic word in the dictionary; and how sagely they would deliberate upon public events some months after they had taken place.

The opinions of this junto were completely controlled by Nicholas Vedder, a patriarch of the village, and landlord of the inn, at the door of which he took his seat from morning till night, just moving sufficiently to avoid the sun and keep in the shade of a large tree; so that the neighbors could tell the hour by his movements as accurately as by a sundial. It is true he was rarely heard to speak, but smoked his pipe incessantly. His adherents, however (for every great man has his adherents), perfectly understood him and knew how to gather his opinions. When anything that was read or related displeased him, he was observed to smoke his pipe vehemently, and to send forth short, frequent, and angry puffs; but when pleased, he would inhale the smoke slowly and tranquilly and emit it in light and placid clouds; and sometimes, taking the pipe from his mouth and letting the fragrant vapor curl about his nose, would gravely nod his head in token of perfect approbation.

From even this stronghold the unlucky Rip was at length routed by his termagant wife, who would suddenly break in upon the tranquillity of the assemblage and call the members all to naught; nor was that august personage, Nicholas Vedder himself, sacred from the daring tongue of this terrible virago, who charged him outright with encouraging her husband in habits of idleness.

Poor Rip was at last reduced almost to despair; and his only alternative, to escape from the labor of the farm and clamor of his wife, was to take gun in hand and stroll away into the woods. Here he would sometimes seat himself at the foot of a tree and share the contents of his wallet with Wolf, with whom he sympathized as a fellow sufferer in persecution. "Poor Wolf," he would say, "thy mistress leads thee a dog's life of it; but never mind, my lad, whilst I live thou shalt never want a friend to stand by thee!" Wolf would wag his tail, look wistfully in his master's face, and if dogs can feel pity I verily believe he reciprocated the sentiment with all his heart.

In a long ramble of the kind on a fine autumnal day, Rip had unconsciously scrambled to one of the highest parts of the Kaatskill Mountains. He was after his favorite sport of squirrel shooting, and the still solitudes had echoed and reëchoed with the reports of his gun. Panting and fatigued, he threw himself, late in the afternoon, on a green knoll, covered with mountain herbage that crowned the brow of a precipice. From an opening between the trees he could overlook all the lower country for many a mile of rich woodland. He saw at a distance the lordly Hudson, far, far below him, moving on its silent but majestic course, with the reflection of a purple cloud, or the sail of a lagging bark, here and there sleeping on its glassy bosom, and at last losing itself in the blue highlands.

On the other side he looked down into a deep mountain glen, wild, lonely, and shagged, the bottom filled with fragments from the impending cliffs, and scarcely lighted by the reflected rays of the setting sun. For some time Rip lay musing on this scene; evening was gradually advancing; the mountains began to throw their long blue shadows over the valleys; he saw that it would be dark long before he could reach the village, and he heaved a heavy sigh when he thought of encountering the terrors of Dame Van Winkle.

As he was about to descend, he heard a voice from a distance, hallooing, "Rip Van Winkle! Rip Van Winkle!" He looked round, but could see nothing but a crow winging its solitary flight across the mountain. He thought his fancy must have deceived him, and turned again to descend, when he heard the same cry ring through the still evening air: "Rip Van Winkle! Rip Van Winkle!"—at the same time Wolf bristled up his back, and giving a low growl, skulked to his master's side, looking

257

fearfully down into the glen. Rip now felt a vague apprehension stealing over him; he looked anxiously in the same direction, and perceived a strange figure slowly toiling up the rocks, and bending under the weight of something he carried on his back. He was surprised to see any human being in this lonely and unfrequented place; but supposing it to be someone of the neighborhood in need of his assistance, he hastened down to yield it.

On nearer approach he was still more surprised at the singularity of the stranger's appearance. He was a short, square-built old fellow, with thick bushy hair and a grizzled beard. His dress was of the antique Dutch fashion: a cloth jerkin strapped round the waist, several pair of breeches, the outer one of ample volume, decorated with rows of buttons down the sides, and bunches at the knees. He bore on his shoulder a stout keg, that seemed full of liquor, and made signs for Rip to approach and assist him with the load. Though rather shy and distrustful of this new acquaintance, Rip complied with his usual alacrity; and mutually relieving one another, they clambered up a narrow gully, apparently the dry bed of a mountain torrent. As they ascended, Rip every now and then heard long rolling peals like distant thunder, that seemed to issue out of a deep ravine, or rather cleft, between lofty rocks, toward which their rugged path conducted. He paused for a moment, but supposing it to be the muttering of one of those transient thundershowers which often take place in mountain heights, he proceeded. Passing through the ravine, they came to a hollow, like a small amphitheatre, surrounded by perpendicular precipices, over the brinks of which impending trees shot their branches, so that you only caught glimpses of the azure sky and the bright evening cloud. During the whole time Rip and his companion had labored on in silence; for though the former marveled greatly what could be the object of carrying a keg of liquor up this wild mountain, yet there was something strange and incomprehensible about the unknown, that inspired awe and checked familiarity.

On entering the amphitheater, new objects of wonder presented themselves. On a level spot in the center was a company of odd-looking personages playing at ninepins. They were dressed in a quaint, outlandish fashion; some wore short doublets, others jerkins, with long knives in their belts, and most of them had enormous breeches of similar style with that of the guide's. Their visages, too, were peculiar; one had a large beard, broad face, and small piggish eyes; the face of another seemed to consist entirely of nose, and was surmounted by a white sugar-loaf hat, set off with a little red cock's tail. They all had beards, of various shapes and colors. There was one who seemed to be the commander. He was a stout old gentleman, with a weather-beaten countenance; he wore a laced doublet, broad belt and hanger, high-crowned hat and feather, red stockings, and high-heeled shoes, with roses in them. The whole group reminded Rip of the figures in an old Flemish painting in the parlor of Dominie Van Shaick, the village parson, which had been brought over from Holland at the time of the settlement.

What seemed particularly odd to Rip was, that though these folks were evidently amusing themselves, yet they maintained the gravest faces, the most mysterious silence, and were, withal, the most melancholy party of pleasure he had ever witnessed. Nothing interrupted the stillness of the scene but the noise of the balls, which, whenever they were rolled, echoed along the mountains like rumbling peals of thunder.

As Rip and his companion approached them, they suddenly desisted from their play, and stared at him with such fixed, statue-like gaze, and such strange, uncouth, lackluster countenances, that his heart turned within him, and his knees smote together. His companion now emptied the contents of the keg into large flagons and made signs to him to wait upon the company. He obeyed with fear and trembling; they quaffed the liquor in profound silence, and then returned to their game.

By degrees Rip's awe and apprehension subsided. He even ventured, when no eye was fixed upon him, to taste the beverage, which he found had much of the flavor of excellent Hollands. He was naturally a thirsty soul and was soon tempted to repeat the draught. One taste provoked another; and he reiterated his visits to the flagon so often that at length his senses were overpowered, his eyes swam in his head, his head gradually declined, and he fell into a deep sleep.

On waking, he found himself on the green knoll whence he had first seen the old man of the glen. He rubbed his eyes—it was a bright, sunny morning. The birds were hopping and twittering among the bushes, and the eagle was wheeling aloft and breasting the pure mountain breeze. "Surely," thought Rip, "I have not slept here all night." He recalled the occurrences before he fell asleep. The strange man with a keg of liquor— the mountain ravine—the wild retreat among the rocks—the woebegone party at ninepins—the flagon—"Oh! that flagon! that wicked flagon!" thought Rip, "what excuse shall I make to Dame Van Winkle?"

He looked round for his gun, but in place of the clean, well-oiled fowling-piece, he found an old firelock lying by him, the barrel incrusted with rust, the lock falling off, and the stock worm-eaten. He now suspected that the grave roisterers of the mountain had put a trick upon him and, having dosed him with liquor, had robbed him of his gun. Wolf, too, had disappeared, but he might have strayed away after a squirrel or partridge. He whistled after him and shouted his name, but all in vain; the echoes repeated his whistle and shout, but no dog was to be seen.

He determined to revisit the scene of the last evening's gambol, and if he met any of the party, to demand his dog and gun. As he rose to walk, he found himself stiff in the joints and wanting in his usual activity. "These mountain beds do not agree with me," thought Rip, "and if this frolic should lay me up with a fit of the rheumatism, I shall have a blessed time with Dame Van Winkle." With some difficulty he got down into the glen; he found the gully up which he and his companion had ascended the preceding evening; but to his astonishment a mountain stream was now foaming down it, leaping from rock to rock and filling the glen with babbling murmurs. He, however, made shift to scramble up its sides, working his toilsome way through thickets of birch, sassafras, and witchhazel, and

His companion now emptied the contents of the keg into large flagons.

sometimes tripped up or entangled by the wild grapevines that twisted their coils or tendrils from tree to tree and spread a kind of network in his path.

At length he reached to where the ravine had opened through the cliffs to the amphitheater; but no traces of such opening remained. The rocks presented a high, impenetrable wall, over which the torrent came tumbling in a sheet of feathery foam and fell into a broad, deep basin, black from the shadows of the surrounding forest. Here, then, poor Rip was brought to a stand. He again called and whistled after his dog; he was only answered by the cawing of a flock of idle crows, sporting high in air about a dry tree that overhung a sunny precipice; and who, secure in their elevation, seemed to look down and scoff at the poor man's perplexities. What was to be done? The morning was passing away, and Rip felt famished for want of his breakfast. He grieved to give up his dog and gun; he dreaded to meet his wife; but it would not do to starve among the mountains. He shook his head, shouldered the rusty firelock, and, with a heart full of trouble and anxiety, turned his steps homeward.

As he approached the village he met a number of people, but none whom he knew, which somewhat surprised him, for he had thought himself acquainted with everyone in the country round. Their dress, too, was of a different fashion from that to which he was accustomed. They all stared at him with equal marks of surprise, and whenever they cast their eyes upon him, invariably stroked their chins. The constant recurrence of this gesture induced Rip, involuntarily, to do the same, when, to his astonishment, he found his beard had grown a foot long!

He had now entered the skirts of the village. A troop of strange children ran at his heels, hooting after him and pointing at his gray beard. The dogs, too, not one of which he recognized for an old acquaintance, barked at him as he passed. The very village was altered; it was larger and more populous. There were rows of houses which he had never seen before, and those which had been his familiar haunts had disappeared. Strange names were over the doors—strange faces at the windows—

everything was strange. His mind now misgave him; he began to doubt whether both he and the world around him were not bewitched. Surely this was his native village, which he had left but the day before. There stood the Kaatskill Mountains— there ran the silver Hudson at a distance—there was every hill and dale precisely as it had always been. Rip was sorely perplexed. "That flagon last night," thought he, "has addled my poor head sadly!"

It was with some difficulty that he found the way to his own house, which he approached with silent awe, expecting every moment to hear the shrill voice of Dame Van Winkle. He found the house gone to decay—the roof fallen in, the windows shattered, and the doors off the hinges. A half-starved dog that looked like Wolf was skulking about it. Rip called him by name, but the cur snarled, showed his teeth, and passed on. This was an unkind cut indeed—"My very dog," sighed poor Rip, "has forgotten me!"

He entered the house, which, to tell the truth, Dame Van Winkle had always kept in neat order. It was empty, forlorn, and apparently abandoned. This desolateness overcame all his connubial fears; he called loudly for his wife and children; the lonely chambers rang for a moment with his voice, and then again all was silence.

He now hurried forth and hastened to his old resort, the village inn—but it, too, was gone. A large, rickety wooden building stood in its place, with great gaping windows, some of them broken and mended with old hats and petticoats, and over the door was painted, "The Union Hotel, by Jonathan Doolittle." Instead of the great tree that used to shelter the quiet little Dutch inn of yore, there now was reared a tall naked pole, with something on the top that looked like a red nightcap, and from it was fluttering a flag, on which was a singular assemblage of stars and stripes—all this was strange and incomprehensible. He recognized on the sign, however, the ruby face of King George, under which he had smoked so many a peaceful pipe; but even this was singularly metamorphosed. The red coat was changed for one of blue and buff, a sword was held

263

in the hand instead of a scepter, the head was decorated with a cocked hat, and underneath was painted in large characters, GENERAL WASHINGTON.

There was, as usual, a crowd of folk about the door, but none that Rip recollected. The very character of the people seemed changed. There was a busy, bustling, disputatious tone about it, instead of the accustomed phlegm and drowsy tranquillity. He looked in vain for the sage Nicholas Vedder, with his broad face, double chin, and fair, long pipe, uttering clouds of tobacco-smoke instead of idle speeches; or Van Bummel, the schoolmaster, doling forth the contents of an ancient newspaper. In place of these, a lean, bilious-looking fellow, with his pockets full of handbills, was haranguing vehemently about rights of citizens—elections—members of Congress—liberty—Bunker's Hill—heroes of seventy-six—and other words, which were a perfect Babylonish jargon to the bewildered Van Winkle.

The appearance of Rip, with his long grizzled beard, his rusty fowling-piece, his uncouth dress, and an army of women and children at his heels, soon attracted the attention of the tavern politicians. They crowded round him, eyeing him from head to foot with great curiosity. The orator bustled up to him, and, drawing him partly aside, inquired "on which side he voted." Rip stared in vacant stupidity. Another short but busy little fellow pulled him by the arm, and, rising on tiptoe, inquired in his ear, "whether he was Federal or Democrat." Rip was equally at a loss to comprehend the question; when a knowing, self-important old gentleman, in a sharp cocked hat, made his way through the crowd, putting them to the right and left with his elbows as he passed, and planting himself before Van Winkle, with one arm akimbo, the other resting on his cane, his keen eyes and sharp hat penetrating, as it were, into his very soul, demanded in an austere tone, "what brought him to the election with a gun on his shoulder, and a mob at his heels, and whether he meant to breed a riot in the village."—"Alas! gentlemen," cried Rip, somewhat dismayed, "I am a poor quiet man, a native of the place, and a loyal subject of the king, God bless him!"

Here a general shout burst from the bystanders—"A tory! a

tory! a spy! a refugee! hustle him! away with him!" It was with great difficulty that the self-important man in the cocked hat restored order; and, having assumed a tenfold austerity of brow, demanded again of the unknown culprit what he came there for, and whom he was seeking? The poor man humbly assured him that he meant no harm, but merely came there in search of some of his neighbors, who used to keep about the tavern.

"Well—who are they?—name them."

Rip bethought himself a moment, and inquired, "Where's Nicholas Vedder?"

There was a silence for a little while, when an old man replied, in a thin, piping voice: "Nicholas Vedder! why, he is dead and gone these eighteen years! There was a wooden tombstone in the churchyard that used to tell all about him, but that's rotten and gone too."

"Where's Brom Dutcher?"

"Oh, he went off to the army in the beginning of the war: some say he was killed at the storming of Stony Point; others say he was drowned in a squall at the foot of Antony's Nose. I don't know—he never came back again."

"Where's Van Bummel, the schoolmaster?"

"He went off to the wars too, was a great militia general, and is now in Congress."

Rip's heart died away at hearing of these sad changes in his home and friends, and finding himself thus alone in the world. Every answer puzzled him too, by treating of such enormous lapses of time, and of matters which he could not understand: war—Congress—Stony Point; he had no courage to ask after any more friends, but cried out in despair, "Does nobody here know Rip Van Winkle?"

"Oh, Rip Van Winkle!" exclaimed two or three. "Oh, to be sure! that's Rip Van Winkle yonder, leaning against the tree."

Rip looked, and beheld a precise counterpart of himself, as he went up the mountain; apparently as lazy, and certainly as ragged. The poor fellow was now completely confounded. He doubted his own identity, and whether he was himself or another man. In the midst of his bewilderment, the man in the cocked hat demanded who he was, and what was his name.

"God knows," exclaimed he, at his wit's end; "I'm not myself —I'm somebody else—that's me yonder—no—that's somebody else got into my shoes—I was myself last night, but I fell asleep on the mountain, and they've changed my gun, and everything's changed, and I'm changed, and I can't tell what's my name, or who I am!"

The bystanders began now to look at each other, nod, wink significantly, and tap their fingers against their foreheads. There was a whisper, also, about securing the gun, and keeping the old fellow from doing mischief, at the very suggestion of which the self-important man in the cocked hat retired with some precipitation. At this critical moment a fresh, comely woman pressed through the throng to get a peep at the gray-bearded man. She had a chubby child in her arms, which, frightened at his looks, began to cry. "Hush, Rip," cried she, "hush, you little fool; the old man won't hurt you." The name of the child, the air of the mother, the tone of her voice, all awakened a train of recollections in his mind. "What is your name, my good woman?" asked he.

"Judith Gardenier."

"And your father's name?"

"Ah, poor man, Rip Van Winkle was his name, but it's twenty years since he went away from home with his gun and never has been heard of since,—his dog came home without him; but whether he shot himself, or was carried away by the Indians, nobody can tell. I was then but a little girl."

Rip had but one question more to ask; and he put it with a faltering voice:—

"Where's your mother?"

"Oh, she too had died but a short time since; she broke a bloodvessel in a fit of passion at a New England peddler."

There was a drop of comfort, at least, in this intelligence. The honest man could contain himself no longer. He caught his daughter and her child in his arms. "I am your father!" cried he—"Young Rip Van Winkle once—old Rip Van Winkle now! Does nobody know poor Rip Van Winkle?"

All stood amazed, until an old woman, tottering out from among the crowd, put her hand to her brow, and peering under it in his face for a moment, exclaimed, "Sure enough, it is Rip Van Winkle—it is himself! Welcome home again, old neighbor— Why, where have you been these twenty long years?"

Rip's story was soon told, for the whole twenty years had been to him but as one night. The neighbors stared when they heard it; some were seen to wink at each other and put their tongues in their cheeks; and the self-important man in the cocked hat, who, when the alarm was over, had returned to the field, screwed down the corners of his mouth and shook his head—upon which there was a general shaking of the head throughout the assemblage.

It was determined, however, to take the opinion of old Peter Vanderdonk, who was seen slowly advancing up the road. He was a descendant of the historian of that name, who wrote one of the earliest accounts of the province. Peter was the most ancient inhabitant of the village, and well versed in all the wonderful events and traditions of the neighborhood. He recollected Rip at once and corroborated his story in the most satisfactory manner. He assured the company that it was a fact, handed down from his ancestor the historian, that the Kaatskill Mountains had always been haunted by strange beings. That it was affirmed that the great Hendrick Hudson, the first discoverer of the river and country, kept a kind of vigil there every twenty years, with his crew of the Half Moon; being permitted in this way to revisit the scenes of his enterprise and keep a guardian eye upon the river and the great city called by his name. That his father had once seen them in their old Dutch dresses playing at ninepins in a hollow of the mountain; and that he himself had heard, one summer afternoon, the sound of their balls like distant peals of thunder.

To make a long story short, the company broke up and returned to the more important concerns of the election. Rip's daughter took him home to live with her; she had a snug well-furnished house and a stout, cheery farmer for a husband, whom Rip recollected for one of the urchins that used to climb upon his back. As to Rip's son and heir, who was the ditto of himself, seen leaning against the tree, he was employed to work on the farm; but evinced an hereditary disposition to attend to anything else but his business.

Rip now resumed his old walks and habits; he soon found many of his former cronies, though all rather the worse for the wear and tear of time; and preferred making friends among the rising generation, with whom he soon grew into great favor.

Having nothing to do at home, and being arrived at that happy age when a man can be idle with impunity, he took his place once more on the bench at the inn door and was reverenced as one of the patriarchs of the village and a chronicle of the old times "before the war." It was some time before he could get into the regular track of gossip, or could be made to comprehend the strange events that had taken place during his torpor. How that there had been a revolutionary war—that the

country had thrown off the yoke of old England—and that, instead of being a subject of his Majesty George the Third, he was now a free citizen of the United States. Rip, in fact, was no politician; the changes of states and empires made but little impression on him; but there was one species of despotism under which he had long groaned, and that was—petticoat government. Happily that was at an end; he had got his neck out of the yoke of matrimony and could go in and out whenever he pleased, without dreading the tyranny of Dame Van Winkle. Whenever her name was mentioned, however, he shook his head and cast up his eyes, which might pass either for an expression of resignation to his fate or joy at his deliverance.

He used to tell his story to every stranger that arrived at Mr. Doolittle's hotel. He was observed, at first, to vary on some points every time he told it, which was, doubtless, owing to his having so recently awaked. It at last settled down precisely to the tale I have related, and not a man, woman, or child in the neighborhood but knew it by heart. Some always pretended to doubt the reality of it and insisted that Rip had been out of his head, and that this was one point on which he always remained flighty. The old Dutch inhabitants, however, almost universally gave it full credit. Even to this day they never hear a thunderstorm of a summer afternoon about the Kaatskill but they say Hendrick Hudson and his crew are at their game of ninepins; and it is a common wish of all henpecked husbands in the neighborhood, when life hangs heavy on their hands, that they might have a quieting draught out of Rip Van Winkle's flagon.

A THING OF BEAUTY

John Keats

A thing of beauty is a joy for ever;
Its loveliness increases; it will never
Pass into nothingness; but still will keep
A bower quiet for us, and a sleep
Full of sweet dreams, and health, and quiet breathing.

Nathaniel Hawthorne
THE GREAT STONE FACE

ILLUSTRATED BY *Walter R. Sabel*

ONE afternoon, when the sun was going down, a mother and her little boy sat at the door of their cottage, talking about the Great Stone Face. They had but to lift their eyes, and there it was plainly to be seen, though miles away, with the sunshine brightening all its features.

And what was the Great Stone Face?

Embosomed amongst a family of lofty mountains, there was a valley so spacious that it contained many thousand inhabitants. Some of these good people dwelt in log huts, with the black forest all around them, on the steep and difficult hillsides. Others had their homes in comfortable farmhouses and cultivated the rich soil on the gentle slopes or level surfaces of the valley. Others, again, were congregated into populous villages, where some wild, highland rivulet, tumbling down from its birthplace in the upper mountain region, had been caught and tamed by human cunning and compelled to turn the machinery of cotton factories. The inhabitants of this valley, in short, were numerous, and of many modes of life. But all of them, grown people and children, had a kind of familiarity with the Great Stone Face, although some possessed the gift of distinguishing this grand natural phenomenon more perfectly than many of their neighbors.

The Great Stone Face, then, was a work of Nature in her mood of majestic playfulness, formed on the perpendicular side of a mountain by some immense rocks, which had been thrown together in such a position as, when viewed at a proper distance, precisely to resemble the features of the human countenance. It seemed as if an enormous giant, or a Titan, had sculptured his own likeness on the precipice. There was the broad

271

arch of the forehead, a hundred feet in height; the nose, with its long bridge; and the vast lips, which, if they could have spoken, would have rolled their thunder accents from one end of the valley to the other. True it is, that if the spectator approached too near, he lost the outline of the gigantic visage, and could discern only a heap of ponderous and gigantic rocks, piled in chaotic ruin one upon another. Retracing his steps, however, the wondrous features would again be seen; and the farther he withdrew from them, the more like a human face, with all its original divinity intact, did they appear; until, as it grew dim in the distance, with the clouds and glorified vapor of the mountains clustering about it, the Great Stone Face seemed positively to be alive.

It was a happy lot for children to grow up to manhood or womanhood with the Great Stone Face before their eyes, for all the features were noble, and the expression was at once grand and sweet, as if it were the glow of a vast, warm heart, that embraced all mankind in its affections and had room for more. It was an education only to look at it. According to the belief of many people, the valley owed much of its fertility to this benign aspect that was continually beaming over it, illuminating the clouds, and infusing its tenderness into the sunshine.

As we began with saying, a mother and her little boy sat at their cottage door, gazing at the Great Stone Face, and talking about it. The child's name was Ernest.

"Mother," said he, while the Titanic visage smiled on him, "I wish that it could speak, for it looks so very kindly that its voice must needs be pleasant. If I were to see a man with such a face, I should love him dearly."

"If an old prophecy should come to pass," answered his mother, "we may see a man, some time or other, with exactly such a face as that."

"What prophecy do you mean, dear mother?" eagerly inquired Ernest. "Pray tell me all about it!"

So his mother told him a story that her own mother had told to her, when she herself was younger than little Ernest; a story, not of things that were past, but of what was yet to come; a

story, nevertheless, so very old, that even the Indians, who formerly inhabited this valley, had heard it from their fore-fathers, to whom, as they affirmed, it had been murmured by the mountain streams, and whispered by the wind among the treetops. The purport was, that, at some future day, a child should be born hereabouts, who was destined to become the greatest and noblest personage of his time, and whose counten-ance, in manhood, should bear an exact resemblance to the Great Stone Face. Not a few old-fashioned people, and young ones likewise, in the ardor of their hopes, still cherished an en-during faith in this old prophecy. But others, who had seen more of the world, had watched and waited till they were weary and had beheld no man with such a face, nor any man that proved to be much greater or nobler than his neighbors, con-cluded it to be nothing but an idle tale. At all events, the great man of the prophecy had not yet appeared.

"O mother, dear mother!" cried Ernest, clapping his hands above his head, "I do hope that I shall live to see him!"

His mother was an affectionate and thoughtful woman, and felt that it was wisest not to discourage the generous hopes of her little boy. So she only said to him, "Perhaps you may."

And Ernest never forgot the story that his mother told him. It was always in his mind, whenever he looked upon the Great Stone Face. He spent his childhood in the log cottage where he was born, and was dutiful to his mother and helpful to her in many things, assisting her much with his little hands, and more with his loving heart. In this manner, from a happy yet often pensive child, he grew up to be a mild, quiet, unobtrusive boy, and sun-browned with labor in the fields, but with more intelligence brightening his aspect than is seen in many lads who have been taught at famous schools. Yet Ernest had had no teacher, save only that the Great Stone Face became one to him. When the toil of the day was over, he would gaze at it for hours, until he began to imagine that those vast features recognized him and gave him a smile of kindness and encouragement, responsive to his own look of veneration. We must not take upon us to affirm that this was a mistake, although the Face may have looked no more kindly at Ernest than at all the world besides. But the secret was that the boy's tender and confiding simplicity discerned what other people could not see; and thus the love, which was meant for all, became his peculiar portion.

About this time there went a rumor throughout the valley that the great man, foretold from ages long ago, who was to bear a resemblance to the Great Stone Face, had appeared at last. It seems that, many years before, a young man had migrated from the valley and settled at a distant seaport, where, after getting together a little money, he had set up as a shopkeeper. His name—but I could never learn whether it was his real one, or a nickname that had grown out of his habits and success in life—was Gathergold. Being shrewd and active, and endowed by Providence with that inscrutable faculty which develops itself in what the world calls luck, he became an exceedingly rich merchant and owner of a whole fleet of bulky-bottomed ships. All the countries of the globe appeared to join hands for the mere purpose of adding heap after heap to the mountainous accumulation of this one man's wealth. The cold regions of the north, almost within the gloom and shadow of the Arctic Circle, sent him their tribute in the shape of furs; hot Africa sifted for him the golden sands of her rivers and gathered up the ivory tusks of her great elephants out of the forests; the

274

East came bringing him the rich shawls, and spices, and teas, and the effulgence of diamonds, and the gleaming purity of large pearls. The ocean, not to be behindhand with the earth, yielded up her mighty whales, that Mr. Gathergold might sell their oil, and make a profit on it. Be the original commodity what it might, it was gold within his grasp. It might be said of him, as of Midas in the fable, that whatever he touched with his fingers immediately glistened, and grew yellow, and was changed at once into sterling metal, or, which suited him still better, into piles of coin. And, when Mr. Gathergold had become so very rich that it would have taken him a hundred years only to count his wealth, he bethought himself of his native valley, and resolved to go back thither, and end his days where he was born. With this purpose in view, he sent a skillful architect to build him such a palace as should be fit for a man of his vast wealth to live in.

As I have said above, it had already been rumored in the valley that Mr. Gathergold had turned out to be the prophetic personage so long and vainly looked for and that his visage was the perfect and undeniable similitude of the Great Stone Face. People were the more ready to believe that this must needs be the fact, when they beheld the splendid edifice that rose, as if by enchantment, on the site of his father's old weather-beaten farmhouse. The exterior was of marble, so dazzlingly white that it seemed as though the whole structure might melt away in the sunshine, like those humbler ones which Mr. Gathergold, in his young play-days, before his fingers were gifted with the touch of transmutation, had been accustomed to build of snow. It had a richly ornamented portico, supported by tall pillars, beneath which was a lofty door, studded with silver knobs, and made of a kind of variegated wood that had been brought from beyond the sea. The windows, from the floor to the ceiling of each stately apartment, were composed, respectively, of but one enormous pane of glass, so transparently pure that it was said to be a finer medium than even the vacant atmosphere. Hardly anybody had been permitted to see the interior of this palace; but it was reported, and with good semblance of truth, to be far more gorgeous than the outside, insomuch that whatever was iron or brass in other houses was silver or gold in this; and Mr. Gathergold's bedchamber, especially, made such a glittering appearance that no ordinary man would have been able to close his eyes there. But, on the other hand, Mr. Gathergold was now so inured to wealth that perhaps he could not have closed his eyes unless where the gleam of it was certain to find its way beneath his eyelids.

In due time, the mansion was finished; next came the upholsterers, with magnificent furniture; then, a whole troop of black and white servants, the harbingers of Mr. Gathergold, who, in his own majestic person, was expected to arrive at sunset. Our friend Ernest, meanwhile, had been deeply stirred by the idea that the great man, the noble man, the man of prophecy, after so many ages of delay, was at length to be made manifest to his native valley. He knew, boy as he was, that there were a thousand ways in which Mr. Gathergold, with his vast wealth, might transform himself into an angel of beneficence and assume a control over human affairs as wide and benignant as the smile of the Great Stone Face. Full of faith and hope, Ernest doubted not that what the people said was true, and that now he was to behold the living likeness of those wondrous features on the mountainside. While the boy was still gazing up the valley and fancying, as he always did, that the Great Stone Face returned his gaze and looked kindly at him, the rumbling of wheels was heard, approaching swiftly along the winding road.

"Here he comes!" cried a group of people who were assembled to witness the arrival. "Here comes the great Mr. Gathergold!"

A carriage, drawn by four horses, dashed round the turn of the road. Within it, thrust partly out of the window, appeared the physiognomy of the old man, with a skin as yellow as if his own Midas-hand had transmuted it. He had a low forehead, small, sharp eyes, puckered about with innumerable wrinkles, and very thin lips, which he made still thinner by pressing them forcibly together.

276

"The very image of the Great Stone Face!" shouted the people. "Sure enough, the old prophecy is true; and here we have the great man come at last!"

And, what greatly perplexed Ernest, they seemed actually to believe that here was the likeness which they spoke of. By the roadside there chanced to be an old beggar-woman and two little beggar-children, stragglers from some far-off region, who, as the carriage rolled onward, held out their hands and lifted up their doleful voices, most piteously beseeching charity. A yellow claw—the very same that had clawed together so much wealth—poked itself out of the coach-window, and dropped some copper coins upon the ground; so that, though the great man's name seems to have been Gathergold, he might just as suitably have been nicknamed Scattercopper. Still, nevertheless, with an earnest shout, and evidently with as much good faith as ever, the people bellowed,—

"He is the very image of the Great Stone Face!"

But Ernest turned sadly from the wrinkled shrewdness of that sordid visage and gazed up the valley, where, amid a gathering mist, gilded by the last sunbeams, he could still distinguish those glorious features which had impressed themselves into his soul. Their aspect cheered him. What did the benign lips seem to say?

"He will come! Fear not, Ernest; the man will come!"

The years went on, and Ernest ceased to be a boy. He had grown to be a young man now. He attracted little notice from the other inhabitants of the valley; for they saw nothing remarkable in his way of life, save that, when the labor of the day was over, he still loved to go apart and gaze and meditate upon the Great Stone Face. According to their idea of the matter, it was a folly, indeed, but pardonable, inasmuch as Ernest was industrious, kind, and neighborly, and neglected no duty for the sake of indulging this idle habit. They knew not that the Great Stone Face had become a teacher to him, and that the sentiment which was expressed in it would enlarge the young man's heart and fill it with wider and deeper sympathies than other hearts. They knew not that thence would come a better

277

wisdom than could be learned from books and a better life than could be molded on the defaced example of other human lives. Neither did Ernest know that the thoughts and affections which came to him so naturally, in the fields and at the fireside, and wherever he communed with himself, were of a higher tone than those which all men shared with him. A simple soul,— simple as when his mother first taught him the old prophecy,— he beheld the marvelous features beaming adown the valley and still wondered that their human counterpart was so long in making his appearance.

By this time poor Mr. Gathergold was dead and buried; and the oddest part of the matter was, that his wealth, which was the body and spirit of his existence, had disappeared before his death, leaving nothing of him but a living skeleton, covered over with a wrinkled, yellow skin. Since the melting away of his gold, it had been very generally conceded that there was no such striking resemblance, after all, betwixt the ignoble features of the ruined merchant and that majestic face upon the mountainside. So the people ceased to honor him during his lifetime and quietly consigned him to forgetfulness after his decease. Once in a while, it is true, his memory was brought up in connection with the magnificent palace which he had built, and which had long ago been turned into a hotel for the accommodation of strangers, multitudes of whom came, every summer, to visit that famous natural curiosity, the Great Stone Face. Thus, Mr. Gathergold being discredited and thrown into the shade, the man of prophecy was yet to come.

It so happened that a native-born son of the valley, many years before, had enlisted as a soldier and, after a great deal of hard fighting, had now become an illustrious commander. Whatever he may be called in history, he was known in camps and on the battlefield under the nickname of Old Blood-and-Thunder. This war-worn veteran, being now infirm with age and wounds and weary of the turmoil of a military life, and of the roll of the drum and the clangor of the trumpet, that had so long been ringing in his ears, had lately signified a purpose of returning to his native valley, hoping to find repose where he remembered to have left it. The inhabitants, his old neighbors and their grown-up children, were resolved to welcome the renowned warrior with a salute of cannon and a public dinner; and all the more enthusiastically, it being affirmed that now, at last, the likeness of the Great Stone Face had actually appeared. An aide-de-camp of Old Blood-and-Thunder, traveling through the valley, was said to have been struck with the resemblance. Moreover the schoolmates and early acquaintances of the general were ready to testify, on oath, that, to the best of their recollection, the aforesaid general had been exceedingly like the majestic image, even when a boy, only that the idea had never occurred to them at that period. Great, therefore, was the excitement throughout the valley; and many people, who had never once thought of glancing at the Great Stone Face for years before, now spent their time in gazing at it, for the sake of knowing exactly how General Blood-and-Thunder looked.

On the day of the great festival, Ernest, with all the other people of the valley, left his work and proceeded to the spot where the sylvan banquet was prepared. As he approached, the loud voice of the Rev. Dr. Battleblast was heard, beseeching a blessing on the good things set before them and on the distinguished friend of peace in whose honor they were assembled. The tables were arranged in a cleared space of the woods, shut in by the surrounding trees, except where a vista opened eastward and afforded a distant view of the Great Stone Face. Over the general's chair, which was a relic from the home of Washington, there was an arch of verdant boughs, with the laurel profusely intermixed, and surmounted by his country's banner, beneath which he had won his victories. Our friend Ernest raised himself on his tiptoes, in hopes to get a glimpse of the celebrated guest; but there was a mighty crowd about the tables anxious to hear the toasts and speeches and to catch any word that might fall from the general in reply; and a volunteer company, doing duty as a guard, pricked ruthlessly with their bayonets at any particularly quiet person among the throng. So Ernest, being of an unobtrusive character, was thrust quite into the background, where he could see no more of Old Blood-and-Thunder's physiognomy than if it had been still blazing on the battlefield. To console himself, he turned towards the Great Stone Face, which, like a faithful and long-remembered friend, looked back and smiled upon him through the vista of the forest. Meantime, however, he could overhear the remarks of various individuals, who were comparing the features of the hero with the face on the distant mountainside.

"'Tis the same face, to a hair!" cried one man, cutting a caper for joy.

"Wonderfully like, that's a fact!" responded another.

"Like! why, I call it Old Blood-and-Thunder himself, in a monstrous looking glass!" cried a third. "And why not? He's the greatest man of this or any other age, beyond a doubt."

And then all three of the speakers gave a great shout, which communicated electricity to the crowd and called forth a roar from a thousand voices, that went reverberating for miles among the mountains, until you might have supposed that the Great Stone Face had poured its thunder-breath into the cry.

All these comments, and this vast enthusiasm, served the more to interest our friend; nor did he think of questioning that now, at length, the mountain visage had found its human counterpart. It is true, Ernest had imagined that this long-looked-for personage would appear in the character of a man of peace, uttering wisdom, and doing good, and making people happy. But, taking an habitual breadth of view, with all his simplicity, he contended that Providence should choose its own method of blessing mankind, and could conceive that this great end might be effected even by a warrior and a bloody sword, should inscrutable wisdom see fit to order matters so.

"The general! the general!" was now the cry. "Hush! silence! Old Blood-and-Thunder's going to make a speech."

Even so; for, the cloth being removed, the general's health had been drunk, amid shouts of applause, and he now stood upon his feet to thank the company. Ernest saw him. There he was, over the shoulders of the crowd, from the two glittering epaulets and embroidered collar upward, beneath the arch of green boughs with intertwined laurel, and the banner drooping as if to shade his brow! And there, too, visible in the same glance, through the vista of the forest, appeared the Great Stone Face! And was there, indeed, such a resemblance as the crowd had testified? Alas, Ernest could not recognize it! He beheld a war-worn and weather-beaten countenance, full of energy, and expressive of an iron will; but the gentle wisdom, the deep, broad, tender sympathies, were altogether wanting in Old Blood-and-Thunder's visage; and even if the Great Stone Face had assumed his look of stern command, the milder traits would still have tempered it.

"This is not the man of prophecy," sighed Ernest to himself, as he made his way out of the throng. "And must the world wait longer yet?"

The mists had congregated about the distant mountainside, and there were seen the grand and awful features of the Great Stone Face, awful but benignant, as if a mighty angel were sitting among the hills, and enrobing himself in a cloud-vesture of gold and purple. As he looked, Ernest could hardly believe

but that a smile beamed over the whole visage, with a radiance still brightening, although without motion of the lips. It was probably the effect of the western sunshine, melting through the thinly diffused vapors that had swept between him and the object that he gazed at. But—as it always did—the aspect of his marvelous friend made Ernest as hopeful as if he had never hoped in vain.

"Fear not, Ernest," said his heart, even as if the Great Face were whispering him,—"fear not, Ernest; he will come."

More years sped swiftly and tranquilly away. Ernest still dwelt in his native valley and was now a man of middle age. By imperceptible degrees, he had become known among the people. Now, as heretofore, he labored for his bread and was the same simple-hearted man that he had always been. But he had thought and felt so much, he had given so many of the best hours of his life to unworldly hopes for some great good to mankind, that it seemed as though he had been talking with the angels and had imbibed a portion of their wisdom unawares. It was visible in the calm and well-considered beneficence of his daily life, the quiet stream of which had made a wide green margin all along its course. Not a day passed by, that the world was not the better because this man, humble as he was, had lived. He never stepped aside from his own path, yet would always reach a blessing to his neighbor. Almost involuntarily, too, he had become a preacher. The pure and high simplicity of his thought, which, as one of its manifestations, took shape in the good deeds that dropped silently from his hand, flowed also forth in speech. He uttered truths that wrought upon and molded the lives of those who heard him. His auditors, it may be, never suspected that Ernest, their own neighbor and familiar friend, was more than an ordinary man; least of all did Ernest himself suspect it; but, inevitably as the murmur of a rivulet, came thoughts out of his mouth that no other human lips had spoken.

When the people's minds had had a little time to cool, they were ready enough to acknowledge their mistake in imagining a similarity between General Blood-and-Thunder's truculent

283

physiognomy and the benign visage on the mountainside. But now, again, there were reports and many paragraphs in the newspapers, affirming that the likeness of the Great Stone Face had appeared upon the broad shoulders of a certain eminent statesman. He, like Mr. Gathergold and Old Blood-and-Thunder, was a native of the valley, but had left it in his early days and taken up the trades of law and politics. Instead of the rich man's wealth and the warrior's sword, he had but a tongue, and it was mightier than both together. So wonderfully eloquent was he, that whatever he might choose to say, his auditors had no choice but to believe him; wrong looked like right, and right like wrong; for when it pleased him, he could make a kind of illuminated fog with his mere breath, and obscure the natural daylight with it. His tongue, indeed, was a magic instrument: sometimes it rumbled like the thunder; sometimes it warbled like the sweetest music. It was the blast of war,—the song of peace; and it seemed to have a heart in it, when there was no such matter. In good truth, he was a wondrous man; and when his tongue had acquired him all other imaginable success,—when it had been heard in halls of state and in the courts of princes and potentates,—after it had made him known all over the world, even as a voice crying from shore to shore,—it finally persuaded his countrymen to select him for the Presidency. Before this time,—indeed, as soon as he began to grow celebrated,—his admirers had found out the resemblance between him and the Great Stone Face; and so much were they struck by it, that throughout the country this distinguished gentleman was known by the name of Old Stony Phiz. The phrase was considered as giving a highly favorable aspect to his political prospects; for, as is likewise the case with the Popedom, nobody ever becomes President without taking a name other than his own.

While his friends were doing their best to make him President, Old Stony Phiz, as he was called, set out on a visit to the valley where he was born. Of course, he had no other object than to shake hands with his fellow citizens, and neither thought nor cared about any effect which his progress through the country might have upon the election. Magnificent preparations were made to receive the illustrious statesman; a cavalcade of horsemen set forth to meet him at the boundary line of the State, and all the people left their business and gathered along the wayside to see him pass. Among these was Ernest. Though more than once disappointed, as we have seen, he had such a hopeful and confiding nature, that he was always ready to believe in whatever seemed beautiful and good. He kept his heart continually open, and thus was sure to catch the blessing from on high when it should come. So now again, as buoyantly as ever, he went forth to behold the likeness of the Great Stone Face.

The cavalcade came prancing along the road, with a great clattering of hoofs and a mighty cloud of dust, which rose up so dense and high that the visage of the mountainside was completely hidden from Ernest's eyes. All the great men of the neighborhood were there on horseback; militia officers, in uniform; the member of Congress; the sheriff of the county; the editors of newspapers; and many a farmer, too, had mounted his patient steed, with his Sunday coat upon his back. It really was a very brilliant spectacle, especially as there were numerous banners flaunting over the cavalcade, on some of which were gorgeous portraits of the illustrious statesman and the Great Stone Face, smiling familiarly at one another, like two brothers. If the pictures were to be trusted, the mutual resemblance, it must be confessed, was marvelous. We must not forget to mention that there was a band of music, which made the echoes of the mountains ring and reverberate with the loud triumph of its strains; so that airy and soul-thrilling melodies broke out among all the heights and hollows, as if every nook of his native valley had found a voice, to welcome the distinguished guest. But the grandest effect was when the far-off mountain precipice flung back the music; for then the Great Stone Face itself seemed to be swelling the triumphant chorus in acknowledgment that, at length, the man of prophecy was come.

All this while the people were throwing up their hats and shouting, with enthusiasm so contagious that the heart of

Ernest kindled up, and he likewise threw up his hat and shouted, as loudly as the loudest, "Huzza for the great man! Huzza for Old Stony Phiz!" But as yet he had not seen him.

"Here he is, now!" cried those who stood near Ernest. "There! There! Look at Old Stony Phiz and then at the Old Man of the Mountain, and see if they are not as like as two twin-brothers!"

In the midst of all this gallant array came an open barouche, drawn by four white horses; and in the barouche, with his massive head uncovered, sat the illustrious statesman, Old Stony Phiz himself.

"Confess it," said one of Ernest's neighbors to him, "the Great Stone Face has met its match at last!"

Now, it must be owned that, at his first glimpse of the countenance which was bowing and smiling from the barouche, Ernest did fancy that there was a resemblance between it and the old familiar face upon the mountainside. The brow, with its massive depth and loftiness, and all the other features, indeed, were boldly and strongly hewn, as if in emulation of a more than heroic, of a Titanic model. But the sublimity and stateliness, the grand expression of a divine sympathy, that illuminated the mountain visage and etherealized its ponderous granite substance into spirit, might here be sought in vain. Something had been originally left out or had departed. And therefore the marvelously gifted statesman had always a weary gloom in the deep caverns of his eyes, as of a child that has outgrown its playthings or a man of mighty faculties and little aims, whose life, with all its high performances, was vague and empty, because no high purpose had endowed it with reality.

Still, Ernest's neighbor was thrusting his elbow into his side and pressing him for an answer.

"Confess! confess! Is not he the very picture of your Old Man of the Mountain?"

"No!" said Ernest bluntly, "I see little or no likeness."

"Then so much the worse for the Great Stone Face!" answered his neighbor; and again he set up a shout for Old Stony Phiz.

But Ernest turned away, melancholy, and almost despondent;

286

for this was the saddest of his disappointments, to behold a
man who might have fulfilled the prophecy, and had not willed
to do so. Meantime, the cavalcade, the banners, the music, and
the barouches swept past him, with the vociferous crowd in the
rear, leaving the dust to settle down, and the Great Stone Face
to be revealed again, with the grandeur that it had worn for
untold centuries.

"Lo, here I am, Ernest!" the benign lips seemed to say. "I
have waited longer than thou, and am not yet weary. Fear not;
the man will come."

The years hurried onward, treading in their haste on one
another's heels. And now they began to bring white hairs and
scatter them over the head of Ernest; they made reverend
wrinkles across his forehead and furrows in his cheeks. He was
an aged man. But not in vain had he grown old: more than the
white hairs on his head were the sage thoughts in his mind;
his wrinkles and furrows were inscriptions that Time had
graved, and in which he had written legends of wisdom that
had been tested by the tenor of a life. And Ernest had ceased
to be obscure. Unsought for, undesired, had come the fame
which so many seek, and made him known in the great world,
beyond the limits of the valley in which he had dwelt so quietly.
College professors, and even the active men of cities, came
from far to see and converse with Ernest; for the report had
gone abroad that this simple husbandman had ideas unlike
those of other men, not gained from books, but of a higher

tone,—a tranquil and familiar majesty, as if he had been talking with the angels as his daily friends. Whether it were sage, statesman, or philanthropist, Ernest received these visitors with the gentle sincerity that had characterized him from boyhood, and spoke freely with them of whatever came uppermost, or lay deepest in his heart or their own. While they talked together, his face would kindle, unawares, and shine upon them, as with a mild evening light. Pensive with the fullness of such discourse, his guests took leave and went their way; and passing up the valley, paused to look at the Great Stone Face, imagining that they had seen its likeness in a human countenance, but could not remember where.

While Ernest had been growing up and growing old, a bountiful Providence had granted a new poet to this earth. He, likewise, was a native of the valley, but had spent the greater part of his life at a distance from that romantic region, pouring out his sweet music amid the bustle and din of cities. Often, however, did the mountains which had been familiar to him in his childhood lift their snowy peaks into the clear atmosphere of his poetry. Neither was the Great Stone Face forgotten, for the poet had celebrated it in an ode, which was grand enough to have been uttered by its own majestic lips. This man of genius, we may say, had come down from heaven with wonderful endowments. If he sang of a mountain, the eyes of all mankind beheld a mightier grandeur reposing on its breast, or soaring to its summit, than had before been seen there. If his theme were a lovely lake, a celestial smile had now been thrown over it, to gleam forever on its surface. If it were the vast old sea, even the deep immensity of its dread bosom seemed to swell the higher, as if moved by the emotions of the song. Thus the world assumed another and a better aspect from the hour that the poet blessed it with his happy eyes. The Creator had bestowed him, as the last best touch to his own handiwork. Creation was not finished till the poet came to interpret and so complete it.

The effect was no less high and beautiful, when his human brethren were the subject of his verse. The man or woman,

288

sordid with the common dust of life, who crossed his daily path, and the little child who played in it, were glorified if he beheld them in his mood of poetic faith. He showed the golden links of the great chain that intertwined them with an angelic kindred; he brought out the hidden traits of a celestial birth that made them worthy of such kin. Some, indeed, there were, who thought to show the soundness of their judgment by affirming that all the beauty and dignity of the natural world existed only in the poet's fancy. Let such men speak for themselves, who undoubtedly appear to have been spawned forth by Nature with a contemptuous bitterness; she having plastered them up out of her refuse stuff, after all the swine were made. As respects all things else, the poet's ideal was the truest truth.

The songs of this poet found their way to Ernest. He read them after his customary toil, seated on the bench before his cottage door, where for such a length of time he had filled his repose with thought, by gazing at the Great Stone Face. And now as he read stanzas that caused the soul to thrill within him, he lifted his eyes to the vast countenance beaming on him.

"O majestic friend," he murmured, addressing the Great Stone Face, "is not this man worthy to resemble thee?"

The Face seemed to smile, but answered not a word.

Now it happened that the poet, though he dwelt so far away, had not only heard of Ernest, but had meditated much upon his character, until he deemed nothing so desirable as to meet this man, whose untaught wisdom walked hand in hand with the noble simplicity of his life. One summer morning, therefore, he took passage by the railroad and, in the decline of the afternoon, alighted from the cars at no great distance from Ernest's cottage. The great hotel, which had formerly been the palace of Mr. Gathergold, was close at hand; but the poet, with his carpetbag on his arm, inquired at once where Ernest dwelt and was resolved to be accepted as his guest.

Approaching the door, he there found the good old man, holding a volume in his hand, which alternately he read and then, with a finger between the leaves, looked lovingly at the Great Stone Face.

"Good evening," said the poet. "Can you give a traveler a night's lodging?"

"Willingly," answered Ernest; and then he added, smiling, "Methinks I never saw the Great Stone Face look so hospitably at a stranger."

The poet sat down on the bench beside him, and he and Ernest talked together. Often had the poet held intercourse with the wittiest and the wisest, but never before with a man like Ernest, whose thoughts and feelings gushed up with such a natural freedom, and who made great truths so familiar by his simple utterance of them. Angels, as had been so often said, seemed to have wrought with him at his labor in the fields; angels seemed to have sat with him by the fireside; and, dwelling with angels as friend with friends, he had imbibed the sublimity of their ideas and imbued it with the sweet and lowly charm of household words. So thought the poet. And Ernest, on the other hand, was moved and agitated by the living images which the poet flung out of his mind, and which peopled all the air about the cottage door with shapes of beauty, both gay and pensive. The sympathies of these two men instructed them with a profounder sense than either could have attained alone. Their minds accorded into one strain and made delightful music which neither of them could have claimed as all his own, nor

290

distinguished his own share from the other's. They led one another, as it were, into a high pavilion of their thoughts, so remote, and hitherto so dim, that they had never entered it before, and so beautiful that they desired to be there always.

As Ernest listened to the poet, he imagined that the Great Stone Face was bending forward to listen too. He gazed earnestly into the poet's glowing eyes.

"Who are you, my strangely gifted guest?" he said.

The poet laid his finger on the volume that Ernest had been reading.

"You have read these poems," said he. "You know me, then,—for I wrote them."

Again, and still more earnestly than before, Ernest examined the poet's features; then turned towards the Great Stone Face; then back, with an uncertain aspect, to his guest. But his countenance fell; he shook his head, and sighed.

"Wherefore are you sad?" inquired the poet.

"Because," replied Ernest, "all through life I have awaited the fulfillment of a prophecy; and, when I read these poems, I hoped that it might be fulfilled in you."

"You hoped," answered the poet, faintly smiling, "to find in me the likeness of the Great Stone Face. And you are disappointed, as formerly with Mr. Gathergold, and Old Blood-and-Thunder, and Old Stony Phiz. Yes, Ernest, it is my doom. You must add my name to the illustrious three and record another failure of your hopes. For—in shame and sadness do I speak it, Ernest—I am not worthy to be typified by yonder benign and majestic image."

"And why?" asked Ernest. He pointed to the volume. "Are not those thoughts divine?"

"They have a strain of the Divinity," replied the poet. "You can hear in them the far-off echo of a heavenly song. But my life, dear Ernest, has not corresponded with my thought. I have had grand dreams, but they have been only dreams, because I have lived—and that, too, by my own choice—among poor and mean realities. Sometimes even—shall I dare to say it?—I lack faith in the grandeur, the beauty, and the goodness which my

291

own works are said to have made more evident in nature and in human life. Why, then, pure seeker of the good and true, shouldst thou hope to find me in yonder image of the divine?"

The poet spoke sadly, and his eyes were dim with tears. So, likewise, were those of Ernest.

At the hour of sunset, as had long been his frequent custom, Ernest was to discourse to an assemblage of the neighboring inhabitants in the open air. He and the poet, arm in arm, still talking together as they went along, proceeded to the spot. It was a small nook among the hills, with a gray precipice behind, the stern front of which was relieved by the pleasant foliage of many creeping plants that made a tapestry for the naked rock, by hanging their festoons from all its rugged angles. At a small elevation above the ground, set in a rich framework of verdure, there appeared a niche, spacious enough to admit a human figure, with freedom for such gestures as spontaneously accompany earnest thought and genuine emotion. Into this natural pulpit Ernest ascended, and threw a look of familiar kindness around upon his audience. They stood, or sat, or reclined upon the grass, as seemed good to each, with the departing sunshine falling obliquely over them and mingling its subdued cheerfulness with the solemnity of a grove of ancient trees, beneath and amid the boughs of which the golden rays were constrained to pass. In another direction was seen the Great Stone Face, with the same cheer, combined with the same solemnity, in its benignant aspect.

Ernest began to speak, giving to the people of what was in his heart and mind. His words had power, because they accorded with his thoughts; and his thoughts had reality and depth, because they harmonized with the life which he had always lived. It was not mere breath that this preacher uttered; they were the words of life, because a life of good deeds and holy love was melted into them. Pearls, pure and rich, had been dissolved into this precious draught. The poet, as he listened, felt that the being and character of Ernest were a nobler strain of poetry than he had ever written. His eyes glistening with tears, he gazed reverentially at the venerable man and said

"Good evening," said the poet. "Can you give a traveler a night's lodging?"

within himself that never was there an aspect so worthy of a prophet and a sage as that mild, sweet, thoughtful countenance, with the glory of white hair diffused about it. At a distance, but distinctly to be seen, high up in the golden light of the setting sun, appeared the Great Stone Face, with hoary mists around it, like the white hairs around the brow of Ernest. Its look of grand beneficence seemed to embrace the world.

At that moment, in sympathy with a thought which he was about to utter, the face of Ernest assumed a grandeur of expression, so imbued with benevolence, that the poet, by an irresistible impulse, threw his arms aloft, and shouted,—

"Behold! Behold! Ernest is himself the likeness of the Great Stone Face!"

Then all the people looked, and saw that what the deep-sighted poet said was true. The prophecy was fulfilled. But Ernest, having finished what he had to say, took the poet's arm, and walked slowly homeward, still hoping that some wiser and better man than himself would by and by appear, bearing a resemblance to the GREAT STONE FACE.

FOLLOW THE GLEAM

Alfred Tennyson

Not of the sunlight,
Not of the moonlight,
Not of the starlight!
O young Mariner,
Down to the haven,
Call your companions,
Launch your vessel,
And crowd your canvas,
And, ere it vanishes
Over the margin,
After it, follow it,
Follow the Gleam.

Eric P. Kelly

THE BROKEN NOTE

ILLUSTRATED BY *Lynd Ward*

IT WAS in the spring of the year 1241 that rumors began to travel along the highroad from Kiev in the land of Rus that the Tartars of the East were again upon the march. Men trembled when they heard that news and mothers held their children close to their breasts, for the name "Tartar" was one that froze folks' blood in their veins. As the weeks went on, the rumors grew thicker, and there began to come through to Poland, our land of the fields, the news that the country lands of the Ukraine were ablaze. Then it was heard that Kiev had fallen, then Lvov, the city of the Lion, and now there was naught between the savage band of warriors and the fair city of Krakow, save a few peaceful villages and fertile fields.

The Tartars came through the world like a horde of wild beasts. They left not one thing alive nor one green blade of wheat standing. They were short, dark men of shaggy beards and long hair twisted into little braids, and they rode on small horses which they covered with trophies that they had gained in war. Brave they were as lions, courageous they were as great dogs, but they had hearts of stone and knew not mercy, nor pity, nor tenderness, nor God. On their horses they carried round shields of leather and iron, and long spears often trailed from their saddles. About their shoulders and thighs they wore skins of animals. Some decorated their ears with golden rings— here and there one wore a gold ring in the nose. When they traveled, the dust rose high into the sky from beneath the hoofs

294

of their little horses, and the thunder of the hoofbeats could be heard many miles away. They were so numerous that it took days for the whole horde to pass any one given point, and for miles behind the army itself rumbled carts bearing slaves, provisions, and booty—usually gold.

Before them went always a long, desperate procession of country people driven from their humble homes by the news of the coming terror; they had already said farewell to the cottages where they lived, the parting from which was almost as bitter as death. So it has always been in time of war that the innocent suffer most—these poor, helpless peasants with their carts and horses and geese and sheep trudging along through the dust to escape, if God so willed, the terrible fate which would befall them were they left behind. There were old people in that procession too feeble to be stirring even about a house, mothers nursing children, women weak with sickness, and men broken-hearted at the loss of all that a lifetime of labor had brought. Children dragged themselves wearily along beside them, often bearing their pets in their arms.

To this company Krakow opened her gates and prepared for defense. Many of the nobility and rich citizens had, in the meantime, fled to the west or taken refuge in monasteries far to the north. The brothers of the monastery at Zvierzyniec, a short distance outside the city, took in all the refugees that the building could accommodate and then prepared to stand siege. But the great, weary, terror-mad mob that had fled ahead of the band of Tartars was content enough to make the city itself its destination. And once within its walls all turned their faces toward the south. For there, in the south of the city, towering on its rocky hill high over the Vistula River, was the great, irregular, turreted mass that was the Wawel—the fortress and castle of the kings of Poland from the time of Krakus, the legend king, and the home of the dukes and nobles who formed the king's court.

It had been decided to make no attempt to defend the city outside the castle gates, since that would entail a great loss of life; and so for several days the city dwellers who remained and

these refugees from all the country about poured into the forti-
fication and were housed inside its walls. The old castle gates
which were then on Castle Highway opposite the Church of
St. Andrew were at last shut and barricaded, and the walls were
manned with citizen soldiery prepared to give their lives for
the protection of the city and their families.

The Tartars fell upon the city in the night and, after burning
the outlying villages, pillaged the districts that lay about the
churches of St. Florian, St. John, and the Holy Cross. The whole
night long was one of hideous sounds—the crackling and fury
of flames, the snarling and yelling of the enemy when they
found that the prey had fled, their roars of triumph when they
came upon gold and treasure. As morning dawned the watchers
from the Wawel looked out over the town and saw but three
churches not already in flames. These were the Church of Our
Lady Mary near the great market, the Church of St. Andrew
with its stalwart towers at the Castle Gate, and the Church of
St. Adalbert in the market place. Already a colony of Jews in
the Black Village had perished, also those refugees and town
dwellers who had not rushed inside the walls of defense. There
remained but one man—or rather a youth—still alive in the
midst of all that destruction.

He was the trumpeter of the Church of Our Lady Mary, and
he had taken solemn oath to sound the trumpet each hour of
the day and night from a little balcony high up on the front of
the church. As the first golden rays of the sun changed the
Vistula from a dark line to a plash of dancing gold, he mounted
this balcony to sound the Heynal—the hymn to Our Lady which
every trumpeter in the church had in the past sworn to play
each hour of the day and night—"until death." He felt with a
strange joy the glow of the sun as it fell upon him that morning, for the night had been very dark both with its own shadow
and with the gloomy blackness of men's ruthlessness.

About his feet, down in the town highway, stood groups of
short, fierce men gazing up at him curiously. Here and there
the roof of a house was shooting upward in flames and belching
forth clouds of black smoke. Hundreds of dwellings lay charred

and ruined by the conflagration. He was alone in the midst of a terrible enemy—he might have fled on the previous day and gained the castle with the refugees and the town dwellers, but he had been true to his oath and remained at his post until he should be driven away. Now it was too late to retreat.

He was a very young man, perhaps nineteen or twenty, and wore a dark cloth suit that was caught at the knees with buckles, like the knickerbockers of a later generation; dark, thick hose extended from the knees to the tops of his soft, pointed sandals, and a short coat falling just below the waist was held together in front by a belt. The head covering was of leather and something like a cowl; it fell clear to his shoulders and ran up over the head in such a way that only his face and a bit of hair were visible.

"My mother and sister are safe," he thought. "May God be praised for that! They are gone these ten days and must be now with the cousins in Moravia."

It came to him then what a sweet thing life is. The sun over the Vistula was now reflected in the windows of the Cathedral of the Wawel where the priests were already saying mass. At the tops of all the gates he could see guards in full armor upon which the sunlight flashed. A banner with a white eagle hung in the air above the gate at the great draw.

"Poland lives," he thought.

And then it came to him, young as he was, that he was part of the glorious company of Polish men that was fighting for all Christendom against brutal and savage invaders. He had not seen much of death before that minute—he had heard of it only as something vague. And now, he himself was perhaps going out to meet it, because of his oath, because of his love for the Church, because of his love for Poland.

"I shall keep my word," he mused. "If I die it shall be for that. My word is as good as my life."

Had a painter caught his expression then, he would have caught only the expression of a very great peace—an expression that signified somehow that God was very close. There was no moment of weakness, no faltering, no suffering even—for he did

298

not think of what might come after his duty was performed. The sand in the hourglass already marked the hour for the trumpet to sound.

"Now, for Poland and Our Lady I will sound the Heynal," he said, and raised the trumpet to his lips.

Softly he blew at first—then, thrilled with a sense of triumph, he felt in his heart a joy that was almost ecstatic. He seemed to see in a vision that though he might now die alone and for naught save what perhaps some scoffing ones might call a foolish honor, still that bravery was to descend as a heritage to the people to whom he belonged and was to become a part of their spirit, their courage, their power of everlasting—all this that moment brought.

A Tartar below crouched to his bow and drew back the arrow as far as he could draw. The string whirred. The dark shaft flew like a swift bird straight for the mark. It pierced the breast of the young trumpeter when he was near the end of his song—it quivered there a moment and the song ceased. But still holding to the trumpet the youth fell back against the supporting wall and blew one last glorious note; it began strongly, trembled, and then ceased—broken like the young life that gave it birth, and at that moment those below applied the torch to the wooden church and it, too, rose in flames to Heaven, with the soul of the youth among them.

299

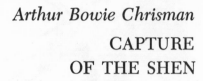

Arthur Bowie Chrisman

CAPTURE
OF THE SHEN

ILLUSTRATED BY *Robert Sinnott*

KUA HAI City stands on a plain in northern China. The plain is called Wa Tien, and it is very smooth and fertile, giving many large melons. . . . Life there is good. The plain is likewise extremely low. Any reliable geography will tell you that Kua Hai is below sea level. And that, I know, is a fact, for I, lazily seated in my garden, have often gazed at sailing ships, large-eyed—wide-staring-eyed junks as they fetched into the Bay of The Sharp-Horned Moon, and to view them I had to raise my eyes. It is very true. I had to look up, as one looks up to behold the sky-hung eagles of Lo Fan.

I had as often wondered if the sea ever broke through its restraining walls and flooded Kua Hai. A storm coming down from the northeast would most likely thrust billows to overtop the wall. So I said to my gardener, Wu Chang: "Wu Chang, did fishes ever swim up the Street of A Thousand Singing Dragons? Did the sea ever come into Kua Hai?" Wu Chang paused in his scratching among the *hung lo po* (the radishes). Since thinking it over, I am inclined to believe that he welcomed an opportunity to change from the working of his fingers to the working of his tongue. "Once, and once only, Honorable One, has the sea invaded Kua Hai. But it can never do so again. Chieh Chung was fooled once, but he was far too clever to be fooled twice. He buried the bottle, perhaps in this very garden, for who knows? He buried it so deep that no ordinary digging shall discover it. And so, the sea may look over the walls of Kua Hai, but it may not enter."

"Indeed?" said I. "And pray, who *was* this Chieh Chung? And what was in the bottle?"

Such astounding ignorance gained me a look of compassion from old Wu Chang. "The Honorable One is surely jesting. He, of course, knows that Chieh Chung was the first King of Wa Tien."

"Oh, to be sure," I interrupted. "It was Chieh Chung who invented—hum—er radishes." That was a guess, and a miss.

Wu Chang corrected me. "Not radishes, but writing. A mistaken thing to do, in my opinion. But beyond doubt he did a great service when he bottled the water demons. Ho. Ho. Ho. He bottled the demons as if they were melon pickles. Ho. Ho. Ho."

"Sit here in the shade, Wu Chang," said I. "So Chieh Chung pickled the water demons—and then what?"

"Not pickled, Honorable One, bottled. Chieh Chung bottled the demons. Ho. Ho. Ho. . . . You must understand that in those days the plain hereabouts was much lower than it is now. It had not been built up. And the sea was much higher in those days, for then there were no heavy ships to weigh it down and flatten it. The sea was very high then-a-days, far too high for its breadth. On every side the land held it back, and it was retarded and had no freedom of motion. So the Shen, the demons of the sea, got them together and took thought. They said: 'Our sea is far too small. We must have more room. We are mighty, are we not? Then let us take some land and occupy it, so that our sea may expand.'

"Accordingly, the water demons swam along the coast, seeking land to conquer. They passed the shores of Fu Sang without stopping, for that region is high and mountainous. They passed the region of San Shen Shan, for in that place lives the powerful land demon named Hu Kung. The water demons were in no great haste to gain Hu Kung's hatred. They passed without a second glance. But when the Shen swam up to Kua Hai, it was to rejoice. The demons looked over the wall; they

smiled down upon Kua Hai and said, 'This land we shall take
for our beloved sea. It is low and suited to our purpose. Right-
fully it is ours. Yes, we shall take Kua Hai, and all the vast
plain hereabout.' But the ocean demons were possessed of
decency. They did not dash over the walls, calling on their sea
to follow, and so drown all the people of Kua Hai. Demons
though they be, the Shen that time had mercy in their hearts.
While the night dew lay upon the fields of Wa Tien, those
demons, to the number of seven, made their way into Kua Hai.
There they waited in the garden of the palace.

"When King Chieh Chung, who ruled over Wa Tien, took
him to the garden for an early morning stroll, he discovered the
demons waiting. He knew at once they were no ordinary men.
Not once did they *kou tou* (knock their heads on the ground)
as men should do. Nor did they look like the men of Wa Tien.
Their mouths were wide mouths, like those of codfishes. Their
bodies were covered with iridescent scales. Nevertheless, Chieh
Chung permitted the Shen to approach. 'What manner of men
are you?' asked the King. 'And what is your pleasure?'

" 'We are the Shen, demons of the sea,' answered the seven.
'We are Shen of the ocean, and we come to claim our own.'
'And what is that?' asked the King, smiling tolerantly upon
them, though in truth he felt more like weeping, for he knew
what would be the answer.

" 'We have come to possess ourselves of the city and all the
low plain that surrounds it. It is our right, and our might—we
mean to have it.' Then Chieh Chung's heart dropped down to
a level with his sandals. His heart was weighted as if with
millstones, as if weighted with Mount Tai. Long he stroked his
beard, pondering, grieving, praying. And the water demons
danced in the dew. Jubilant were they, flinging their toes high,
spattering dewdrops upon the palace roof, and singing the
terrible song of the ocean.

"Finally the King answered. 'Shen,' said he, 'what time do
you grant me? Kua Hai is a large city. In it are half a million
souls. It will be moons and moons before I can count my people
safely upon the Mountain of The Yellow Ox.' One of the

demons was shaking a *pai shu* (shaking a cypress tree), so that its dew fell upon him and upon his companions, for already the sun was up, and they were beginning to feel the day and its dryness. 'What time?' said the Shen, taking his answer from the *pai shu*. 'We shall give you until this tree is in flower. Have all your people gathered upon high ground when this *pai shu* blossoms, for at that time we shall lead the sea upon Wa Tien, and the sea shall stand three *li* deep above your palace. That is our answer. And now we must go for the sun has lit his fire.'

"The Shen made a move as if to depart, but no sooner were they out of the shadows than they halted abruptly, murmuring in displeasure. And small wonder. The sun had dispelled the dew, and there was no moisture upon the land. A water Shen cannot exist where there is no moisture. In that respect he is like the *yin yu* and the *shih pan* (fishes). So the Shen turned to Chieh Chung and said, 'Is there water here, O King, where we may spend the day hours?' 'There is little,' said Chieh Chung; 'I dare say too little for your purpose. But in such quantity as it is, you are welcome.' He pointed to a crystal bowl in which burgeoned a sacred lily. There was water in the bowl, water surrounding the lily bulb. Too, there were stones in the bowl—blue lapis lazuli, and green jade, and yellow topaz (precious stones, as befitted a palace garden), for that is the way sacred lilies are grown—in bowls filled with water and pretty pebbles. 'You are quite welcome to it,' reiterated the King. The Shen shook their heads half in despair. 'It is too little,' groaned they, 'far too little.' 'But,' said Chieh Chung, 'you are demons—hence magicians. Why do you not make yourselves smaller? Why not change yourselves into red *hung pao shih* and recline in the bowl amid the lily roots? I am sure you would make handsome rubies. Beyond a doubt, my courtiers would say "Ah" and "How lovely" and admire you greatly when they saw you. Of a certainty, you would make resplendent gems, dazzling and superb.' 'Well,' agreed the Shen, somewhat dubiously, 'we shall try it. If you have no more water it is the only thing we *can* do.' And so, in a twinkling the Shen were gone, and seven beautiful rubies appeared in the crystal bowl.

" 'How lovely,' said Chieh Chung—and deliberately winked at the cypress tree, first with one eye and then with the other. He went to a cabinet that stood in his chamber, and from the cabinet took a bottle fashioned out of *fei yu* (a cloudy jade). And the bottle had a wide mouth. Into it Chieh Chung poured water. Returning to the lily bowl, he quickly took therefrom the seven red *hung pao shih* and dropped them into the jade bottle—closing the mouth securely.

" 'Now,' exulted the King, 'my city is saved. My people may walk in security and without fear. The seven water demons are in my keeping, and please Heaven may they never escape my hand.' And in his joy, King Chieh Chung ordered that ten thousand catties of rice be given to the poor.

"Weeks lengthened into months. Lengthened the months to years. Still languished the water demons in the clouded jade bottle. Still broke the sea on Kua Hai's walls—but did not enter. Chieh Chung added to his kingdom and ruled with beneficence. His name was heralded throughout the length of the world. Not by the spear, but by wisdom he added to his dominions. Peoples of far-distant regions came seeking to place themselves under the rule of Chieh Chung—wisest and best.

"At length came ambassadors from Wei Chou, yes, even from distant Kou Pei, offering to give their allegiance to Chieh Chung. Ah, but that was a great day, a day of all proud days. The ambassadors were a hundred for number, haughty mandarins all. There was a great stir about the palace, you may well believe, retainers rushing hither and thither to provide food and drink and entertainment for the foreign great men.

"A foolish servant, ransacking cupboard and closet for what victuals and drink he could find, came upon the dusty jade bottle that stood in Chieh Chung's cabinet. 'Ah,' said the servant, trying to peer through the cloudy jade. 'Beyond a doubt, here is something of rare excellence. This will do for the highest of the mandarins, for the red-button mandarins with peacock feathers. It rattles—rock candy in it.' And the foolish one removed the stopper. A thousand pities he was not stricken dead before the seal was broken.

"Chieh Chung came into the chamber and saw what had happened. For a moment he was stunned. Then, 'Let me have the bottle.' The bottle was empty, all save for a bit of water. 'They are gone,' said the King. 'The Shen have escaped. But even so, I may baffle them, for they promised with binding oaths not to take my kingdom until the *pai shu* blossoms. And—in this region the cypress tree never blossoms—it *never* comes into flower.' The King smiled in spite of himself.

"Meanwhile, the water demons, having escaped from the bottle, hastened through the palace toward the garden. They were very angry—were those demons, gnashing their teeth with a noise like that of waves lashing a rock-guarded coast. They were determined on vengeance.

"The Wei Chou ambassadors were encamped in the palace garden. Their servants had been washing garments, brilliant-hued garments such as the wealthy and noble of that land wear. The garments had been hung on the cypress tree to dry. And there the garments hung when the water demons appeared. The tree was aflame with color. Instantly the Shen raised a great shout. 'Come billow. Come ocean.' They shouted in triumph. 'The *pai shu* blossoms (the cypress tree blooms)'—for they thought the garments were flowers—'and our promise is ended. Kua Hai is ours.'

"Fathoms deep, roaring, grinding, relentless, the sea swept over Kua Hai, buried the city, buried the plain. The water demons raced before it, calling it on. They who had been the people of Kua Hai rode upon white-crested billows—without life—drowned. Out of all the vast population perhaps a thousand escaped. And among those who escaped was the King.

"Chieh Chung sat under a pine tree on the mountain, grief-stricken, heartbroken, gazing upon what had been a city, and now was sparkling sea. Hour after hour sat the King, grieving and thinking, meditating a way to regain his country. Now and then the seven water demons appeared before him, mocking, splashing him with spray.

"One day, having meditated long, Chieh Chung arose and shouted exultantly: 'I have it. I know how I shall regain my

307

city. I shall go immediately and put the plan in writing, while it is fresh in my mind.' Having said, he walked to the little hut that served for his palace and sat down at a table to write. On the table stood a crystal bowl, with a lily, and with green, blue, and yellow stones.

"Chieh Chung sat writing meaningless stuff upon parchment. All the while he kept an eye on the crystal bowl. Lo! There appeared seven red stones at the root of the lily. The demons had come to spy upon the King's writing. They had come to learn his plan, and so triumph over him. But they, unwittingly, were giving themselves into bondage again. For Chieh Chung quickly thrust them into a bottle and sealed it against all escape. Six of the demons he thus imprisoned. The seventh, who was a small fellow, Chieh Chung threw back into the sea. 'Go,' said the King, 'and take your sea with you. Take your sea, and never trouble me again. Else I shall most certainly destroy your six brothers. It is a warning.'

"So the seventh demon sped away, taking the sea with him. Then did Chieh Chung descend to Kua Hai and build up the city, people coming in from far countries. Once more the city was inhabited, and the land was more rich, by reason of its flooding.

"And the six Shen, the six water demons are buried deep, in a jade bottle—perhaps under this very garden."

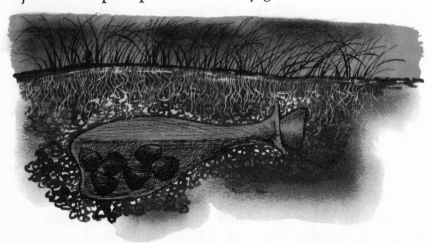

Cornelia Meigs

THE TALE OF SIR GARETH OF ORKENEY THAT WAS CALLED BEAUMAINS

RETOLD FROM THE WORKS OF SIR THOMAS MALORY

ILLUSTRATED BY *Henry C. Pitz*

KING ARTHUR of Britain had the custom, at certain festivals of the year, to say that he would not sit down to feast until he had heard of some strange marvel or some new adventure. At this season of Whitsuntide, in the warm May weather, he was holding the feast at Kynkenadon, on the bright sands of Wales, and had gathered the whole company of his knights of the Round Table to keep the festival with him. As he sat waiting before meat, Sir Gawaine came in to him to say that he had seen a company approaching that must indeed mean some strange errand or adventure. Into the great hall, where the knights of the Round Table sat assembled, there entered three men and a dwarf, all well and richly dressed. No word was said, but all watched in silence as the three walked up to the high throne where the King sat. It was the man who walked in the middle of the three who caught the eyes of all, for he stooped and leaned on the shoulders of the others, but when he stood before the king he raised himself upright and showed that he was a good foot and a half taller than anyone in the Hall, and showed also that he had big awkward hands and feet, and that he was very young.

"Most noble King Arthur, God bless you and all your fellowship," he said, "and especially the fellowship of the knights of the Table Round. I have come here to ask you for three gifts, nor will it be of any hurt or loss to you to grant them. But there is only one of them that I will ask for now."

"Ask and you shall have," returned the King, for it was his custom to grant every petition possible that was made to him at the feast of Whitsuntide.

"What I wish is that I may abide here in your household and that you shall give me meat and drink for a twelvemonth," the boy said. "And at the end of that time I beg for leave to ask you for two things more."

"You could have had more than that," Arthur declared, for he thought that this lad was one of the goodliest that he had ever seen. "But what you have requested shall be granted. Now we should like to have your name."

"I cannot tell you my name," the young man answered. Nor could anyone bring him to say more.

King Arthur called his steward, Sir Kay, and gave orders that the boy should have the best of meat and drink for the whole year to come. But Sir Kay was sour and unwilling and thought that it was wasteful to grant such a strange wish to a young man of whom they knew nothing. "I am certain that he is a low-born fellow," he growled, "for if he had been a gentleman he would have asked for a horse and armor, knowing that he could have them. And since he has no name I will give him one. Those great hands of his are strangely white, as though he were unwilling to work. I will call him Beaumains, or Fair Hands, and he shall be sent to the kitchen, to spend his time there and eat broth and grow fat to his heart's content."

So Beaumains was sent to the kitchen where he slept among the kitchen boys and was bullied and scorned by Sir Kay and his followers. The boy was willing and good-natured, and took no offense, bearing for a whole long year everything that was put upon him. But whenever the knights were practicing at arms, he would go out to stand watching with all his eyes. And when there was matching of skills among the younger squires, he was allowed to take part and showed that he had great strength and could cast an iron bar or a stone two yards farther than could any other. Sir Launcelot and Sir Gawaine took interest in him and spoke friendly words to him, but when anyone praised him Sir Kay was always there to say, "How do you like my kitchen boy?"

Whitsuntide came round again, and this year Arthur held the feast at Carleon, and once more he waited to sit down to meat until he should hear of some adventure. And this time it was a young damsel who came in and stood before the King. "I pray you for help," was her greeting, and the King answered, "For whom is the help and what is the adventure?"

Her sister, the young woman explained, was a very great lady, and she had been shut up in her castle by a wicked knight and her lands laid waste because she would not accept his love and marry him. This evil enemy was called the Red Knight of the Red Plains, but the sister's name and her own the girl did not reveal. "And since it is said that here are all the noblest

311

knights of the world," she ended, "I have come to you to ask for succor."

"That Red Knight is one who has the strength of seven men," said Sir Gawaine. "Once I did battle with him and hardly escaped with my life." Sir Gawaine was nephew to King Arthur and son of the King of Orkeney. All knew him to be a mighty fighter. No other knight spoke, nor did anyone come forward to offer himself for such an adventure.

"There are brave knights here who would ride to the rescue of your lady and do their utmost for her," Arthur said, "could they but know her name. But without it no one will offer."

"Then I must seek farther," said the damsel, and she went toward the door.

But meanwhile word of these matters had got to Beaumains in the kitchen, and he came hurrying in to stand before the King. "I have had good living in your household for a twelvemonth, Sir King," he declared, "and now I have come to ask for my two other favors. One is that I may have the adventure of this damsel, and the other is that Sir Launcelot shall ride after me, and if he sees me prove myself worthy, shall make me a knight. I will be made knight by no hand but his."

"All this shall be done," said the King, but the damsel burst out in anger.

"Fie on you," she cried. "I came to ask for a champion, and all you have for me is a knave out of the kitchen." And she went out and mounted her horse.

But now word was brought in to Beaumains that "his horse and armor were come for him," and there outside stood the dwarf who had been with him at his first coming, holding a horse and bearing rich clothes and arms for the lad out of the kitchen. He was a goodly sight when he had arrayed himself in rich cloth of gold and went in to bid good-bye to the King and to Sir Gawaine, and to beg that Sir Launcelot would indeed come after him. Everyone went outside to see him mount, and a few followed a little way as he rode after the damsel. But Sir Kay, full of curiosity, took his horse and went behind him, ready to mock him still. Beaumains made a fine figure on the

great horse, but he had as yet neither shield nor spear such as a
knight carried.

He had just come up with the damsel when Sir Kay came
spurring behind. "Kitchen boy, do you remember me?" he
asked mockingly as Beaumains turned about.

"I remember you for an ungentle knight who has put scorn
on me for a whole long year," Beaumains cried. "Now, therefore, beware of me." With only his sword against Sir Kay's
spear he rode down upon him, struck the spear from the
knight's hand, and wounded him in the side, so that he fell
headlong from his horse and lay as though he were dead.
Beaumains got down, took Sir Kay's spear and shield, ordered
his dwarf to mount Sir Kay's horse, and rode away.

And now another horseman came spurring up behind, and
Beaumains, angry and excited, was ready without a word to
fight again. They charged together, and both were carried from

313

their saddles; the other man leaped up and helped Beaumains get free of his horse, but Beaumains raised his sword to do battle on foot. For an hour they fought, trampling the grass, feinting, dodging, advancing and retreating. Beaumains laid about him like a giant, and the other, with all his skill, could scarcely defend himself. At last he spoke.

"Beaumains, do not fight so sorely. Your quarrel and mine is not so great a one." It was Launcelot.

Beaumains lowered his sword. "That is surely true," he answered. "But it does me good to feel the might and power of your fighting. Yet I did not fight you to the end, my lord."

"You had no need to," Launcelot replied. "By the faith of my body, I had as much as I could do to hold my own against you. You need have no fear of any earthly knight you may meet in combat."

"Do you—could you believe that I will some day be worthy to be made a knight?" Beaumains asked.

"Fight always as you have fought today, and I will swear you are worthy," Launcelot answered. Beaumains knelt down upon the trampled grass.

"Then I pray you to give me the Order of Knighthood now," he said.

"First I must know your name, and who are your kindred," Launcelot told him.

"And will you discover it to no one?" Beaumains asked.

"By my faith, I will discover it to no one," Launcelot promised.

"Then," said Beaumains, "know that my name is Gareth, and I am the King of Orkeney's son. I am nephew to King Arthur and brother of Sir Gawaine."

Launcelot laid his sword across Gareth's shoulders and spoke the words which made him a knight. The boy stood up and took his arms again.

"I must leave you now and go forward with this damsel," he said. All this time she had waited at a little distance, sitting upon her horse. Now she put it in motion once more and moved away.

Launcelot rode homeward, stopping by the way to see how Sir Kay had fared. He had men sent out to carry him on his shield back to the King's castle, where he was tended and healed, although he had barely escaped with his life. "You should know more of a man's birth before you dare to cast scorn upon him," Sir Launcelot said to him, and Sir Kay had no answer.

The new-made knight rode forward to overtake the damsel and was greeted thus— "What are you doing here, kitchen boy? You have the very smell of the pots about you, and your clothes reek of grease and tallow. Do not boast to me that you have just killed two knights. It was only by shameful accident. I know well enough just who you are. Sir Kay named you Beaumains and said you were a sluggard, a fellow just good enough to wash ladles and turn the spit for roasting."

"Damsel," answered Beaumains, "You can say what you will. I have promised King Arthur to carry out your adventure, and that I will do or die for it."

"Finish my adventure indeed," she exclaimed. "You will presently meet an enemy so terrible that not for all the broth you have ever supped would you dare look him in the face."

"As for that I will try it," Beaumains returned, and they rode onward.

They had not gone far before they met a man running in wild flight. "Ah, my lord, help us," he cried, "for my master is set upon by six thieves, and they have bound him to a tree to rob and slay him."

The thieves scattered as Beaumains came spurring upon them; he pursued them and struck them down, and came back to set the bound man free. The rescued knight wished to give him great reward, but Beaumains said,—

"Sir, this day I have been made a knight by the noble Sir Launcelot. I will take no reward but that which God gives me." But on the knight's urging, the damsel consented to take lodging that night at his castle, although she would not let the kitchen boy sit at the table with her.

Next morning, when they went upon their way, their first

adventure was the meeting with two knights who stood at the ford of a river to forbid their passing. Beaumains rode into the water and overthrew them both, so that he and the damsel and the dwarf could go forward in safety. "The knight fell only because his horse stumbled in the water," the girl said.

It was toward evening that they came to a wide clearing in a wood and in the midst of it a black-trunked hawthorne tree. Beside it was a great black horse and on its back a man clad all in black armor. "You had better flee down the valley," the damsel said low to Beaumains, "for you can never face this terrible knight." But the man had seen them and called out,—

"Maiden, have you been to the court of King Arthur and brought this knight to be your champion?"

"No," she answered, "this is only a boy who sat in the kitchen and lived on charity. He has done some strange deeds and overthrown some knights, but it was all by accident. I wish you could rid me of him in any way except by slaying him."

"I will not slay him, I will only take away his horse and armor," said the Black Knight.

"You get no horse and armor of mine," cried Beaumains. "I am of as high rank as you and will prove it fairly on your body."

They rode their horses apart to the opposite ends of the glade, wheeled, laid their spears in rest, and came together with a shock like thunder. The Black Knight's lance shattered, and Beaumains' spear wounded him in the side. Nonetheless he fought on bravely with his sword until suddenly he dropped from his horse in a swoon and died. It had been no wish of Beaumains' to slay him, but now, seeing that his horse and armor were better than his own, he got down and took possession of them, then mounted the black horse to follow the damsel. "Ride out of the wind, kitchen boy," she said, "for the smell of your clothes still troubles me. Now here is one coming who will pay you for what you have done, so again I counsel you to flee."

It was a knight in green armor who was riding toward them, brother of the Black Knight and ready to avenge his death. Him also Beaumains overthrew from his horse and then gave him such a buffet on the helmet that he fell to his knees and was forced to beg for mercy that he should not be slain. "You beg in vain," Beaumains told him, "unless this damsel shall pray to me to save your life."

"I will never pray to you for his life," the girl said, "for I will not be so much in your debt."

"Then he shall die," returned Beaumains, and began to unlace the knight's helmet.

"Do not suffer me to be slain for the want of speaking a word of mercy," the Green Knight begged. "I will forever be your man," he promised Beaumains, "and will give you my service and that of thirty knights who are under my commands."

"In the devil's name," the girl cried, "that a kitchen knave should have your service and that of thirty knights. But let be, slay him not, for if you do you will greatly repent it."

"Damsel," said Beaumains, "your command is my pleasure, and his life shall be spared." The Green Knight knelt upon the grass and swore homage to Beaumains, who directed him to go and yield himself to King Arthur whenever he should receive word to do so. They lodged that night in the Green Knight's castle and went on their journey the next morning. And on that day they met another brother of the slain Black Knight.

Him also Beaumains overcame. Then the damsel prayed that his life might be spared and then this warrior also promised his own service and that of fifty knights. But as they went on once more, the girl was still chiding Beaumains and finding fault with him.

"It is most uncourteous of you so to rebuke me," he declared at last. "And it is no matter what you say, I tell you fairly that I will not depart from you."

And now they came in sight of a rich, bright city, and before it a wide field, new mown of its grass and covered with tents, where banners flew and shields hung at their doors, all the color of indigo. And the greatest and finest pavilion of all was that of the Blue Knight, who, like the others, was brother to the Black Knight whom Beaumains had slain. "He is the lordliest knight that you have ever looked upon," the maiden told him, "and you had better flee from him while there is time."

"If he is so lordly a knight as you say," Beaumains said, "he and his men will set upon me only one at a time, and I will go on meeting them as long as my life lasts."

"Sir," she answered, "I begin to wonder who you are and of what kindred you come. For you act and speak boldly, as I have well seen. Therefore truly I pray you to save yourself while you can, for you and your horse have had heavy labor, and I fear that now at last you will come to great harm. We are now not far from the place where my sister is besieged, and while this Sir Persaunte, the Blue Knight, is strong and mighty, he is as nothing beside that lord who lays siege to the lady my sister."

"Be that as it may," Beaumains replied, "by the grace of God I will so deal with this knight that by two hours after noon I shall have overcome him, and we can reach the place of the siege of your sister's castle while it is still daylight. I have striven to do you gentlemen's service, and peradventure I shall serve you better still before I depart from you."

"Alas," she sighed, "fair Beaumains, forgive me all that I have said and done against you."

"With all my will I forgive you," he told her. "And perhaps your harsh words have made me fight the better. But now that you speak kindly to me, I feel that there is no knight living that I am not able to meet."

And now Sir Persaunte came riding forth against him, and the two charged down upon each other in fearful combat. The Blue Knight was a powerful fighter but at last Beaumains struck him down with a terrible blow and, standing over him, began to unfasten his helmet. Then the Blue Knight yielded and asked for mercy, promising his own homage and that of a hundred knights. The damsel, too, came close to plead for his life.

"He shall have it," Beaumains said, "for it were a pity that so noble a knight should die."

As before, their beaten adversary begged them to lodge at his castle that night, and in the morning, before they set out, he held some talk with them. "Whither are you leading this young man?" he asked, and the girl answered,—

"He is going to the Castle Dangerous, where my sister is besieged."

"Ah," said Sir Persaunte, "it is the Red Knight of the Red Plains who there lays siege; he is the most dangerous knight now living and a man without mercy. God save you, young Beaumains, from such a one. He has done great wrong to that lady, who is one of the fairest in the world. And you damsel, are her sister? Is not your name Lynet?"

"That is what I am called," she told him, "and my sister is the lady of Lyones."

"Now I will tell you," Sir Persaunte went on, "that this Red

Knight of the Red Plains has laid siege to her castle for two years, and many times he could have taken it, if he had wished. But he has spun out the time, for he has hoped that Sir Launcelot would come from King Arthur's court to do battle with him, or Sir Tristram or Sir Lamorak or Sir Gawaine, and this is the reason for his long tarrying. But be strong and of a good heart, my lord Beaumains, for at least you know that you are to give battle to a mighty champion."

"I will do my best against him," Beaumains answered.

"Sir," said the damsel Lynet, "before this gentleman fights my sister's enemy, I beg that you will make him a knight."

"With all my heart," Sir Persaunte agreed, "if he will take the Order of Knighthood at the hands of so simple a man as I am."

"I thank you, sir," Beaumains said, "but the noble Sir Launcelot has already made me a knight."

"No greater hand could have made you one," Sir Persaunte declared, "for out of all others he may be called the chief of knighthood. It is said by all that knighthood is divided between these three, Sir Launcelot du Lake, Sir Tristram de Lyones, and Sir Lamorak de Galys. And if you can prove a match for the Red Knight you shall be called the fourth knight of the world.

"It is my hope to be of good fame and of good knighthood," Beaumains said, "and if you and this damsel will keep it close I will tell you now of what kin I am. My name is Sir Gareth of Orkeney; King Lott of Orkeney is my father, and my mother is King Arthur's sister, Queen Morgawse. Sir Gawaine is my brother, and Sir Agravaine and Sir Gaheris, also, and I am the youngest of them all. But neither King Arthur nor Sir Gawaine knows who I am." And now he and the damsel Lynet took up their journey again, for there was but a little way further to go.

They had come through the edge of a green forest and could look across a plain to the roofs and towers of a fair city. There were walls all about it, and on one side, beyond the wall, they could see water and the sails of ships, and they could hear the voices of sailors as they sang and heaved together to raise an anchor. Close beside them was a big sycamore tree and hanging from it a huge horn, made from an elephant's tusk. Upon this

321

Beaumains must blow to challenge the Red Knight of the Red Plains. And farther away, among the trees, he could catch sight of something colored, hanging and swinging from the lower branches.

"Do you see yonder," said Lynet. "This Red Knight, when he has overcome someone who comes against him, does not spare his life even when the knight cries out that he will yield. He hangs him shamefully upon those great trees, with his shield and arms hanging with him. Oh, sir, I pray you, do not blow the horn, or wait at least until it is afternoon, for the Red Knight grows in strength through the morning, and at this hour he has the force of seven men."

"For shame, damsel," Beaumains returned. "I will fight like a true knight or die like one." And he pressed forward to blow the horn until the plain and the city walls rang with the echo of the blast.

And now there came riding toward them the great Red Knight of the Red Plains; blood red was his armor as were his shield, and even the spurs on his heels. "There," said Lynet, "there is your deadly enemy. But look beyond and you will see my sister, the lady of Lyones, watching from a window above the city wall." And she pointed with her finger.

Beaumains raised his eyes and, even so far away, he could see the fair figure of the besieged lady and knew how beautiful she was. And she, knowing from afar that here was her champion come to rescue her, made him a deep curtsey, holding up both her hands.

"Come," shouted the Red Knight, "leave your staring and look on me instead. That lady is mine, and for her I have fought many men before you."

"Then you have fought in vain," Beaumains returned. "For she has made it plain that she does not love you, and to love one who cares nothing for you is great folly. And know this, Sir Red Knight, that I love her and will rescue her, or else I will die for her."

"Then make ready," said the Red Knight, "and talk no more to me."

They laid their spears in rest and charged, coming together with such force that the straps, the cruppers, and the girths of their saddles burst, and they both fell to the ground. So heavy was the shock that they both lay for a moment motionless, and those who watched from the walls thought that their necks were broken. "We never yet saw any man bring down the Red Knight," they told each other wondering.

But the two arose, lightly and easily, raised their shields, and rushed together like two fierce lions; they struck blows upon each other's helmets, they reeled, they staggered, panted, fell back bleeding, and then rushed into the fight again. The sun stood straight above for noon, and they stopped a moment to breathe. So furious had been the strokes of the swords that their armor was battered and rent, they had only their swords to ward off the terrible blows. Then they fought again, and the hours of the afternoon passed, the sun was dropping, and neither had got the victory. By common consent they paused again to rest; the Red Knight's page and Beaumains' dwarf came forward and unlaced their helmets, so that they could feel the cool air blow upon their faces. Beaumains looked up and saw again the Lady of Lyones looking down upon him from the window.

"Now make ready again," he said to his enemy, "for this time we will battle to the very end."

The Red Knight was watching keenly for his chance and when Beaumains made a great thrust past him he struck the boy across the hand, so that his sword flew out of his grasp. This he followed with a blow upon the helmet that brought Beaumains face downward on the earth. The Red Knight flung himself upon him to hold him down.

Then the voice of the damsel Lynet rose high and shrill. "Sir Beaumains, Sir Beaumains, where is your courage? The lady my sister is watching; she is crying out and weeping, Beaumains."

At that the young knight put forth his giant strength, staggered to his feet, caught up his sword again, and fell to the attack. His blows rained down with double power; the Red Knight reeled backward, dropped his sword and, smitten upon the

324

helm, measured his length upon the ground. Beaumains tore
open his helmet and raised his blade for the final blow, but the
Red Knight cried out in a loud voice, "O noble knight, I yield
me to your mercy."

"How can I spare your life," said Beaumains, "when you
brought so many knights to shameful death, even when they
had yielded to you?"

The Red Knight answered, "The reason for that I will make
clear to you. I once loved a lady whose brothers were slain by
either Sir Launcelot or Sir Gawaine of King Arthur's Round
Table. She prayed me, if I loved her truly, to put to a villian's
death any of King Arthur's knights that I would overcome. I
swore to her that I would do as she begged to any or all of the
knights of King Arthur's Round Table."

Meanwhile, out of the tents and from before the city came
a throng of richly dressed earls and barons and knights, who
fell on their knees before Beaumains and prayed for the life of
their lord. "Let him give you his homage," they besought him,
"let him hold his lands of you. His death will be of little use
to you."

"He has done ill and shamefully," Beaumains said, "but if
it was for a vow that he had made, his blame is not so great.
He must promise me upon his life that he will go into the castle

and ask forgiveness of the lady he has so long besieged, he must make amends to her for all the harm that he has done her. And then he must journey to King Arthur's court and there ask mercy and forgiveness from Sir Launcelot and Sir Gawaine. Then I will release him." Thus the Red Knight of the Red Plains and all his earls and barons with him, swore homage and obedience to the young knight, Sir Beaumains. "And now," Beaumains said to the damsel Lynet, "I would that I might see the lady your sister."

"You shall see her," Lynet answered.

Beaumains, armed and on his horse, with his spear raised and his helmet opened, rode to the city gate to seek his lady. But the drawbridge was raised, the portcullis was down, and armed men guarded the gates. The lady of Lyones looked down upon him from above.

"Not yet, Sir Beaumains," she said. "Not even by what you have done can you earn a lady's whole love until time as well

326

as deeds has proved you a true knight. For that a year must pass. Go your way and be of good comfort, for twelve months will soon go by. Trust me, fair knight, for neither your great labors nor your true love shall be lost. I will be true to you and not fail you, for to my death I shall love you and none other."

Twelve months had passed away, and this year King Arthur was holding the feast of Whitsuntide at Carleon. There, as the knights of the Round Table gathered together, came three warriors, the Green Knight with fifty others, his brother with sixty, and the Blue Knight, Sir Persaunte, with a hundred. All came to yield themselves to King Arthur in the name of "a young knight that had a damsel with him, and she called him Sir Beaumains." And even as Arthur was marveling, Sir Launcelot came to tell him that some great person was approaching with a company of five hundred knights, and these too had come to do homage to King Arthur at the orders of Sir Beaumains. "I am called the Red Knight of the Red Plains," said this great lord, "and Sir Beaumains defeated me in fair battle, hand to hand, as no knight had done to me for twenty years."

"You have long been a bitter enemy to me and my court," Arthur declared. "And now I trust to God that you shall be my friend. But where may we find this knight, Sir Beaumains?"

"That I cannot tell you," answered the other, "for such young knights when they are away on their adventures, have no abiding place."

Now King Arthur could sit down to meat for here, indeed, had come great marvels. But presently another company entered, his sister the Queen of Orkeny with her ladies and knights. "What have you done with my young son, Gareth? she cried as she came before him. "He was here with you a twelvemonth, and you made a kitchen knave of him. But where is he now?"

"Mother," said Sir Gawaine, "I did not know him," and Arthur echoed,—

"I did not know him. But he shall be found, if he is within our seven realms."

The King sent out letters, directing his messengers first of all to seek the lady of Lyones whom Beaumains had gone forth to rescue. And since the twelve months were over, Beaumains, after many adventures, had come back to her, and they journeyed together to the court of King Arthur. The King decreed that they should be wedded at Michaelmas, at Kynkenadon, by the seaside in Wales, a fair and plenteous country. Beaumains, who was now called by all Sir Gareth, bade for his wedding guests all those knights and barons and earls whom he had sent to do homage to King Arthur. The Bishop of Canterbury came thither to marry them, and on the same day Sir Geheris, Gareth's brother, married the damsel Lynet, and his other brother, Sir Aggravaine, wedded dame Laurel, niece of the lady of Lyones. And with the brides were given rich gifts, so that they might all live royally to their life's end.

SONG OF KING ARTHUR'S KNIGHTS

Alfred Tennyson

Blow trumpet, for the world is white with May!
Blow trumpet, the long night hath rolled away!
Blow through the living world—Let the King reign!
Shall Rome or Heathen rule in Arthur's realm?
Flash brand and lance, fall battle-axe on helm,
Fall battle-axe, and flash brand! Let the King reign!
Strike for the King and live! his knights have heard
That God hath told the King a secret word.
Fall battle-axe, and flash brand! Let the King reign!
. . . Strike for the King and die! and if thou diest,
The King is king, and ever wills the highest.
Clang battle-axe, and clash brand! Let the King reign!
Blow, for our Sun is mighty in his May!
Blow, for our Sun is mightier day by day!
Clang battle-axe, and clash brand! Let the King reign!
The King will follow Christ, and we the King,
In whom high God hath breathed a secret thing.
Fall battle-axe, and clash brand! Let the King reign!

Eleanor Hull

CUCHULAIN'S ADVENTURES IN SHADOW-LAND

ILLUSTRATED BY *Kay Lovelace*

WHILE Cuchulain was still a little lad, but strong and brave and full of spirit, it came into his mind that he would like to go out into the world to perfect himself in every kind of soldierly art, so that he might not be behind any warrior in feats of strength and skill. He went first to the Glen of Solitude in Munster, but he did not long remain there, but returned to Ulster, to invite his companions to go with him to visit the woman-warrior Scáth who dwelt in "Shadow-land." Where the land was, Cuchulain knew not, but he thought it was in Alba, or mayhap in the Eastern world.

Three of the chiefs of Ulster consented to go with him, Conall, whom men in after days called The Victorious, because of his many combats, and Laery the Triumphant, and Conor, Ulster's king.

These three friends set out together in Conall's boat the "Bird-like," which needed not to be guided or rowed, but which sped at its own will across the deep-green, strong-waved ocean, like the winging flight of a swift bird. It took its own way to strange lands, where none of those who traveled in the boat had ever been before, and they came at last to a dark, gloomy shore where dwelt a fierce woman-warrior, Donnell the Soldierly, and her daughter, Big-fist.

Huge and ugly and gruesome were they both, with big gray eyes, and black faces, and rough bright-red hair, and so cruel

329

and vengeful were they that it was dangerous to quarrel with either of them. Yet they knew many feats of arms, so that the three warriors stayed with them a year and a day, learning all they knew. But Cuchulain was fain to go away from them, for the darkness and the gloom of the place and the ugly deeds of Big-fist troubled him, and he liked not at all to remain with her.

The year and the day being past, Cuchulain was walking by the brink of the sea revolving these things in his mind, when he saw close beside him, sitting on the shore, a man of enormous size, every inch of him from top to toe as black as coal. "What are you doing here?" said the big black man to Cuchulain. "I have been here a year and a day learning feats of prowess and heroism from Donnell," said the little lad. "How so?" said the big black man. "If you want to learn true knightly skill and feats of valor, it is not here that you will learn them." "Is that true?" said Cuchulain. "It is true, indeed," said the big black man. "Is there any woman-champion in the world who is better than the woman-champion that is here?" said Cuchulain. "There is indeed," said the big black man; "far better than she is Scáth, daughter of Ages, King of Shadow-land, who dwells in the Eastern world." "We have heard of her before," said Cuchulain. "I am sure you have," said the big black man; "but great and distant is the region of Shadow-land, little man." "Will you tell me all about it, and where it is, and how to find it?" said Cuchulain, eagerly. "Never will I tell you a word about it to the end of time," said the black man surlily. "O hateful, withered specter, now may knowledge and help fail you yourself, when most you stand in need of them," cried the boy, and with that the phantom disappeared.

Cuchulain did not sleep a wink that night thinking of the great far-distant country of which the big black man had told him; and at break of day on the morrow he sprang from his bed and sought his companions, Conor and Conall and Laery. "Will you come with me to seek for Shadow-land?" he asked, when he had told them the tale of the big black man. "We will not come," said they, "for last night a vision appeared to each of us, and we could not put it away from us. We saw before us our own homes, and the kingly courts of Emain Macha standing right before us in the way, and we heard the voices of our wives weeping for our absence, and the call of our clans and warriors for their chiefs; therefore today we bid you farewell, for we return together to our homes. But go you on to Shadow-land and perfect yourself in feats with Scáth, daughter of Ages, and then return to us." It seemed to Cuchulain that it was the big black man who had raised this vision before the chiefs, that they might separate themselves from him, so that he might find his death traveling to Shadow-land alone. So he bade the chiefs farewell with a heavy heart, and they set off for Erin in Conall's boat, the "Bird-like"; and as soon as it was out of sight, speeding over the waves of the blue, surging ocean, Cuchulain set out alone along the unknown road. For he was determined to reach Shadow-land, or to die in the attempt. He went on for many days over great mountains and through deep impenetrable forests, and dark, lonely glens, until he came to a wide-spreading desert and a lightless land. Black and scorched and bare was that desert, and there was no path or road across it, and no human habitation was in sight. Cuchulain stood wondering and fearing to adventure forth alone across that terrible stony trackless waste, for he knew not whither to turn, or how to go. Just then he saw a great beast like a lion coming out of the forest on the border of the desert, and advancing towards him, watching him all the time. Now Cuchulain was but a little lad, and he had no weapons with him, and he was afraid of the mighty beast and tried to escape from him; but whichever way he turned, the beast was there before him, and it seemed to Cuchulain that it was a friendly beast, for it made no attempt to injure him, but kept turning its side to Cuchulain, inviting him to mount. So Cuchulain plucked up his courage and took a leap and was on its back. He did not try to guide it, for of its own accord the lion made off across the plain, and for four days and nights they traveled thus through the dim, lightless land until Cuchulain thought they must have come to the uttermost bounds of men. But they saw a small loch and a boat on it, and boys rowing the boat backward and forward amongst the reeds of the shore, and the boys laughed at the sight of the hurtful beast doing service to a human being. Then Cuchulain jumped off the back of the lion, and he bade it farewell, and it departed from him.

The boys rowed him across the loch to a house where he got meat and drink, and a young man with a face bright like the sun conducted him on his way until he came to the Plain of Ill-luck, and there he left him. Difficult and toilsome was the journey across the Plain of Ill-luck; on one half of the plain the feet of the wayfarer would stick fast in the miry clay, so that he could not move on, but thought he would sink into the earth at every step; and on the other half of the plain the grass would rise up beneath his feet and lift him up far above the ground upon its blades, so that he seemed to be walking in the air.

No road or comfortable way ran across that plain, and Cuchulain could not have made his way across, but that the young man with the face like the sun had given him a wheel to roll before him, and told him to follow wherever the wheel led. So he rolled the wheel, and bright shining rays darted out of the wheel and lighted up all the land. The heat that came out of the wheel dried up the clay, so that it became hard and firm to walk upon, and it burned up the grass, so that it made a clear path before Cuchulain all the way. And the noisome evil airs of the plain were sucked up by the heat and sunshine of the wheel, so that Cuchulain went on gladly and cheerfully until he came to the Perilous Glen. Then Cuchulain was afraid again, for he saw before him a narrow glen between high, rocky mountain fastnesses, and only one road through it, and that as narrow as a hair. And on either side of the road and among the rocks were cruel savage monsters waiting to devour him. But the youth with the shining face had given him an apple, and he rolled the apple before him as he went along, and when the monsters saw the apple, they ceased watching Cuchulain and sprang after the apple. But the apple ran on and on, so that they could not come up with it, and as it ran, the narrow path grew wider, so that Cuchulain could follow it with ease. By that means he passed the Perilous Glen, and he took the road that led across the terrible high mountains, until he came to the Bridge of the

Leaps. And on the other side of the bridge was the isle where Scáth or Shadow, daughter of Ages, lived.

Now this is how the Bridge of the Leaps was made. It was low at the two ends, but high in the middle, and it passed over a deep and precipitous gorge, up which came foaming the waters of the wild, tempestuous ocean. And fearful strange beasts and fishes were moving about in the waters below, which made a man's heart quail with fear to look upon, for it was certain that if he should fall, they would seize him in their jaws and devour him.

On the near side of the bridge were many youths playing hurley on the green, and Cuchulain saw amongst them champions from Ulster, Ferdia, son of Daman, and the sons of Naisi, and many others. They greeted him kindly and gladly, and they asked news of Ulster and of their friends and companions in Erin; and Cuchulain was glad to see the faces of his friends, for he was weary and fatigued after his journey and after the terrors of the way across the Plain of Ill-luck and the Perilous Glen. Then Cuchulain asked Ferdia, for he was older than he, "How shall I get across the Bridge of the Leaps, to reach the fort of Scáth?" "You cannot cross it," said he; "for this is the manner of that bridge; when anyone steps on one end of the bridge the other end leaps up and flings the passenger off again upon his back. Not one of us has crossed the bridge as yet, for there are two feats that Scáth teaches last of all, the leap of the Bridge, and the thrust of the spear that is called the Body Spear, which moves along the water. When we have achieved valor, she will teach us the leap of the Bridge, but the thrust of the Body Spear she will not teach to any man of us at all, for she reserves that feat for the champion who excels in all other feats, and who is, out of all her pupils, the one whom she likes best.

"Tell me, O Ferdia, how Shadow herself crosses the bridge when she comes to teach you feats," said Cuchulain. "Only by two leaps can that bridge be crossed," they all replied; "that is, one leap into the very center of the bridge, and one upon the firm ground beyond; but if the leap is missed, it is likely that the passer-by will fall into the gulf below, and woe to him if

333

he should fall." Then Cuchulain looked at the bridge, and he looked at the foaming gorge below and at the openmouthed monsters in the tossing waves, and he waited awhile until his strength was returned. But as evening fell he rose, and gathering all his forces together, he leaped upon the bridge. Three times he tried to cross it, and three times it flung him again upon the bank, so that he fell upon his back; and the young men jeered at him, because he tried to cross the bridge without Scáth's help. Then Cuchulain grew mad with anger, and he leaped at one bound upon the very center and ridge of the bridge. Here he rested a moment, and then he leaped again, and he gained the firm ground on the further side, and he strode straight up to the fort of Shadow and struck three thunderous knocks upon the door.

"Truly," said Scáth, "this must be someone who has achieved valor somewhere else," and she sent Uthach the Fearful, her daughter, to bring him in and welcome him to the fort.

For a year and a day he remained with Scáth and learned all that she could teach him, and he became the most renowned warrior of his time, or of any other time; and because Shadow loved his skill and his strength and comeliness, she taught him the feat of the Body Spear, which she had never taught to any before. And she gave the spear into his own keeping. When Ferdia saw the spear, he said, "O Scáth, teach me also this feat, for the day will come when I shall have need of it." But she would not, for she wished to make Cuchulain invincible, and that he should have one feat that was not known to any but himself. And she gave him the Helmet of Invisibility, which Manannan mac Lir, the ocean god, brought out of Fairy-land; and the mantle of Invisibility made of the precious fleeces from the land of the Immortals, even from the Kingdom of Clear Shining; and she gave him his glorious shield, with knobs of gold, and chased all round with carvings of animals, and the combats of fighting men, and the sea-wars of the gods. And he became companion and arms-bearer to Ferdia, because he was the younger and because they loved each other, and all the time he was with Scáth they went together into every danger, and every peril, and they

took journeys together, and saw strange sights. And because the twain loved each other, they swore that never in life would either hurt or wound the other, or do combat or quarrel with the other, but that forever and forever they twain would aid and support each other in war and in combat, and in all the pleasant loving ways of peace. But Scáth knew that other days were coming, for she was a seer, and when Cuchulain bade her farewell, to return to Ireland, she spoke to him these words out of her prophet's shining ken: "Blessing and health go with thee! Victorious Hero, Champion of the Kine of Bray! Chariot Chief of the two-horsed chariot! Beloved Hero of the gods! Perils await thee; alone before the foe I see thee stand, fighting against a multitude, fighting thy own companion and friend. Red from many conflicts are thy warrior weapons; by thee men and champions will fall; the warriors of Connaught and of Meave, the hosts of Ailill and of Fergus scatter before thy sword. The Hound of Ulster will be renowned. At his death will the glory of Ulster fail, the glory of Erin will depart from her. . . . Farewell, farewell, Cuchulain."

Then Cuchulain parted from her and turned to go back to Erin, and a magic mist overtook him, so that he knew not how he went, or by what road he came to the borders of the white-flecked, green-waved ocean, but he found Manannan's horses of the white sea foam awaiting him near the shore upon the surface of the mighty main, and he caught their tossing white-tipped manes, and they bore him out across the waves, and so he came to Ireland again. It was on the night of his return that he found and caught his two chariot horses, the Gray of Macha, and the Black Steed of the Glen, and this is how he caught them. He was passing along the borders of the Gray Lake that is near the Mountain of Slieve Fuad, pondering on the fate that was before him and the work that he would do. Slowly he walked along the reedy, marshy ground that lay along the lake, till he saw a mist rise slowly from the mere and cover all the plain. Then, as he stood to watch, he saw the form of a mighty steed, gray and weird and phantom-like, rise slowly from the center of the lake and draw near to the shore, until it stood with

336

its back to him among the rushes of the water's edge. Softly Cuchulain crept down behind the steed; but it seemed not to hear him come, for it was looking out towards the center of the lake. Then with a sudden leap, Cuchulain was on its neck, his two arms clasped upon its mane. When it felt the rider on its back, the noble animal shuddered from head to foot, and started back and tried to throw Cuchulain, but with all his might he clung and would not be thrown. Then began a struggle of champions between those two heroes, the King of the Heroes of Erin and the King of Erin's Steeds. All night they wrestled, and the prancing of the steed was heard at Emain Macha, so that the warriors said it thundered, and that a great storm of wind had arisen without. But when it could by no means throw Cuchulain from its back, the horse began to career and course round the island, and that night they fled with the swiftness of the wind three times round all the provinces of Ireland. With a bound the wild steed leaped the mountains, and the sound of its coursing over the plains was as the break of the tempestuous surf upon the shore. Once only did they halt in their career, and that was in the wild and lonely glen in Donegal that is called the Black Glen, where the ocean waves roll inward to the land. From out the waters arose another steed, as black as night, and it whinnied to the Gray of Macha, so that the Gray of Macha stopped, and the Black Steed of the Glen came up beside it and trotted by its side. Then the fury of the Gray of Macha ceased, and Cuchulain could feel beneath his hand that the two horses were obedient to his will. And he brought them home to Emain and harnessed them to his chariot, and all the men of Ulster marveled at the splendor of those steeds, which were like night and day, the dark steed and the light, and one of them they called the Gray of Macha, because Macha was the goddess of war and combat, and the other they called the Black Steed of the Glen.

Margaret Prescott Montague

BIG MUSIC

ILLUSTRATED BY *Lynd Ward*

OGGONE it! I wished Tony Beaver would
quit being so all-fired reckless! Why, I b'lieve some day that
feller'll turn the world right spang upside down jest for to
see how would she look thataway! There was more times than
one up Eel River when I was skeered right down to bedrock
and would of laid back my years and shot for home if Tony
hadn't of named me the Truth-Teller and laid a kind of a sacred
trust on me, so I knowed I had to stay with the job and hang
onto the truth no matter where it might take me—and it sure
tuck me into some strange places.

I'm mighty glad though, I happened to be in camp when
the big music busted in, for that sure was a great time, and
folks have tole so many lies about it that I'm glad to give you-all
the straight truth in this here tale that's been all tried out with
that paper of Tony's, and every lie sifted outer it.

Well, Tony sure was fooling with somepen powerful dangerous that time, and yit the whole thing commenced with nothing
more'n a little drop of dew: jest pure common dew like what
a person kin see any nice summer morning laying over the
leaves and grass and swinging onto the spider webs. That's
what started the business, but mebbe even Tony wouldn't of
been so reckless if there hadn't a-been so much spite work

going on in camp. Aw, you know how it is, sometimes a camp'll all go right sour with spite. Every feller'll have a gredge erginst the next feller, and there'll be more mean tales passing from mouth to mouth behind hands than you kin shake a stick at. Every feller'll git so techy that if a person happens to say "Hand the biscuits" kinder short, 'stead of "I'll thank you for them sody biscuits, if you please," there'll be a fight and a sulk right that minute.

Well, that was what struck the Eel River camp whilst I was up yonder. Aw, I dunno how the thing come to pass: mebbe it was dog days, or mebbe they vittles had kinder turned erginst 'em, anyhow every feller's temper was on a hair trigger, couldn't nobody open his mouth 'cept for a mean word, all the good healthy cussing and fooling had done went in the ground, and every job was tied up, 'cause there wa'n't no good fellowship to grease the wheels of work.

"What's the matter with this camp is that it's done froze up. What you-all need is somepen that'll git you above yerselves and thaw you out, so's you'll be running all loose and free ergin," Tony says looking around at all them sour dough faces, with they under jaws set and they lips pouting out. "And I'll jest have to figger out somepen that'll do it," he says.

With that he goes off into the woods all to hisself, for Tony kin allus figger better when he's out in the deep woods all alone.

Well, the very next morning he was 'way off on the top of a high ridge all to hisself jest at sunup, when he ketched a wink from a little dewdrop what was laying out there on a bunch of green moss. And seeing's he was all alone, Tony he winked back at the critter, for you know, stranger—you fellers what's reading this book—a person'll do a heap of nice fool things when there ain't any other feller round to laf.

Well, sirs! the minute he done that, it seemed like somepen inside him jumped up and hollered, "Dewdrop! Dewdrop! Look at it, you great big two-fisted Jim-bruiser, you ain't never seen a dewdrop afore! Look at it! Look at it!"

Tony he did. He jest looked and looked at that dewdrop with

339

all the looks he had. It was filled with frosty light, and yit it had a rainbow in it too, and furst the sun would twinkle it on one side, and then it would twinkle it on the tother. And all the time it kep' setting there so round and pretty, like it was the whole of creation and knowed a heap more'n it was aiming to tell. That kinder made Tony mad.

"Hey! You doggoned sassy little cuss!" he bawls at it. "Don't you know I could bust yer head off with one finger?"

But the little critter didn't sass him back nor nothing. It jest kep' right on twinkling along there to itself, and the more Tony looked at it, the more awestruck he got, for he seen he was looking right into the very heart of creation itself.

By now all the little birds had done chirped the sun up right high, and Tony tuck a great skeer that his little dewdrop would melt. So all in a hurry he commenced plucking up leaves and moss to kiver it over. He worked like he couldn't work fast enough, and when he had it all safe, he was dripping wet, and panting like he'd run a mile—for you know a feller's bound to sweat if he aims to beat the sun.

Then, having got sorter acquainted with one dewdrop, Tony commenced to see all of 'em like it was for the furst time. 'Peared like, everywhere he'd look the sun was winkling and twinkling dewdrops at him. Tony set there in a maze, jest fa'rly carried away with the sight, and seemed like he could hear every last one of them sparklers hollering out at him, "Brother! Brother!"

By now the sun commenced to lap them dewdrops up off'n the leaves and spider webs, and all of 'em went like they was glad to go, hopping away in the sun like they was jumping into their daddy's lap.

About then a right peculiar thing come to pass. There was a little feller in camp what all the hands called Fiddling Jimmy, 'count of him allus playing tunes on his fiddle, and now as Tony set there kinder dazed, watching them dewdrops hop off into the sun all so round and pretty, it seemed like he heared that little fiddler playing a tune somewhere right close. The tune it come nigher and nigher, 'til d'rectly Tony thought he was

340

riding erway on it, like he was riding a saw-log downstream. But when the last little dewdrop had hopped away to—well to wherever it is they does go—he found hisself still setting there with his mouth gapping open.

"Well, I will be dogged!" he says. "An' *that's* what happens every morning, and me never knowing it afore!"

Then he peeked down at the twinkle of dew he'd saved, and right that minute he knowed he'd ketched there a drop outer the heart of all the world, and that what was in it was the sap in him too, and in all the varmints and critters, and rocks and rivers, and green things in all creation.

When Tony bumped erginst that big thought he goose-fleshed up all over, for he seen he was thinking too wide, and in another pair of seconds he'd slip right out over the edge and be where—well it's the truth, I don't know where he would be! And Tony didn't know neither, but he give a powerful jump back in his mind from all that wide kinder thinking, and it seemed like he couldn't git back where other humans was fast enough. He stuffed his little dewdrop into the bosom of his shirt and lit out for camp so fast he fa'rly burnt the trail up behind him.

Well, when Tony hit camp and smelled sweat and sawdust, it eased up that cold feeling down the spine of his back, and he ketched his breath, looking around for a good place to hide his dewdrop.

He'd jest got it all kivered up nice under the roots of a white pine when he turns about and seen that little hand by the name of Fiddling Jimmy leaning up erginst a sapling looking at him.

Now there was somepen right peculiar about that little feller. He was mighty clear and wide betwixt the eyes, and had a look like he knowed a heap more'n he could tell with his tongue, so he had to try to git it out by fiddling. Mebbe you remember me speaking of him when I furst hit camp.

Tony seen right off that the little feller sensed he'd been fooling with somepen powerful dangerous, so he lighted into him furst.

"Hey!" he bawls, "what in the thunder was you doing fid-

dling when every other hand was on the job?"

"Me?" says the tother looking s'prised.

"Yes, *you!* I heared you fiddling out in the woods this morning jest at sunup."

"Jest at sunup!" Jimmy hollers, pricking up his years mighty quick and looking kinder awe-struck too. "Aw no, Tony, that wa'n't me. *You* know what it was."

"I'll be dogged if I do!" Tony answers him back.

"It was the *big music,*" the tother says, letting the words slip right out soft and respectful like.

"THE BIG MUSIC!" Tony whispers, his mouth gapping open, and the goose flesh walking up the spine of his back ergin.

"Look a-here, Tony, you better tell me all erbout it," the Fiddler says mighty earnest and solemn.

And looking at him Tony seen he'd better. So he hands it all out to him, how he got acquainted with his dewdrop, and how all at onced he seen dewdrops and everything else different from what he ever had seen 'em afore, and then how the music come so close it seemed like he was riding erway on it.

"Tony, you'd better mind how you go looking and looking at dewdrops and hearing music jest at sunup," the Fiddler warns him, "or the furst thing you know you'll look a hole spang through to the tother side, and *then* the big music'll bust in on us sure 'nough!"

"Well, I wouldn't keer if the big music *was* to come!" Tony hollers out, looking powerful mad and dangerous. "Things has got mighty hidebound and mean-spirited round this here camp, and you know there's a heap of spite going on. Mebbe if the big music busts in it'll kinder sweep things cl'ar ergin. An' anyhow," he lets fly at the Fiddler, "it ain't for *you* to talk! You been fiddling holes all round this camp ever since you struck it. Why look a-here!" he bawls, jabbing his finger into the air. "Here's a place right this minute, where you fiddled 'My Old Kaintucky Home' what's so thin a person kin nigh run his whole hand through it. And what with you all the time playing 'Dixie' and 'The West Virginia Hills,' and all them other tunes, you got the whole place punched as full of holes as a porous plaster, and why we ain't had the big music in on us afore this is a wonder to me!"

"Well, if she comes, she comes! And *I* don't keer!" the Fiddler says cutting a kind of a pigeon-wing.

"I don't keer neither!" Tony hollers out, all fired up. "It's jest the very thing this camp needs. And by the breath of the gray rocks, I'll turn that there dewdrop loose tomorrer jest at sunup!"

"*Jest at sunup!* Great Day in the Morning!" Jimmy busts out, his eyes dancing, and him dancing with 'em.

Well, now you-all kin easy see what sorter dangerous doings Tony and the little fiddler was up to that time. They didn't say nothing to nobody, not even to me, but the next morning jest at daybreak, Tony tuck that powerful big cow's horn of hisn that's a whole sight bigger'n any natcheral born cow ever did have, and standing out there on a gray rock, he blowed sech er blast it fetched every feller tumbling outer the bunkhouse on the jump.

"Fellers," says Tony, looking mighty strange an' tall in the gray light, "it's glimmering for dawn, and I want you all to take a right good look at this little dewdrop and keep on looking at it when the sun hits it, for it's my belief that not a one of you

343

great big two-fisted Jim-bruisers ever really seen a dewdrop afore." With that he showed 'em the little critter still laying on its green moss, all so round and pretty.

Well, that sure was mighty reckless talk, and right that minute old Preacher Moses Mutters, what's allus sech a calamity hunter, tuck a powerful skeer.

"Oh, my *lands*, Tony!" he screeches out, "you'll have us in every kinder trouble d'rectly! Do pray take keer!"

"Man!" says Tony, flashing a crisscross look at the ole feller that twisted him into a corkscrew, "who ever seen me take keer?"

And it's the truth, not a hand there had ever seen Tony take it.

Well, all us hands done like Tony told us to and jest looked and looked at that little dewdrop. And the more we looked, the more still and awe-struck we got.

Fiddling Jimmy had tuck a stand on a cliff er rock at the head er the holler, and he kep' a-looking and a-looking off into the dawn, holding his fiddle, and kinder stretching up on tiptoe like he was listening for somepen. Right about then a yeller strand of sunlight come wavering down the mountain and hit that little dewdrop, and the little feller commenced to burn with a spark o' fire, and while we was a-looking at it so awe-struck like, it burned brighter and brighter, 'til it burned itself right up into the sun and was gone. When that happened every feller there felt the stillness inside of him kinder bust wide open, and he knowed he was right on the edge of somepen powerful big.

Jest that minute Fiddling Jimmy, off on his rock, let loose with a powerful yell: "She's busted! She's busted!" he hollers. "*Great Day in the Morning!* The big music's busted through!" And with that he commenced to dance and to fiddle fit to kill hisself.

"Oh, my lands! Somepen terrible is coming!" ole Brother Mutters screeches out, flinging both arms round a right stout pine tree to kinder anchor hisself to the ground.

By now all us fellers could hear the strangest kinder music

344

coming from 'way off yonder somewheres, and it looked like Jimmy's fiddling up there on his rock was kinder blazing a trail for that tother music to come in by.

Well, *sirs!* the next thing that come to pass was a whole panel of rail fencing floating over the ridge and down the holler, like it was riding a river a person couldn't see. And *whoop-ee!* In another pair of seconds that panel busted itself all to pieces, and every last one o' them gray rails up-ended and commenced to dance, whirling around and bowing to one another, back and forth and hither and yon!

"O my lands! O my lands! Jest *look* at that now!" pore ole Brother Mutters bellers out, taking a strangle holt of his pine tree, with his hair all bristling up and his eyes hanging out of his head.

The next thing that come was a fat old lady of a haystack dancing over the ridge and down the holler, bowing and kicking up, and carrying on like she was a two-year-old. And you better b'lieve every hand there made tracks to git outer *her* way in a hurry! Next there come the prettiest little pair of young maple saplings, skipping and dancing with they branches on they hips, and cakewalking along together jest as sassy as you please.

That was jest the beginning! In another pair of seconds the full tide of the big music busted in on us, pouring down the holler in a kind of torrent, like a river in flood. Every kind of a tune a person every did hear, and every kind of a critter and varmint and growing thing dancing to the tunes, all of 'em wove together in the wildest sort of a jamboree. There was 'possums and rabbits and groundhogs, 'til you couldn't rest, and there was b'ars and wildcats in plenty too, and strange critters what never had been seen in these mountains afore. And there was trees and bushes and sawlogs and rocks, all jumbled and dancing together, and tunes—Whoop-ee! Every tune what ever was! A feller could see 'em as well as hear 'em, every color of the rainbow weaving in and out amongst all them dancing critters. Every varmint and critter there blowing along by them tunes was dancing and laffing fit to kill theyselves. A old she b'ar with her cubs come rolling and bounding in, doing a kind of a breakdown along a little pink strand of a tune, and laffing so hard she jest natcherly had to clap her paws to her sides to hold 'em in place.

All a feller had to do was jest to jump into a tune and let it carry him on away. For when the *big* music comes it ain't like little musics, you don't dance *to* it, *it* dances you. And you'd *better* dance! For if you try to hold out erginst it, it sure will treat you mighty rough like it done pore old Brother Mutters.

Well, all us hands in the Eel River crew, we jest let ourselves go to it, and one tune after another picked us up and swirled us off. And all the time Fiddling Jimmy was up there on his rock dancing and fiddling and singing like he was plum *de*stracted.

The fellers they all tuck partners if they could find 'em, but if they couldn't they jest flapped they arms and danced by theyselves. The Sullivan feller picked him out a right stout saw-log, and danced so hard with it that the chips flew outer the log like popcorn hopping outer a hot griddle. That little Eyetalian hand, he found a monkey along of all the stream of foreign critters the music fetched in. They two sure was glad to see one another and stepped off together to the strangest kind of a wild dance ever was seen up Eel River. I can't reely tell you what-all I danced with I was so busy watching the tother fellers.

But *whoop-ee!* I wished you-all could of seen Big Henry, doing the polka with that old lady haystack what come over the ridge at the start! Big Henry was sorter bashful at the beginning, but onced they got acquainted, they cert'n'y was dancers from Dancerville! That haystack, for all she was right up in years, sure was a light stepper. And courtesy—Great Day! She'd draw off from Big Henry and bob right down to the ground and up ergin and never drap a straw! Big Henry cert'n' was taken with her, and the last the fellers seen of the two together they was going on down the stream of music with Big Henry's arm around the lady's waist—as fer that is as it would go—and him talking matrimony to her to the tune of "I seen my lover go round the bend."

Tony Beaver jest danced with every last thing and critter

346

that come by. Furst off he tuck up with a big gray rock what
come footing it down the ridge early in the game. "Hey,
brother! Fall to it!" Tony sings out, and they ketched aholt of
one another some way, and had a high old time together. But
it's the truth, that rock was so all-fired heavy every step it tuck
it went down waist deep in the music, and splashed the tunes
and songs up all over everybody like they was showers of rain.
And having the music splashed over 'em like that jest sent
every feller off dancing harder'n ever.

Well, Tony he danced with his rock a spell, and then he
broke loose from it and tuck a whirl around with a whole string
of little young squirrels, what come by all sorter strung together,
frisking they tails and jumping and barking and cracking out
jokes like they was cracked nuts. Then Tony he tuck up with a
field mouse and a hoppy toad, what was riding around together

on the tune of "A frog he would a-wooing go." And then he
danced a spell with a dogwood tree what had all busted out in
full bloom ergin, though its right time of flowering was over
and done with nigh a month back. It sure was a pretty sight
to see that tree all kivered over with its white blooms, as graceful as a young bride, with its branches waving and twinkling
to the tunes. Tony he had it for a partner for a right smart
spell, and after that he danced with any and every thing that
come by, and between whiles he'd kick up high and low and
whirl round all to hisself.

But about then, that little boy what's sech a great buddy of
Tony's got wind of the jamboree, and come a-running and
a-limping into the camp as best he could on his crippled foot,
holding out his hands and hollering, *"Take me!* Take me, Tony!
I wan'a dance too!"

"Sure! Come on, buddy! *You* kin dance to the big music with
the best of 'em!" Tony hollers back, ketching aholt of him, and
yonder the two of 'em went off together, laffing and dancing,
bounding, whirling around, and carrying on with every last tune
in the bunch, and I'll be dogged if that there little feller, for all
his crippled foot, didn't outdance the whole shooting match.

It sure was one of the biggest sights a feller ever did see, all
them hands and critters dancing and laffing there together, with
the pink tunes and blue ones and red and yeller, whirling 'em
all about; and Fiddling Jimmy up there on his rock, fiddling
and singing, and jest carried away in a kind of a glorification.

It was a funny thing what kind of a tune the different critters
would pick out to be danced by. It's like I say, when the big
music comes it dances you, you don't dance to it, but every
feller's free to pick his own tune. Take that string of thorn
bushes now, the pretty little round kind that a person kin see
most any time growing in a old run-out field: they come dancing in to the tune of "Here we go 'round the mulberry bush."
All they little leaves was winkling and twinkling and clapping
theyselves together, and all of 'em was giggling out the prettiest
little green giggles a person ever did hear.

It was all right for them bushes to pick a baby song like

348

that, but it sure was a funny thing to see them powerful big steers of Tony's jest natcherly carried away by the tune of "Bye Baby Bunting." When it come by in all that tangle of music, them beasts they jest got right up on they behind legs, slung they tails over they arms, and let it walse 'em away for mile upon mile. Them critters is so powerful and large that when they dances they tromples down trees and kicks great cliffs of rock outer the mountainside, and I bet "Bye Baby Bunting" never had no sech a swath cut to *it* afore. But pshaw! A person can't never say *what* they'll do when the big music busts in.

And it's like I say, when it comes you better mind and dance, or you're mighty apt to see the same rough time ole Brother Moses Mutters seen. That ole preacher, pore feller! He sure did set a great store by his soul, and he was allus powerful oneasy for fear it might git lost, and if it *was* lost what in the H——— Excuse me! What in the *thunder* would he have to travel on when he hit the next world?

So when he seen them rails dancing over the ridge, and heard the big music coming, he knowed they was in for somepen all outer plum with his kinder religion, and he ketched aholt of that pine tree like I said to sorter anchor hisself down, for he knowed dancing was a sin and powerful onhealthy for the soul. But pshaw! I tell you, you *got* to dance when the big music hits you! And try as he might that pore ole feller jest *couldn't* keep both foots to the ground at onced. Furst one little tune and then another'd come tickling round, and h'ist his leg up in time to it, and 'fore he could holler out, "*Aw my soul!*" and git that foot jammed down nice and pious to the ground ergin, here'd be the tother up in the air shaking a dance step to every jig that come by. It sure was a right pitiful sight to see that poor old feller hanging on tight to his pine tree, trying so hard to save his soul, while furst one leg and then the tother was danced out from under him, and waving up in the air like a cat shaking its foot when it steps in water. His ole buddy Ain't-That-So had been swept off by the tunes long since, for he ain't got the staying powers of the preacher.

350

But d'rectly his pine tree failed Brother Mutters too! Whoop-*ee!* When the full tide of that music come down the holler, that tree give a great heave and a bound, and busting its roots loose, it jumped up outer the ground, and commenced to toss its branches and to dance with the best of 'em, swirling pore ole Brother Mutters round and round with it, high and low, up and down.

Well, *sirs!* That ole pine it muster lost *its* soul long since, for it sure did take to dancing natcheral! And you better b'lieve it was a strange sight to see that tree dancing for all it was wurth, with the pore ole preacher feller dangling on to its trunk, his coat tails spread out right straight behind him, and him groaning and moaning over his soul. He didn't want to dance with the tree, but onced he'd got aholt of it, he was skeered to let loose. And looked like the tree didn't want to dance with him nother, for it jest turned itself loose and did every kind of a scan'lous worldly step a person ever heard tell of, fox-trotting and cheek-dancing with the ole feller 'til you couldn't rest. And every now and ergin if the preacher wa'n't mighty spry the tree'd tromp down right hard on his toes—and you all know a pine tree ain't got no light tread.

But after a spell the tree, it got plum out-*done* with sech a flat-footed, mean-spirited partner, and it give a great bound and a kick and slung Brother Mutters up to a high ledge of rock 'way above all that tide of music. After that the pine tree hucked branches with a red oak, and the two of 'em went downstream together kicking out jigs and cutting pigeonwings and dancing so hard the sap sweated out in great beads all over 'em.

Ole Brother Mutters, he lay up there on his ledge all tousled to pieces, yammering and moaning and panting out, "Oh my soul! *It's lost! It's lost!*" and peeking down over the edge at all that swirl of music and dancing down below, like he was looking to see where his soul had done went. The hands and critters what was dancing, they got pretty nigh tickled to death over the old feller and his soul, and 'fore they hardly knowed it, they was all dancing out a game, acting like they was hunting for the preacher's soul. They made up a little song, "Has anybody

351

seen Brother Mutters's soul?" It went off real nice to the tune of "Has anybody here seen Kelly?" 'Course Tony Beaver, *he* had to start the thing. Him and his little buddy walsed over to Big Henry and his haystack, splashing the music up every which away as they come, and bows and sings out, "Has anybody seen Brother Mutters's soul?" Big Henry and his partner, they danced it on to that string of little young squirrels, Big Henry he bowed to the squirrels, and the hayrick she bobbed a courtesy to 'em, and both together they sings, "Has anybody seen Brother Mutters's soul?" The squirrels they jerked they tails and frisked and barked it out all up and down the line, 'til d'rectly the whole shooting match, hands and critters, trees, rocks, and varmints, was all doing the ladies' chain to the tune of "Has anybody seen Brother Mutters's soul?" all of 'em skipping and laffing fit to bust they heads off. It sure was scan'lous, but it's the truth when the big music is dancing you around, the thing that'll tickle you most is to have anybody think they *kin* lose they souls.

And all the time Fiddling Jimmy stood up there on his rock, with all that stream of music and dancing critters splashing and bobbing and whirling past him. One little tune after another'd come lapping up round his ankles, asking him to come on with it, but he jest kep' on where he was, fiddling and dancing all to hisself, and waiting. And then, by and by, a wonderful big tune come rolling in that was bigger and grander than any of us rough hands up Eel River ever had heard afore. It was all blue in the middle where the soft notes was, and pink up high, and way down gray in the low notes. It come in to a long thundering march, mighty solemn and beautiful, like the skies had opened and stood back for to let it come through, and like it was rolling outer the heart of all creation. Fiddling Jimmy, he tuck one look at that big tune and hollers out, *"Here I am!"* mighty high and joyful, like they'd been a-looking for one another since the world commenced, and with that he jumped right out into the heart of it. The tune it never broke its stride, but it ketched the little fiddler up and went on rolling away all so grand and beautiful. And all them other little tunes, they drawed up on both sides and all the dancers with them, making a kinder rainbow lane of sound, as you might say, for that big tune and the fiddler to pass down. After that—? Well, that was all. The minute that big tune passed away, all the rest of the big music sorter gathered itself together and blowed off to—Well, to wherever it had come from. The sound and the sight of it all died away; the hole where it had busted through closed right up tight; all the critters and varmints scuttled away into the woods, the trees jumped back into the ground, and in the shake of a lam's tail there wa'n't nothing to show for it all but jest a few gray rocks laying around outer place, a little dogwood sapling in full bloom a month outer season, a parcel of husky hands all outer breath, and ole Brother Moses Mutters still lamenting up there on his ledge. Fiddling Jimmy we never did see no more, but we didn't feel too bad about that 'cause the feller looked so all-fired happy when him and that there big tune ketched hands and danced off together thataway.

But every hand there felt mighty limber and free. All the meanness and spite work was clean swep' away, for we'd seen a dewdrop for the furst time, and we'd danced to the big music,

353

and we was all kinder stretched up above our common selves.

More'n that there was another grand big thing come outer it all. Whilst we was all laying round, sorter ketching our breaths, and feeling mighty friendly to each other 'count of all the spite work having clean blowed away, all to onced that little buddy of Tony's hollers out, "Aw, *look!* Look at *me*, Tony!"

And when we looks there was the little feller, running and jumping, and cutting up capers jest to beat the band, for I'll be dogged if the big music hadn't straightened his crippled foot all out, so's it was jest as limber and free as the tother.

"Aw, *look*, Tony! Watch me—*watch!*" he kep' a-hollering out, jumping and cutting up, and laffing all carried away with his-self.

Well, sirs! All us hands bust loose with a great shout at that, and Tony ketched his little buddy high up on his shoulder and went off into another wild dance, with the young-un setting up there, his arm hugged right tight round Tony's neck, kicking his heels, and singing out a little song, "I kin walk! I kin walk! Tony, I kin walk!"

For you see, strangers, that little feller had danced to the big music jest right. He hadn't helt back or been mean-spirited or skeered, he'd jumped right into the middle of it and let it dance him on away jest anywheres it pleased.

And that's what you better mind and do too. If the big music comes, you mind and dance to it, for if you don't you're mighty apt to git treated like it done Preacher Moses Mutters. That ole brother, pore feller! His coat tails was all tore to strings, his whiskers was raveled out, and it's the *truth!* he ain't had a sprig of hair on his head from that day to this—no, sir! *Not one sprig!*

And if any of you readers don't trust me and the lie-paper to hand you out the truth, all you have to do is to go up Eel River for yerself, and any hand there kin show you a kind of a crinkled place on the face of one of the highest cliffs up yonder, what marks the spot where the big music busted in—and *then* mebbe you'll know the truth when you see it!

G. W. Cox

ROLAND
AND HIS HORN

ILLUSTRATED BY
Henry C. Pitz

THE battle of Roncesvalles, like the entire legend of Roland, has a real basis in history, although the actual enemies were the Basques, not the Saracens. The battle was fought in the eighth century, and this version of it comes from the fourteenth century. Ganelon was Roland's stepfather and was jealous of his favor with the king. Ganelon's punishment for his treachery was death, with all the pagans.

CHARLES the Great, King of the Franks, had fought seven years in Spain, until he had conquered all the land down to the sea, and there remained not a castle whose walls he had not broken down, save only Saragossa, a fortress on a rugged mountaintop, so steep and strong that he could not take it. There dwelt the pagan King Marsilius, who feared not God, but served Mohammed.

'King Marsilius sat on his throne in his garden, beneath an olive tree, and summoned his lords and nobles to council. When twenty thousand of his warriors were gathered around him, he spoke to his dukes and counts, saying: "What shall we do? Lo! these seven years the great Charles has been winning all our lands, till only Saragossa remains to us. We are too few to give him battle, and man for man we are no match for his warriors. What shall we do to save our lands?"

Then up spake Blancandrin, a wily counselor: "It is plain we must be rid of this proud Charles; Spain must be rid of him; and since he is too strong to drive out with the sword, let us see what promises will do. Send envoys to him and say that we will give him great treasure in gold and cattle. Say that we will be his vassals, and do him service at his call. Say that we will forsake our God and call upon his God. Say anything, so long as it will persuade him to ride away with his army and quit our land." And all the pagans said, "It is well spoken."

Charles the Emperor held festival before Cordova and rejoiced, he and his host, because they had taken the city, had overthrown its walls, and had gotten much booty, both of gold and silver and rich raiment. The emperor sat among his knights in a green meadow. Round about him were Roland, his nephew, the captain of his host, and other princes, as well as fifteen thousand of the noblest born in France. The emperor sat upon a chair of gold, beneath a pine tree; white and long was his beard, and he was huge of limb and noble of countenance. When the messengers of King Marsilius came into his presence, they knew him straightway, and alighted quickly from their mules, and came, meekly bending at his feet.

Then said Blancandrin, "God save the king, the glorious king, whom all men ought to worship. My master, King Marsilius, sends greeting to the great Charles, whose power no man can withstand, and he prays thee make peace with him. Marsilius offers gifts of bears and lions and hounds, seven hundred camels, a thousand falcons, of gold and silver, as much as four hundred mules harnessed to fifty chariots can draw, with all his treasure of jewels. Only make peace with us and retire with thy army to Aachen, and my master will meet thee there at the feast of Saint Michael. He will be baptized in thy faith, and will hold Spain as thy vassal. Thou shalt be his lord, and thy God shall be his God."

The emperor bowed his head while he thought upon the message; for he never spake a hasty word and never went back from a word once spoken. Having mused awhile, he raised his head and answered: "The King Marsilius is greatly my enemy. In what manner shall I be assured that he will keep his covenant?" The messengers said: "Great king, we offer hostages of good faith, the children of our noblest. Take ten or twenty, as it seemeth good to thee; but treat them tenderly, for verily at

Marvelous and fierce was the battle.

the feast of Saint Michael our king will redeem his pledge and come to Aachen to be baptized and pay his homage and his tribute."

Then the king commanded a pavilion to be spread, wherein to lodge them for the night. And on the morrow, after they had taken their journey home, and the king had heard mass, he called his barons to him. There came all the chiefs of his army and with them many thousand noble warriors. Then the king showed them after what manner the messengers had spoken, and asked their advice. With one voice the Franks answered, "Beware of King Marsilius."

Then spake Roland and said: "Trust him not. Remember how he slew the messengers whom we sent to him before. Seven years have we been in Spain, and now only Saragossa holds out against us. Be not slack to finish what is now well-nigh done. Gather the host. Lay siege to Saragossa with all thy might. Conquer the last stronghold of the pagans and end this long and weary war."

But Ganelon drew near to the king and spake: "Heed not the counsel of any babbler, unless it be to thine own profit. What has Marsilius promised? Will he not give up his God, himself, his service, and his treasure?" And all the Franks answered, "The counsel of Ganelon is good."

So Charles said, "Who will go up to Saragossa to King Marsilius and make terms of peace with him?"

Roland answered, "Send Ganelon," and the Franks said, "Ganelon is the man, for there is none more cunning of speech than he." So King Charles sent Ganelon as his envoy. But Ganelon was a traitor and gave evil counsel to King Marsilius, saying: "Send back the hostages to Charles with me. Then will Charles gather his host together and depart out of Spain and go to Aachen, there to await the fulfillment of thy promise. But he will leave his rear guard of twenty thousand, together with Roland and Oliver, and his noblest knights, to follow after him. Fall on these with all thy warriors; let not one escape. So shall the pride of Charles be broken; for the strength of his army is not in his host, but in these, and in Roland his right arm.

357

Destroy them, and thou mayest choose thy terms of peace, for Charles will fight no more. The rear guard will take their journey along the narrow valley of Roncesvalles. Surround the valley with thy host, and lie in wait for them. They will fight hard, but in vain."

When Ganelon came before Charles, he told him King Marsilius would perform the oath which he swore, and was even now setting out upon his journey, to pay the price of peace and be baptized. Then Charles lifted up his hands towards heaven, and thanked God for the prosperous ending of the war in Spain.

On the morrow the king arose and gathered to him his host to go away to keep the feast of Saint Michael at Aachen and to meet Marsilius there. And Olger the Dane he made captain of the vanguard of his army which should go with him. Then said the king to Ganelon, "Whom shall I make captain of the rear guard which I leave behind?" Ganelon answered, "Roland; for there is none like him in all the host." So Charles made Roland captain of the rear guard. With Roland there remained behind Oliver, and the twelve knights, and Turpin the Archbishop, who for love of Roland went with him, and twenty thousand well-proved warriors. Then said the king to his nephew: "Good Roland, behold, the half of my army have I given thee in charge. See thou keep them safely." Roland answered: "Fear nothing. I shall render good account of them."

So they took leave of one another, and the king and his host marched forward, till they reached the borders of Spain. They had to travel along steep and dangerous mountain ways and down through silent valleys made gloomy by overhanging crags. And when the king thought upon his nephew whom he left behind, his heart grew heavy with the thought of ill. So they came into France and saw their own lands again. But Charles would not be comforted and would sit with his face wrapped in his mantle; and he often said that he feared that Ganelon had wrought some treason.

Now Marsilius had sent in haste to all his barons to assemble a mighty army, and in three days he gathered four hundred thousand men at Roncesvalles, in the western Pyrenees, and

there lay in wait for the rear guard of King Charles. And a great number of the most valiant pagan kings banded themselves together to attack Roland in a body and to fight with none other till he was slain.

Now when the rear guard had toiled up the rocky pass and climbed the mountain ridge, they looked down on Roncesvalles, whither their journey lay. And behold! all the valley bristled with spears, and the valley sides were overspread with them, for the multitude was like blades of grass upon a pasture; and the murmur of the pagan host rose to them on the mountain as the murmur of a sea.

Then when they saw that Ganelon had played them false, Oliver spake to Roland: "What shall we now do because of this treason? For this is a greater multitude of pagans than has ever been gathered together in the world before. And they will certainly give us battle." Roland answered: "God grant it; for sweet it is to do our duty for our king. This will we do: when we have rested we will go forward." Then said Oliver: "We are but a handful. These are in number as the sands of the sea. Be wise; take now your horn, good comrade, and sound it; per-

haps Charles may hear and come back with his host to rescue us." But Roland answered: "The greater the number, the more glory. God forbid I should sound my horn and bring Charles back with his barons, and lose my good name, and bring disgrace upon us all. Fear not the numbers of the host; I promise you they shall repent of coming here; they are as good as dead already in my mind."

Three times Oliver urged him to sound his horn, but Roland would not, for he said, "God and His angels are on our side; through Him we shall do great wonders, and He will not see us put to shame before His enemies." Yet again Oliver pleaded, for he had mounted up into a pine tree and seen more of the multitude that came against them; far as the eye could see they reached; and he prayed Roland to come and see also. But he would not. "Time enough," he said, "to know their numbers, when we come to count the slain. We will make ready for battle."

Roland ranged his trusty warriors and went to and fro among them, riding upon his battle horse, by his side his good sword Durendal. There was not a man but loved him unto death and cheerfully would follow where he led. He looked upon the pagan host, and his countenance waxed fierce and terrible; he looked upon his band, and his face was mild and gentle. He said: "Good comrades, lords, and barons, let no man grudge his life today; but only see that he sells it dear. A score of pagans is a poor price for one of us. I have promised to render good account of you. I have no fear. God knows the result of the fight, but we know that much glory and worship await us upon earth, and crowns in Paradise." Then he gave the word, "Forward!" and with his golden spurs pricked his steed. So, foremost, he led the rear guard down the mountainside, down into the Valley of Death, called Roncesvalles. Close following came Oliver, Archbishop Turpin, and the valiant Twelve, the guard pressing forward with shouts and bearing the snow-white banner of their king aloft.

Marvelous and fierce was the battle. Roland's spear was good, for it crashed through fifteen pagan bodies, through brass and hide and bone, before the trusty ash broke in his hand and he drew Durendal from its sheath. The Twelve did wondrously; nay, every man of the twenty thousand fought with lion-like courage; and no man counted his life dear to him. Archbishop Turpin, resting for a moment to get fresh breath, cried out, "Thank God to see the rear guard fight today!" and then spurred in again among them. Roland saw Oliver still fighting with the butt of his spear and said, "Comrade, draw thy sword"; but he answered: "Not while a handful of the stump remains. Weapons are precious today."

For hours they fought, and not a Frank gave way. Wheresoever a man planted his foot, he kept the ground or died. The guard hewed down the pagans by crowds, till the earth was heaped with full two hundred thousand heathen dead. Of those kings who had banded together by oath to fight him, Roland gave good account, for he laid them all dead about him in a ring, and Durendal to its hilt dripped with blood. But many thousands of the Franks were slain, and of the Twelve there now remained but two.

Marsilius looked upon his shattered host and saw them fall back in panic, for they were dismayed because of the Franks. But Marsilius heard the sound of trumpets from the mountain-top, and a glad man was he, for twenty strong battalions of

361

Mohammedans were come to his help, and these poured down the valleyside. Seeing this, the rest of the pagans took heart again, and they pressed about the remnant of the guard and shut them in on every hand. Nevertheless Roland and his fast-lessening band were not dismayed. So marvelously they fought, so many thousand pagans they hurled down, making grim jests the while as though they played at war for sport, that their enemies were in mortal fear and doubted greatly if numbers would suffice to overwhelm these men, for it seemed as if God's angels were come down to the battle. But the brave rear guard dwindled away, and Roland scarce dared turn his eyes to see the handful that remained. Dead were the Twelve, with all the flower of the guard.

Then Roland spake to Oliver, "Comrade, I will sound my horn; perhaps Charles may hear and come to us." But Oliver was angry, and answered: "It is now too late. Hadst thou but heeded me in time, much weeping might have been spared the women of France, Charles would not have lost his guard, nor France her valiant Roland." "Talk not of what might have been," said Archbishop Turpin, "but blow thy horn. Charles cannot come in time to save our lives, but he will certainly come and avenge them."

Then Roland put the horn to his mouth and blew a great blast. Far up the valley went the sound and smote against the mountaintops; these echoed it on from ridge to ridge for thirty leagues. Charles heard it in his hall and said: "Listen! what is that? Surely our men do fight today." But Ganelon answered the king: "What folly is this! It is only the sighing of the wind among the trees."

Weary with battle, Roland took the horn again and blew it with all his strength. So long and mighty was the blast, the veins stood out upon his forehead in great cords. Charles heard it in his palace and cried: "Hark! I hear Roland's horn. He is in battle or he would not sound it." Ganelon answered: "Too proud is he to sound it in battle. My lord the king groweth old and childish in his fears. What if it be Roland's horn? He hunteth perchance in the woods. Forsooth, a merry jest it would be for

him were the king to make ready for war and gather his thousands and find Roland at his sport, hunting a little hare."

The blood ran fast down Roland's face, and in sore pain and heaviness he lifted the horn to his mouth and feebly blew it again. Charles heard it in his palace and started from his seat; the salt tears gathered in his eyes and dropped upon his snowy beard; and he said: "O Roland, my brave captain, too long have I delayed! Thou art in evil need. I know it by the wailing of the horn! Quick, now, to arms! Make ready, every man! For straightway we will go and help him." Then he thrust Ganelon away and said to his servants, "Take this man and bind him fast with chains; keep him under guard till I return in peace and know if he has wrought us treason." So they bound Ganelon and flung him into a dungeon; and Charles the Great and his host set out with all speed to come to Roland.

Fierce with the cruel throbbing of his wounds, and well-nigh blinded with the blood that trickled down his face, Roland fought on, and with his good sword Durendal slew the pagan prince, Faldrun, and three and twenty mighty champions. The little company that was left of the brave rear guard cut down

363

great masses of the pagans and reaped among them as the reapers reap at harvest-time, but one by one the reapers fell ere yet the harvest could be gathered in. Yet where each Frank lay, beside him there lay his pile of slain, so any man might see how dear he had sold his life. But a pagan king espied where Oliver was fighting seven abreast and spurred his horse and rode and smote him through the back a mortal wound. Yet even when the pains of death took hold on Oliver, so that his eyes grew dim and he knew no man, he never ceased striking out on every side with his sword; and then Roland hastened to his help and, cutting the pagans down for a wide space about, came to his horse. But Oliver struck him a blow that brake the helm to shivers on his throbbing head. Nevertheless, Roland, for all his pain, took him tenderly down and spake with much gentleness, saying, "Dear comrade, I fear that thou art grievously wounded." Oliver said, "Thy voice is like Roland's voice; but I cannot see thee." Roland answered, "It is I, thy comrade." Then he said: "Forgive me if I smote thee. It is so dark that I cannot see thy face; give me thy hand; God bless thee, Roland; God bless Charles and France!" So saying, he fell upon his face and died.

A heavy-hearted man was Roland; little cared he for his life since Oliver, his good comrade, was parted from him. Then he turned and looked for the famous rear guard of King Charles the Great. Only two men were left besides himself.

Turpin the Archbishop, Count Walter, and Roland set themselves together to sell their lives as dearly as they might; and when the pagans ran upon them in a multitude with shouts and cries, Roland slew twenty, Count Walter six, and Turpin five. Then the pagans drew back and gathered together all the remnant of their army, forty thousand horsemen and a thousand footmen with spears, and charged upon the three. Count Walter fell at the first shock. The Archbishop's horse was killed, and he, being brought to earth, lay there dying, with four wounds in his breast.

Then Roland took the horn and sought to wind it yet again. Very feeble was the sound, yet Charles heard it away beyond the mountains, where he marched fast to help his guard. And the king said: "Good barons, great is Roland's distress; I know it by the sighing of the horn. Spare neither spur nor steed for Roland's sake." Then he commanded to sound all the trumpets long and loud; and the mountains tossed the sound from peak to peak, so that it was plainly heard down in the Valley of Roncesvalles.

The pagans heard the trumpets ringing behind the mountains, and they said: "These are the trumpets of Charles the Great. Behold Charles cometh upon us with his host, and we shall have to fight the battle again if we remain. Let us rise up and depart quickly. There is but one man more to slay." Then four hundred of the bravest rode at Roland; and he, spurring his weary horse against them, strove still to shout his battle cry, but could not, for voice failed him. And when he was come within spearcast, every pagan flung a spear at him, for they feared to go nigh him, and said, "There is none born of woman that can slay this man." Stricken with twenty spears, his faithful steed dropped dead. Roland fell under him, his armor pierced everywhere with spearpoints. Stunned with the fall, he lay there in a swoon. The pagans came and looked on him and gave him up for dead. Then they left him and made all speed to flee before Charles should come. They hastened up the mountainsides, and left the gloomy valley piled with dead, and fled away towards Spain.

Roland lifted his eyes and beheld the pagans fleeing up the mountain passes; and he was left alone among the dead. Then in great pain he drew his limbs from underneath his horse and got upon his feet, but scarce could stand. He dragged himself about the valley and looked upon his dead friends and comrades. Roundabout each one there lay a full score of pagan corpses, and Roland said, "Charles will see that the guard has done its duty." He came to where Oliver lay, and he lifted the body tenderly in his arms, saying, "Dear comrade, thou wast ever a good and gentle friend to me; better warrior never broke a spear nor wielded sword; wise wert thou of counsel, and I repent me that once only I hearkened not to thy voice. God

365

rest thy soul. A sweeter friend and truer comrade no man ever had than thou." And in the Valley of Death, Roland wept for the last of his friends.

When he found death coming on him, Roland took his sword Durendal in one hand and his horn in the other and crawled away about a bowshot to a green hillock, whereupon four marble steps were built beneath the trees. There he lay down in his agony. A certain pagan was plundering there among the dead, and watched till Roland ceased to moan in his pain; then, thinking there was no more breath in him, the thief stole slowly up, and seeing the glitter of the hilt of Durendal, put forth his hand and drew it from its sheath. Roland lifted his eyes and saw the thief bend over him with the sword in his hand. He seized the horn from beside him, and dealt the man a blow upon the crown that broke his skull.

Then he took Durendal into his hands and prayed that it might not fall into the power of his enemies. He said: "O Durendal, how keen of edge, how bright of blade thou art! God sent thee by his angel to King Charles, to be his captain's sword. Charles girt thee at my side. How many countries thou hast conquered for him in my hands! O Durendal, though it grieves me sore, I had rather break thee than that pagan hands should wield thee against France." Then he prayed that God would now give him strength to break his sword; and lifting it in his hands, he smote mightily upon the topmost marble step. The gray stone chipped and splintered, but the good blade broke not, neither was its edge turned. He smote the second step; the blade bit it and leaped back, but blunted not, nor broke. The third step he smote with all his might; it powdered where he struck, but the sword broke not, nor lost its edge. And when he could no more lift the sword, his heart smote him that he had tried to break the holy blade; and he said, "O Durendal, the angels will keep thee safe for Charles and France!"

Then Roland, when he felt death creep upon him, lay down and set his face toward Spain and toward his enemies, that men should plainly see he fell a conqueror. Beneath him he put the sword and horn. Then lifted he his weary hands to heaven and

closed his eyes; and whilst he mused God sent his swift arch-angels, Gabriel and Michael, to bear his soul to Paradise.

Gloom fell; the mists went up, and there was only death and silence in the valley. The low red sun was setting in the west.

Charles and his host rode hard, and drew not rein until they reached the mountaintop and looked down on the Valley of Roncesvalles. They blew the trumpets, but there was no sound, and there was no answer but the echoes on the mountainsides. Then down through the gloom and mist they rode and saw the field; saw Roland dead, and Oliver; saw the Archbishop and the twelve valiant peers, and every man of the twenty thousand chosen guard; saw how fiercely they had fought, how hard they died.

There was not one in all the king's host but lifted up his voice and wept for pity at the sight they saw. But Charles the king fell on his face on Roland's body, with a great and exceeding bitter cry. No word he spake, but only lay and moaned upon the dead that was so dear to him. Then the king left four good knights in Roncesvalles to guard the dead from birds and beasts of prey and set out in chase of the pagans.

In a vale the Franks overtook them, hard by a broad and swift river. There being hemmed in, the river in front, and the fierce Franks behind, the pagans were cut to pieces; not one escaped, save Marsilius and a little band who had taken an-other way and got safe to Saragossa. Thence Marsilius sent letters to the king of Babylon, who ruled forty kingdoms, pray-ing him to come over and help him. And he gathered a mighty army and put off to sea to come to Marsilius.

Now after this Marsilius and the king of Babylon came out to battle with King Charles before the walls of Saragossa. But Charles utterly destroyed the pagans there, and slew the two kings, and broke down the gates of Saragossa, and took the city. So he conquered Spain and avenged himself for Roland and his guard.

Index